*Mistaking her Character* ... broken family connections, and suspense ... riveted. - J Dawn King

## Praise for Maria Grace

"Grace has quickly become one of my favorite authors of Austen-inspired fiction. Her love of Austen's characters and the Regency era shine through in all of her novels." **Diary of an Eccentric**

"A great read for any Jane Austen fan-fiction lover. With great characters, witty writing, and a swoon-worthy romance, Maria Grace's Given *Good Principles* series is a solid addition to your bookshelf." **Austenprose**

Grace sprinkles in enough of the familiar, while still allowing room for change and growth to highlight her creativity and abilities in weaving a tale. I believe that this is what she does best, blend old and new together to create a story that has the framework of Austen and her characters, but contains enough new and exciting content to keep me turning the pages. … For those that enjoy a classic Jane Austen reimagining this is a no-brainer. Grace's style is not to be missed.. **From the desk of Kimberly Denny-Ryder:**

# Mistaking Her Character

Maria Grace

White Soup Press

## Published by: White Soup Press

Mistaking Her Character
Copyright © 2015 Maria Grace

All rights reserved including the right to reproduce this book, or portions thereof, in any format whatsoever.

The characters and events portrayed in this book are fictitious or are used fictitiously. Any similarity to actual persons, living or dead, events or locales is entirely coincidental and not intended by the author.

For information, address
author.MariaGrace@gmail.com

ISBN-10: 0692453547
ISBN-13: 978-0692453544 (White Soup Press)

Author's Website: RandomBitsofFaascination.com
Email address: **Author.MariaGrace@gmail.com**

# Dedication

For my husband and sons.
You have always believed in me.

# Chapter 1

*The more I see of the world, the more am I dissatisfied with it; and every day confirms my belief of the inconsistency of all human characters, and of the little dependence that can be placed on the appearance of merit or sense."*
— Jane Austen, Pride and Prejudice

ELIZABETH SQUINTED AT THE mantle clock. The final rays of afternoon light glared off the crystal, but if she turned her head just so…splendid! A quarter of an hour remained before they needed to depart.

Betsy tucked a few more pins into her hair. The splotchy dressing table mirror confirmed her unruly mass of curls had been tamed into submission. Bits of lace and ribbon framed her face. A pretty effort indeed

Mama swept into Elizabeth's room without knocking, feathers fluttering and taffeta rustling. Elizabeth steeled herself. Was there a fresh crisis requiring her attention, or had Mama come to remind her yet again—

"Betsy, attend Jane."

Betsy dropped a timid curtsey and disappeared.

"Jane requires Betsy's complete attentions. It is her night, after all."

Yes, Jane's night—a tiresome reminder indeed, but preferable to a fresh calamity demanding her intervention.

Mama flicked her skirts as she positioned herself between the dressing table and the bed. "I will finish your hair. Betsy's arrangements are far too fussy. You do not object, do you?"

Elizabeth contemplated Mama's reflection in the looking glass. The set of her mouth, the glint in her eye—Mama had already resolved the matter in her own mind. Best not attempt to answer at all.

Why was she so uneasy about this evening? None of the usual vexations had occurred. No dresses required mending, no hairpins or ornaments were mislaid. Even Kitty and Lydia had not lamented their lack of invitation.

Mama picked at her curls and wound one into place, securing it a bit too forcefully with a sharp hair pin. Did she have to be so rough? Elizabeth's own mother—she swallowed a familiar lump in her throat—had been so gentle and composed.

"You are looking very well. Very well indeed. You will never be as handsome as Jane, of course, but tonight you might even be considered pretty."

"Thank you, Mama."

"Up, up, and let me see." She pulled Elizabeth's elbow. "Turn about for me. I am surprised at how cleverly you reworked my old gown."

"Most of the trims came from my older dresses. The last time we dined with Lady Catherine, she was so adamant about demonstrating economy in our dress. I hoped to please both you and her with it." It probably would not do to note she liked it, too.

Mama harrumphed. "I grant your intentions were appropriate. I wonder if perhaps you have done a mite too well with it."

Elizabeth balled her fists, focusing on the sharp stab of her nails.

"Lady Catherine is hosting this dinner to introduce your sister to a prospective match. Jane must be the center of attention this evening. You look well enough for conversation to be directed to you instead of her."

Such compliments! If Mama was not careful, they might truly go to her head. No, that attitude would not suit for an evening in company. She forced her features into a suitably contrite mask. "Jane is so lovely and her gown brand new. No one will pay notice to me in this reworked frock."

"Another night it might not be such an issue, but tonight … The blue dress you wore last week—"

"Mrs. Bennet! Lady Catherine's carriage approaches," Papa called from the base of the stairs. He used his commanding, not-to-be-argued-with air that always raised Mama's ire.

Both of them short-tempered and in the coach together—what joy was hers.

"We are coming, Dr. Bennet." Mama pulled a fichu from the dresser's top drawer. "We cannot keep your father waiting. Put this on and be downstairs quickly." She tossed the lace at Elizabeth. "I can count on you to help me make everything about Jane?"

"You know I would never do anything to injure Jane."

Elizabeth settled into the soft velvet of Lady Catherine's oldest coach. The upholstery reeked of Lady Catherine's perfume—stale roses and something else that combined into a most fitting stink.

How many carriages did she own? This one, the barouche box, the chaise, the landau, oh yes, and Miss de Bourgh's little phaeton. No wonder she could afford to maintain Papa on retainer as her personal physician.

Mama leaned close to Jane, offering further advice on how best to comport herself to please their patroness and her gentlemen guests.

Why? Jane hardly needed such a lecture. She was Mother's spit and image—beautiful and gracious in all things, and everyone's favorite.

"Is that Charlotte and Mr. Collins in Lady Catherine's chaise?" Elizabeth asked.

Papa glanced out of the side glass and grunted. His dark coat, well-brushed beaver and buckskin breeches cut a very fine figure indeed.

"Charlotte?" Mama's face squeezed into her special look of disgust, reserved for all things Collins. "I find your familiarity most unbecoming."

"If you prefer, I will not address her so in public."

"See that you do not. I would much prefer it if you did not exchange intimacies with her at all," Mama said.

"I do not see what is wrong with Lizzy having a particular friend," Jane said.

Mama cocked her head and furrowed her brow. Elizabeth gritted her teeth for the lecture that would invariably follow.

"You do not see what is wrong?" Mama half rose from her seat, flinging her hands in the air. "That woman is an interloper. She should not even be among us!"

Papa grumbled. "You would do well to remember, she is my cousin's wife."

"A place she does not deserve. By all rights, Lizzy should have been mistress of the parsonage, not her." Mama planted her hands on her hips, jabbing Papa in the chest with her elbow.

"Collins did us enough of a favor when he recommended me to Lady Catherine. We can hardly require him to marry one of our girls as well."

"Whom else should he have married? Lady Catherine herself presented Lizzy as a suitable match for him. He would not have gone against her will had Lizzy behaved as she ought."

"As I recall, he expressed more interest in Jane." Papa might have corrected an entire room full of children with that tone.

"What man would not be attracted to her?" Mama patted Jane's knees. "That is precisely why Lady Catherine deemed she must marry higher than a vicar. Mr. Collins was quite good enough for Lizzy, though."

"And yet he still chose elsewhere. What does that tell you, Mrs. Bennet?"

"Lizzy should be more attentive … "

Not a day had passed since Mr. Collins's marriage that Mama failed to deliver the familiar tirade—usually followed by lamentations on the expense of keeping an unmarried daughter—who ought to be married—in the house.

Elizabeth's jaw dropped and she covered her mouth with her hand. Ah, no wonder Mama fluttered so anxiously tonight. Bad enough to have one daughter who had failed in the marriage mart, a second would be intolerable.

"… your failure to secure Mr. Collins is costing your sisters dearly. Mary will not be able to order a new gown, and my poor dears Kitty and Lydia …"

Mary did not need a new gown to catch a beau. She alone of them already had the eye of a reliable young man neither too high nor too low for her station—not that Mama would appreciate a reminder right now. As for Kitty and Lydia—

"We are nearly arrived!" Mama lurched across the coach and squeezed in beside Jane, smashing Elizabeth into the side wall.

The brass handle jabbed Elizabeth's side. What a lovely bruise it would leave.

Mama pinched Jane's cheeks hard enough to make her wince. "Sit up straight, Jane. No man will look at a slouch. Remember, you are the guest of honor. Lady Catherine has selected these gentlemen specifically with you in mind."

Papa huffed and pushed his glasses higher up his nose. "Hardly. As I understand, her nephews are visiting, and happened to bring several friends with them."

"Perhaps, perhaps," she tugged Jane's bodice a bit lower.

Elizabeth winced. Any lower would be indecent. Poor Jane!

"Still, she noted Jane as suitable company for these young men of quality. Do not squander this opportunity, my dear. Since we are no longer in London, we cannot afford to waste—"

The driver opened the door and dropped the steps in a bone-rattling clank. Elizabeth hung back to be the last one out. A few moments spent in the fresh air would provide just the tonic to compose her suitably for the evening ahead.

Lady Catherine must have chosen the tallest man in all of England for her butler. He towered head and shoulders, and perhaps another head again, above Elizabeth. His deep gravel timbre and somber countenance might have intimidated her, but he winked before he led her inside.

Dozens of candles lit the over-decorated foyer, glinting off mirrors and crystal. Their scent bespoke beeswax, an extravagance reserved for Rosings. Lady Catherine insisted Mama and Mrs. Collins order only tallow candles, as they were far more suitable for a small income.

"I will choose my own candles without … "

"What is that, Lizzy?" Mama asked.

"I was merely noting the lovely candles." Her cheeks burned hot as the candle flames.

"Stop muttering." Papa gazed up at the ornate ceiling moldings and clenched his hand—a warning she dare not ignore.

"Yes, sir."

The butler ushered them into the parlor. It should have been called the throne room; an overstuffed palatial chamber in which Lady Catherine held court, dispensing her opinions upon anyone she lured or trapped within.

"The Bennets, madam." The butler bowed and left, giving Elizabeth one last twitch of his eye as he passed.

Appropriate bows, curtsies and greetings were exchanged with the already arrived Collinses.

"The time, Dr. Bennet, have you noticed the time?" Lady Catherine pulled herself straighter in her imposing gilt chair. Her foot beat a rapid tattoo on the carpet, narrowly missing the golden sphinxes supporting her throne. Good that she did not have a scepter, or she might have struck him with it. "The Collinses preceded you by a full ten minutes at least."

"Pray excuse us, your ladyship." Mama clasped her hands. "Consider though, two young ladies—"

"I require you to be the first to arrive, Dr. Bennet. Always. Anne must not suspend her evening's enjoyment waiting for your consultation."

"Of course, your ladyship. I assure you, it will not happen again." Papa bowed low, glaring at Elizabeth on the way down. "I will attend to her now."

"Go on then." She waved him away and pointed her long, bony finger at a settee. "Sit down. I will not have you stand about stupidly."

Mama and Jane sat down. Elizabeth took stock of the remaining space. No, not even Miss de Bourgh might fit in those tight quarters. She hurried across the room and sat beside Charlotte.

Lady Catherine glowered. Goodness, what did the woman expect, for her to sit upon Jane's lap? Perhaps perch on the settee's arm like some sort of royal pet—a pug mayhap? She dare not ignore the command altogether.

"You look very well tonight, Lizzy," Charlotte whispered.

"Thank you, Mrs. Collins." Elizabeth shifted her eyes toward Mama.

Charlotte rolled her eyes to the ceiling. She was simply, but neatly, dressed. Her wide face with round cheeks could hardly be declared pretty, much less beautiful, but her heart was kind and her sense of the ridiculous well refined.

Lady Catherine cleared her throat and flipped a wrinkle out of her skirt. "As I was saying…"

All eyes turned to her.

"My nephews and a party of friends arrived yesterday and need company to amuse them in the evenings. I insist you attend us often whilst they visit.

"Certainly, your ladyship. I can think of nothing better for my girls—"

"My wife and I are always present to serve you in any way possible." How did Mr. Collins manage to bow despite being still seated?

"While your daughters could undoubtedly benefit from well-bred company," Lady Catherine sniffed in Elizabeth's direction, "except for my niece who has just come out, the party's ladies are merely tradesmen's daughters seeking to improve themselves. Though their wealth gives them some standing, no one with so new a fortune can be considered of consequence."

"No, your ladyship." Mr. Collins's head wobbled so hard it might have fallen off, save for his securely tied cravat. Plump and round-faced, his well-oiled hair stuck to his head and his brow usually glistened with sweat.

"A family name and good connections are no small things in the world."

"And a connection to Rosings Park is a most valued one indeed." Mama's words tumbled out almost on top of Lady Catherine's, earning Mama a withering raised eyebrow.

"Although they have been educated in the best girls' seminary their parents could *afford.*" Lady Catherine sneered at the word. "We must prepare ourselves for vulgarity of manner and coarseness of opinion. I expect their conversation will be unpolished and their accomplishments of little note."

"Those are not unredeemable faults, though," Elizabeth said. "Fine company and examples such as yourself and Miss de Bourgh might be the very tonic to cure their malady."

Charlotte pressed her lips into a tight line. Dear friend that she was, she would save her rebuke for a private moment. And Charlotte would be right. Comments in that vein would probably not serve her well.

"Perceptive of you, Miss Elizabeth, most astute. That is precisely why I have permitted them to come. I take the responsibility of rank quite seriously. I cannot shirk my duty to offer betterment to those willing to seek it, no matter the inconvenience to me."

"Indeed you are all that is gracious and kind," Mr. Collins said.

"My girls have blossomed under your tutelage, my lady."

"And Mrs. Collins."

Charlotte flinched and turned the same rich red as the settee. Perhaps she might blend in and avoid further notice.

"Of course, who could imagine anything else?" The sweeping plume on Lady Catherine's turban bobbed, amplifying each nod into a grand gesture fit for a royal audience. "How could anyone fail to bloom in the shadow of Rosings? You may take comfort in knowing dear Anne has suffered no ill effects from the tradesman's daughters' presence … "

Elizabeth balled her fists and pushed them deep into the settee. Miss de Bourgh suffer harm from them? The very thought! With her highhanded remarks and her ill-informed opinions, her guests were the ones in danger of being ruined by that scrawny, spoiled, freckled—

"What say you, Miss Elizabeth?" Lady Catherine asked.

"Excuse me, your ladyship?"

"Pay attention, young woman. How many times have I—"

"Forgive me. When you mentioned Miss de Bourgh, I recalled all her notable qualities and fell lost in consideration of what more I might learn from my acquaintance with her."

Charlotte stepped on her foot, hard.

Lady Catherine fixed narrowed eyes upon her whilst Mama gaped at Lady Catherine. No one breathed, though the loudly ticking clock reminded them perhaps they should.

"Of course you were—and who could blame your distraction." The turban feathers dipped slowly.

"We hired the new maid you recommended," Charlotte said.

"Naturally, why would you do otherwise?"

"What my dear wife means," Mr. Collins leaned forward and slightly in front of Charlotte, "is we are humbly grateful for your advice in the matter. She is everything you promised and a boon to our household already." He snuck a pointed look over his shoulder at Charlotte and Elizabeth.

Odious man! How could Mama have ever expected her to marry him? Poor, poor Charlotte, now forced to endure him the rest of her life.

Lady Catherine rose and everyone else followed suit. She took several steps toward the doorway. "Ahh, Anne, you have been sorely missed tonight."

Miss de Bourgh made her grand entrance, stopping two steps into the room. No doubt to give them a moment to bask in her majestic presence. A girl of four and twenty, she appeared no more than four and ten by stature and figure alone. Her sallow complexion turned positively jaundiced against the rich coral silk of her pouffed sleeves. The full skirt and train weighed her down and made any movement a prodigious effort. No wonder she was late. It was a great wonder she had arrived downstairs at all.

She leaned on the arm of a tall, well-built gentleman. He carried himself like a soldier, confident and proud. The line of his nose and jaw resembled Miss de Bourgh and Lady Catherine enough to pronounce him kin. Behind them another gentleman, escorting a much taller, handsome young lady, waited to be admitted. Shadows shifted and shuffled, bespeaking more persons waiting in the hall behind them.

"Pray, take our place, Miss de Bourgh." Mr. Collins bowed and gestured toward the settee.

Miss de Bourgh approached with tiny, mincing steps so unhurried she might never reach her destination. Two more ladies and three gentlemen filed in. Papa closed the procession and stationed himself near Miss de Bourgh. He helped her sit, offering her additional pillows and blankets until she waved him off with a flick of her frail hand.

The rest of the party stared at the room, their shoes, and Lady Catherine.

"Are you going to introduce us, Aunt, or shall we all just gawk dumbly at one another?" Miss de Bourgh's escort asked. His ramrod straight spine did little to belie a glint of mischief in his eyes.

"Nephew." *Her* glare would have withered most plants and all but the most stalwart of men. "Colonel Fitzwilliam, Mr. Darcy, Miss Darcy, may I present my vicar, Mr. Collins, Mrs. Collins, my physician, Dr. Bennet, Mrs. Bennet, Miss Bennet and Miss Elizabeth Bennet."

Mr. and Miss Darcy were no doubt siblings, given the way they favored one another, and perhaps cousins to Miss de Bourgh and Colonel Fitzwilliam. Brother and sister shared the same uneasy posture and uncomfortable set of their jaws. Did they not like company, or perchance Lady Catherine?

Lady Catherine looked at the Collinses and Bennets. "May I present my nephews' friends, Mr. and Mrs. Hurst, Mr. Bingley, Miss Bingley and Mr. Wickham."

How kind of her to draw the distinction of rank so clearly.

Mr. Darcy and Colonel Fitzwilliam rearranged the room to permit all to sit in the great lady's presence. The Hursts seemed all too pleased to be near *her;* Miss

Bingley, too, though with slightly more dignity. Mr. Wickham and Mr. Bingley took seats next to Jane. At least Mama did not cackle aloud with glee.

Clearly the Darcys and the colonel had endured an audience with Lady Catherine before. They sat as far from *her* as possible.

Elizabeth waited for the others to be seated and took the one remaining place, between Charlotte and Colonel Fitzwilliam. His warm, easy manner marked him a likely jester in the Lady's court.

Mr. Collins leaned toward the Darcys. If he did not attend his posture, he might soon topple from his chair. "I understand your party arrived—"

"Just yesterday, they arrived yesterday," Lady Catherine said, "traveling in three coaches with drivers and six outriders."

"We could have driven ourselves, but that sends her mad," Colonel Fitzwilliam murmured, lips barely moving. "I was sorely tempted."

Elizabeth blinked rapidly and stole a sidelong look, but his serene countenance betrayed nothing.

"Had you a pleasant journey?" Mama asked.

Mr. Darcy glanced at his sister. Tall and pretty as an Almack's fashion plate, she seemed to have everything in her favor, save courage. Poor dear shrank into her chair each time Lady Catherine turned her way.

Mr. Darcy inclined forward as if to shield Miss Darcy from view. His broad shoulders and imposing presence made a formidable barrier. "It was—"

"Tolerable. Travel is at best tolerable. A necessary evil, I always say. It is much more agreeable for one to receive company than to be received. Do you not agree?" The creases in her forehead made it clear a response was neither expected nor welcome.

"She has obviously not visited the right houses," Colonel Fitzwilliam whispered

What an uncanny trick, to speak without moving one's lips. She ought to petition him to teach her. Elizabeth hid her chuckle with a hearty cough.

"Are you unwell, Miss Elizabeth?" Lady Catherine's voice cut sharp as a surgeon's knife.

"Certainly not!" Mama wrung her hands in her lap. "We would never allow anyone with signs of illness to come—"

"No, no, your ladyship, I was merely taken by the unique wisdom and insight of your words."

"Oh," she settled into her seat, "as you should be."

Colonel Fitzwilliam sputtered and choked.

Charlotte kicked Elizabeth's heel and pointed her chin toward Papa.

He hovered near Miss de Bourgh, eyes dark and sharp and ominous as a raven's.

She studied garish patterns in the carpet. Mama's ire she could endure. Papa's she could not. What did he expect when everything about this situation was so entirely ridiculous?

Talk, mostly Lady Catherine's, swirled around her. How far had they traveled? They came from London under fair weather and on fine roads. *She* made pronouncements on the best inns and the evils of travel by post.

How interesting, considering she traveled little herself and certainly never by post.

The butler appeared in the doorway. "Dinner is served."

Lady Catherine rose. Papa and Mr. Collins offered their arms in escort. She strode past them both and took Mr. Darcy's arm.

His mask was too practiced to discern him pleased or aggrieved. He was well-favored though, his features as refined and regular as chiseled marble. Had he merely been blessed by nature, or had Lady Catherine ordered it so?

Papa escorted Miss de Bourgh. Elizabeth lingered near the wall as the higher ranking ladies and gentlemen exited until she was left alone with Miss Bingley.

"It is uncomfortable when the ladies outnumber the gentlemen," Miss Bingley murmured. She was angular and birdlike, with plumage that far outshone her wit.

"I am one of five sisters. I find it a most common occurrence."

"You have no brothers? How shocking. One would think, if anyone could get sons, a doctor would."

"One might, but clearly he could not. Worse still, he chose to be born the second son of a country gentleman, with only a profession to supply his fortune."

Miss Bingley drew a breath, but paused, mouth open, her brows drawn together in an odd little crease. Elizabeth halted a step and ushered the poor confused woman ahead.

Footmen stood like pillars around the heavily laden table. A multitude of mirrors multiplied their numbers into a veritable army of attendants. While impressive, the effect rendered the dining room far too crowded.

Lady Catherine reigned at the head of the table. An ornate, armed chair stood in admirably for her regular throne. Colonel Fitzwilliam occupied the foot with Anne at his right. Interesting, Mr. Darcy did not occupy a place of honor. Rather, he sat away from both ends, beside his sister. Had he displeased *her* in some way, or was he continuing as bodyguard for the fragile Miss Darcy?

The only seat open for Elizabeth suited her well, in the middle of the company and easily overlooked. She slipped in between Charlotte and Mr. Wickham.

His unaffected smile and twinkling eyes recommended him as a dinner companion. She pulled her chair tight under the table. The footmen would require room to perform their office, and they deserved consideration.

A plate of crayfish soup appeared before her, fragrant perfume wafting from its surface. For all its flaws, Rosings Park possessed a splendid kitchen staff and served memorable meals.

"You are Dr. Bennet's daughter?" Mr. Wickham asked, tucking his napkin into his collar over his elaborately tied cravat.

"One of five, sir." She sipped her soup, likely to be the chiefest pleasure of her evening.

"Five? That is rather a large number of sisters? Have you any brothers?"

What original questions and stunning conversation. "No, sir, I do not."

He whispered in intimate tones. "I imagine Lady Catherine has already informed you that is an ill-advised strategy for a family."

Elizabeth set her spoon beside her plate and dabbed her mouth. "Indeed, she has also offered her sage advice on what may be done to remedy the situation." She caught his gaze. "Very specific recommendations. In the drawing room."

Mr. Wickham choked and sputtered into his napkin.

"Are you well, sir?" She must not react at all lest Lady Catherine take notice.

"Yes, yes, I am thank you." He slapped his chest. "And your father, he is not … troubled by her—"

"Certainly not. Everyone knows her counsel is of uncommon value, always worth careful attention."

He snorted and took up his napkin again.

She returned to her soup.

"What is that? I could not hear you clearly." Lady Catherine leaned forward on her elbows. "I must have my share of the conversation."

Naturally, none could evade her notice, but still, how rude to call down the table. Elizabeth turned toward her and her throat pinched, lifting her pitch half a note. "I was merely telling Mr. Wickham how we all rely upon your advice in all matters."

Papa's eyes bored into her; color rose along his jaw.

"Who else amongst us speaks to the variety of subjects, with the level of authority you do, your ladyship? We all spend many hours discussing the wisdom you condescend to dispense."

*She* relaxed into her chair, hands folded into her lap. "Few are so attentive to their betters when they speak. It does you and your family credit that you are."

Papa grunted and took another sip of his soup, the unattractive hue fading from his jowls.

Conversation resumed around the table.

Why was Mr. Wickham staring at her? "Have I spoken untruths?"

"I am all astonishment, Miss Elizabeth. I have been told I am glib, but I do believe I have met my equal." He beamed, a glittering, warm, utterly distracting expression. His eyes, though, made it clear he knew exactly the effect of that mien.

A smile in return would have been appropriate, but the vile taste in her mouth precluded one. "How am I to discern what kind of compliment I have been paid, sir?"

"Excuse me?"

"Is it a desirable thing to be your verbal equal, or some dire pronouncement to be avoided by all polite society?"

"I encountered many at school who would have considered it a compliment."

Lady Catherine rang a silver bell, and the footmen leapt into action, removing platters and plates. They folded the first tablecloth with great ceremony, revealing a pristine cloth underneath.

Elizabeth sat perfectly still lest she jostle any of the servants. Lady Catherine did not tolerate clumsiness in her staff.

New delicacies filled the table, and Lady Catherine introduced the new dishes, some quite exotic indeed. Her servants and many of the parish would eat well tonight and tomorrow. Had *she* any idea the quantity of food sold from the kitchen's back door?

Lady Catherine turned the table and addressed her new conversation partner. Elizabeth faced Charlotte. She would not repine the loss of Mr. Wickham's conversation, but she peeked over her shoulder at him.

He was, all told, a well-looking man, in a dangerous, intriguing sort of way.

"You may wish to stop staring before someone notices," Charlotte whispered.

Elizabeth shook her head and ducked away from his spell.

"You are welcome." Charlotte dabbed her chin with her napkin. "I give you leave to like him, though, even if he is quite handsome."

"Why has he been singled out for your particular approbation?"

"Not my approval, Lizzy, Lady Catherine's."

Elizabeth set her fork alongside her plate. "Pray, tell me your meaning."

"Miss Bingley heard Lady Catherine decree Mr. Wickham would do very well for you."

A vague chill coursed down her spine. "Indeed? What have you discovered? Is he a gentleman?"

"I understand he is studying the law. Miss Bingley said he has recently been granted admission to the Inn of Courts."

"How fortunate for him." Elizabeth pushed vegetables around her plate.

"You seemed content with his attentions a few minutes ago. You have changed your mind now? Even you are not so contrary."

"I was not well pleased, and I am not being contrary." Elizabeth stabbed a slice of meat with her fork. "I have merely learned my desires are rarely the same as *hers*."

"Therefore, you must necessarily reject whatever she recommends?"

"It is a useful shorthand."

"I cannot believe it of you. You may say it, but I cannot allow you would act on it. You are far more sensible."

Yet her good sense informed that very opinion. What would Charlotte think if she knew Lady Catherine had intended Elizabeth for mistress of the parsonage and heartily disapproved of Mr. Collins's choice?

"You have remarkable faith in my prudence." Elizabeth sipped her wine.

"You shall not convince me otherwise. I know no one who speaks more superior sense than you."

"Which is precisely why you are my friend. I must have someone in my life who thinks me clever."

Lady Catherine cleared her throat. Conversation ceased, and all eyes turned to her.

"Mr. Collins shall now say the grace—briefly."

Oh, how it hurt containing her snicker, as did the weight of Charlotte's heel on her toes. At least Charlotte had a sense of humor about her husband's imperfections, including his legendary long-windedness.

Truly, he had chosen better for himself than had Lady Catherine.

"… Amen."

Lady Catherine rose. "We shall all adjourn to the drawing room."

Everyone stood.

What excellent fortune! The ladies would not be granted a private audience with her ladyship tonight. Surely the realization the gentlemen would carry a conversation without *her* having a share of it was too much for her ladyship to bear.

The drawing room glittered with as many candles as the dining room. Ormolu covered nearly every surface not already upholstered or inlaid with fine woods. Ancient oil paintings glowered down on the party, reminding them of the prodigious condescension permitting them admission to this chamber.

"You should open our entertainment, Georgiana." Lady Catherine lowered herself onto a grand chair, placed front and center in the rows of seats surrounding the pianoforte. Few in England might boast more true enjoyment in music than she. With her natural taste, if she had only learnt, she would have been a proficient.

Elizabeth hid her face in her shoulder. Probably best not to recall the great lady's words so well.

Miss Darcy jumped up, hand pressed to her chest. "Before so many people?"

She was a tall girl, not the gangly tallness that could be considered an affliction, but rather that elegant columnar stature that harkened to classic lines and sophisticated beauty. The fringe of her embroidered white shawl trembled.

Lady Catherine's eyes bulged, a bit too much like Charlotte's pug. It was a wonder she did not growl.

Miss Darcy blanched white as her gown. The tremors moved from her fringe to her hands. If she quivered any harder, Papa might mistake it for a seizure.

Mr. Darcy tensed, ready to spring to his sister's defense. For Jane's sake, that must not happen.

Elizabeth slipped to Miss Darcy's side. "Our group is not so very intimidating, truly. Would it be helpful if I turn pages for you? I could even stand between you and your onlookers. You might pretend I am the only one watching."

"I … I …"

"I am genuinely impressed by anything more accomplished than a simple scale."

Miss Darcy giggled, though her eyes glistened, and her hands still shook. She peeked over at Mr. Darcy whose towering stance eased. The most formidable furrows faded from his forehead.

"I … thank you. You are very kind." Miss Darcy sniffled and picked her way to the pianoforte.

Elizabeth followed. "What do you wish to play?"

"Miss Elizabeth, give her the selection uppermost in the folio on the instrument. I acquired it particularly for her." Lady Catherine pointed without looking while she talked to Colonel Fitzwilliam.

Elizabeth retrieved the music. Poor Miss Darcy, required to execute so complicated a score. "Are you—"

"The music is fine," Miss Darcy whispered and perched on the piano stool. "I just—" she peeped at her audience and gulped.

"You prefer to be in the audience, not their subject." Elizabeth shifted to block Miss Darcy's view of her onlookers. "Better?"

"Yes, yes, I suppose."

An accomplished musician who needed blinders like a horse? Though beastly inconvenient, her modesty did Miss Darcy credit. "Shall I procure the screen from the corner and place it around you?"

"Oh, would you?"

Elizabeth snickered. "I would gladly, but I ought to warn you, the japanware clashes terribly with your gown."

Miss Darcy clapped her hand to her mouth, giggling.

"Oh, you must not! Her ladyship is most opposed to laughter." Elizabeth arranged the crisp sheets. "Shall I ask her to wait whilst I rearrange the furniture again?"

Miss Darcy laughed harder.

Lady Catherine cleared her throat, her preferred form of reprimand.

"Perhaps not." They shared a conspiratorial glance, and Miss Darcy lifted her hands to the keys.

The black notes on the score came to life, cavorted though the bric-a-brac and skipped amongst the candles. This was the performance of a true proficient. Lady Catherine certainly would not have become one—had she only learnt.

Miss Darcy graced them with another piece while Elizabeth remained at her post. A trivial enough favor to perform as their enjoyment should not come at the expense of the poor girl's equanimity. Miss Darcy even offered her a weak imitation of a smile. Though whether for her assistance, or relief that her ordeal was over, was not clear.

Lady Catherine ordered Miss Bingley to play next.

She sauntered to the instrument. No doubt displaying her accomplishments—and her figure—brought her great pleasure and no few accolades.

"Pray, Miss Elizabeth, sit beside me." Miss Darcy patted the cushion next to her.

"I should not. Her ladyship prefers to preserve the distinction of rank. It is not my place—"

"I insist, Miss Elizabeth." Mr. Darcy towered over her, dark eyes warm and rich as his voice. He gestured toward the spot.

What could she do but obey?

He hung close behind them, daring his aunt to express displeasure. Clearly, he was fashioned of sterner stuff than his sister, and gallant enough to apply it for her good.

"Miss Bingley plays very well," Elizabeth whispered.

"Yes, though her grasp of dynamics is not quite right. Listen—this passage, can you hear? She does not manage the light-handed parts right at all."

Elizabeth closed her eyes. Were the keys crying in pain as she hit those notes? "The piece feels—unbalanced?"

"You have a good ear. Do you play?"

"A little and very ill indeed. I only play in duet with my sister Jane. She covers for all the passages I fudge and slur. She is hardly proficient, though."

Jane sat beside Mr. Bingley, hanging on his every word. He basked in her glow.

"She is beautiful. Is she always so …" Miss Darcy asked.

"Angelic? Yes. She is precisely as she seems to be. I confess, having a sister so perfect can be a trial. It is my burden to bear, and I think I make a good show of it, most times. I regard no one more highly, even if she hides her true feelings beneath her reserve. Some consider her too serene, but they do not know how deeply she feels."

"I am pleased to hear it."

"You suspect your aunt's judgment enough to distrust the match she selected for him?"

Miss Darcy crushed her skirts in her knotted hands. "Oh, I mean no criticism to your sister. Truly, I meant no offense, Miss Elizabeth."

"None taken, I assure you. I am sure you are unaware that *she* declared I was for Mr. Collins."

Miss Darcy gaped at Mr. Collins. He leaned so far toward Lady Catherine that, if anything startled him, he would surely fall out of his chair.

Mr. Darcy grunted something sounding suspiciously like a clandestine laugh. He wore the same impassive mask, but the barest hint of a dimple appeared in his right cheek.

Miss Bingley ended her sonata with a final crescendo.

Elizabeth applauded because she should. Considering their bland expressions, most of the others did likewise. Mr. Bingley nearly missed his cue to clap, saved only after Jane nudged him and gestured toward the pianoforte.

"Tell me of the gentleman our benefactress has chosen for my sister."

"I like him very much—"

Lady Catherine waved toward the piano. "Miss Bennet, you shall now play. Mrs. Collins, Miss Elizabeth, sing for us."

The burning started in her chest and reached up her neck to her face. At least she had not been ordered to play. That would have been truly mortifying following such truly accomplished musicians. Perhaps she might beg Miss Darcy to perform the same service she herself had recently rendered.

Lady Catherine cleared her throat. Perhaps a cup of warm tea and honey would help her clear away that nasty tickle. Then again, rapid obedience to her orders might work better.

Jane sat at the pianoforte, hands clenched in her lap. "I cannot play nearly as well as either—"

"Do not try." Elizabeth reached for the music folio. "Let us have some simple, gay melodies that cannot, by their very nature, be compared to the previous concertos." She placed sheet music on the stand, several familiar country songs, the kind of tunes people actually enjoyed.

Charlotte pointed to one. Jane played the first notes.

Lady Catherine scowled through the entire piece, yet the subtle turn of her lips suggested she appreciated the simplicity of their recital. Mr. Bingley, though, beamed, his eyes never leaving the pianoforte.

The first song drew to a close, and Mr. Wickham approached. "May I join you?"

"Do you meet the standards of our accomplished little band?" Elizabeth bobbed a small curtsey.

"It will be challenging, but I am up to the effort, if you will have me." His smile revealed excellent teeth, enhancing the warmth in his dark eyes.

Elizabeth glanced at Jane and Charlotte, who shrugged. "We shall be happy for you to join us, if you fulfill your promises."

Jane played another song. Mr. Wickham's rich baritone filled the room, as engaging and entrancing as his visage. Jane's fingers tangled, and she stumbled over the next chord, but quickly regained her composure.

Elizabeth nearly missed her cue. How impertinent she had been. Few men sang so well, and she had intimated he was not a worthy partner.

Mama was right; her teasing would be her undoing.

She fought to focus on the music, but the words blurred. How she envied Jane her occupation and her self-control. Jane never found herself in such humiliating circumstances.

The final chords faded away and enthusiastic applause replaced the music. Mr. Wickham bowed. He clearly enjoyed displaying as much as Miss Bingley.

"Give us another."

"Yes, yes do."

"Shall we?" Mr. Wickham turned his stammer-inducing charm on her.

Elizabeth sucked in a deep breath. "Pray go on without me. I must take some air." She curtsied and strode away lest he do any more to test her resolve.

Darcy stepped aside as Miss Elizabeth rushed past. Had the raging fire in both fireplaces affected her so—or had Wickham?

The musicians began another piece. At least Miss Bennet had the modesty to restrict herself to pieces she could perform passably well. Better than forcing them to endure a mediocre attempt at a more impressive work, even though it encouraged Wickham's display.

What had he said to Miss Elizabeth?

Darcy slipped half a step backward and peered into the corridor. Old Long Tom, the butler, held her captive midway down the hall. Blast and botheration! He would terrorize the poor girl just as he did Georgiana.

Miss Elizabeth did not deserve such inhospitable treatment, particularly after her sensitivity to Georgiana. He taped tapped Georgiana's shoulder and pointed through the doorway with his chin. Her eyes grew wide, and she waved him out.

He stopped two steps outside the door. Cool air embraced him. How good to be free of the cloying atmosphere of the drawing room.

A peculiar barking filled the hall. How? It was simply not possible. Long Tom smiling? The butler was laughing with Miss Elizabeth. What matter of enchantment had been woven here?

He approached, but they both fell into mirth before he could make out their conversation.

Long Tom jerked upright and tugged his coat. His normal fierce mien snapped into place.

"Mr. Darcy?" Miss Elizabeth examined him with such peculiar, penetrating intensity, as though she recognized things that no one else did.

What did she see? He should reply, but her spell stole away his words.

Her lips quirked into an entirely unique, captivating expression no other woman had ever worn in his company. How utterly delightful.

"You will not give away our secret, will you?"

"Certainly not." He glanced up at the butler who did not even blink. Had he really just seen the man laugh? "Did you need some fresh air?"

"Ah … yes … I did." She adjusted her fichu.

What had Wickham done?

He yanked his shirt cuffs past his coat sleeves. "May I accompany you?"

"As you wish."

The butler stepped aside, allowing them to pass.

"The parlor is overwarm." Not the most original topic of conversation, but an improvement over awkward silence.

"I believe my father recommends keeping it so for Miss de Bourgh's comfort." Her slippers barely whispered across the polished marble tile.

"My aunt is pleased a proper physician cares for Anne now. She never considered surgeons and apothecaries suitable to the task."

"No more pleased than my father is for such an illustrious patroness." She did not look at him.

Would that she train her charming gaze on him once more.

"I am grateful for your care toward my sister tonight. Few would have marked her distress or come to so elegant a solution for it. We—she—feels ill-qualified to recommend herself to strangers."

"That is her natural disposition, I suppose? She does not bear the timidity of one wounded by society."

"You are quite astute." Astonishingly so. How long had it taken her to reach that conclusion? Minutes, seconds?

"She seems a very sweet girl, and only in need of a modicum of encouragement. Perhaps a touch of laughter to find her way across this transition."

"And that is your prescription, Miss Elizabeth? Is laughter your favorite tonic?"

"I confess it is. I dearly love to laugh."

Why did shadows linger around her eyes when she confessed that?

"It seems to have served you well."

She squared her shoulders, her back straight like a soldier prepared for inspection. "My poor mother reminds me that it is considered unladylike at best."

No doubt, she had been made to endure those sentiments often. Not unlike Georgiana, subjected to Aunt Catherine's constant admonishments.

They reached the end of the corridor. When had the hall become so short?

"Will you be staying long in Kent?" she asked.

"Our current plan is three weeks, but I expect—"

"It will be closer to six before Lady Catherine grants you permission to leave?"

"How came you to that conclusion?"

"Lady Catherine summoned us from London nearly two years ago. We have been in the shadow of Rosings Park ever since," she said.

"I do not follow."

"Two years is sufficient time in which to become quite well acquainted with a person's manner and habits."

"So you have made a study of my aunt?" Hairs on the back of his neck rose. Did she think his character like *hers*?

"After a fashion, I suppose. Pray do not infer any nefarious intentions on my part. When it is incumbent upon one to please a patron—"

Or a mother perhaps?

"—seeking to understand them and their ways is, in my experience, a wise course of action."

"You are skilled observer and keen judge of persons."

"I would never don such airs, sir. It would be both immodest and untrue."

"Yet you trust your own conclusions and take your own counsel in matters of …managing those around you?"

"Managing others is not my place in life." The tips of her ears flushed bright red. "But I endeavor to minister to as many needs as are within my means."

"You discerned my sister's temperament quite accurately."

Three, four, five steps in silence.

What had he said wrong? Was she trying to punish him?

"I know this is forward, but I would very much like to further my acquaintance with her, unless you object, sir."

She certainly was not of Georgiana's station. Aunt Catherine would not approve. Oh balderdash! What matter what she thought? Miss Elizabeth was a gentleman's daughter and, more importantly, possessed the kind, gentle nature Georgiana needed in a friend. "It would benefit her to have a companion at Rosings."

"She seems lonely and uncomfortable around Miss de Bourgh."

"I…how?"

"Miss Darcy chose a seat far away from Miss de Bourgh and the other ladies of your party. She stayed close to you—her protector, I expect."

Darcy stopped mid-step and stared at her. She did not flinch as so many did when he studied them.

"I meant no offense sir. She idolizes you, much as Miss de Bourgh does."

Darcy ran a finger along the inside of his collar. It would forever be a loss to the legal community that Miss Elizabeth could not sit at the bar.

"Clearly, you are worthy of such respect. With a man like Colonel Fitzwilliam looking to you as his commander in this action and Mr. Bingley attending your every word, emulating your dress—"

"No—"

"He has recently begun knotting his cravat after yours—"

"Nonsense!"

"Look carefully, and you will see. His valet has not yet mastered the craft of it. It must be new to him. Given it is the way yours is tied, I can hardly fathom another reason."

She noticed his cravat? "I had not—"

"Of course not. To do so would be prideful—arrogant even. With two respectable gentlemen and several young ladies who esteem you so much, it is obvious you are neither. Undoubtedly, you put yourself out for their welfare and are apt to sacrifice your own happiness for your duty to others."

"And how do you determine that?"

"You are at Rosings, though you would rather be elsewhere."

"Excuse me? You cannot know—" No one had ever so quickly or accurately gauged him—not that any had ever tried.

Her dark eyes sparkled in the candlelight. She was a handsome woman—not the ethereal beauty of her sister, but attractive in the way that would blossom through the years, deepening every day—

"Am I wrong, sir?"

Not wrong, but he would not confess so easily either. He broke eye contact and with it her spell. "I come each spring to assist the steward with matters of the estate—"

"Your own estate requires your attention as well." Her eyebrow arched high. "I expect you have worked numerous long nights in anticipation of this journey. The dark shadows under your eyes are not of the kind caused by traveling with a large party of friends."

His jaw dropped. How could he reply?

"Do not worry—your secret is most safe with me."

"You keep many secrets?"

"I must."

A few more steps and the parlor door loomed. The corridor was definitely too short. How lacking in taste of Aunt Catherine to allow it to be so.

"I should return before my absence causes consternation. Thank you for your company." She dipped in a shallow courtesy and left him.

Darcy remained in the doorway as Miss Elizabeth rejoined Georgiana. The corridor echoed, empty and lifeless without her.

Long Tom appeared and loomed very close, his stony mask shadowed and dark. "May I help you, sir?"

A shiver skittered down Darcy's back. Miss Elizabeth had a protector.

"No, I just need some air." Darcy strode away.

---

Later in the evening, Colonel Fitzwilliam queried Elizabeth's opinion and struck up a lively debate regarding the Tudor monarchs. Not that it could be truly called a debate—no opinion but Lady Catherine's could be tolerated. After she expressed her thoughts once, Elizabeth dropped the matter entirely, but her acquiescence alone was not sufficient. They were not dismissed from Lady Catherine's presence until each proclaimed hers the only right judgment on the matter.

Elizabeth climbed into Lady Catherine's coach, glad in equal measure for the transportation and for the exhausted silence of her companions.

What was Colonel Fitzwilliam's true view on the issue? He was not a mean spirited sort of man, just one easily bored and in search of a spot of fun. Most likely he agreed with Lady Catherine, but could not resist toying with her entirely predictable responses.

Interesting how he failed to notice the uncomfortable looks exchanged in his wake. The only other one in the room who appeared to enjoy the entire affair was Mr. Wickham, who goaded him on from the far side of the room.

Good that Lady Catherine did not intended Colonel Fitzwilliam for Jane. Her tender heart could not enjoy his variety of amusement. Mr. Bingley, though, proved surprisingly acceptable. He spent the evening most attentive to Jane, with pleasing manners and correct opinions.

How scandalous! She agreed with Lady Catherine? Then again, even a broken clock was right twice a day, so perhaps. Elizabeth sniggered. As long as Jane was pleased, so would she be.

## Chapter 2

THE NEXT MORNING, Elizabeth slept far later than usual, savoring the rare sensation of doing absolutely nothing. She had barely dressed when Papa called up from the stairwell.

"Miss de Bourgh is unwell. I must go. Lizzy, attend me." He hurried away.

Elizabeth slipped on her pelisse, gathered her workbag, and pelted after him.

Mama caught them at the front door. "Must Lizzy accompany you to Rosings again? Why do you not bring Jane to assist you?" She followed them out and down the steps.

"Jane has not the constitution for the sick room." Papa loaded his satchel and Elizabeth's workbag under the gig's seat.

"She can sit with Miss de Bourgh as well as Lizzy."

"If she does so, she will not be available for Mr. Bingley's attentions." Papa's face tightened in a mask that only a simpleton could mistake for a smile.

Did Mama recognize his patronizing tone?

"I suppose, but she will be much closer to him at Rosings. Lady Catherine might care to invite … "

"Mama, remember Miss de Bourgh is ill. If the surgeon comes to let blood, or there are skin eruptions to dress, or she casts up her accounts—"

Mama wrinkled her nose. "Must you bring up those unsavory—"

"Precisely the point, Mrs. Bennet. I am not paying a social call. Those 'unsavory' aspects, as you call them, are part and parcel of why I am going to Rosings."

Mama huffed—and was that a dainty stamp of her foot? Pray let not Papa notice, lest his mood sour further.

Elizabeth touched Mama's arm as Jane did when trying to calm her. "You do not wish Lady Catherine or her guests to associate Jane with the sick room. I can hardly imagine what Mr. Bingley—"

"When you put it that way, I have no choice but to agree." Mama pouted.

Papa settled his hat firmly in place and handed Elizabeth into the compact gig.

"While you are there, Lizzy, be sure to pay proper attention to that Mr. Wickham fellow Lady Catherine has chosen for you. He is to be a barrister, and it would be useful to have one in the family. Oh, and afford yourself of every opportunity to compliment Jane to Mr. Bingley. He must not forget about her in her absence."

"I will be certain to mention her at every opportunity." She would of course have so many opportunities as she would be constantly in the presence of the healthy denizens of Rosings. After all, Miss de Bourgh's illness was of no concern at all. She must not mutter. That would only provoke Papa.

"And try to persuade Lady Catherine to include Kitty and Lydia in a future invitation. They would so love to be part of the company there."

Papa clucked his tongue and flicked the reins. The gig lurched into motion. Elizabeth clutched her bonnet with one hand and the side rail with the other. Quite an effective, if tooth rattling, means to end a conversation.

At Rosings, a young groom took the gig from Papa and Long Tom let them in. Though his expression hardly changed, the tension in his shoulders was different, increased. Elizabeth caught his gaze. He closed his eyes and shook his head.

This was not one of Miss de Bough's ordinary spells.

"Shall I see Miss de Bourgh directly, or does Lady Catherine desire an audience first?" Papa handed his hat to the closest footman.

"Lady Catherine awaits you in the morning room." Tom turned and led them to the morning room in strides so long they scurried to keep up. Their steps echoed more loudly than usual in the long, empty hall, lending an eerie, ominous air to the gloomy chamber.

Long Tom announced Papa, but Elizabeth waited just outside the door.

"Is Miss de Bourgh very bad this time?" she asked.

"Mrs. Jenkinson and Dawson spent all night tending her. They are quite alarmed."

"Have they been giving her the willow bark tincture Papa ordered?"

"No. The apothecary declares it useless for rheumatic fever, though he is happy enough to sell it. Mrs. Jenkinson agrees." He murmured something else under his breath.

Probably best she not attempt to decipher it.

"Is there any in the house?"

"Mrs. Jenkinson poured out the last bottle and replaced it with a mix of brandy and poppy tea. She and the apothecary believe it more … ah … efficacious … for Miss de Bourgh's complaints."

"Which does Miss de Bourgh precious little good." Elizabeth pressed her clasped hands to her chin.

"As you say, Miss."

"You have discussed this behavior with them?"

Tom's voice honed to a knife's edge. "They answer to Lady Catherine directly, not to me. Mrs. Jenkinson is certain she acts in Miss de Bourgh's best interest."

"I shall speak with her myself."

"Now?" She must not laugh at the hopeful lilt in his voice.

"No, call for the gig to be brought around. Papa will insist on more willow bark tincture, and the sooner it is here, the better for all of us." Especially herself. Papa invariably blamed her if he lacked the necessary supplies.

"Shall I arrange a driver?"

"No. That will take far too long, and I fear tempers will be short. You know how impatient Papa can be."

"You know her ladyship does not approve—"

Of course, *she* did not approve. "However, she approves even less of Anne's distress when Papa and Mrs. Jenkinson argue, which they will if he finds no willow bark in the house. No doubt, words will be exchanged, but perhaps this way, they might be held off until out of Miss de Bourgh's presence."

Long Tom nodded and signaled a footman to carry his message to the stable. He ushered her to a side door where the gig soon appeared

"Do you require anything else?" He bowed.

"You obeisance is quite stiff this morning. Do you need more liniment for your back?"

He squared his shoulders and looked away.

"I asked you to tell me, not leave me to guess," she muttered. Stubborn, irritating— "Does Cook still have her stomach decoction?"

He shut his eyes.

"Pray, simply tell me all the needs in the household without forcing me to go through them one by one."

He drew a neatly written list from his pocket and passed it to her.

"Why did you not give this to me first?" Elizabeth lifted her hand. "Wait, I know. *She* does not wish for you to disturb Dr. Bennet with the complaints of the staff."

"Yes, Miss."

"I am sorry my father's attendance at Rosings means the apothecary rarely visits anymore."

He grunted. Tom could hardly mention such a thing to Lady Catherine, but perhaps the steward might be prevailed upon to make arrangements. One more thing she would have to remember.

He handed her up to the gig's seat.

"I shall make it a point to request your list in the future." She gathered the reins in her palm and set off.

None of her sisters knew how to drive the gig. Lydia and Kitty did not even ride. Mama would rather forget that Elizabeth could do either. Those were not among the ladylike accomplishments she preferred her daughters to acquire. Still, in the country, they were useful, even if it would result in a scolding from Lady Catherine and Papa after her. What joy to anticipate.

If Miss de Bourgh's episode was truly bad, Papa would require a host of other items. What had he called for the last time?

The horse tossed its head and looked over its shoulder. A rider approached.

"Miss Elizabeth?" Mr. Wickham, atop a tall, chestnut horse, maneuvered alongside her gig, matching her pace.

"Good morning, Mr. Wickham." His dark green coat and well brushed beaver did not yet sport road dust. Interesting, the knot in his cravat was not the same as Mr. Darcy's.

"Out driving for pleasure this fine morning?"

"No, my father waits on Miss de Bourgh. I am on an errand for him."

"I was unaware she was ill today."

"How remarkable. The whole household is generally alerted. They must tread very carefully so as not to disturb her when she has a spell."

Mr. Wickham's eyes twinkled as they had the previous night. How singular. He was caught in a fabrication and pleased about it?

"I confess, after we left the drawing room last night, Hurst and I secreted ourselves away in a distant part of the house and enjoyed our hostess's excellent collection of port."

"But not her company."

"Indeed, though I would say that only enhanced our enjoyment." His eyelid twitched in the barest wink. "You do not agree?"

"Whatever faults you or any other might find with Lady Catherine, she is my father's patroness. Her attentions have been a boon to my family."

"So you will not hear any criticism of the great lady?"

"I will not engage in it myself, nor will I encourage conversations which perpetuate any disrespect toward her."

"You are exceedingly loyal."

"Loyalty is not the issue, sir. Courtesy is."

"You are not loyal to Lady Catherine? Your family is in her service, but does not declare their fealty?"

The audacity! A knot wrenched in her belly. "You are clever with words, sir, but I will not allow you to divert one matter with another. The only concern of which I speak is the debt of courtesy owed between one level of society and another."

"So you owe her a debt—"

Oh, that he would stop talking! "We all owe one another a debt of common politeness and dignified treatment."

"Which is why even the grumpy old butler, who has never spoken to anyone in his entire life, speaks to you?" His eyebrows climbed his forehead.

"I do not appreciate either your tone or your implications, Mr. Wickham." She urged her horse faster.

Another horseman approached. "Wickham!"

Mr. Darcy here as well?

Her horse startled and jerked the gig forward.

"Steady now." Elizabeth pushed her left hand down and pulled up the reins with her right. "No need for a to-do." *Pray let him not bolt!*

The gelding settled back into an easy walk.

"Forgive me, Miss Bennet," Mr. Darcy said.

"He is generally a steady animal, but not accustomed to so many other horses close-by."

"Perhaps I should go?"

"There is no need. Mr. Wickham was just taking leave."

"Indeed I was. Good day." He kicked his horse and trotted off.

*Oh, that he would take the knots in her stomach with him as he rode away!*

---

Darcy stroked his horse's neck. It should not be so satisfying to see Wickham turned away. Pity the horse that had to carry him though. "May I share the road with you?"

"If my horse is agreeable, then so shall I be."

Her horse snorted and plodded on.

"It seems I have been granted approbation."

She chuckled, the melody of dappled sunlight and soft breezes.

"You are an accomplished driver." And a beautiful one—her bearing elegant and strong, with reins and whip in hand. The wind rippled the brim of her bonnet, revealing the soft pink flush on the crest of her cheeks.

"That is a very generous of you." She turned aside so that her bonnet shadowed her profile once more. How beastly unfair.

"You will find I am not prone to idle remarks, kind or not. Most women I know would have been unable to keep their horse under control. Those that could, would not have maintained such poise in the process."

"I am pleased my driving meets your standards. While I would not attempt a four-in-hand, I enjoy the freedom and usefulness our modest equipage provides." She peeked at him.

Who knew a compliment might be so delightfully rewarded?

"I must agree. It is quite needful for a lady in the country to be able to manage a horse well. I have encouraged my sister to learn."

"My mother does not share your view, but I am glad your sister has your support."

She approved of his opinion! That should not please him so, but it did. Her girlish blush at his praise thrilled him like a school boy. Dear God, he had complimented her! Good that Fitzwilliam had not heard.

"Did Wickham trouble you?" he asked.

"No, sir, not at all. Why do you ask?"

"You prevaricate."

"No—"

"Look at your feet. You are not the only keen observer."

She glanced down at the floor boards. Her toes were pressed hard into the wood, but her heels were lifted and widely splayed.

"A horsewoman with your skill would never drive in that attitude unless quite distracted."

"Oh!" She tucked her feet neatly side by side.

"And obviously your horse did not cause your discomposure."

"You are most astute, sir." She looked away.

The turn of her head and the height of his mount conspired to afford him such a view! Sweat prickled under his cravat. She was lovely—and would be mortified if she knew what he saw—or that he was looking in the first place!

By Jove! What kind of a man was he?

"It appears now, sir, you are distressed."

Such concern in her dark eyes?

"I … I … in what way did Wickham impose upon you?"

"It is interesting that you so quickly assume my perturbation might be connected with your friend."

"Is it not?"

"Might I not be alarmed for Miss de Bourgh's health? Perhaps I am anxious that my father will not be able to cure her. I might fear the results of Lady Catherine's displeasure if her daughter does not recover."

"Plausible alternatives, for they also weigh upon your mind, I am sure."

"Why were you so disturbed your friend might have offended me?"

"Friend is not the correct description."

"He came with your party, did he not?"

"He is the son of my father's steward. We were great friends as children."

"But now your stations in life separate you? An up and coming barrister is not worthy of your association?" Her eyes narrowed.

Had she faced such prejudice because of her father's gentlemanly profession?

"He told you he was to be a barrister?"

"No, the intelligence comes from Miss Bingley."

"He applied for admission to the Inn of Courts, but is unlikely to be accepted."

"You have withdrawn your support?"

She did think him like his aunt. Damn.

"A few unwise dalliances have cost him a position at the bar."

"I see." A hint of color rose from her neckline. "I did not realize."

"So now, he has petitioned me for the position of steward of Pemberley."

"You are displeased at the prospect?"

He had not even spoken to Fitzwilliam on the matter. How had she drawn this from him, and why was he willing to tell her? There could be no good reason, but that ending the conversation would be a far worse punishment.

"I am."

"Because of his dalliances?"

"I find it difficult to trust him with the welfare of my tenants."

She shaded her eyes with her hand and looked in the direction Wickham had ridden off. "He and I shared an … instructive tête-à-tête. While he never precisely said anything—I found his meaning essentially clear."

"That is very like him." How long had Wickham been perfecting that trick? As long as Darcy remembered.

"If I may ask, why did he come to Kent with you and your friends?"

"I appointed my Aunt's steward a number of years ago—"

"Mr. Michaels is a fine, fair man."

"I am glad you approve." Surprisingly glad. The thought left him warm and comfortable. "My father thought well of the elder Mr. Wickham. He extracted from me a promise to help young Mr. Wickham establish himself in the world. I brought him to sit under Michaels' tutelage. I will not hire him myself, but Michaels' recommendation should be adequate to secure him a situation elsewhere."

"How did he come to stay at Rosings?"

"Word he was already a barrister, not just in preparations to be one, made its way to my aunt, by his machinations no doubt. She declared it unseemly that a man in his position stay with Michaels and installed him in one of the small guest rooms."

"What will happen when she becomes aware of his true situation?"

"I hope to remove him from Rosings before such a time. My aunt does not suffer mistakes, even her own, gladly."

Only her eyes smiled. "Mr. Michaels will not endorse him and will probably refuse to train him."

"You are very certain."

"I have had many an occasion to speak with him. He does not indulge those who are not plain spoken. I suspect he would not be pleased to have such a man work with him for even a brief time."

"It seems Mr. Wickham has not your approval either?"

"I do not share Lady Catherine's tastes in acceptable suitors."

"She wishes to match you with him?" What a travesty!

"She and my mother have directed me to pay him appropriate courtesies, for *she* has declared him a suitable young man. I must beg you to excuse me though. We come upon the apothecary's now."

How could she leave him on that note? But what could he say? He tipped his hat. "Good day then, Miss Elizabeth."

The old gig turned down the lane, kicking up a little cloud of dust in its wake.

He should have ridden off, but he stayed to watch her safely inside.

What would Aunt Catherine do when she found out Wickham's true standing? Would she rescind her support of him as a suitor to Miss Elizabeth? Possibly, but her stubbornness might well prevent any retraction on her part.

He stroked his chin. If he could come by some means by which to send Wickham away, Miss Elizabeth would be safe from his attentions and Aunt Catherine's scheming. Moreover, he might be able to enjoy the pleasure of her conversation without Wickham's intrusions.

He turned his horse back toward Rosings. *How to get Wickham from Kent?*

---

Mr. Lang, the apothecary, was a decent enough fellow and always pleased for her visits. Of course, her long shopping list likely contributed to the warmth of her welcome. He chatted on about all matters of local gossip as he completed her order. He, not the old women, was the surest source of information in the village. She listened dutifully, though she dismissed most of the intelligence, until he made mention of a putrid infection at the Marsh house.

Papa must be informed. Every precaution must be taken to keep Miss de Bourgh from contact with septicity. The poor girl seemed to draw illness to herself. Since Papa began isolating her from sickness, she suffered fewer spells.

The apothecary helped her carry her packages, which nearly filled the floor of the gig, and she made haste back to Rosings.

Long Tom waited outside the kitchen door and handed her down.

"Lady Catherine has learned of your errand and wishes to see you at once." He loaded parcels into his arms.

"I am not surprised. However, I must get this and this," she took two boxes from him, "and some vital news to my father, directly."

"Her ladyship wishes to see you, immediately."

"You have said so." That earned her a stern glare. "I will brave her wrath, Tom. My first priority is the health and welfare of Miss de Bourgh. Though piqued, *she* always comes to agree my priorities are correct."

"As you say, Miss, though it pains us all to hear you endure another tongue lashing from her ladyship."

She squeezed his wrist. "That is very dear of you—all of you. I cannot tell you how much your concern means, but I have a great deal of experience in weathering displeasure. Pray, see that these are distributed to the staff. I have each one labeled according to your list. If you have any questions—"

"I will seek you out myself. No one will trouble Dr. Bennet."

"Very good. I shall return for my audience with *her* as soon as Papa releases me." She dashed upstairs, her footfalls nearly silent along the marble steps.

Miss de Bourgh's door stood ajar, but no light came through. Her eyes must be sensitive again, or at least she was convinced that they were. How a body was to improve in a dark, hot stuffy room eluded her, but Papa was the doctor. She must not question his wisdom.

She slipped in past the maid who stood ready by the door. The blazing fire behind the fire screen provided more heat than light. Tiny beads of sweat dotted her forehead. Elizabeth shrugged off her pelisse.

Papa stalked to her and pulled her into the hall by the elbow. "How dare you disappear when I most needed you? Where on earth have you been? What possessed you—"

She pressed boxes into his hands. Did he notice her trembling? "There was no willow bark tincture in the house."

He lifted the lid off the first box.

"I visited the apothecary. I brought a double supply of the tincture and good measures of everything else you prescribe for Miss de Bourgh."

"And how do you know I will not—"

She straightened her spine. Her courage always rose with every attempt to intimidate her—or at least that is what Mother had told her. "You always recommend the same course of treatments for her. Even if you require something further, is it not best she has these immediately?"

"I do not like you anticipating me, Lizzy."

"You also do not like to wait."

He rolled his eyes.

What a disagreeable expression. Was he angry with her or Miss de Bourgh's condition?

"You drove there alone, I suppose?"

"I did."

"You realize Lady Catherine—"

"Does not approve. I am very well aware of it and am certain she shall remind me of it soon enough. I saw little choice, though. I could hardly command one of Rosings' servants to attend me. Besides, I have important news regarding the welfare of your patient, sir."

"What exactly would that be?" His eyes narrowed as if to challenge her to offering him something meaningful.

"A putrid infection has broken out at the Marsh farm. Two of the children are already sick with it. The oldest girl is a scullery maid here."

He slammed his fist into his palm. "Blast and botheration! That is precisely—"

"I will see that Tom keeps her from the house until the disease has run its course."

"And three weeks beyond. I will not take any chances."

"I will make certain of it, sir."

"Miss Elizabeth?" Miss de Bourgh's cry barely reached the corridor.

Elizabeth pushed past Papa to the imposing poster bed. Curtains were drawn across three sides and blankets piled high over the counterpane. Miss de Bourgh barely peeked out above the mounds of wool.

"I am here, Miss de Bourgh. I brought the medicines Papa ordered for you."

"The tonic Mrs. Jenkinson gave me did not taste the same as I remember." She rolled toward Elizabeth, but the heavy blankets fought her back. "She complained of a cough … this morning. She is confined at the other side of the house."

"I will see to her—"

"No, Dawson can manage her well enough. I am without … my companion … until she recovers. Stay with me until she does."

Would that she could endure Mrs. Jenkinson' cough instead. "She will not be away from you that long. Besides, I am not an appropriate companion for you."

"You are gently born and know how to manage my medicine. You can read to me and play pianoforte—well enough—to give me distraction from my suffering. I do not need a chaperone or someone to improve my accomplishments now. I need comfort, which you are aptly able to provide."

Papa clucked his tongue. "You mother is well able to spare you, and I would rest easier with you attending her."

She jumped and turned toward him. He held up a small cup of the reddish willow bark tincture.

"If Papa thinks it wise, then of course, I will stay until Mrs. Jenkinson returns."

"Do be a good girl then, and tell Mama it is all settled." Had Miss de Bourgh's voice been any stronger, Elizabeth would have balked. But it was a threadbare whisper that engendered pity, not ire.

Tom met her at the foot of the stairs.

"You have a new scullery maid here?" she asked.

"The girl from the Marsh farm?"

"Yes. Papa's orders she must not come into the house until everyone there is well and three weeks beyond."

"I shall discuss it with the housekeeper. We will manage the situation." He ushered her ahead. "Her ladyship awaits you in the parlor."

"Well, I can avoid it no longer, so into the lioness' den." She smoothed her skirt.

Mr. Collins assured his congregation that life would not bring more than one could bear. Waiting on Lady Catherine's wrath gave her pause to wonder if it were true.

Long Tom announced her.

Though sunlit, the room greeted her with a cold chill, a pointed reminder she was underdressed for such an audience.

"Lady Catherine." She curtsied so deeply her knee brushed the garish carpet.

"You have kept me waiting far too long, Miss Elizabeth Bennet." Lady Catherine perched on her throne. All she needed was a scepter and a ruff, and she might be mistaken for a portrait of Queen Elizabeth.

"I beg your pardon, your ladyship. I undertook an urgent errand for my father."

"Before he even sent you?"

"You have decreed that she must not be kept waiting."

Lady Catherine's eyes squeezed into tiny slits behind her sharp nose. "You drove to the village."

Why was there always one who hurried to report her every action to *her*?

"Have I not adequately impressed upon you the impropriety of young women driving alone? Or perhaps you were not attentive—"

"I have been most attentive to your instructions."

"And still you disobey me, repeatedly." She drummed her fingers along the arm of her throne.

"Only for the sake of Miss de Bourgh. Her welfare is the only consideration that could induce me to disobedience."

Lady Catherine huffed and screwed her mien into a peculiar expression that normally portended good. "What did you obtain from the apothecary?"

She removed a wrinkled paper from her pocket.

"All of this for Anne?"

"No, my Lady. The first six items were for her. The rest were for members of your staff, to alleviate their temptation to approach Papa."

Lady Catherine worked her lips into six variations of a frown, finally settling into the one that most creased her features. "You are remarkably good at avoiding blame, young woman."

Elizabeth ducked her head. The golden sphinxes supporting the throne stared back. Best not speak what came to mind. The creatures could be of a mind to bite. "Miss de Bourgh asked me to stay with her whilst Mrs. Jenkinson recovers from her cough, though I am sure she will not be abed long enough to warrant—"

"I shall order a room readied for you. Whilst you are here, though, should you need to drive out again, a scullery maid will accompany you. I shall accept no excuses on this point. You are a gentleman's daughter. I shall not have it said that an errand for me caused you to behave as less than one."

"Yes, madam." She choked back her retort. How horribly inconvenient.

"I also expect you to pay appropriate attentions to Mr. Wickham whilst you are here as well. Do not waste this opportunity—"

"Excuse me, Aunt Catherine?"

Mr. Darcy strode in, coat covered with road dust. Sweat trailed through the dust on the side of his face. Why would he be reporting to Lady Catherine after a long, hard ride?

"Darcy? Why are you standing there in that condition?"

"I just spoke with Dr. Bennet. He asked me to convey news of a putrid infection at the Marsh farm."

She slammed her hands on the chair arms. "How dare they! I have given specific instruction that no one—"

Elizabeth summoned her reserves of self-control. How good of Papa to insure she could not handle the matter quietly. "They cannot choose when they will take ill or to what disease they will succumb, your ladyship."

"My Anne must be protected at all costs."

"She shall. I spoke to the butler, and measures are already underway to isolate the farm as my father has ordered."

Lady Catherine grumbled a muffled lioness's roar.

"Shall I tell him to send the apothecary to the Marshes? Hastening their recovery can only benefit Miss de Bourgh."

She harrumphed. "Yes, yes, make it so."

Mr. Darcy stepped forward. "I also learned Mr. Wickham and Mr. Bingley were out fishing and spent the day on that property. I do not believe, though, they had contact with anyone on the farm."

"Keep them away from my house." Lady Catherine half rose in her throne, her color high. If she did not calm soon, Papa might have a second patient.

"Papa prefers to err on the side of caution. It might be best that the gentlemen be kept from Rosings until it is clear they have not drawn illness to themselves."

"Yes, yes." Lady Catherine resettled in her seat. "Send them to the Bennets."

"Excuse me?" Mr. Darcy and Elizabeth said simultaneously.

"Where is the difficulty? Miss Elizabeth, you will be here with Anne. Your mother will have room for guests."

The audacity! The overbearing, arrogant—

"Do not lounge about stupidly. These are your friends, Darcy. I expect you to manage them. Go, now." She waved her hands toward the door.

Elizabeth curtsied and hurried out, Mr. Darcy on her heels.

Long Tom intercepted them just outside the door. "I will make preparations for your rooms and for the gentlemen's removal. A man will be waiting to deliver a note to your mother and the apothecary." Tom bowed and strode away.

"He is nothing if not efficient." Mr. Darcy turned his intense gaze upon her.

Her skin tingled and heart raced. Why did he affect her so?

"He has been here as long as I can remember. He is the kind of servant one assumes will always be with the house." He fingered his lapel. "I apologize for my Aunt's imposition upon your family's hospitality. Bingley and Wickham," he said the latter name in the tone one described a soggy pudding, "are part of my party, and I feel responsible—"

"There is no need—"

He edged a half step closer than proper. His dark eyes, flecked with gold, trained on her with an intensity she had never encountered. He smelled of sandalwood, sweat and horse, scents of a man who took himself and his responsibilities seriously.

"Do not brush my concerns aside so lightly, Miss Elizabeth. Your family owes me nothing, and to impose on them is abhorrent to me." He leaned nearer. "I will be happy to install them at the local inn."

How different he was from his aunt, a true gentleman. Her pretty speech fled from her mind, chased away by the thundering double time of her heart.

His eyebrow lifted just a little.

She must not continue to gape at him, dumb. "You are most gracious, but my father would not dare flaunt Lady Catherine's orders. Moreover, I expect my mother will not find the guests a trial. On the contrary, she will be quite pleased to host Mr. Bingley."

Darcy's forehead furrowed and creases appeared beside his eyes.

"You are wary of match-making mamas."

He looked away, clearly too polite to speak the epithets evident on his face.

Poor man, what must he have endured in the ton's marriage mart?

"While my mother might have her ambitions, my sister does not. She will not accept a man she does not like very much."

"Am I so transparent?" His breathy whisper caressed the back of her neck, sending shivers along her spine.

"You are not one to give up your secrets easily." She licked her lips.

"You have tried to discern them?"

When he quirked his brow just that way, it demanded she stroke it smooth.

"I … that is to say—"

"Miss Elizabeth!"

They both jumped.

Lady Catherine loomed in the parlor doorway, her features gathering into her darkest, most menacing scowl. "A word, if you please." She turned on her heel and disappeared into her lair.

Elizabeth dropped a small curtsey and rushed into the parlor to brave the dragon in all her fury. If only she had remembered to bring her sword in her workbag.

Lady Catherine ascended her throne, a stony mask of creases, gnarls and shadow firmly in place.

Was that the scent of burning sulfur in the air?

"Your ladyship?"

"You think I am ignorant of what you are about, young woman?"

"I have not the pleasure of your meaning, madam."

"None of your cheek here, girl. I know. Oh, I know." She shook her finger toward Elizabeth. "You have ambitions beyond your station, beyond all propriety and decency."

"Excuse me?" Elizabeth grabbed the back of the nearest chair to shore up her liquid knees.

"It is written upon your face—clear in that indecent display I just walked in upon."

"Mr. Darcy?" She gasped. "You assume far too much. I only met him yesterday."

"Entirely long enough to form designs upon his person and fortune. You spurned Mr. Collins—I am sure—in the hopes of someone of greater consequence whom you have now found in the person of my nephew."

The upholstery tore a tiny bit beneath her fingernails. "I assure you, madam, I never considered such a thing. Mr. Collins and I ... our temperaments are so different, we could never have made a good match. I am convinced he has a much happier situation with Mrs. Collins."

"Are you suggesting happiness may be found in disobeying me?"

"By no means."

"Then turn your attentions to Mr. Wickham. He studies at the Inn of Courts—."

"He does not, nor is he likely to, having offended a very influential member."

She flushed puce.

That could not be healthy.

"Where do you come by this information?"

"Mr. Darcy—"

Lady Catherine slapped the arms of her chair and heaved to her feet. "What were you doing talking to my nephew?"

"We met on the road this morning."

"While you were driving, unchaperoned, as I have expressly forbidden."

Her shoulders drew up and she tucked her elbows close into her sides. "Yes, your ladyship."

One, two, three steps. Lady Catherine stood so close their skirt hems touched. She waved her bony finger under Elizabeth's nose. "I will make this very plain to you, young woman, so that even you, in all your cleverness, cannot pretend to misunderstand me. Darcy is for Anne. From their cradles, they have been promised to one another. It was the fondest wish of his mother and me. No upstart like you is going to interfere with those plans."

"What am I compared to Miss de Bourgh?"

"What are you—exactly! Exactly! But do not play coy with me." She circled Elizabeth, a hungry cat stalking a bird. "We both know you have arts and allurements to distract him from his duty to his family. You have no delicacy, exposed to the basest things of life—of men."

How did one respond to such raving? Perhaps best not.

"Have you considered why I have been trying to find you a match? Even with your connection to me, few decent men will ally themselves with a woman like you. Despite your youthful airs and arrogance, I have had—and will continue to have—your best interests in mind—unless—" She stabbed her sharp finger into Elizabeth's chest.

Elizabeth jumped back.

"—unless you insist on preying upon Darcy. You are not his equal and would bring shame upon his name and all his family."

"Shall I leave Rosings?"

"No, Anne requires your presence. I will not deny her any comfort, no matter how little I fathom it."

"Then shall I ignore him? Turn my back as the servants do when he approaches?"

"You are not … not … a servant."

"How am I to behave?"

"With every civility, but nothing more."

"As you wish, your ladyship."

"I will be watching you, Miss Elizabeth. Do not think you can escape my notice if you disobey. Now leave me."

She curtsied and strode away, fists balled so tightly her arms shook.

Two steps into the corridor, Mr. Darcy blocked her path. She stopped short and barely held back a tiny shriek. How tall he was, towering—or was that, hovering over her.

"I hardly know what to say, my aunt—"

She raised an open hand. "Pray forgive me, sir, but I am truly in no state for conversation at the moment."

"Will you speak with me later?"

"I do not know, sir. Excuse me." She curtsied and hurried away.

---

Darcy's urge to chase after Miss Elizabeth was an irrational one to be sure. Gentlemen of his station did not race after young ladies. He shook the thought from his head. That statement had the sound of Aunt

Catherine to it. Certainly not the specter he wanted haunting his consciousness.

Aunt Catherine had treated her abominably, yet Miss Elizabeth had maintained her dignity and grace. No weeping or vapors, no scraping apologies or false humility. Though he had known her but a day, he could sketch her character clearly. She might not possess wealth, or so he had been warned, but she possessed other attributes far more valuable.

"Darcy? What do you want?" Aunt Catherine demanded in something just short of a shriek.

When had he wandered into her lair? More importantly, why?

"Darcy?"

A shudder trailed down his spine. That voice! It had tormented him as a child and yanked him back to that place even now. "Yes, Aunt."

"You came to me—I did not summon you, though I am glad you are here. I just finished instructing Miss Elizabeth Bennet that she is not to interfere with you."

"Did I complain of being disturbed?"

She sniffed, one side of her nose curling back. "I am no fool. I saw the way you looked at her in the hall."

"Excuse me?" Surely he could not have been so obvious.

"You will remember your duty to Anne." She leaned forward, hands braced on the carved scrolls of the chair's arms.

"My duty to Anne?"

"Do not toy with me, Darcy. When she recovers from this spell, you will marry her and unite our houses at last."

His favorite discussion. "That is impossible. Anne cannot—"

"Do not say it. I am all too aware of a man's nature. She cannot satisfy your basest urges." She flicked her bony hand and rose. The beads in the chair's valance clacked in her wake.

"She cannot bear children. Surely you realize, I must have an heir—"

"Every man in your position is in need of an heir. That is not the only consideration."

"Instruct me, Aunt, what other considerations—"

"My daughter deserves a fine match for whatever time she has."

"What you insist is not—"

"You must and you will marry Anne directly. If you require someone for the exercise of your urges, find a mistress or keep the one you have. Only be discreet. Anne must never know."

His gut knotted so hard, bile burned his tongue. "Did I understand you correctly? You suggest I should deceive her in … everything?"

"If a bit of deceit is necessary to see her happy, it is a price I am willing to pay."

"You assume I am a willing pawn in your scheme."

"Remember, Rosings will be yours for your trouble." She jabbed his shoulder, punctuating each terse word.

His fists screamed to be put to use. Had she been a man—but she was not. Apparently, that meant she could insult his integrity with impunity.

"This way—my way—when you get yourself heirs, you will be able to provide estates for several sons, not just the eldest." She circled him, arms folded over her chest. "Would you not like to save your sons from Fitzwilliam's fate?"

"You appear to have my life entirely planned out for me."

"As almost your nearest relation, I am entitled—"

"To nothing, madam, absolutely nothing. Keep your schemes and plans to yourself. You are nothing short of pretentious, and I will not admit such interference."

She sneered. "I have heard that from you before, but in the end, you will do your duty by your family. It is in your Fitzwilliam blood." She returned to her chair and ran her hand along the red velvet, leaving a trail in her fingers' wake. "You may go now. I must attend my correspondence."

Fitzwilliam blood be damned. It was the Darcy will that governed his resolve. It would not be bent to her purposes.

He marched to the stables. How quickly could his hunter be readied? A brisk ride might be the only way to curb his tongue right now. A mistress indeed! How dare she even consider whether he kept one, much less assume that he did.

## Chapter 3

ELIZABETH SAT BLEARY-EYED beside Miss de Bourgh. Beneath mounds of blankets, she slept fitfully, but the relevant issue was that she slept. At last. Elizabeth rubbed her palms into her eyes. How long had she been keeping watch in the sickroom?

Gracious heavens, it had been a se'nnight! Days and nights all blurred into an unending stream of treatments and tonics and trials. How was it that Papa was the physician, but the real work of ministering to Miss de Bourgh fell to her?

The door cracked open, and a young maid peeked through.

"A note just come for you, Miss." She handed Elizabeth a carefully folded paper bearing her stepmother's handwriting.

"Stay with Miss de Bourgh until I return. I will be in the sitting room across the hall. Fetch me if she awakens." Elizabeth directed the maid to succeed her at the bedside vigil.

The hard chair had extracted its vengeance upon her every joint. They mutinied against her, stealing any grace she might have possessed. She hobbled into the hallway, bent and gnarled like the ancient oak in their front yard.

Midday sun streamed through the hall windows nearly blinding her. After so many days in the fire-lit darkness of Miss de Bourgh's chamber, she had almost forgotten that golden, painful brightness existed in the world at all.

She stamped her feet and rubbed her arms, throwing off the heat-induced lethargy. A note from Mama was rarely a welcome event. Still, anything that excused her from the sickroom, even for a little while, must be welcomed.

What joy—heaven truly favored her this moment. Not a soul to be seen in the hall or the sitting room. Within, she might savor a few moments to explore her own meditations, uninterrupted and uncorrected by those who knew best what she should think and feel. What better gift could she desire?

She pushed the window open and gulped in fresh air. Anyone who saw her would believe her half drowned, and she was—suffocating in pretense and overbearing interference. At Rosings, she could hardly draw breath without instruction on how to carry it out more properly, more elegantly, more to *her* satisfaction.

The worn blue velvet bergère invited her, and she nudged it to the sunny window. The upholstered arms and back wrapped around her, snug and comfortable.

Surely Lady Catherine had not chosen this chair. It was far too agreeable to suit *her* tastes.

Mama would scold her appalling attitude. Elizabeth ought to be grateful for all the blessings Lady Catherine's patronage afforded. She let her head fall against the upholstery. Mama would never grasp the myriad ways Lady Catherine inspired spleen at every turn. As their patron and their superior, it was her right to demand whatever she saw fit, even the sun to rise and set at her fancy. Gah! Even Jane would be taxed by the constant scrutiny.

And she was definitely not Jane.

She sighed and opened Mama's note. At least the penmanship looked happy.

*My dearest Lizzy,*

*What a clever girl you are! I do not know how you managed to accomplish it—more than I dared hope for! Mr. Bingley and Mr. Wickham have been comfortably installed upstairs for several days now. Can you imagine my astonishment when I received word of their being sent to us?*

*Mr. Bingley is happy to be so much in Jane's company. She entertains him with all the grace and animation I have instilled in her—*

Elizabeth choked and sputtered. What gall! Any admirable qualities in Jane or herself came from their esteemed mother. Mama's only contribution was providing a model not to follow.

*I have every hope of joyous news before the quarantine ends. I trust you shall do whatever you can to ensure it lasts as long as possible.*

*I regret Mr. Wickham cannot be at Rosings with you. But we shall play the cards we have been dealt. He seems to very much enjoy Lydia's society. Who knows—perhaps she shall be the first of you girls to marry.*

Oh, Lydia! She would be the one among them to find Mr. Wickham's companionship pleasing. Perhaps, Mr. Darcy might be willing to warn Papa about Mr. Wickham's past dalliances. That might incite Papa to protect Lydia.

Or not—particularly if Mama wished to encourage the match. He rarely opposed Mama in matters concerning her three younger step-sisters. What better way for Mama to prove herself as the fittest Mrs. Dr. Bennet than for Lydia to marry first?

How was she to even approach Mr. Darcy now that Lady Catherine decreed—the audacity! The arrogance and conceit of her to proscribe to whom Elizabeth may speak! Were there no limits to her reach?

Clearly Papa had no intention of stopping *her* intrusions into his family. Neither did Mr. Collins. Only last week, her ladyship cancelled Charlotte's order at the butcher when *she* deemed them ordering wasteful quantities of lamb.

Soon Lady Catherine would be decorating their homes and instructing them on what to wear each day. A cold flush spread across Elizabeth's face, and she rose to her feet. Heaven forfend! *She* already did those things, too. Had she not trimmed her dinner dress according to Lady Catherine's instruction? The arrangement of the Bennet's drawing room and Charlotte's dining room were directed by *her*. The shelves in Elizabeth's own closet had been designed and ordered by *her*.

Was there no part of her life not under her ladyship's control? If Elizabeth did not halt its insidious spread now, she might spend the rest of her life ensnared by the Queen of Rosings Park.

She jumped to her feet. No, no, no! She might owe Lady Catherine her father's livelihood, but her soul was her own.

This queen's reign would end, quietly, but it would end. Should Mr. Darcy wish to speak to her, she would accept or decline on her preference alone, without regard to Lady Catherine or Miss de Bourgh.

Oh, that he might do just that! His dark eyes held greater depths than she had yet discerned. He was a tantalizing puzzle, one well worth solving.

The door creaked open. The maid peeked in and beckoned her. She tucked that pleasing thought close to her heart and returned to Miss de Bourgh.

Elizabeth passed two more interminable days cajoling Miss de Bourgh to eat and bathing her skin lesions and contorted swellings. Between those endeavors, she sang and read aloud until the rasp of her own raw voice grated her nerves. Surely, an infant could not be more demanding. Even a wet nurse had occasion to sleep now and then.

If only Miss de Bourgh might suffer like Jane did when she took ill—pleasant and considerate to all who ministered to her. That was probably unfair and uncharitable. In truth, few could be so good as Jane.

A maid arrived to issue the nightly summons to dinner. Elizabeth rubbed her sandy eyes and pushed herself up. After a full day shut up in the sweltering sickroom, even time in Lady Catherine's presence was welcome.

The cool hallway air revived her mind and spirits, and a fresh gown reminded her life still went on beyond her genteel captivity. On the way to the parlor, she encountered Miss Darcy.

"Good evening." Elizabeth curtsied.

"I have missed your company all day. I am pleased you are you come to dinner with us. How fares Anne?" Miss Darcy asked.

"She is quite ill, I fear. My father is still hopeful she will recover. It might be several weeks or even months before she is strong enough to come downstairs again, though."

"That is welcome news ... that she is likely to recover, I mean." Miss Darcy's cheeks colored all the way to her shoulders, and she cringed.

"I understood what you meant. It is your aunt? She makes you anxious?"

Miss Darcy wrung her hands. "She is quite apt to correct whatever does not meet her approval."

"And a great deal about you does not?"

Miss Darcy gulped and tripped over the next stair.

Elizabeth caught her elbow and stared into her gold-flecked eyes. Just like Mr. Darcy's—did they favor their mother or their father? They glistened, ready to overflow.

"Come." She took Miss Darcy by the arm and led her upstairs.

The forgotten sitting room and blue bergère welcomed them.

"But we are expected for dinner." Miss Darcy scanned the room like a nervous bird. Did she expect Lady Catherine lay in wait to ambush them?

"We have time. Mr. Hurst is not yet dressed. The maid who fetched me said he seems to be having difficulty with the fit of his breeches."

Miss Darcy giggled into her hands.

"Much better." She pressed a handkerchief into Miss Darcy's hands. "Dry your eyes now. You have no need for tears."

"But she was so angry this afternoon. You do not know—"

"Oh, I know very well." Elizabeth rolled her eyes.

"How can you tolerate it with such equanimity?"

Elizabeth snickered. Surely laughter should not leave a bitter taste in one's mouth. "I am not sure that is the word with which I would describe my reactions."

"How can you bear her ill-humor?"

"You must not allow Lady Catherine to upset you so much."

"But how is such a thing to be accomplished? My aunt is so forceful."

"Indeed she is; however, would your brother ever allow her to injure you?"

"No … no, he would not. He is so very good to me."

"Then what is there to fear?"

Miss Darcy's brave mask crumpled, but she restrained a freshet of tears. "She is so … loud."

"Yes, she is, but so is a summer thunderstorm. It passes quickly and ends with the sunshine and, at times, a rainbow."

"I do not like thunderstorms."

"Few of us relish the thunder and lightning, but you do not hide under your bed from storms any longer, do you?"

"Not usually."

"Much better. Now," she straightened the lace at Miss Darcy's sleeve, "simply regard her as a summer thunderstorm. Remember, no matter how fierce, the storm soon passes, and all is well once more."

"Will you sit beside me and give me courage?"

"Certainly." She hooked her arm in Miss Darcy's and led her to the stairs.

Mr. Darcy met them at the parlor and escorted Miss Darcy inside. He tipped his head toward Elizabeth before retreating within.

Would that he had offered his arm to her.

Foolish thought! A man like Mr. Darcy could have little use for a doctor's daughter. With a mere twenty-five hundred pounds, her dowry would only be of interest to a middling sort of man.

But were that true, why would Lady Catherine be so concerned she might distract Mr. Darcy?

Papa sidled up close. "How is Miss de Bourgh?"

Elizabeth started. "She sleeps now, but restlessly. Despite all the medicines, her fever has not yet passed."

He rapped his knuckle against his teeth. "I may need the surgeon to bleed her if the fever does not abate."

"Shall I send for him and the apothecary to come?"

"I do—"

Mr. Hurst rushed in, face red and breeches far too tight. His belly bulged over the waistband like a sausage burst in cooking.

"Perhaps I should send for a tailor as well. His breeches may cause him a rupture," Elizabeth muttered.

"Elizabeth! That a most indelicate remark. You will guard your tongue as befits a young woman of your age and station."

"Yes, Papa." He was right, of course. How could she have been so indiscreet?

"I do not expect to be kept waiting, Mr. Hurst." Lady Catherine rose from her throne, staring down her nose at the wheezing, sweating Hurst. The sphinxes beside her added their glare to hers.

"No, no, of course not, your ladyship. I beg your pardon." He bowed, but stopped only halfway down.

The claw hammer tails of his coat revealed a seam taxed to breaking, a sight she would be happy to spend her whole life without witnessing. Elizabeth averted her eyes and prayed his tailor's stitching would hold fast.

"See it does not happen again." She lifted her chin and paraded past him, her skirts swishing and rustling a rebuke. "Dinner is served."

Elizabeth hung back as the gentlemen offered their arms to the ladies. Entering the dining room last and alone was difficult, though better than a tray in the sick room. Jane would admonish her to think on that, but then Jane was rarely the one left alone.

They ate in the smaller dining room with Lady Catherine at the head of the table and Mr. Darcy at the foot. She found a place between Miss Darcy and Mrs. Hurst.

The soup's aroma arrived before the soup plate—turtle. Elizabeth squeezed her eyes shut.

"You do not like it either?" Miss Darcy whispered.

"The last time I ate it, I enjoyed three days spent violently ill. Papa and Lady Catherine declared it could not have been caused by anything from her kitchen. Yet, since then, I can hardly look at it."

"Follow my example." Miss Darcy stirred the soup, took a tiny bit in her spoon and raised it to her mouth. She made all the motions of sipping it, but the portion in the spoon did not change. "If necessary, hold your breath as it approaches your nose. If you do this whilst everyone else eats, the staff will remove your plate when they clear the course. You will escape unscathed."

"What is that you are saying to Miss Elizabeth, Georgiana?" Lady Catherine leaned so far forward her ample bosom nearly tipped her soup plate.

"Miss Darcy was merely instructing me in the finer points using of a soup spoon, madam."

"You would do well to listen to her, Miss Bennet. Georgiana has impeccable manners and excellent, if untutored, taste. Hers is a desirable model to follow."

"I am grateful for her willingness to assist me."

"The Fitzwilliam nature is to be magnanimous to those lower in station and dutiful to their family." *She* glowered at Darcy.

His eyes narrowed, and he held his ground against her imperious stare.

What conversation inspired that contest?

Lady Catherine retreated from the skirmish and returned her attention to the rest of her guests. "We have been told our condescension might go so far as to be a fault. But I suppose, if one must have a flaw, that of too much Christian charity is preferable to any other vice of excess."

Mr. Darcy pinched his temples and looked aside while Miss Darcy winced. Colonel Fitzwilliam grumbled something without moving his lips.

Elizabeth patted Miss Darcy's hand under the table. "It is difficult to deem too much virtue a vice, your ladyship."

"Well said, Miss Elizabeth." Colonel Fitzwilliam dipped his head in an odd mixture of amusement and satisfaction. "A toast to the virtue of the Fitzwilliam family. May it continue to overflow and be the most apparent of its vices." He lifted his goblet.

Elizabeth took a dainty sip of wine. Mr. Darcy only pretended to drink. What a singular reaction. Why—

Long Tom's heavy tap on her shoulder startled her. She removed her napkin from her lap, and he pulled her chair out.

"Pray excuse me. Miss de Bourgh requires attention." She followed Tom out before anyone could comment.

They paused at the sweeping marble stairs. The ever present creases in his forehead were just a bit deeper than usual and his brows drawn more tightly over his eyes.

"You are worried for her?"

He nodded, once.

She rubbed her hands together. "Send for the surgeon and apothecary. We will likely need them before the evening is out. Keep them from Miss de Bourgh until Papa sends for them, though. Have the kitchen keep a supply of hot water available all night. Instruct the maids to bring up fresh linens, toweling and blankets as well."

"Yes, miss." He bowed. "I shall have a tray sent up to you—without turtle soup."

"Thank you." Hopefully he was the only one who noticed.

He disappeared down the hall, and she trudged up the marble staircase. How many times had she climbed it in the last ten days, fetching and carrying for—

"Where is she? Why has she left? I want her here." Miss de Bourgh's keening had the same piercing quality as her mother's, a screeching metal-on-metal tone.

She opened Miss de Bourgh's door, pausing a moment to allow her eyes to adjust to the oppressive, dark room.

"Miss Elizabeth?"

"I am here. Your mother insisted I attend dinner downstairs. I asked to be summoned if you awoke, and now I am here."

Miss de Bourgh pushed up on her elbows and kicked the blankets away. "I did not ask you to stay with me, only to awaken alone."

"You were not alone. The maid attended you."

"I still do not like it."

Elizabeth sat beside her. "I cannot disregard your mother's wishes."

Miss de Bourgh harrumphed and wound her arms around her waist, so much like Lydia. She must not give in to the temptation to scold.

"Let me straighten your sheets and plump your pillows. I am sure that will ease you." Elizabeth pulled the sheets aside.

Miss de Bourgh's sweat-soaked nightgown clung to her frail body. She began to shiver, teeth chattering. Red splotches covered her legs. Swollen nodules, some as large as a small egg, clustered near knees and ankles.

"I hurt—everywhere." Her words ended in a plaintive wail.

Elizabeth pressed her hand to Miss de Bourgh's forehead.

"You are burning with fever. We must get you into something warm and dry." Elizabeth rushed to a large press and removed a nightgown.

A maid burst in, arms piled high with linens. In quick order, they had Miss de Bourgh clothed in a fresh gown, wrapped in a dressing gown and seated by the fire. While the maid changed the bed clothes, Elizabeth pressed a small glass of willow bark tincture into Miss de Bough's shaky hands. "Drink this."

"I do not want to." She pushed it away and turned up her nose.

"I asked not if you wanted to. I told you to drink it." Elizabeth guided her hands toward her mouth.

"It tastes terrible."

"That is why it is not served at the dining table alongside the wine."

Miss de Bourgh giggled but pulled away from the glass. "My throat hurts, and it burns when I swallow."

"It cannot be helped. I shall make you some tea with honey after you drink this." She glanced at the maid who nodded and scurried out.

"It makes my stomach hurt."

"I will give peppermint lozenges—after you drink it."

"You are unkind to me."

"That is why you require me to sit with you when you are ill. Now drink." Elizabeth moved the glass to her mouth.

Miss de Bourgh made a sour face and drank down the entire tincture in a single large gulp. She gasped and sputtered.

Elizabeth poured her a glass of wine and water. "This will help."

"Oh! Oh, this burns too!" she cried and spilled the liquid.

"Here, let me take that. The maid will be back soon with the hot water for tea. I will get you a fresh gown."

Elizabeth changed Miss de Bourgh into another clean gown. The maid arrived with the hot water and a dinner tray, without turtle soup. Elizabeth prepared tea with honey.

"Look, broth and gruel for you."

"I am not hungry." They locked gazes. Miss de Bourgh looked away. "But you did not ask if I was and shall give me no peace if I do not try to eat."

"Why not sip the broth whilst the gruel cools. Papa says you must eat as much as you can to speed your recovery."

Miss de Bourgh harrumphed, but took the bowl of broth, grimacing at each sip. "It does not taste good."

"Nothing tastes good right now. You are not taking it for the taste, but for strength. Here is your tea. I trust you will find it palatable."

Miss de Bourgh took the teacup and drank. "It will do."

"I am glad to hear it. The gruel is ready for you."

She took several tiny spoonfuls, but pushed away the bowl before eating even a quarter. "I cannot. It hurts my throat too much," she whispered. "And my stomach hurts."

Elizabeth took the dish. "Do you wish to play cards, or shall I read to you?"

"Eat your dinner, and then read to me. We have not finished that novel yet." She lay back on the pillow with a small groan.

Elizabeth read for several hours, entertaining Miss de Bourgh with theatrical voices for each character. While excellent medicine for her spirits, it did naught to alleviate her rising fever or sick stomach. After the third time she cast up her accounts, something had to be done.

"I must get Papa. I will return shortly." She hurried away before Miss de Bourgh could argue.

Long Tom intercepted her at the foot of the stairs.

She panted. The staircase grew longer each time she traversed it. "Have the surgeon and apothecary arrived?"

"They are in the kitchen, dining."

"They will need it. I fear it will be a very long night."

"Shall I direct them upstairs?"

"Not until Papa has seen her first. Send up at least three large basins and more towels and linen. "

He bowed, and Elizabeth forced herself to the drawing room.

Miss Darcy sat at the pianoforte, her brother standing guard between her and her audience. She played very well, and her choice of music was infinitely better than Miss Bingley's. How disappointing she could not stay to listen.

Blast and botheration! Papa sat with Lady Catherine. Though the sick room did not need one more advisor, there was little to be done for it. She slipped in and whispered in Papa's ear.

He sprang up and followed her out.

"She had some broth and tea … oh, and a few bites of gruel, as well as. I gave her the willow bark, but her fever is rising, as is her pain. She expelled all she has eaten, and I fear she is becoming delirious as well."

They started up the stairs.

"The surgeon and apothecary are waiting in the kitchen—"

He halted mid-step. "What are they doing here?"

"You told me to summon—"

"I most surely did not. You take far too much upon yourself, and I am quite tired of it."

She flinched as though slapped. That would have stung less. He had asked for them! No point in arguing now—or later. Once he made up his mind, little would alter his perceptions. No wonder Mama called him a vexing man.

Papa hurried up the stairs. He stopped short at the top.

"You said they were in the kitchen."

The two men paced outside Miss de Bourgh's room. The surgeon, Mr. Peters, stalked in long storklike steps behind Mr. Lang, the apothecary. Mr. Peters' gravelly lecture resonated in the hall. When they reached the end the far wall, they turned and changed roles, Mr. Lang waving his short, stocky arms in time to his strident speech.

"This is most unhelpful, Elizabeth. You have done me and Miss de Bourgh a great disservice this night." Papa tugged his sleeves, thrust out his chest and approached them in long, confident strides.

Elizabeth sagged against the wall, eyes burning. Cook's fine supper soured in her stomach. She wrapped her arms around her waist. If she could just hold on tightly enough, the pain would pass. Why did he have to be so trying?

She huffed out a ragged breath. To be fair, Papa was anxious for his patient and his patron. He and Mr. Peters disagreed and argued regularly, but the surgeon was a necessary evil when a vein needed to be bled or some other such task was required. Papa was often short with her in these circumstances. After the crisis passed, he would regain his good humor and not even remember his harsh words to her.

But she would.

Papa led the others in to examine their patient. No point in following. She would only be in their way.

Several sets of footsteps clattered down the corridor. Lady Catherine bustled toward her, Mr. Darcy and Colonel Fitzwilliam an arm's length behind. Though *she* lost none of her regal bearing, the creases in her skirt where she had clutched it, bespoke her anxiety. They stopped at Elizabeth's side.

"Papa, Mr. Peters and Mr. Lang are all with her right now."

"Should we join them?" Colonel Fitzwilliam asked.

Mr. Darcy rubbed his thumb in his palm. "Best we know what they—"

The door flew open and Papa herded Mr. Peters and Mr. Lang into the hall. He closed the door and led them a few steps further away. They regarded at each other in silence, bruisers sizing one another up before they contested for chief cock of the walk.

"She must be bled, sweated and purged." Mr. Peters ticked off the points on his impossibly long fingers.

"Cupping is preferred to leeches in these cases—" Mr. Lang perched his fists on his ample hips. He resembled a stout, stone pitcher and poured out opinions as readily.

"If there is bleeding to be done, it will be by a surgeon." Mr. Peters leaned forward just enough to tower over Mr. Lang.

Mr. Lang pursed his lips, round cheeks puffing with each labored breath. "I should think an emollient clyster most appropriate in this case. I can prepare one immediately."

"A purge must come before the clyster." Mr. Peters shook his head violently. "And sweating—it is critical these things are done in the proper order."

"Did you not see the sweat on her brow, or the pile of bed linen in the corner? She is already sweating profusely. Inducing more is unnecessary. She needs gentle cooling and fresh air." Papa crossed his arms, thumbs up and drumming a rapid beat along his upper arms.

Mr. Lang turned scarlet. "You would not advise a purgative—"

"She has done so naturally, several times. Why prompt further?" Papa said.

"Surely you can see the inflammation with the fever demands bleeding." Mr. Peter slapped the back of his hand into his palm.

Papa leaned close to Mr. Peters. "Too much bleeding in my experience—"

"What experience?" Mr. Peters shouted. "You never do the job yourself. When properly bled, patients inevitably prosper. That and a steady dose of laudanum—"

"No!" Papa snapped.

---

"Certainly not," Darcy muttered.

He and Fitzwilliam stormed toward the argument. Let them debate their bleeding, purging and clysters. Darcy would do away with them all if he could, but he would defer to their learning if pushed. Laudanum, though, was another matter altogether.

They shouldered their way into the conversation.

Bennet shuffled aside, almost treading on Lang's toes. "I only recommend laudanum for the most occasional administration: when her pain is too great; the cough too severe; or the purging uncontrollable." The defiant glint in his eye invited challenge.

"We agree entirely." Fitzwilliam's practiced officer's scowl sent Peters retreating, his back to the wall.

"You speak of things you have not the training to understand." Lang folded his arms over his ample paunch.

If Lang had as much brains as guts, what a clever fellow he would be. Darcy rolled his eyes.

"I supply Mrs. Jenkinson with laudanum for Miss de Bourgh to take regularly in brandy—"

"You bloody fool!" Dr. Bennet stepped forward. He might just throttle the man, and from the look of it, Fitzwilliam might just help.

Lang edged out of arm's reach.

"You damnable fool! You gave her that poison in place of the willow bark I—"

"Willow bark! What kind of remedy is that?" Lang's face darkened to nearly purple.

"No one recommends its use in these cases." Peters pressed his way into the conversation. "You risk her life by—"

"You countermanded my orders." Bennet balled his fists.

Surely he desired to put them to use. Perhaps it would not be such a bad thing.

"Your ill-conceived, arrogant—" Peters towered over Bennet.

"You would judge my recommendations? A surgeon instructing a physician?"

"I will do so when he is wrong."

Bennet's eyes narrowed and his tone assumed a dangerous edge. "And how do you come by that judgment?"

"A good ten years more experience than you, Bennet." Peters poked him in the chest.

"I care not for the experience of a self-important fool."

Lang broke away and strode toward Anne's door.

"Where are you going?" Bennet followed him.

"You two will argue until dawn. Miss de Bourgh needs my help, and I shall administer it."

"You shall do no such thing. She is my patient."

Lang stomped to Darcy. "I beseech you, sir. On behalf of Miss de Bourgh, put a stop to this endless debate. Decide which of us you will have treat her, and the rest of us shall leave."

Peters hurried to join Lang. "You have known us many years, sir. You can be certain of the efficacy of our methods."

"No, I am not," Darcy said.

Peters and Lang turned to Fitzwilliam.

"Sir, you cannot—"

"Enough!" Fitzwilliam's command rang like gunfire in the hall. "Bennet, attend her."

Peters and Lang jumped back.

"You two, go downstairs and wait in the kitchen. You will be summoned if you are required. If you interfere with Dr. Bennet again, you shall lose Rosings' patronage entirely. Need I remind you, there are other surgeons and apothecaries with whom we may consult?"

They tried to stammer something resembling 'yes, sir' but Long Tom's sudden appearance cut short their attempts. One had to credit the man for his impeccable sense of timing.

The butler grunted and gestured toward the stairs. Peters and Lang nearly tripped over each other in their haste to obey.

Bennet straightened his cravat. "I am sorry you were privy to that disagreeable display. Those men are useful in their place. They can bleed a vein and mix a decoction when needed, but I am afraid they have become too high handed."

"You do not rely on the heavy use of laudanum, sir?" Fitzwilliam asked.

"No, I do not."

"On what basis?" Fitzwilliam squared his shoulders, every inch an officer.

"If you are trying to persuade me differently, you waste your time. Better men than you have tried. I remain unmoved."

"Why?" Darcy stared at him.

Bennet held his gaze steadily. Only men of powerful conviction would stand up to Darcy's dark look.

"Those who use too much laudanum come to need it like their daily bread. It weakens them, sometimes fatally. Miss de Bourgh is far too weak to risk the possibility."

"Those are very unusual ideas, sir," Fitzwilliam said.

"Surely you have seen what I describe. Wounded soldiers are apt—"

Fitzwilliam raised his hand. "Note, I never said I disagreed with you. Only that your ideas are unique."

"If you do not disagree, then to what point is this discussion? My patient requires attention."

Darcy and Fitzwilliam exchanged a brief glance.

"When Anne regains her strength, there is another case we would present for your consultation," Darcy said.

"I can make no predictions on when that may be. Perhaps I might recommend—"

Fitzwilliam shook his head. "No. Your expertise, none other."

"Very well. I must attend Miss de Bourgh now. We may speak more of this later." Bennet bowed and disappeared into the sick room.

"I confess, I am surprised." Fitzwilliam leaned against the wall. "Who would have thought that useless vicar could have made such an apt recommendation?"

"I am certain it was luck that his cousin happened to be a useful physician."

Fitzwilliam snorted. "There is a family resemblance, though. Bennet seems prone to boot licking."

"At least, not as profoundly as Collins." Darcy stroked his chin. "He does seem to profess opinions entirely his own, though, and with enough conviction that Aunt Catherine allows him his head in Anne's care."

"Few hold that kind of sway with her. Knowing our aunt accepts him may help my father do the same." Fitzwilliam tipped his head toward Anne's closed door.

"Let us hope so, for your brother's sake."

---

The next three days blurred together in an endless sequence of warm baths, cooling teas, tinctures, decoctions and compresses, punctuated with meals of gruel and roasted apples. Miss de Bourgh refused to eat unless Elizabeth coaxed her. Afterwards, Elizabeth read novels until nearly too hoarse to cajole her patient to drink her medicines. They played cards when Miss de Bourgh was strong enough. When she fell confused and delirious in her fevers, Elizabeth sat at her bedside and held her hand. If Elizabeth left for even a few moments, Miss de Bourgh called and cried for her like a lost child.

Sometime in early on the fourth morning, Miss de Bourgh's fever finally broke, and she slept peacefully. Utterly spent, Elizabeth dragged herself to her room and collapsed on the bed, fully dressed.

She awoke, startled and disoriented, wearing night clothes, hair braided down her back. Mid-morning sun shone through the windows. When had the maid come in to help her change? She squeezed her eyes shut and tried to picture it. The shadows had been long then—it must have been late in the afternoon. Her stomach grumbled and pinched. Had she slept through the entire day and night?

She fell back into the soft pillows and groaned. Someone would no doubt be displeased with her for sleeping so long. Someone was always upset with her.

No, that was uncharitable and doubtless unfair. But was it wrong to be a bit ungracious after such an ordeal?

Probably.

A tray of food sat on the dainty, inlaid table near the window. Bless whoever thought to send it. Surely she would be more agreeable after a meal.

She drew on her dressing gown and stretched her aching muscles. Definitely too many hours abed. She was not made for idleness, even in a room as lovely as this. It might be one of the meanest rooms Rosings had to offer, but the fine linens, soft mattress, and quality appointments provided an air of luxury that one must appreciate—even when one was hungry, sore and tired.

She sat down with the tray. Cheese and cold meat, compote, fresh bread and scones. Quite a tolerable meal.

Her door creaked open.

"Papa?" She started to rise, but he waved her down.

"I was beginning to worry you might be taking ill yourself."

"Come sit with me, and tell me of Miss de Bourgh."

He sat, pulled off his glasses and rubbed his eyes. His face was lined, his cheeks sunken. No doubt he had eaten and slept poorly himself.

"Her improvement continues. The fever has not returned, but neither has her strength. She will be many weeks recovering." He replaced his glasses. "I shall impose upon your mother's hospitality for some time longer though. I would keep Mr. Bingley and Mr. Wickham away from here at least a fortnight more."

"Do you think that—"

"I am of no mind to venture any risks. Besides, your mother does not object to her guests." He removed a letter from his pocket. "As she most eloquently informed me."

"Her last letter to me said something similar. She revels in the opportunity to play hostess to guests late of Rosings Park."

He opened Mama's note to reveal another folded within. "I believe Jane writes to you."

She took the paper. It was indeed Jane's handwriting. A perfect sweet course with which to finish her meal. "What of Mrs. Jenkinson?"

"Her cough turned to a sore throat. She has been removed to the parsonage to recover."

Poor Charlotte!

"Every servant who sneezes will be dismissed?"

"It is possible."

She ground her teeth. "Surely you would not support so drastic a measure? Think of what suffering that would cause amongst the staff."

"They are not my primary concern."

"But—"

Papa grunted, a sound that always presaged a stern conversation—one she had no wish to partake in.

She looked down to her plate. "Scones, Papa?"

"Thank you." He picked one up and bit into it. "In Mrs. Jenkinson's continued absence, Miss de Bourgh requests you stay at Rosings as companion to her."

"Her companion, Papa?"

"No complaining now, Lizzy. Lady Catherine wills it as well. Despite your unfortunate penchant for impertinence …" he peered over his glasses.

Why must he resort to that censorious glare?

"… her ladyship is comforted by your presence."

She might well do herself an injury biting her tongue and not rolling her eyes. "Does not Mama require me at home?"

"With four other girls in the house, your mother can very well spare you. Make no mistake, with all the favor Lady Catherine has to offer, it would be folly not to take full advantage of your situation here and oblige her small request."

"Yes, Papa."

"Whilst you are here, I have a task for you. Colonel Fitzwilliam and Mr. Darcy mentioned a case for which they desire my consult, following Miss de Bourgh's recovery. They refused to offer me any further details, though. In the course of your time here, you must talk with them. Encourage them to reveal any information about the case, so I may prepare for whatever they might require of me. The colonel is the Earl of Matlock's son. Connections to that family would be most beneficial to us all."

"But, Papa, I—"

"You carry on as if I have asked you to flirt or otherwise conduct yourself improperly. Do be a sensible child and not missish! You are a clever girl and a most observant one. I have every faith in your ability to find a way to accomplish this little favor for me."

"You do not understand—"

"No more protests." He rapped the table with his knuckles. "I need your cooperation, not just for me, but for your mother and sisters as well. Remember, you have three younger sisters in need of husbands. Think of the kind of young men a peer might put your sisters in a way to meet. You might raise Mary's prospects beyond a mere steward."

Of course it mattered little that Mary actually liked that mere steward.

"What of—"

"Must you think of only yourself, Lizzy? I am sure they might perform introductions for you as well, though they will have heard from Lady Catherine of your refusal of Mr. Collins and Mr. Wickham, and may very well deem you too particular for your own good."

"You believe I should have accepted Mr. Collins? I thought you yourself said—"

"That is not the point, Elizabeth! You must perform this service for your sisters. Your younger sisters' dowries are small, even compared to yours. It is in your best interests to see each other all well settled."

She bit her tongue hard. Best she not speak just now.

"There is a good girl. I am glad I brought you with me." He kissed the top of her head and left.

The door shut. She rose, fists clenched and trembling with the effort. It was good she had practice holding her tongue, or she would certainly scream. She rubbed her hands along her arms and paced the room.

Jane's letter caught her eye.

*Dear Lizzy,*
*It has been very odd at home without you. Mama's spirits have been very high of late—*

So Mama was flitting and fluttering and silly without Elizabeth to dampen her spirits. How comforting to know.

No, that was unfair. Jane would never suggest such a thing.

*I dearly miss your company, but our guests offer some consolation. Mr. Bingley's company is quite agreeable. Had it not cost me your society, I would call it one of the pleasantest things all year. Mama encourages us to be often with one another.*

*Mr. Wickham takes it upon himself to entertain all of our younger sisters. You might not think a single man could be up to such a daunting task, but he manages tolerably well. He endures his captivity with great equanimity.*

*Mama encourages Lydia to make the most of her time with Mr. Wickham. I hope you will not be distressed, but I believe Mr. Wickham prefers Lydia.*

*I know Lady Catherine intended him for you—*

She tossed the letter aside. Gah! Papa still knew nothing of Mr. Darcy's intelligence regarding Mr. Wickham. He would surely not believe her now.

A dull throbbing drummed at the base of her skull. Perhaps this should wait until the headache subsided. She climbed into bed and slept until the next morning.

---

Darcy swung into his hunter's saddle despite the storm clouds gathering on the horizon. All the more the reason to get out and ride now, while the rest of Rosings Park still slept. This might well be his only opportunity for quiet and repose before Aunt Catherine demanded his full attention.

In the two days since Anne's fever had broken, Bingley's dreadful sister had barely left his side. She clung to him like a thistle, purple and prickly and prattling one inanity after another. Even when she chanced upon some intelligent remark, it became drivel when it fell from her tongue.

Poor Georgiana was at the end of her patience with Miss Bingley. She fled from Miss Bingley's presence whenever possible, her steps pounding out the same rhythm as his horse's trot beneath him. Mrs. Hurst was no better, though she had the decided advantage of having very little occasion to speak when Miss Bingley was present. Darcy cringed. What might that woman utter if given the opening, considering the ill-informed opinions of her husband?

In the interest of protecting Georgiana's delicate sensibilities, he sent his own valet to speak to Hurst's regarding the cut of the gentleman's breeches. Whilst the garment should be flattering, some things were certainly not complimented by excessive constriction. The corner of his lips drifted up. Miss Elizabeth would surely have some fascinating observation about the situation.

She was the only one of their party who might have relieved his yearning for substantive conversation. Yes, she remained absent from his sight. Though invited to join them for dinner last night, a headache kept her abed. Was it truly a headache, or had Aunt Catherine's earlier tirade dissuaded her from keeping company? Dreadful meddling—

How was he to convince Aunt Catherine that he would not marry Anne? As if her brief life expectancy might make the prospect any more enticing. He spat the sour tang from his mouth. Nothing she might say could persuade him to degrade the sacrament of marriage that way. The very idea showed how poorly Aunt Catherine knew him.

Perhaps he had set his standards impossibly high. Not everyone could have a relationship like his parents. Still, to have a woman know him, understand him—as his mother did his father— and to be able to do the same for her in return, that was his notion of a proper marriage.

Yes, one more impossible Darcy ideal to add to the rest that Aunt Catherine failed to comprehend.

He urged his horse around a gentle curve in the garden path.

A solitary figure in a pale gown and shawl strolled along the garden wall. It was not Georgiana, and the Bingley sisters would never rise at this hour. Miss Bennet?

His horse, ever perceptive, increased his pace, but Darcy slowed him to a walk. Startling her would be rude.

She acknowledged him with a curtsey. He dismounted and led his horse to her.

"Good morning, Miss Elizabeth."

"Good morning to you, sir, and your most charming mount." She smiled—oh, that smile!

How could the same expression appear so affected on Miss Bingley and so utterly delightful on Miss Elizabeth?

His hunter tossed his head and pressed his nose toward Miss Elizabeth. Fortunate creature to be welcomed acting on his desires.

She stroked the horse. "You are an early riser by habit, sir?"

"Indeed, I have always thought the countryside most appealing by the light of sunrise. You are as well?"

She chuckled. "With four sisters in the house, I find it is the only time for quiet and contemplation."

"Am I interrupting? I can go." He had no desire to, but would abide by her wishes, if asked. Pray, let her not ask.

"Not at all, sir. With only Miss de Bourgh for company and my own babble for entertainment, conversing with another person holds great appeal." Her cheeks flushed just enough to give her a nearly irresistible glow.

What Miss Bingley would give to look so well with so little effort. But no, that was certainly not a fitting topic of conversation.

They set off along the bridle path, his hunter between them.

"Your father says Anne's condition improves."

"You wish to ascertain the extent to which that is said to please your aunt and the degree of concern you should have for your sister's health after keeping company with Miss de Bourgh?"

His heart skipped a beat, and he nearly stumbled. "How do you come by that conclusion?"

She gave him a brief, sidelong glance and looked away. "You spoke to my father. Why would you ask me, except for information you could not rightly expect to get from him? "You surely could not ask him if his prognosis was for his patron's benefit. That would be insulting, and you are not a rude man. Similarly, you rightly assume Papa would be reluctant to openly say he feared for those keeping company with Miss de Bourgh. At the same time, you are singularly protective of your sister and most concerned for her safety."

A shiver coursed down his spine. She was intrusive, presumptuous and right—the latter being the most disconcerting.

"Forgive me, sir. I have been far too forward. Pray excuse me." She darted away.

His horse tried to follow.

"No! Wait." He dodged in front of the horse and grabbed her arm.

Blast! How ungentlemanly, but he could not allow her to go. He tucked her hand into the crook of his elbow. "No, no, you were entirely correct."

"I should not have spoken so."

"There was nothing improper in what you said. I am not accustomed to …" He licked his lips. "To being so quickly understood, by anyone—"

"Particularly impudent young ladies who usually look at you in terms of what you have to offer." She squeaked a repentant sound and pressed the back of her hand to her mouth. "Forgive me. I hardly know what has come over me."

"Whatever it is, I hope you do not stop."

She paused mid-step and stared at him.

"I find your honesty and openness—"

"Shocking."

"Refreshing and intriguing."

"Your taste in manners is astonishing, sir."

"Your company is quite remarkable." Had his compliment occasioned that pleasing blush?

They rounded a turn in companionable silence. A sharp breeze, tasting of rain, swirled about them, whipping stray hairs into her face. Her remarkable eyes made even that disarray appealing.

"Would you be willing to grant me an answer to my original question?"

"The one you stated or the ones you intended?" Her eyes issued a sparkling tease.

"Both, if you do not object." If only he could attend to her answers whilst faced with the utterly distracting pressure of her hand in his arm.

"Miss de Bourgh is improving, though she remains very weak. There is reason to hope for a good recovery, but it is unlikely she will return to her former strength."

"And that is to be the way of things? Each attack leaving her increasingly feeble?"

"Her last several spells have left her weaker, in both body and mind. On good days, it is difficult for her even to climb the stairs without pausing for breath at the landing. But mine is an untutored opinion."

"Fear not, I shall not share it with anyone."

"Thank you."

There was something so vulnerable, so exposed, in those words. Every fiber of his being jumped to defend her—but from what? Whom?

"As to your sister," she plucked a tall weed and offered it to his horse, "my father believes there is no danger to those keeping company with Miss de Bourgh."

"And you agree?"

"Not that it signifies, but yes, I do." She bowed her head.

How unfair her lovely visage should be hidden by her bonnet.

"Might I ask a favor of you?"

She stiffened, just a little. "Certainly, sir. What may I do for you?"

The warmth left her voice, replaced by something which mimicked it closely enough most would ignore the change. He could not.

"My sister, she is painfully shy and lonely. She has no fitting companion here."

She pulled away. "You wish me to be her companion?"

Something in the way she spoke the word 'companion' gnawed at him. No! What a bumbling fool he was! "Pray forgive me. I did not speak well at all. I was not offering you employ as her companion."

She paused, but kept her face turned away. "What then did you mean?"

He chewed the inside of his cheek. Pray he find the right words, lest she be irredeemably offended. "You once asked permission to become better acquainted with her. I hope you will continue your acquaintance."

"You wish to ensure she is entertained? That does not sound like you."

"She is melancholy, and I know something troubles her."

"You wish me to be your spy?" Dainty eyebrows rose high on her forehead.

Was she teasing?

"Certainly not—although …"

"Then you do."

"No. She needs a friend—one with good character and sound judgment. She has passed the age where she desires me to be privy to all her thoughts."

"And you do not expect me to report all her secrets to you?"

"Not unless you ascertain she is in some sort of danger. Then I insist."

"Of course." She bit her lower lip. "I will be happy to be her friend."

Was she aware of how enticing a demonstration that was? Especially when combined with the tiny hint of pleasure in her eyes.

"Do you fear Lady Catherine will object?"

"Whatever for?"

She choked on the thought and offered him an expression that might well wither the surrounding roses.

"My aunt has no say over matters concerning Georgiana. Fitzwilliam and I are her guardians. I shall inform her that you are—"

"You inform Lady Catherine?"

He snickered. "I suppose that sounds rather ridiculous."

"Rather like a mouse informing a cat of what she should have for her dinner."

He chortled. "I believe her sphinxes might find a juicy mouse quite an acceptable eventide meal."

"Only if prepared by her French chef."

"In a fine pastry crust."

"What does one serve with a fine mouse pie?"

"Imported cheese."

She pressed her fist to her mouth, but laughed in spite of her efforts.

Fitzwilliam would deem him daft. Who knew such a ridiculous topic might be so delightful!

"Perhaps the book of fairy stories I read to Miss de Bourgh has addled my mind." Her manner turned somber. "Did you know, Lady Catherine asked me to be companion to Miss de Bourgh until Mrs. Jenkinson recovers?"

No wonder she had her back up. "I can only imagine what my aunt said to you. I cannot apologize enough."

She looked up at him, her gaze penetrating, alluring and sad. How was it she could give voice to so little and speak so profoundly?

"Why?"

Could she not read his face and know? "It was on all accounts rude and thoughtless. She likes to direct the lives of those around her, even those not hers to direct."

"You are not under her direction?"

"Hardly. In many ways, she is under mine. Fitzwilliam and I come each spring to ensure the estate is in order and to arrange her affairs."

"I see."

"I appreciate your willingness to care for my cousin, but I hardly expect that you would be obedient to all my aunt's desires." He extended his arm, and she slipped her hand into the crook of his elbow once more.

Exactly where it should be. She leaned into him ever so slightly. Yes, exactly as it should be.

"My aunt is not at liberty to direct my conversation."

"And you do not fear it would trouble Miss de Bourgh for you to … converse freely with anyone of your choosing?"

He paused until he held her full attention. "No. Her opinions have no bearing on my actions either."

Miss Elizabeth's eyebrow arched high into what was fast becoming a favorite expression.

"May I ask a favor of you? I recognize our acquaintance brief for such a thing, but —"

"Think nothing of it. How may I be of assistance to you?" Pray, let it be as least as substantial a request as he had asked of her.

"Mr. Wickham is staying at our house until the fear of contagion is past."

"Of course! I must speak to your father. No doubt he believes whatever misapprehensions Aunt Catherine told him of Wickham."

"Jane wrote to say Mr. Wickham was keeping my younger sisters well entertained."

He squeezed his eyes shut. Why, of all things, did she ask him to remedy an oversight of his own making? "I will speak to him as soon as possible."

"Thank you."

Why did she thank him when he was the cause of her troubles in the first place?

"You need not look so uneasy, though. Jane is much pleased with Mr. Bingley's company—despite the fact that Lady Catherine says she should be."

He guffawed.

"Forgive me. I fear my sense of humor rather impudent."

"And utterly delightful."

"I mean no disrespect to your aunt."

"Only to make sport with her as you do of everyone else."

She blushed darker, almost the color of the blossoms lining the path.

"It seems you are well acquainted with my reputation."

"You are well respected for your kind heart and ready assistance to all."

"You flatter me."

"Disguise is my abhorrence." Besides only a fool would attempt to lie to Miss Elizabeth.

"I shall keep that in mind. Of what else have you such decided opinions, sir?"

They walked and talked through a full circuit along the bridle path. How well read she was, with well-informed and argued opinions, and on topics not generally regarded as proper for female education. She was altogether an enchanting companion. Better still, she agreed to meet him again to walk together in the early hours.

Her company made for the most satisfying morning spent at Rosings, ever. Not that the pleasure would last. He and Fitzwilliam were to meet with the steward and tour the estate.

Wickham should accompany them—yes, that would be most appropriate. Perhaps he might even see Dr. Bennet as well. When they next walked, he might tell her of accomplishing her favor, and she would thank him with her smile.

## Chapter 4

AFTER BREAKFAST, DARCY, Fitzwilliam and Michaels rode toward the Bennets' house by way of the eastern fields. A brisk wind held the rains at bay, though the skies remained gloomy and threatening. Michaels insisted they pause on their way while he looked over an overgrown, muddy field. He pulled out a notebook and pencil from his coat and scribbled furiously.

"Remind me why we are seeking out Wickham's company?" Fitzwilliam asked.

"He has neatly avoided the very purpose of bringing him on this trip. It is high time for him to apply himself to what he came for."

"Why put forth so much effort finding a situation for him? The man has little intention of doing any sort of work. Unless, of course, you call soaking and wenching and getting cleaned out work?"

"My father's dying wish. He wanted to see Wickham established in the world in a gentlemanly profession—or at least an honest one."

"Good God, man! Dying wish or not, Uncle Darcy would have written the blighter off after he lost his invitation to the Inn of Courts. Wash your hands of him already."

Darcy grumbled and pinched the bridge of his nose.

"You are entirely too responsible and too serious. You need to live a little. When we have finished with Aunt Catherine's affairs, come with me to London. I will show you how to enjoy yourself.

"Thank you all the same. I would rather return to Pemberley."

"Do you not get lonely, isolated from good society? It is not healthy for you to always be alone. It is high time you find a wife."

"Fitzwilliam!" Hopefully, he would recognize the warning tones and cease this line of conversation. But Fitzwilliam was not always known for taking a warning well. "It is enough Aunt Catherine pressures me to marry Anne as soon as she leaves her sick bed. I will not endure it from you as well."

"I have no idea of you marrying Anne." He shuddered. "What a horrible thought … her sickly, pale frame in your—"

"Enough!" Darcy raised a hand and prepared to kick his horse if Fitzwilliam uttered another word. He fought to keep that particular image at bay often enough.

"I would not wish that upon you. No, but perhaps a pair of fine eyes and a wry wit has garnered your attention. Indeed, anyone who can charm old Long Tom must be rather remarkable."

Darcy's eyes narrowed.

"I knew it. I knew it. You have taken notice of the doctor's daughter. If she were richer, I would have sought her out myself."

"You are referring to a gentlewoman, not a convenient article—"

"Do not get your back up on me now. That is a thought, though. There is a way you might please everyone at once."

Darcy's horse shook its head. The perceptive creature saved him the trouble of doing the same.

"See here, it would not be difficult. Set Miss Bennet up in Lambton or Derby, if you prefer to do it in style. Keep her there, under your protection, whilst you marry Anne—"

"What you suggest is repugnant. You have been too long in your brother's company—"

"Easy there, Darcy. I have no need of your moral outrage. You would hardly be the first. It is all the kick among the *ton*. You could have Rosings and your pretty bit of muslin on the side. Miss Elizabeth gains a nice establishment apart from her dreadful family."

"And any self-respect."

"Promise to marry her, what … two, three months after you put out your mourning wreath. It cannot be very long before that happens, anyway."

"I shall pretend I did not hear that."

"Aunt Catherine suggested it too, eh?" Fitzwilliam threw his head back and hooted. "She's a thoughtful old bat; is she not?"

Darcy clutched his temples. Had his entire family lost all respectability? No, merely the Fitzwilliams—

who perhaps never had it in the first place. "I will not dishonor two respectable women."

"You reckon them both respectable? You are very generous. Anne is hardly a woman. Miss Bennet is one misfortune away from genteel poverty or, in all likelihood, something far worse. It is in your power to save them both."

"When did you sink so low?"

"When did you lose sight of practical concerns? You have spent far too much time alone in your walled garden of Pemberley. Money, the carnal act, a bit of sport and a splash of good liquor to keep it all well washed; that is the way of our world."

"Your world perhaps, but not mine." Darcy said.

"Think of your children. You would lose Rosings when you could assure them a gentleman's existence?"

"It has never been mine in the first place. It should go to a Fitzwilliam, not a Darcy. If you are so nuts upon it, you marry Anne and take it all." Darcy worked his tongue against the roof of his mouth.

"Now, there's an idea." Fitzwilliam screwed his lips into a thoughtful pucker. "Not that I had have not considered it, but since you and Anne have always been destined for each other—"

"You have my blessings. I will press your suit to Aunt Catherine and encourage her to find you acceptable."

The levity left Fitzwilliam's countenance. "You are certain? You are giving up a great deal."

"Swear to me you will be faithful to Anne as long as she lives. She deserves that much."

"You would sell Rosings for so meager a price?"

"You would purchase it for the same? I should think you would count the cost quite dear." Darcy glanced over his shoulder at Michaels. "As to Rosings, you know as well as I, even with Michaels' efforts, it will be a monumental task getting the estate out of debt. Seeing it prosperous once again may well be the work of a lifetime. You suppose I am giving up a great deal, but perhaps my willingness should give you pause to reconsider what you are taking on."

"You are an odd man, Darcy. Given the opportunity, my brother would have married Anne without a second thought. What is it to him to mortgage away another estate?"

"Thank heavens he did not have the option. Neither Anne nor the tenants deserve that grief."

"No, I imagine not. He certainly would not tolerate your conditions." He rolled his eyes. "Do you suppose Bennet will be able to help him?"

"His attitude is very different from the others we sought out, so perhaps …"

"You might suggest he bring her along, you know."

"What?"

"Have Bennet bring his daughter when we send him to Matlock. Invent some excuse—Georgiana might invite her as a particular friend. Once there …"

That might allow him to see her without the specter of Aunt Catherine—

Michaels rode up. "Pray, forgive me. That field's drainage needs improvement. Nothing will grow there left as it is."

Michaels was right. The field, like most at Rosings, was in poor condition. Did Fitzwilliam realize just how poor? Probably not, especially if his idea of life was reduced to the carnal pleasures offered by the *ton*. Still, he was unlikely to do a worse job managing Rosings than Aunt Catherine. If he were determined, he might even do better. Regardless, the chances of the estate prospering in this generation were slim at best. More likely, it would struggle to avoid debt, debt Darcy did not want to finance from Pemberley's coffers. No, that was for legacies for his younger children … what an outstanding mother Miss Elizabeth would be.

*Where had that thought come from?*

---

Three days later, Miss de Bourgh's entertainment required a book that had been loaned to Charlotte. No other tome would suffice. Elizabeth set out to fetch the article, though a footman or a maid might have been sent in her stead.

The afternoon sun offered just the right amount of light and warmth. She slowed her pace, craving the sunbeams' kisses on her skin. Her bonnet fell back, and she lifted her face to the sky. Mary teased that she should have been a peony in Mama's garden for the way she loved the sun. Perhaps she was right.

The gardens were now her favorite place at Rosings. Mr. Darcy met her there now every morning before anyone else rose. Some days, like today, they said little, keeping amiable company with only the occasional stray remark. Other mornings, they spoke at length on a great variety of topics.

He was certainly a man of information and pronounced opinions—not entirely unlike his aunt in that regard. He, however, proved far more amenable to discussion and debate. A common strength of character ran through them both, but he applied it to far nobler efforts. How different the experiences of his tenants to hers.

Clearly, he resented *her* attempts at running his life. Yet she seemed utterly blind to his rebellion. How frequent had her remarks regarding his marriage to Anne become?

Elizabeth plucked a tall weed and swished it through the air. That point would come to a head soon. Would that she could be far away when it did, lest the blame land squarely in her lap.

It was a shame—a very great shame—that he was the most agreeable man in her acquaintance. She would very much like to continue their friendship. She sighed, though Mama had told her numerous times it was an unattractive gesture. That wish, like so many others, had little potential for fulfillment.

At least Jane's desires had hope. If her letters were to be believed— and Jane's always were—Mr. Bingley showed her every attention and admiration. Perhaps this once, Lady Catherine had stumbled on to an appropriate match.

As she approached the parsonage, a white flash in the garden caught her eye. Charlotte! Even better, Mr. Collins was nowhere in sight. She ran the last few paces.

"Charlotte!"

"Lizzy! How delightful to see you." Charlotte extended both hands. Her apron was streaked with garden dirt and the basket on her arm filled with cut flowers.

"I have been temporarily released from my gilded cage, on a mission of mercy for Miss de Bourgh."

"You come to reclaim Mrs. Jenkinson?"

"No, that would be a mission of mercy for you."

Charlotte giggled and covered her mouth. It did not help. She only laughed harder. "Oh, dear, it has been too long since I have seen you."

"You must indeed be in desperate need of humor."

"I suppose so. Mr. Collins is not exactly one to encourage levity—"

"At least not intentionally?"

Charlotte gasped and snickered. "Lizzy! You should not say—"

"Is it somehow untrue?"

"Not untrue, but perhaps unwise." Charlotte glanced towards the lane.

"You may be correct. I have been away from polite society too long."

Charlotte clutched her forehead and chuckled. "You really must stop. One day, you will forget yourself in the wrong company.—"

"I apologize for taxing your ears with my rampant misbehavior."

"Will you come inside and sit with me a bit?" A v-shaped crease formed between Charlotte's eyes, the way it always did when there was something serious on her mind.

"No one in your house has taken ill since Mrs. Jenkinson's arrival, so I am sure Papa would not object. Perhaps, we might find the novel Miss de Bourgh insisted you borrow several weeks ago."

Charlotte led her into the house. "Oh dear, she wants it back? I have not had time—or inclination—to read it."

"I shall not tell her."

"But what if she quizzes me on it? You know the great joy she takes in that sport."

~110~

Elizabeth winked. "Offer me tea, and I shall relate to you everything you need to know to answer her questions most suitably. If you desire, I shall even tell you your opinions of the characters. The hero is hardly swoon-worthy, though the heroine has some potential to be tolerable enough, I suppose."

"Then tea you shall have." Charlotte spoke a few words to her maid and ushered Elizabeth into the parlor.

The room faced the back garden—not an ideal view—but Mr. Collins liked to keep watch of the road, so the front room was left for him. He dared not risk the possibility of Lady Catherine driving past and not being there to greet her appropriately.

Despite the view, the back parlor was neat and snug. Lady Catherine had her share of influence over all facets of the room: the shelves, the carpets, the curtains, the paper hanging and the paintings. Charlotte, though, still managed to insert her touch in every corner with her flowers, a sampler, a fancy work pillow. How cleverly she maintained her dignity under the reign of the Queen of Rosings Park.

In the time it took to bring tea, Elizabeth related the plot and details of the novel Charlotte had avoided reading.

"I must confess, I am glad I did not read it." Charlotte poured tea.

"It is not to your taste?"

"I am surprised it was to yours."

Elizabeth took a teacup. Lady Catherine had obviously chosen the china, but Charlotte had blended the tea to her own likings. "I never said that."

"But you describe it so well."

"I read it to Miss de Bourgh during her last bout of illness. Several times."

"Oh, Lizzy! I know of no one else so willing to do disagreeable things simply because those around her expect it." Charlotte uncovered a second small teapot and peeked inside.

Elizabeth shrugged. "I suppose it is easier than weathering the consequences of refusing."

"You puzzle me exceedingly. How is it you are, on one hand, so ready to speak your mind and yet, in the next moment, you agree to perform that which you clearly have no desire to?"

Elizabeth's cheeks burned as if slapped. How could Charlotte understand the price to be paid for disagreeing? Her throat tightened almost too constricted to breathe. Though Papa appeared mild, his temper, when finally revealed, was a fearsome force. The strength and tenacity of his resentment rivaled Lady Catherine's. How lovely it would be to say 'no' when she felt the urge, but it was a luxury she could ill-afford.

"Is that ginger I smell?" Elizabeth asked.

"Yes, I have grown fond of ginger tea."

"No, you have not." She peered into Charlotte's face. "It is disagreeable, and I know you think it, too. There is only one reason you would drink it. To settle your stomach—"

Charlotte looked away.

Elizabeth leaned across the table until she could see Charlotte's eyes once more. "Are you … you are!"

Charlotte pressed her hands over the tiny bulge in her middle.

"I am so pleased for you. I have suspected for weeks—"

"Of course you have. Why do I even bother to tell you anything? You know everything before I speak it." Charlotte sipped her tea.

"Well, I am glad you have told me as now we can speak of it freely."

"You do not consider it indelicate?"

"For the drawing room, yes, of course. But not in private, between us. With Mama's many lying-ins and attending Papa's consultations, I dare say I have been exposed to far more than a delicate, unmarried, woman should be. But we shall let that be our secret."

"I shall be glad of someone in whom I may confide." Charlotte blotted her eyes.

"What is wrong? You are afraid?"

"I am being foolish, I suppose."

"The travail frightens you?"

"I was with Mama during her last lying in. It was midwinter, and a snowstorm prevented the midwife from attending. She finally arrived, but it had already gone on a night and a day. There was so much blood!" She shuddered.

Elizabeth took her hand. "I am sorry."

"All I can think of now are her screams and the blood and her fever afterwards. We feared she would not survive. It took six months before she began to regain her strength. And the baby …" A tear escaped but she brushed it away with the back of her hand. "Mr. Collins tells me I am being a goose cap, but he has no experience with such things. He has no grasp of what may happen and declares I should consult with Lady Catherine on the matter."

Elizabeth cringed. What an ugly conversation that would be. "Perhaps you should speak to Mama instead. She had seven lying-ins and will be able to advise you much better."

"I would like it if she would. May I ask something else of you? Would you speak to your father?"

"Would not a midwife be more appropriate?"

"After the midwife who attended Mama, I want nothing to do with one. Lady Catherine is so particular about Dr. Bennet treating anyone but Anne. Mr. Collins insists I should not ask. He plans to arrange whatever midwife Lady Catherine recommends or none at all, if that is her fancy."

"That is not his place. The birthing room is not the purview of any man, save perhaps a medical one."

"He is my husband—"

"He is a fool." Elizabeth rose and paced beside the table. "Forgive me, Charlotte, but this is beyond the pale. He has no business interfering. I will certainly petition Papa on your behalf. Mama has made certain he is most sympathetic to a woman's concerns at such a time. She will be of great comfort to you as well, though, perhaps too much comfort."

Charlotte sagged against the back of her chair. "You are the one person I could rely upon to understand. You always are."

---

Darcy paced the hall near the stairs. Five days Bennet managed to elude him. Easier he should capture a wraith! This could go on no longer.

Bennet was trapped in the parlor with Aunt Catherine while Darcy waited in ambush. He would have his meeting at last.

The door squeaked. Finally! He rushed to the parlor door, but Bennet was already disappearing down the corridor.

"Dr. Bennet, A word with you, if you please."

Bennet stopped. "Certainly, sir."

Darcy scanned the corridor. As always, Long Tom lurked in the shadows. Did that man never leave? How did he manage to accomplish anything when all he did was stand about?

"Not here. Let us take some fresh air, if you will." Darcy gestured down the hall.

"I must call upon the apothecary. Perhaps you would care to ride with me?"

"That will suffice." His horse could use the exercise since he had forgone morning rides for clandestine walks with Miss Elizabeth.

It must be the anticipation, but he found each encounter with her more agreeable than the last. She was altogether pleasing: her intelligence, her humor, the gentle thoughtfulness that suffused everything about her. Nothing was below her notice, not the scullery maid's chilblains, nor Long Tom's aching back, nor Aunt Catherine's sleeplessness.

What did she notice about him?

They headed for the stables, late morning sun dappling the path as it cut through the trees.

What an odd man this doctor was. Intelligent and acerbic, but innovative in his treatments. Certainly Anne improved under his care. Still, he acquiesced to Aunt Catherine's meddling interference in his household far too readily.

How could Darcy respect a man who was not master over his own home? Much less one who treated his daughter the way Bennet did. Could not he see the treasure given him? On the surface, he appeared to favor her. In closer reflection, though, he took her assistance and support for granted, dismissing and even insulting her with impunity.

She would endure it all pleasantly, never once taking up for herself. But then, how could she do so in polite company? Still, how many barbs was it right for one to endure?

At least Bennet was a decent horseman. Not Fitzwilliam's caliber, certainly, but good enough not to be an affront to the title 'gentleman'.

"You had something you wished to speak on?" Bennet pulled his horse alongside Darcy's.

The road widened just a bit and they lost the meager shade from the ancient oaks near the manor. At last, a suitable place for a private conversation.

"The case for which you desire consultation, perhaps?" Bennet had none of his daughter's subtlety.

"No, that is for another time. I have a more immediate concern."

"Some physical complaint? I know what often plagues gentlemen of your age and standing. I regret I have little to offer but the conventional treatment for one who is—how they say—burnt."

What? How dare he! Darcy's horse snuffed and shook its head, feeling the affront as deeply as his rider.

"That is not what I wish to discuss."

"No need to take such a defensive posture with me, sir. The malady is common enough." Bennet urged his horse slightly ahead of Darcy's.

Could Bennet possibly be more offensive? A bootlicker for Aunt Catherine but easily insulted by those he regarded more his equal. Interesting dichotomy and not pleasing in the least.

A gig clattered toward them. It was early yet for the driver to be drunk as David's sow, but his control of the equipage said otherwise. Raucous shouts and laughter from its passengers rose above the din of the wheels and pounding horse's hooves.

The driver—Good Lord it was Wickham! The young woman beside him bore a strong resemblance to Miss Elizabeth.

They urged their horses off the road barely in time for the gig to fly by. Wickham did not acknowledge them as they rattled past, but the girl, one hand clutching her bonnet, waved wildly.

Darcy choked on the impropriety and the dust cloud left in their wake. "That is what I desire to talk to you about."

Bennet's lips puckered in something resembling disapproval. "I did not authorize him to drive my gig."

"That is all you have to say? You did not authorize him to drive your equipage? Did you not make out one of your daughters with him?"

"I am full capable of recognizing my own children, thank you."

"Is it not troubling to see your daughter, unchaperoned, in the society of a man?"

"Lady Catherine presented him as a suitable beau for Elizabeth. Why should I object to his keeping company with any of the girls?"

Darcy clenched and unclenched his hands. Shaking the man was not likely to make him any more rational, though it could not hurt, could it?

"Are you not mindful of her reputation—even her person?"

"If Lady Catherine trusts him, then I do as well. Though, I will insist he leave off driving my gig."

"That is all you wish him to leave off? What about escorting your unchaperoned daughter?"

"The gig only holds two; a chaperone would be easier to arrange if they cannot use it."

"His company is not suitable—I know his long unsavory history with young ladies. If you are concerned about someone being burnt, it is to him you should offer your services."

"Lady Catherine told me otherwise. Why should I trust you?" Bennet folded his arms over his chest. "You are eager enough to stroll with Lizzy, unescorted, on Rosings' ground. Nearly every morning for nearly a week now."

Darcy's jaw dropped.

"You thought those walks surreptitious? I am more observant than you think. Lizzy takes after me." He stroked his chin. "It seems to me we have a case of the pot calling the kettle black, son."

Son? Bennet assumed entirely too much familiarity, and looked so smug in the process. This was not to be borne!

"You wish me to cease walking with her?" The possibility was dreadful, but so was Bennet.

"Dismiss the very notion. I would not instruct Lady Catherine's nephew on his comportment. You are engaged to Miss de Bourgh. Lizzy has been nursing her. What is more natural than for you to take the opportunity to communicate regarding Miss de Bourgh's welfare?"

"I am not engaged to Anne."

"Lady Catherine says you are."

What point correcting him? Talking sense to this man would be a sleeveless errand!

"Fear not. I shall not share your secret. In the meantime, enjoy your conversations with my daughter. Let her instruct you on how best to ensure your future wife's health and happiness. None knows that better than my Lizzy." He tipped his hat and rode off.

Darcy started at his back. He had been accused of having the pox, of being engaged to Anne, and of being inappropriate with Miss Elizabeth. All the while, Bennet ignored his warnings about Wickham. This was not the favor he promised Miss Elizabeth. Perhaps, he should resolve the matter of Wickham himself.

---

Four days later, Miss de Bourgh declared herself strong enough to visit below stairs for a short time. The following day, Papa released Wickham and Bingley from quarantine. Lady Catherine invited the Bennets and Collinses to dinner the following evening to celebrate.

Elizabeth helped Miss de Bourgh prepare for her guests. Dawson, her lady's maid, should have performed the service. How interesting and convenient that she had been sent to her sister's house in the village to recover from some ambiguous symptoms.

"You seem in very high spirits tonight, Miss Elizabeth." Miss de Bourgh sniffled and dabbed her nose with her silken handkerchief.

"I have not seen Jane since the night you took ill. I miss her very much."

"Why it should matter so very much to you? The company here at Rosings must be far better than your sister's."

Elizabeth choked back the remark dancing on the tip of her tongue. There was no civil response to such a remark.

"I mean no offense, but even the Bingley woman and her sister are better educated. Since they have been living recently in London—"

"While Miss Bingley and Mrs. Hurst have been to many fine and fashionable places, they are not my particular friends as Jane is."

"I do not understand all the fluff and fluster about a particular friend. Truly, what good is it? I have not one and never cared a jot."

"Perhaps those of your rank have no need of it. Whereas those of us without that comfort must find it elsewhere," Elizabeth replied through gritted teeth.

"Still, I find it a stupid thing. I expected you above such banalities. Is not your companionship to me enough?"

"I … I …"

"I am going to tell Mama to install you as my companion. You are much pleasanter than crusty old Mrs. Jenkinson."

"I do not think that a good idea, Miss de Bourgh." Cold prickles crept across Elizabeth's face. There were not enough words in the King's English to describe how bad an idea it was.

"Nonsense! When I marry my cousin, Darcy, you may come with me to Pemberley and nurse me just as you do now."

"I was not of a mind to seek a position—"

"Well, you should. You will never marry now you have refused two eligible suitors. Mama quite despairs of marrying you off. She is seeking positions for you and anticipates seeing you well-settled in one soon. I do not see why it cannot be with me."

Elizabeth jerked back and twitched her head. She must remember to breathe—swoons would be categorically unsafe around one who would make no attempt to break her fall.

"Her consideration toward you is very great, is it not? Come now, take my arm and walk me downstairs. I should like to enjoy a bit of company tonight. Since you are so looking forward to seeing your sister, you may stay below stairs even when I retire. Am I not good to you? You see how pleasant it is to be my companion?"

Elizabeth stretched her lips into the most insincere smile of her life. The gall! The arrogance! She was every inch her mother's daughter. How dare she think Elizabeth would ever live at Pemberley in any capacity but its mistress?

*Mistress? Heavens, where had that notion come from?*

Everyone in the parlor rose and offered their greetings to Miss de Bourgh. A few looked genuinely excited to have her company. Such disguise was definitely beyond Elizabeth's means. She released her charge and made her way to Jane.

Mr. Bingley, smiling and satisfied, stood beside her. How well they looked together: Jane, angelic and Mr. Bingley adoring her celestial beauty. By all rights she should be very pleased for Jane, but that did nothing to assuage the tightness in her throat. Their sisterly confidences would have to wait. It would be well. She must not be so selfish. Jane should make the most of her opportunity to engage Mr. Bingley now he was no longer resident under Mama's hospitality.

"Lizzy!" Jane kissed her cheek. "I have missed you so."

"Nonsense. How can you say such a thing when we have had such charming guests in her absence?"

Elizabeth turned. "Good evening, Mama."

"You are looking well, Lizzy." Mama's gaze raked her up and down. "Miss de Bourgh is looking well, too. It seems your presence is a great boon to her."

"Papa's care for her has a great deal more to do with that, I am sure."

"Perhaps so, but a woman is always comforted by the companionship of another woman." She peeked over her shoulder toward Miss de Bourgh.

No! Heavens please, let her not be thinking the same thing as Miss de Bourgh!

"I am reminded, Charlotte—Mrs. Collins—is very much in need of motherly affection right now." Elizabeth pressed her belly. "She might not be bold enough to seek you out herself. I know she would be greatly comforted if you would take the time to speak with her."

"Indeed?" She craned her neck to see Charlotte in the crowded room. "The dear girl, so far from her own mother at such a time as this. I will make sure to single her out tonight." Mama patted her arm and wandered toward Charlotte.

Long Tom entered the parlor and announced dinner. Lady Catherine, on Mr. Darcy's arm, led them into the glittering, candle-lit dining room.

The novelty of Miss de Bourgh's attendance at dinner carried the entirety of the conversation. Each of the many dishes had been prepared with her tastes and requirements in mind. Though the overall effect was bland, tepid, and mushy, no one at the table had even the opportunity to remark upon it. Lady Catherine scarcely breathed, or ate, with her running commentary on every imaginable topic.

Her verbosity always grew in proportion to her anxiety. Poor woman was still beside herself with worry for Miss de Bourgh.

Colonel Fitzwilliam glanced at Mr. Darcy and rolled his eyes. Mr. Darcy rubbed his temples. What were his perceptions of his Aunt tonight? Did he think her merely ridiculous, or could he discern her underlying apprehension. Perhaps they would talk about it in the morning.

Colonel Fitzwilliam leaned close to Miss de Bourgh. He whispered something that earned him a smirk that ended in a tiny cough.

The room fell silent, and all eyes turned to Miss de Bourgh. She blushed and chided her cousin for causing unnecessary concern.

Something about Colonel Fitzwilliam's posture had changed since the last time he kept company with Miss de Bourgh. Why was he suddenly paying such attention to a woman previously outside his notice? Best not exert too much thought on the matter.

More disturbing, the meaningful expressions passing between Miss Darcy and Mr. Wickham. Did not Mr. Darcy recognize them?

Lady Catherine adjourned with the ladies, leaving the dining room to the men. Mr. Bingley and Mr. Wickham had been deprived of masculine company these weeks in the Bennet abode, after all.

As usual, oppressive heat permeated the drawing room. Miss de Bourgh sat near the fire. The Bingley sisters crowded close, fawning upon her every word, freeing Elizabeth to seek out Jane.

"Oh, Lizzy!" Jane took her hands and drew her down to the settee beside her. "How I have missed you!"

If they spoke softly, they might escape Lady Catherine's and Mama's notice for a few moments.

"I am surprised you even detected my absence while hosting such agreeable company."

Jane blushed but gave her an admonishing look. "That does not mean you were not missed."

"So tell me, how will you bear the loss of Mr. Bingley and Mr. Wickham now their banishment from Rosings has ended?"

"It will be difficult. Mama has been in such high spirits entertaining them."

"Did you enjoy high spirits as well?"

"You know that is not my nature, Lizzy. No matter how much I like him, I cannot be something I am not."

Elizabeth squeezed Jane's hand. "You have been much pressured for exactly that?"

"Mama is much more pleased with Lydia's manners in a gentleman's society than mine."

"Because she used those means to get Papa."

"Lizzy! You must allow for differences among people. You cannot judge. Just because they are not your ways, does not make them wrong."

"Tell me of Mr. Bingley. You like him very well?"

Jane dropped her gaze and wrung her hands. "I do indeed."

"Looking at him tonight, I am certain the feeling is mutual."

"Do you think it too soon to hope he has formed an attachment to me?"

Elizabeth glanced toward the door. "For some, perhaps, but Mr. Darcy has often mentioned his bewilderment at Mr. Bingley's impulsive nature—"

"That does not sound like a compliment."

"What bewilders him is the degree to which Mr. Bingley's impulsive decisions are correct."

Jane giggled.

"You will forgive me, your ladyship, but on this point, I must disagree."

What was that? Elizabeth started and sat up very straight. Mama never contradicted Lady Catherine.

"Disagree? Disagree? On what basis can you possibly disagree with me?"

"I have three living daughters, your ladyship, and experienced seven lying-ins. I have far and away more experience in all things related to motherhood."

"Experience alone does not make you an expert."

Mama's words had that tone, the one that never ended well. Jane and Elizabeth rose and hurried toward the other ladies.

Charlotte sat between Mama and Lady Catherine while Georgiana looked on with wide eyes and a creeping pallor.

"I should think, Mrs. Bennet, that married to a man of science, you would be quick to recognize science is the best arbiter of experience."

"I thought you believed tradition to be the arbiter of experience." Mama's pitch climbed an octave, rapier sharp to make her point.

Had Mama not learned? It was unwise to remind Lady Catherine of opinions she had declared previous to a current conversation.

"Indeed it is, in some things. But in other matters, like this, it is science. And science dictates—"

"Nonsense! It is not Mrs. Collins' fault she fell with child, now. No means of preventing it is entirely effective."

Charlotte colored almost to match the wine of the upholstery, eyes bulging and begging for deliverance.

"Had she but followed my advice, she might be spared her current situation." Lady Catherine waved her hand, nearly striking Charlotte in the face.

"Spared, why might she wish to be spared? A child is a blessing—the duty of a wife is to provide heirs."

"Summer is a most ill-advised time for a confinement. I told her spring—"

"So you expected Mr. Collins—"

Jane wavered and clutched an overstuffed pillow. Miss Darcy gasped, so pale she might faint.

Elizabeth sprang to her side. "I discovered some music in the sitting room upstairs. Would you come examine it with me? You might enjoy playing it when the gentlemen join us."

Miss Darcy leapt to her feet. "Yes—yes, that is an excellent idea." She grabbed Elizabeth's arm, and they rushed out the door.

A dozen steps from the drawing room, she collapsed against the wall. Poor girl was trembling. Long Tom appeared at Elizabeth's elbow. Miss Darcy shook even harder.

"Fetch Miss Darcy some wine and water. We will be upstairs."

He bowed and strode away.

They trudged their way up the stairs, and Elizabeth guided her to the sitting room's window bench. She pushed the window open. Soft night air, tinged with clean green smells flowed in. "Just sit back. The fresh air will do you good."

Miss Darcy leaned back and closed her eyes. Color gradually returned to her features.

Elizabeth retrieved several sheets of dusty music from the ancient armoire.

"You actually found music here?"

She handed Miss Darcy the neatly penned scores. "Of course, I did. I find it ill-advised to employ deception, especially when a convenient truth is available. These are older pieces, just plain folk songs—"

Miss Darcy traced the line with her fingertip and hummed. "I shall enjoy playing them, and my brother will approve. He likes these simple melodies very well indeed."

"I am glad then. It makes the excuse that much more palatable."

"Thank you for removing me from that conversation. I cannot believe—"

"Yes, thank you."

They both jumped and turned.

Mr. Darcy stood, shadowed in the door way, wine glass in hand. "The butler suggested where I might find you. He intimated my sister might be feeling ill."

"Not ill, brother, only mortified."

"The drawing room conversation took a turn inappropriate for a maiden's ears," Elizabeth said.

"So I gathered." Darcy strode in and handed the glass to Miss Darcy. "The conversation was quite animated when I left. Your father was doing his best to pacify them both. Fitzwilliam suggested the rest of us should adjourn to the music room while they settled matters. We thought you might be willing to play the music Miss Bennet procured."

Elizabeth quirked her brows.

Miss Darcy giggled. "Of course, I think it a very good idea. Shall I go then?"

"Yes, we will follow in a moment."

Georgiana picked up the music and left.

Mr. Darcy offered Elizabeth his arm. His fingers were warm and heavy over hers. Lady Catherine would certainly not approve.

"Thank you for removing Georgiana from that scene. I cannot fathom what possessed my aunt to engage in such a debate, much less with my sister present."

"My mother contradicted Lady Catherine, and her ladyship cannot abide being disagreed with."

"I know that to be true." He turned and gazed into her eyes.

No man had ever looked at her that way, so intensely, seen her so completely. Her skin tingled where his eyes touched it, and her breath came in shallow pants. Why could she not breathe when he stood so close?

His voice turned husky, a music she would never tire of. "I am deeply grateful. My sister is easily distressed by our Aunt."

"Those of a stronger constitution are as well." She chuckled.

"Are you?"

The room swam. Had he actually asked? When was the last time anyone had asked how she felt? Only her grasp on his arm kept her from a swoon.

"Miss Elizabeth?"

"I suppose there are times when it is challenging."

He threw his head back and laughed. The bubbling, joyful melody surely held the power to make everything right in the world. Would that he never stop.

"You are indeed the embodiment of all that is gracious and kind. I have never met the likes of you." His eyes bored into hers, and perhaps into her soul. "Your eyes are utterly arresting."

"Excuse me, sir." Long Tom broached the doorway, hands clasped behind his back, face frozen in an impassive mask.

Of all people to come upon them, thank Providence it was one she trusted.

"Shall I send refreshments to the music room?"

Darcy stared, color creeping up along his jawline. "Ah, yes, that would be …"

"Most agreeable," Elizabeth said.

Tom bowed and disappeared.

"Perhaps, we should adjourn there before we are missed." She did not sound as convincing as she should.

"I am sure you are correct." He pressed her hand to his arm.

She held firm, glad for the support against her weakened knees.

If only the journey to the music room were a fraction longer, they might have had time to talk, even a little. Their morning walks left her greedy for more.

The last strains of a country melody faded away. Jane's playing, no doubt. She peeked in.

Chairs had been rearranged to accommodate the large group and many candles brought in to brighten the dark corners. No ill-tempered paintings censured them from the walls, only filigreed green paper hanging that always left her a little sick to her stomach.

Mr. Bingley applauded loudly. His enthusiasm was nothing if not endearing. Miss Bingley hovered near the piano, obviously waiting to take her turn and remind them all of her superior skill. The Hursts sat nearby, clearly unimpressed by Jane's performance.

Why was Colonel Fitzwilliam sitting so close to Miss de Bourgh and with such a solicitous smile? At least, Miss de Bourgh did not seem to mind. If anything, she appeared inordinately pleased. Elizabeth flexed her shoulders to ease the tension along the back of her neck.

"Mr. Darcy, you have come at last." Miss Bingley called a bit too loudly. "And Miss Eliza …"

Elizabeth cringed. Why did she insist on using that dreadful nickname and insinuate intimacy neither felt? Perhaps the next time she would respond with 'Yes Carrie' and see how well received that was.

Perhaps not, for Jane's sake.

"It would have been a shame to miss an opportunity to hear you play." Elizabeth released Darcy's arm.

Georgiana patted the settee beside her. Elizabeth took her place and folded her hands in her lap.

Mr. Wickham sauntered toward them. "Shall you grace us with your music, Miss Darcy?"

Georgiana giggled and blushed.

Elizabeth's jaw tightened and she edged closer to Georgiana.

"I certainly will, sir, but you must promise to sing with me."

"Sing with you? I did not know you deigned to play such music as an unaccomplished talent like mine might accompany."

"You have a very fine voice."

"Not nearly as fine as your skill." He cocked his head, eyes twinkling.

"You are entirely too kind. Is he not, Miss Elizabeth?" Miss Darcy's cheeks glowed, and she batted her eyes, just a hair's breadth short of coquettish.

"Certainly, he is. Though, one must always question the motives of a man who flatters too much." Her eyebrow arched.

The corners of his mouth dropped just a touch, and he blinked rapidly. "Of what do you accuse me, madam? You cannot think me insincere."

"To say so would be to criticize Miss Darcy's performance, and that I would never do."

"Of course not. None who has heard her play would. Shall we, Miss Darcy?" He offered his arm.

She took his arm, giggling and blushing, and driving a sharp pang through Elizabeth's ribs. They proceeded to the pianoforte, displacing Miss Bingley just before she sat down. Wickham arranged her music and they began.

Miss Darcy's fingers were sure and nimble and Wickham's voice polished. He stood close to her, too close. Did Mr. Darcy approve?

He sat in the corner with his cousins. Why was he so at ease around Miss de Bourgh tonight? What had changed? How could he ignore the inappropriate glances Mr. Wickham and Miss Darcy shared?

They began another song. Mr. Wickham sidled even closer. His hand hovered above her shoulder, not quite touching her, but Miss Darcy blushed as though he did. The audacity of it!

She dare not interrupt Miss de Bourgh to bring it to the attention of Mr. Darcy and Colonel Fitzwilliam. She chewed her knuckle.

Another verse? Would they never finish? Another moment and she would scream. She sprang to her feet. A muttered pleasantry escaped on her way out the door. What an utterly ghastly way to spend an evening.

## Chapter 5

SLEEP TAUNTED AND TEASED, but never settled in place. The first tendrils of daylight wound their way through Elizabeth's curtains. What point fighting for slumber any longer? She slid out of the high bed and pulled a shawl around her shoulders. Little good it did against the morning chill. Her bare feet padded softly on the cool wood floor as she paced the length of the room.

How could Miss Darcy's guardians neglect her so? Did they assume only Bennet sisters vulnerable to Mr. Wickham, and Miss Darcy enjoyed immunity to his charms? Why were they so distracted by Miss de Bourgh? What made her suddenly so interesting to both of them? What puzzle piece was she missing?

Gah, this was maddening!

How long until Mrs. Jenkinson recovered and she might return to her own home? Or would Mama and

Papa insist she stay on as Miss de Bourgh's companion?

Elizabeth stopped and clutched the carved oak bedpost. Heavens, she was trapped and pacing like a caged animal. If only she could run, but where? No one would take her. Wait! Aunt and Uncle Gardiner—they always welcomed her and Jane—surely they would help!

She flung open the curtains and dropped down at the writing table. The early sunbeams cast just enough light to permit her to pen a brief note.

The sealing wax pooled on the missive. Pray, let it find favor in Cheapside.

A maid peeked in. "Her Ladyship wants to see you in the parlor as soon as you are presentable. I am to help you dress."

Great heavens, what now? Had *she* heard of her walks with Mr. Darcy? Or perhaps some helpful servant reported Mr. Darcy had escorted her to the music room last night. Blast and botheration!

"I can dress without your assistance. I will be down shortly. Take this—" She handed the maid her letter. "See that it is in today's post."

"Yes, Miss." The maid curtsied and scurried away.

Elizabeth grumbled under her breath as she pulled on her gown. At home, a plain, comfortable morning dress would do. Oh, but not at Rosings. Here she had to be fit to be seen at all times, even so early in the morning. Dare she simply pin her hair in a simple knot? No, Lady Catherine's ire would be severe enough without one more detail to criticize. She arranged her hair into something slightly more appealing, but only slightly.

~134~

There, acceptable—not excellent, but acceptable. She wrapped her shawl tightly about her and marched toward her fate.

Her slippers grew to the weight of a gentleman's hessians as she approached Lady Catherine's throne room. The lady's sharp tongue would doubtless be used liberally upon her.

Was it ungracious to be weary of these summonses? Papa would insist so. They were a small price to be paid for all the benefits had in an association with Rosings Park.

"You sent for me, Lady Catherine?" She stepped into the dim chamber.

How cold and glum it was in the morning. A balcony on the floor above shaded the west facing windows. Lady Catherine sat on her throne, backlit in the grey light, her face in the shadows.

"You are an early riser, Miss Elizabeth."

She must not roll her eyes, so she curtsied. "Yes, your ladyship."

"You can be at no loss as to why I called you here."

"No, your ladyship. I am afraid I have no idea at all."

"Do not play games with me."

"I am not, your ladyship. Truly, I do not understand the reason for this interview."

She snuffed out a sharp breath, her nostrils flaring like a dragon preparing to breathe fire. "Your behavior yesterday was indiscreet and bordering on disgraceful."

What had she seen or thought she had seen? Elizabeth blinked hard, barely breathing.

"How could you direct Mrs. Collins—"

"Mrs. Collins?" Surely she had misheard.

"Yes, Mrs. Collins—do not interrupt me, young woman. How could you direct Mrs. Collins to anyone but me for advice?"

"Her concerns regarded increasing, and lying in, and confinements. No offence or disrespect intended to your ladyship but—"

"It is taken, I assure you." Lady Catherine clutched the arms of her throne. Any more tightly and the sphinxes below would scream for mercy.

"Your ladyship has but one daughter and, as I understand, been with child only once. My mother has birthed five living children and experienced no less than—"

"You are in no position to offer advice or direction to anyone. It is my place, not yours. If wisdom or knowledge is required, steer my people to me. I will then guide the seeker as I deem fit, not you. Is that understood?"

Elizabeth's jaw dropped. The audacity—the gall! *Her*, the repository of all insight and discernment in her realm?

"Finally struck dumb, Miss Elizabeth? I require a response."

"Yes, your ladyship. I ... I understand."

A thin lipped smile threatened to crack Lady Catherine's face. "See you do not forget. I know you are generally a well-meaning creature, but it is most unbecoming when one forgets her proper place. You may go now."

Elizabeth inched backward. She dare not turn her back on the Queen of Rosings Parks.

"I expect Anne will be quite tired from last night and not in any need of your company today. Take one of those long walks you so favor. Perhaps a bit of fresh air will help you to remember yourself once again." She eased her grip on her throne and laughed a peculiar rasping bark.

Elizabeth stared as the dragon transformed into something still majestic, but less terrible.

Should she flee now?

"You have no idea what to make of me?" *She* cackled and rubbed her hands together. "It is a rare treat to see you speechless."

"It is?"

"Indeed. You see, you do not know as much as you think you do. You would do well to recall that." *She* leaned forward and peered into Elizabeth's eyes. "You regard me as some kind of ogre."

Not an ogre, but a dragon. Still, the effect was the same.

"Do not deny it, girl. I can see."

Elizabeth stammered odd, useless sounds.

Lady Catherine laughed again. Oh, that she would stop!

"I am no ogre. Consider me … a mother hawk, protecting her nest and young."

Her nose did have a hawk-like quality.

"Rosings Park is my nest, girl, and all within it, my keep. It is my role to protect it, by whatever means necessary. I want, and will insure, what is best for all under my wings." *She* spread her hands, the sleeves of her gown rustling like feathers. "Even you."

"Yes, your ladyship."

"Now, I shall forgive you your youthful interference this time, assuming you knew no better. Do not do it again. Now, go on. I have other business to attend." *She* flicked her hand toward the door.

Elizabeth dropped in a curtsey, more reflex than courtesy, and restrained herself to a brisk walk toward the door. She did not stop until outside and well clear of the parlor windows.

A garden wall rose up in her path and offered her support. She slumped against it, the stone cold and sharp against the back of her head. A morning sunbeam kissed her face.

Bah! She had no bonnet! One more transgression to add to her list.

*Elizabeth Margaret Rose Bennet! You will be the death of me, yet. Why can you not be more like Jane?* Mama's shrill voice echoed in her mind.

A chill shiver snaked down her spine. No, she was nothing like Jane and probably never would be.

"Miss Elizabeth?"

Her eyes flew open.

Mr. Darcy stood over her. "Are you well this morning?"

"Oh, I … I … forgive me." She rubbed her forehead. "I just left an interview with Lady Catherine and I am a bit—"

"Shaken?"

She cleared her throat. "That is one word for it, though perhaps not the first one I would have considered. She can be quite formidable."

"I am well acquainted with that aspect of her temperament." He gestured down the path. "Perhaps a turn about the gardens will rally your spirits?"

Returning to the house certainly would not improve her equanimity. She nodded and they set off. "I fear I upset her yesterday."

"She did work herself into a high dudgeon, did she not?" He snorted a little chuckle. "She enjoys directing the lives of others and does not appreciate interference."

His voice was tight and his shoulders held an uncharacteristic tension.

"She has been trying to direct your life as well?"

"Am I so obvious? We have battled over the issue for many years now, but especially since my father's death. As almost my nearest relation, she sees it her right—nay her duty—to manage my life and my sister's."

"I do not imagine her very successful."

He kicked a small stone skipping and bouncing down the narrow path. "It vexes her when I do not immediately capitulate."

"Which is often?"

"And why I have not been to Rosings these last two years."

The back of her throat ached. How soon would he leave and how long until he would return? She dared not ask either of those questions. Some things were too impertinent, even for her.

"That seems a prudent means of handling a difficult situation. It does not appear Miss Darcy would repine the loss of Kent's society."

"Hardly. It is difficult to imagine her repining the loss of any society." He stared into the wispy clouds and exhaled heavily.

"Something is amiss with her?"

"I am afraid so."

"Perhaps, I might be able to help?"

He offered her his arm. His hand was so warm and comforting on hers. Surely it must be wrong to revel in it so.

"I dearly hope so, but I am reluctant to impose upon your gracious nature."

"Any graciousness you see in me is certainly not the product of nature, sir."

"You think too meanly of yourself."

"I merely echo the sentiments of my parents and your most wise and learned aunt."

He muttered something unintelligible.

Foolish girl! He was so easy to talk to, every word invited indiscretion.

He stepped into her path. She stopped short and looked up at him. Oh! His eyes—

"I am grieved to hear they have spoken of you so unjustly."

She should turn away, but his gaze was too insistent, too compelling.

He lifted his fingers, barley not touching her cheek. Her skin burned beneath his fingertips. Would that he only touch her—

"Forgive me." He pulled back. "I am too forward. But pray, do not denigrate yourself in my presence."

"I shall try." She rubbed the side of her neck below her ear. "What … what may I do for you … your sister?"

How was it he managed to discompose her so completely?

He closed his eyes for a moment and offered his arm again. They walked.

Movement was definitely preferable. His direct scrutiny was far too unsettling.

"You have by now noticed that Georgiana is painfully shy."

"Much like her brother."

He shrugged. "Yes and no. I am reticent in company—uncomfortable, but I am not fearful of others."

"No gentleman would admit to being fearful in company."

He looked down at her, his scowl quickly transforming to mild amusement. "Do you regularly tease a person who is trying to discuss matters of a serious nature?"

"Generally, yes. I find it lightens the mood and eases the way to speak frankly."

"I am not accustomed to being teased."

"I can tell." She tugged the stray hairs near her ear. "Should I cease?"

"Perhaps not. I am growing accustomed to it."

Their eyes locked again.

This would not do. All the tingling and fluttering he stirred up would undoubtedly lead her to say something very foolish indeed. She turned her face aside and stepped along the path. "You sister is afraid of unfamiliar company?"

"Very much so. Last month, she turned eighteen. It is time for her to come out. Unlike most girls who long for it, she has begged to delay yet again."

"She is only eighteen. You might safely wait a year, I believe. Perhaps, during that time you might slowly introduce her to small parties at home that she might grow more accustomed to social gatherings."

"Would that it was so simple, but Georgiana has been paying close attention to Anne. She desires to emulate our cousin's example."

Elizabeth's brows knit. What example? Miss de Bourgh kept little company and never went out. Oh!

"Miss de Bourgh expects to marry well without the ordeal of balls and parties and suitors?"

"You see the problem."

"Then perhaps there is a convenient cousin for her to marry? The Colonel or one of his brothers." She licked her lips.

He stopped midstride. "Good God, no!"

"Forgive me. I did not mean to offend." Nettlesome heat coursed across the back of her neck and ears. When would she learn to subdue her impudent humor?

"I would not see my sister married to one of my Fitzwilliam cousins, not whilst I live."

"I … I thought you quite good friends with the Colonel."

"We are friends, yes. I trust him deeply, but he is a worldly man with worldly tastes and ways. His brothers are even worse with their brood of natural children strung across the breadth of England. The eldest has an appetite for opium that is slowly killing him."

That must be the case Papa was concerned about! Dare she ask more? No, now was not the time.

"I recognize I am too forward, forgive me. I must ask, though. Why do you encourage Colonel Fitzwilliam toward Miss de Bourgh if you find him unsuitable for your sister?"

"You are very forward indeed. I should take umbrage at your question."

"Yes, I suppose you should—but will you?"

He sighed. "No, not from you."

"I am flattered."

"You should be." A dear little smile quirked the corner of his mouth. "You are aware my aunt has determined I should marry Anne."

"They hardly make it a secret."

"That is not the kind of marriage I desire for me nor my sister. Neither Fitzwilliam nor Anne expect, or even want, a marriage encumbered by love. They are amiable enough with one another to live peacefully together. He can devote much more to Rosings than I am able."

"And Rosings needs a great deal?"

"You have no idea."

She grimaced. Papa's position was far more precarious than he realized, but for reasons he did not comprehend and she dare not explain.

"What of Miss de Bourgh?"

"Anne has warmed to the idea. It may take some time, but I expect my aunt will also be persuaded."

"This pleases you?"

"Very much so." His voice dropped to a low husky murmur that draped softly around her shoulders in an intimate embrace. How could a voice be so incredibly—

"Miss Elizabeth! Miss Elizabeth!" Tom jogged toward them, his normal implacable mask shattered and left somewhere between the garden and manor.

"What is wrong?" Elizabeth dashed to him.

"My nephew—he drunk half a bottle of laudanum, thought it leftover beer. He cannot stand and barely breathes."

"Half a bottle of laudanum? Dear heavens! Take me to him." She turned to Mr. Darcy. "Ames is one of the junior footmen. Please get my father and bring him below stairs."

"Certainly." He bowed his head and ran off.

Elizabeth picked up her skirts and sprinted alongside Tom. "What has been done for him?"

"The cook brewed a rousing tea, but I do not think it helped."

"How long ago did he take the laudanum?"

"Three hours, I think." Tom had never looked less like himself than he did now—so vulnerable and out of control.

So much time and so much laudanum! Was it possible to survive such a dose? Papa had treated children who died from just a spoonful of the stuff. He knew some ways, but they were not always successful.

Tom led her down the dank servants' corridors to his quarters beside the butler's pantry. The smell of silver polish and tobacco hung heavy in the stale air. The musty darkness of the windowless apartments draped heavily upon her chest and shoulders. She fought to breathe.

Dim shadows from the candlelight flickered against Ames, crumpled on the floor, half in livery, half in night clothes. He did not stir when they entered.

"Ames, boy, look at me. I brought Miss Elizabeth. She will set you to rights. Ames!"

She dropped to her knees beside Ames. His head hung limp, chin to chest, his breath slow and labored, almost like one deep in slumber. She took his wrist and searched for a pulse. Great heavens, where was Papa?

Several sets of footsteps shuffled just outside the room.

"Dr. Bennet." Tom clambered to his feet.

Thank Providence! She sagged against a squat cabinet.

Papa shouldered her out of his way. Mr. Darcy and Colonel Fitzwilliam appeared at her side and helped her to her feet. She held her breath while Papa muttered and checked Ames's eyes, pulse, and breathing.

Papa pushed to his feet and stroked his chin. "The situation is very serious, but not without hope."

Tom caught a strangled cry in his fist. "Thank you, sir."

"We have a difficult row to hoe." He turned to Elizabeth and glowered. "Made far more difficult because of you."

"What have I done?"

"Thanks to your thoughtlessness, Lady Catherine is in high dudgeon today and does not wish me gone from her sight for very long. She is concerned I might ignore her commands and call upon Mrs. Collins if I am gone for more than a few minutes."

"She controls what patients you will see?" Elizabeth whispered.

"She prefers to maintain the belief that she does. I am well able to manage my own affairs if allowed to do so in my own way." He grumbled under his breath. "I must leave in a moment."

"What of Ames? You cannot ignore his need—he will die!"

He adjusted his glasses. "I did not say I would turn my back, just that this would be difficult. I cannot treat him directly. I will give you direction, and you will manage him."

No, he could not possibly mean—

"Sir, it is not proper," Mr. Darcy said.

"Call a maid to assist. Help her yourself if you will. We have little time and few options if he is to be saved."

Elizabeth gulped. "Yes, Papa. What … what must I do?"

"The laudanum must be purged from his system. Is there blue vitriol in the house?"

Tom nodded. "I believe the housekeeper has it."

"Get it and toweling, a basin, warm water. Lizzy, you will want an apron."

"I will get them." Tom hurried out.

Colonel Fitzwilliam dashed after him.

"Mix half a drachm of blue vitriol in water and get him to drink it. He will vomit soon after, perhaps multiple times. Make him drink warm water after he does. You must get him to his feet and keep him moving. Do not let him sleep, or he may never wake."

"How long?"

"Until he recovers, or dies. I must return to her ladyship. I shall come back when I can, perhaps in several hours. Send me word if anything happens that I have not described." He dusted his hands together.

Pray, let him not leave her now. What if she made a mistake? What signs should she watch for? How would she determine—"Papa …"

"Perhaps you will remember this and weigh your future behavior more carefully." He scowled and left.

Her hands trembled, and her knees might buckle at any moment. How could he leave this man's fate to her?

Behind her, Ames moaned.

Darcy's clenched his hands behind his back. How could Bennet blame Aunt Catherine's outrageous demands on Miss Elizabeth? Her eyes shimmered, eyelashes bright with teardrops. His jaw tightened. He would have words with that man yet, especially if Bennet was to treat Fitzwilliam's brother.

"Are you well, Miss Elizabeth?" Clearly she was not. Any fool could see she was hurt and vulnerable and in need of a champion.

She rubbed the back of her hand over her eyes. "I am fine, thank you."

He lifted her chin with one finger. "I am not so certain I agree."

"I am merely embarrassed at my foolishness, sir. As it seems I should be."

"You have received far too much censure for fault not your own. You are far too patient with it."

She dodged his gaze. "You give me far too much credit, sir."

"And you give yourself far too little. I mean to see that change." No, that was not true. What he meant for was to kiss her.

Footsteps pounded in the hall, and she jumped away. Blast and botheration! Why had he not been granted a few more seconds?

Richard burst in, a small, dark jar in one hand, a pitcher and small bowl in the other. "Here." He pushed the bottle at Miss Elizabeth, then searched his pocket and produced several tiny scoops.

"Pour some water." She measured out the blue-green vitriol and added it to the liquid.

Tom stumbled in, laden with towels. A young maid followed with a basin and an apron over her shoulder.

Miss Elizabeth threw the apron over her gown. "Get him upright. Tom, open his mouth."

They jumped into action.

She leaned close to Ames's ear. "You must drink this if you wish to live."

Ames's face creased, and one dilated eye cracked open. He gasped and muttered unintelligible sounds.

Why were they even trying? Even at his worst, the viscount never reached this state. This man was going to die. Would it not be more merciful to allow him to do it peacefully?

How could she be so strong? Darcy rubbed the back of his neck. Any other would have walked away, but her determination alone was enough to make one hope.

Miss Elizabeth poured the mixture down his throat and forced his mouth shut. He coughed and sputtered and tried to spit. She pinched his nose and held a hand over his mouth. He swallowed, and she repeated the process until the bowl was empty.

"Put the basin in front—"

Ames retched and vomited thin brown liquid smelling strongly of laudanum. Only a small portion hit the basin. The rest painted Miss Elizabeth's apron.

Darcy wrinkled his nose and turned aside. That stench! How did she bear it so stoically? He pressed a fist to his lips and swallowed hard.

"Give me a wet towel."

A maid passed her one, and she wiped Ames's face.

"Get me water." She forced him to drink a few sips. "He must walk now."

Tom waved Darcy and Fitzwilliam to his sides.

Ames's head lolled to the side as they hauled up him, dead weight in their arms. Darcy dragged Ames's limp arm over his shoulder and held his wrist tight. What point to this exercise? A man should be allowed to die with dignity, not dragged about like a feed sack.

"I do not …" Darcy muttered.

Her fierce mien arrested him. The force of her will alone would make this man survive, and woe to him that crossed her.

"You must compel him to walk. If he sleeps, he might never awaken." She stepped back, making space for them.

"Come there, Ames, pick up them bloody big feet of yours." Tom clapped very near Ames's ear.

Ames groaned, eyes cracking open. One foot dragged in a slow step.

"Good man! Just like that there." Tom glanced at Miss Elizabeth.

She grabbed his hand and squeezed. "Yes, just like that."

They dragged Ames through three circuits of the room. He cascaded again. This time Tom bore the brunt of his favors.

Darcy's guts did an arsey-varsey tumble along his ribs. How did Miss Elizabeth bear it?

They pulled Ames up and began another course around the room. A few minutes later, he cast up his accounts yet again. The room reeked. If there was a next time, Darcy might well join him.

Two young men, fresh from the stable, burst in. Darcy drank in the fragrance of horse and barn, a veritable perfume in the now fetid room.

"We just heard, sir." The taller of the two panted heavily.

"How can we help?"

"Take the gentlemen's place and keep him walking, down the hall now. He's moving better, now. Ain't he Miss Elizabeth?" Tom motioned them toward Ames.

Darcy ducked under Ames' arm and allowed the groom to take his place. Ames still hung like dead weight, but perhaps Darcy's roiling stomach biased his opinions.

Fitzwilliam straightened his coat and moved beside Darcy. "Is there anything else we might do?"

Tom glanced over his shoulder toward the three men in the hall. "I … I do not wish to leave him."

"If you might find some way to …" She cocked her head, such hope in her eyes that he dare not disappoint.

"Of course, we will see to it. Take care of your nephew. I will manage my aunt," Darcy said.

"Thank you, sir." Tom had never looked so—so human before.

This must be the way Miss Elizabeth always saw him. How did she cut through the masks that fooled others into ignoring the person behind them?

What did she see when her fine eyes turned on him?

Darcy nodded and hurried out, Fitzwilliam on his heels.

They paused at the base of the narrow, roughhewn servants' stairs. Slender rays of sun trickled from a distant window above, painting the confined space in wisps of light and shadow.

"Are you well?" Fitzwilliam asked *sotto voce*.

Darcy worked his tongue against the roof of his mouth. "Well enough. You have seen far worse."

"Indeed." Fitzwilliam's lips molded into a tense, thin line. "At least, there was neither blood nor gunpowder."

Darcy suppressed a shudder. "Do you think he will live?"

"I have never seen anyone ingest that much laudanum and survive, but he just might."

"If Bennet can affect this cure, then—"

"There is hope for my brother. Still, one must wonder how much is Bennet's expertise and how much is his daughter's dogged stubbornness. She has the will of a general I once served under. One did not breathe—or die—without a direct order from him. She would make a formidable commander."

Darcy sniggered. How did Fitzwilliam joke of death so easily?

"Should we leave her alone with him? The maid is there …"

"I do not like it." Darcy flexed his fingers and released them several times. "She is a gentlewoman."

"Indeed she is, acting more like the mistress of Rosings than its mistress. Are you in danger of her?"

Darcy grunted and shuffled his feet.

Fitzwilliam eyes narrowed, and he tilted his head. "You are considering more than merely a carnal attachment with her."

"Excuse me?"

"Our aunt may not see through your bluster, but I am not so easily beguiled."

Darcy turned aside and stared at the wall. A small spider scuttled up from the floorboards and into a small crack. "She owns no fortune."

"You do not need one."

"She is without connections."

"You do not care for the ones you have. Fewer for you to dislike?"

"Her mother is frightful."

"And our aunt is not?" Fitzwilliam nudged Darcy's foot with his own. "I ask you again, are you in peril of falling under her arts and allurements?"

"What arts and allurements? She has no artifice, makes no efforts to put herself forward, nor call attention to herself."

"So you are in no danger—"

"No—"

"Because you have already fallen."

Darcy scrubbed his face with his hands. "I take offense at the way she is treated by our aunt—do you know Anne considers her—"

"To be Mrs. Jenkinson's replacement? Yes, Anne spoke of it yesterday. She expects to bring Miss Elizabeth to Pemberley."

Darcy's eyes bulged. "How did you respond?"

"That Miss Elizabeth was not currently seeking a position and might be offended at such an offer. I suggested that Anne might rather stay at Rosings with me."

"And?"

"You cannot image it could be so easy? She has little intention of staying at Rosings when Pemberley is much pleasanter—and free of her mother. Still, she did not reject my offer outright. Though without a suitable home to offer her, I am not an appealing suitor. You are still her first choice."

"I suppose I should be flattered."

"Do not be. Her preference is less about your person and more about what you can provide. As it has ever been, Anne considers little beyond her own wants."

"Not a desirable trait in a wife, is it?"

Fitzwilliam braced his shoulder against the wall. "No, but a fortune and an estate are. So I shall continue to press my suit."

"I can help you lease a house in town, or elsewhere."

"I would rather usher Lady Catherine to the dower house."

Darcy choked back laughter. "I do not foresee—"

"Nor I. I shall keep your offer in mind."

Moans and coughs floated in the stale air. They turned toward the butler's rooms.

"You know, Darce, if Bennet gets word that Anne wants Miss Elizabeth for a companion, he will probably force her to accept."

Darcy bounced the back of his head against the cold stone wall.

"If that happens, you cannot pursue your interests in her. No, no, hold your ire for a moment, and hear me out. Even were you to marry her, Miss Elizabeth would forever be stained by suspicion over how she got your proposal. Not to mention the taint of having been in service! Her reputation would be tattered, and the *ton* would treat her like rubbish. That would not be fair to you, your children, or her. Better to set her up under your protection—"

"I will do no such thing!"

"I will never understand your rarified notion of marriage. But if you insist upon it, you best act to secure your happiness quickly, or it may be forever lost to you." Fitzwilliam brushed past him and climbed the narrow stairs.

Darcy sank down on the bottom step and drove his elbows into his knees. Bloody hell and damnation! Fitzwilliam was right.

Retching and liquid noises raced through the narrow corridor. He might join the chorus himself very soon.

No woman had ever been so well suited for him or Pemberley. But she was so unsuitable, with nothing but herself to recommend her. Would it even be fair to her to expect her to manage a place like Pemberley? She knew nothing about estates or—no, that was not true—she cared for Rosings, above and below stairs, as much as any proper mistress. With her quick mind and active nature, she would certainly rise to any occasion.

If only he had kissed her. Then he might—gah! He sounded like Fitzwilliam now. She had bewitched him utterly, mind and soul.

Late that evening, Darcy escaped from the drawing room and headed for his chambers. The company without Miss Elizabeth's presence proved unbearable. Near the top of the stairs, he made out Bennet's agitated tirade from the sitting room near Anne's rooms.

He should not snoop at doors. Pemberley's servants would never do such a thing. But this was not Pemberley, and Miss Elizabeth was on the other side of that door.

"You have placed me in a most disagreeable position, Lizzy. I am most displeased."

"Papa, I—"

"No more. It is enough I am now caught between your mother's and Lady Catherine's desires for Mrs. Collins. Had you not meddled, I would have been able to manage the situation as I did with young Ames today. You see how well he faired. Lady Catherine remained untroubled by any of it. I do not need you attempting to manage affairs that are not your own. You have gotten quite highhanded and forgotten yourself."

"Yes, Papa."

Darcy peeked in. Miss Elizabeth stood near the fireplace, a broken doll in her father's shadow. She no longer wore the soiled apron, but her hair was disheveled, tendrils escaping their pins and her lovely eyes, darkly shaded and so very weary.

Bennet tipped her chin up none too gently.

If he attempted to harm her in any way …

"What I am going to do with you? I know somewhere in there you are a very good girl. Why are you so stubborn, willful and steadfastly determined to do whatever is the worst thing for you and your family?"

"But, Papa—"

"Do not interrupt me."

She trembled and a tiny squeak escaped.

Darcy's fists clenched so tightly his fingers cramped.

"I said little, I see now too little, when you refused Mr. Collins. Now, you have lost your chance with Mr. Wickham as well. He seems far more interested in one of your younger sisters—which I can hardly imagine Lady Catherine will approve. It is only because Jane has maintained a proper attitude toward Mr. Bingley—"

"But she likes him, and he her, very much indeed."

"A fortunate thing for her, I agree. She keeps us in Lady Catherine's good graces." He released her chin and turned toward the fire. "You are usually a clever girl. Why do you insist on underestimating our need for her help? Your meager fortune will not attract a good match, particularly with your headstrong ways."

"So you expect me—"

"I do not expect—" he removed his glasses and pinched the bridge of his nose. "Sadly, I do not expect very much of you right now."

Her jaw quivered just enough to threaten Darcy's composure.

"I will not live forever, then what? You are so difficult. Your sisters will not want you living with them. If you have no husband, your dowry will not be sufficient for very much of a life. I know you think me harsh right now, child, but I am only considering what is best for you. I know you can be a sensible girl. I merely want you to begin acting on it." He turned toward the door. "I prefer you take that action and do not force my hand."

Darcy spun on his heel and strode away. Best he not encounter Bennet now. Even his self-control had its limits.

The sitting room door shut, and Bennet's staccato footsteps clacked down the grand staircase. Darcy crept back and pressed his ear to the door. Muffled cries sifted through.

How fortunate his sword was safely at Pemberley, lest he take it up against that despicable man. What an utter wretch to be so insensible to the treasure he had in his daughter? She would have been wasted on Collins. Wickham—the thought alone was disgusting. He scraped the bile from his tongue along the roof of his mouth.

He called her difficult? What about her was difficult? She embodied all that was kind and sympathetic to all around her.

Darcy's hand hovered over the door knob. Should he invade her privacy? No, he should not. It would only embarrass her to be exposed in such a moment. Yet, how could he abandon her in her distress? He slipped inside and closed the door softly behind him.

She knelt near the fireplace, face in her hands, shoulders shuddering. He stole to her side.

What might he say? He had eavesdropped and been party to her father's chastisement, witnessed her disgrace. Would that not wound her more? Perhaps—

"What may I do for you, sir?" she whispered, dabbing her eyes with the corner of her fichu. She stared into the fireplace, a tear still glittering on her cheek.

"I did not come to ask anything of you, but rather—"

"Ames continues to improve." She pushed to her feet and dusted her skirt with her hands. "They are still walking him about below stairs, but he is almost able to stand without support now. He drank a little broth as well. Papa … Papa says if he goes on this way through the night, it will be safe to allow him to sleep again."

"I am pleased to hear it."

"So is Tom. Ames is the only family he has. He raised Ames after his sister and her husband died."

"I had no idea."

Perhaps he should not have intruded. She looked so uneasy. No doubt, she must wish him gone, but the pain in her voice begged protection and comfort.

She moved to the window and stood bathed half in moonlight, half in firelight, stunning in both.

Her hand drifted along the edge of the curtain. "I do not suppose even Lady Catherine is aware. It is not the kind of detail she is apt to dwell upon."

"How came you by such intelligence?"

"I asked." She shrugged and pushed a stray lock from her eyes.

"You took the time to see him as a man and not merely a piece of useful furniture meant for service."

"He is very astute, you know, and has an excellent wit."

"I imagine Rosings gives him great fodder for it."

"He never disparages Lady Catherine."

"Of course not. I did not mean—" Darcy stepped toward her. "He will not come to harm because of anything you say."

"Thank you." She turned toward the door and whisked past him.

He grabbed her hand.

"I should go to him." She took a hesitant half-step away, but he held her hand fast.

"No. You do not need to tend to everyone's problems. Ames has others who are doing an admirable job caring for him. You have more than done your duty to him, Tom, my Aunt and your father."

She gasped and bit her knuckle. Her eyes screwed shut, but several fleet tears squeezed through. "Forgive me," she whispered. "I am being stupid."

He pulled her closer. "No, I do not think you capable of that."

"You do not need to flatter me, sir."

"I am not flattering, merely speaking the truth as I see it."

She peeked at him, eyes swollen and glistening.

Her lips begged a kiss! If only he might—no, that was not a safe thought! How easy it would be and how much it might simplify, though. She would then know … know what? That he was a cad who would exploit her weakest moments?

No, at her most vulnerable, she required the protection of his strength. He would not take advantage of her at a time like this. He must … he would honor her as she deserved, and kiss her only when he made her an offer of marriage. Soon.

If only he might wrap his arms around her and assure her of his purpose. Her shawl lay crumpled on a nearby chair. He snatched it and tucked it around her, a poor substitute for his embrace.

"Will you sit for a few moments?" He guided her to a chair and sat on the footstool before her.

She studied her hands.

How strange for her to avoid him so. What did she desire to conceal?

"What can I do for you, sir?"

"Let me do something for your comfort. Pray, instruct me."

She sniffled and shook her head, more a required gesture than an answer.

"Surely there is something."

"Convince Miss de Bourgh that she no longer requires my presence. Mrs. Jenkinson is well and should resume to her position. I should very much like to return home," she whispered.

Of course she would. His company was not enough—no, that was entirely selfish of him.

"Forgive me." She jumped to her feet. "I should not have—"

"I am not offended. I only hesitate because I am a selfish being and will miss our morning walks."

A nascent smile appeared.

Joy! Nothing she could wear might make her more beautiful than that simple, elegant curve of her lips.

"At home, I often walk in the morning, frequently in the direction of Rosings."

"I am very pleased to know that." He stepped behind her, very close—too close. Her warmth beside him begged to be touched. "May I call on you at your father's house?"

"Lady Catherine will not approve."

"But it would please me very much."

She turned and fixed his eyes with her own, cutting through layers of manners and artifice. Sharper than a surgeon's blade, her gaze demanded he reveal the naked truth of his soul. He flinched. No one had ever demanded so much of him, but if he did not answer, he would have no hope of her. The pain of losing her was far worse than what she required. He met her scrutiny.

She held him with a grip as strong as his bond to Pemberley, and studied, searched him, discerning what no other had ever seen. Blood rushed to his cheeks and he fought to stand fast. How much easier it would be if she had only stripped his body naked, not his heart. She blinked once and made her judgment.

He dare not breathe.

"I … I would be pleased to receive your call."

It would be most improper to take her by the waist and whirl her about. But he could dream of the day he might do just that.

"Thank you." He brushed a curl back from her forehead, his fingertips lingering at her temple. She leaned into him, just the barest hint, but it was enough. He would court her as she deserved, and she would finally be his.

The door creaked open, and they jumped apart.

Tom, face haggard and coat wrinkled, bowed.

He looked so old, like a worn dish cloth at the bottom of a laundry pile, far from the imposing figure he usually struck.

"Is something wrong?" Miss Elizabeth hurried to him.

Darcy held his hands tight to his side. It would not do to pull her back to him.

"No, Miss, just the opposite. I am …" His voice cracked, and he dragged his sleeve over his eyes. "I came to tell you, your father just examined him and … and says he will recover, not much worse for the wear."

"That is splendid news."

Darcy crossed the distance to them in three long strides. "Yes, it is most welcome news."

"Him and me, we have both of you and the Colonel to thank—"

"Papa most of all—"

"No, Miss, you. You were the one who did all the hard work and would not let him or any of us give up. We know where the debt is owed. You can be sure it will be paid back, with percents besides."

"You owe me nothing."

"That boy—" Tom blinked furiously and cleared his throat. "He is everything to me. He is set to marry after he's saved enough. She's a dear girl. They're going to buy a pub with some rooms to let, you know.

They asked me to live with them and help run the place. If it all comes to pass, it will be because of what you did today."

"I hardly think that."

"We won't forget it. Nor your aid, sir." Tom nodded at Darcy. "Know if there is any way I can serve you, you have only to say the word. I should go back to him, though." Tom bowed and disappeared.

"I am relieved Ames will return to health." She drew her shawl around her more tightly. "I should go now. Thank you … for everything." She curtsied and vanished through the door.

Rosings would be a bleak shell without her. He leaned against the wall and let his head fall back with a dull thud.

*How soon until he could take her back to Pemberley?*

## Chapter 6

THE NEXT MORNING, Darcy searched the house only to discover Anne in the music room, leafing through sheet music. An odd place indeed for one who did not play herself.

She had her mother's proud bearing despite her frail frame, but lacked her mother's clarity of mind. As Miss Elizabeth had intimated, this latest spell had taken its toll on Anne's mind, compromising her judgment and accentuating all her least attractive characteristics. As if they were not notable enough on their own.

Anne set the music aside and turned to face him. "It really is a shame Miss Bennet does not play better. That is her greatest flaw as a companion. Do you not agree?"

Not at all. Miss Elizabeth's greatest flaw was her patience with people such as Anne. "Music is not her proficiency, although her voice is very sweet."

"As long as the melody is simple, I suppose her singing is tolerable enough. I still would prefer it if she were more skilled."

Now was not the time for impatience. His shoulders tightened and he clenched his hands behind his back. "You look like your health is much improved today."

"Thank you for noticing, Fitzwilliam." She sidled closer, something barely resembling coyness in her eyes.

He rolled his shoulders away from her, struggling not to jump back. "Now that you are feeling better, there is something we need to discuss."

Her lips pulled into an awkward, unattractive, wholly unsettling expression.

"What shall we talk about, or shall I guess?" She edged toward him until she stood far nearer than propriety or good sense allowed.

He cast about the room. Excellent, nothing stood between him and the door.

"Have you given thought as to your companion?"

Anne stopped short and cocked her head. Her forehead knotted as if thinking that hard gave her pain. "My companion?"

"Yes, Mrs. Jenkinson—"

"That old tabby? Why would I give her any mind?" She flicked her hand. "I do not need her any longer. Miss Bennet is a much more agreeable companion."

"You have imposed upon Miss Elizabeth far longer than you should. She should return home."

"Whatever for? She is of no use to her mother and an affliction on her father. She will never marry. I am doing them all a favor, relieving the burden on her family."

"A favor?"

"Trust me. That garish Mrs. Bennet babbles constantly about the trial her second daughter is to them all."

Best not argue, but how to change her mind? Anne rarely let go of an idea once entrenched in her mind. Richard was going to have his hands full if … no, when … he married Anne.

She minced closer, brushing her shoulder against his. "Besides, I have noticed the attention you pay her."

The breath froze in his lungs. "Excuse me?"

"Do not deny it. Every time you look at her, your mind wanders to those low places men are so apt to travel."

He covered his eyes and pinched his temples. Had he been so intemperate, or was Anne playing some other sort of game?

"See, you do not deny it. Your Miss Bennet is not the only keen observer of persons."

"She is not my Miss Bennet." Not yet.

"You would like her to be."

What was worse, her sly air or the accusation she posited? If only he might shake her and dislodge both.

"Anne, you will cease this line of conversation, immediately."

She laughed—laughed!

The discordant tone could sour milk.

"I am not troubled by your interest in her. In fact, it has led me to devise an excellent plan. When we marry and go to Pemberley—which really must be very soon—I shall bring her with me as companion … to both of us."

"What?" His eyes bulged so hard they hurt, and he clutched the back of the nearest chair.

"It is the perfect solution for us all." She minced around the chair, dancing her fingers along the arm.

Good Lord, if she touched him, he might very well—

"I am far too frail to bear children, you know."

"I will not hear this."

"Oh, do not be so prudish—you are a worldly man. You must possess the desires all men do."

He clenched his jaws. Even she should not hear the invectives that threatened to escape.

"Of course, I will not participate in those disagreeable matters. So Miss Bennet—"

Darcy slapped the seat back. "Enough! How can you so callously direct the lives of others like chess pieces in your little game? Have you no concerns for the feelings, the—"

"What plans could Miss Bennet have greater than what I imagine? She will live in a fine home, above all the servants, taking care of me. I will claim her children as my own. Her son might be heir to Pemberley."

"Stop! Let us be clear on two matters. First, Miss Bennet shall return to her father's house, and Mrs. Jenkinson will resume her place as your companion. Second, I will not marry you."

Anne stared at him a moment. Her face split in a wide, eerie smile and she cackled.

"You are attractive in your indignation, Fitzwilliam. But you must set it aside, if we are to live together peaceably."

"We are not going to live together."

"What of Rosings Park? Do you not want it?"

"Rosings is not the prize you believe it to be. The estate—"

"Is large and the house very fine—"

"And all the debts even finer."

"What is that to me?"

"A much larger problem than you comprehend."

"Richard does not seem to think so. In fact, he finds me quite appealing." She leaned toward him.

Any further her bosom might tumble from her too low bodice.

"Accept Richard's suit. He will find your sorts of plans and expectations much more to his tastes than I."

She pressed her bosom close to his chest and traced his jaw with her fingertip. "You are not jealous?"

He jumped away. "Certainly not."

"He is not so well looking as you. Besides, Mama—"

"Tell her you and Richard have come to an agreement. She will be happy to see Rosings kept in Fitzwilliam hands. I am certain you will find him a much more agreeable husband than me." In so very many ways.

"You will regret me, Fitzwilliam."

"I am willing to take that chance. You will release Miss Bennet?"

"Yes, I suppose so, though Richard might find her—"

He raised his open hand. "No. She is a gentlewoman and will be treated as such."

"Gah! You are quite dicked in the nob to pass by such an offer. You are only hurting her, you know."

"Anne!"

"Very well, perhaps you are right. Richard is far less stubborn."

He bowed from his shoulders and fled the music room.

*How long would it take his man to draw a very hot bath?*

---

A hot bath and a scouring did little to cleanse the ill-ease that clung to his mind. Perhaps his notions were quaint, antiquated and unrealistic, but he would not alter his values for anyone.

Anne and Richard made a far better match than he had dared hope. So much so, he could free Richard from his promise. That should make the couple quite happy indeed.

Still his skin crawled and every muscle twitched. He must away, if only for a short time. He headed for the stable.

A long ride failed to settle his mind. By early evening, his nerves were as raw as during foaling season, waiting for news of his mares. An ideal time for a summons from Lady Catherine.

He trudged to the parlor. Thankfully, the halls were empty of witnesses to his uneasy journey. Why did he feel like a school boy called to the headmaster's office?

Aunt Catherine glowered down from her throne, but said nothing until he stood before her and her sphinx guardians. "Anne tells me you have no intention of marrying her."

"I have told you that on more than one occasion. Only recently, I stood in this room and—"

"She tells me that you mean it."

"Pray, why else would I have said it?"

"Do not take that tone with me, young man. You may be the Master of Pemberley, but I am the daughter of a peer and your nearest relation, matriarch—"

He should not have laughed, it only annoyed her more. "You give yourself airs and distinctions you do not deserve. I do not answer to you in any way, and I shall thank you to remember that."

"Are you finished with your disgusting impertinence?"

"Good day, madam." He turned on his heel.

"Wait right there, Fitzwilliam Andrew Michael Darcy." The beads on her chair's valance clacked an alarm.

He stopped.

Mother called him thusly when cross. It still sent a pang through his belly.

"You see. You do obey me." She descended her throne and circled him, skirts rustling ominously. "From your cradle, we have agreed. You and Anne were to marry."

"I was never a party to your agreement."

"I do not need your agreement, only your obedience."

"You shall have neither. Anne and I are ill-suited to one another, our minds and tastes completely unmatched."

"What has that to do with marriage?"

"The fact you would ask illustrates the problem."

"Marriage is a business about preserving an inheritance and noble blood lines."

He turned his shoulder to her. "This discussion is over."

"It is over when I am satisfied—"

"Your satisfaction is of little concern to me."

"Then why ask Anne to send the Bennet girl back to her father's house?" She leaned far too close to his face. Her breath smelt of cloves. "I will tell you. Her presence tempts you. You wish her away that way you may focus on your duty without distractions."

"Are you accusing Miss Bennet—"

"Hardly, I nipped that possibility in the bud. The chit dare not disobey me." She wagged her finger under his nose. "But young men are easily distracted by a pretty face and a light and pleasing figure."

Good thing she were not a man or this would turn to fisticuffs or more likely pistols at dawn. "Richard will marry Anne."

"This has nothing to do with Richard."

"He is the son of an Earl, so your precious bloodline is preserved."

"He is not suitable."

"He is far more suitable than I. He wants to marry her."

"I do not care what he wants. He is a second son, without title or fortune—"

"Or Pemberley." His eyes narrowed. "This is about Pemberley! You have always wanted it. You tried to gain it through my father, but he did not—"

"That is none of your business. After the Bennet girl is gone, you will see more clearly. In fact, I shall invite her younger sisters here in her stead. They are ill-mannered little creatures and shall help you appreciate Anne properly."

He huffed and squared his jaw. What point in trying to make her listen?

She patted his cheek. "Despite this, I am proud of you. Even distracted, you seek to do your duty. Leave me now. I must make arrangements for her removal. This change will be exactly what you need."

She pushed his shoulder toward the door and hurried out past him, calling for Long Tom.

He groaned and pressed his eyes. How had this turned into such a hubble-bubble? At least, Miss Elizabeth would be freed from Rosings, and he would be free to court her apart from the constant observation of his aunt and her minions.

---

Late the next morning, Lady Catherine's oldest coach rolled to a stop before the Bennet's house. The footman handed Elizabeth out.

"Thank you for what you did for Ames, Miss." Beneath his ill-fitting powdered wig, his dark eyes shone.

"I am thankful he is recovering." She tried to sound pleased, but, even to her own ears, the effort was weak at best.

Mama burst through the front door, a neatly penned note clutched in her left hand. "You clever girl! You very clever girl!" She waved the paper in front of Elizabeth's face.

Of course, Lady Catherine would not have sent her home without explanation. What could *she* have said that would leave Mama declaring her clever?

Mama looped her arm in Elizabeth's and escorted her into the parlor. Late afternoon sun filtered through the windows, bathing the room in a welcoming, soft glow. The room was nothing to even the most modest at Rosings, but it was home.

"Has not Lady Catherine told you?" She handed Elizabeth the letter.

Elizabeth took it and glanced over the spidery words. What were Lydia's and Kitty's names doing on the page? Invited to Rosings? Company for Anne and Miss Darcy? She gasped.

"Is it not wonderful? You must tell me, how did you contrive you sisters' invitation?"

Elizabeth passed the letter back to Mama and shrugged.

"Do not tell me then, but you shall not spoil my delight! You surprised me, child, and I will not forget the service you have done us all." She tossed the letter on a small table. "I fear your father is not going to be very forgiving of this turn of events, though. Neither Kitty nor Lydia is of any use to him. He will not appreciate being forced to work without assistance. I expect he will be very cross with you over this."

Elizabeth avoided Mama's curious gaze. "I had considered that." Dwelt on it the entire way from Rosings, dreaded the possibility the moment Lady Catherine announced she was to leave. Why had she not thought of it before asking for Mr. Darcy's aid? Now she would have to live with the consequences of her impulsivity.

"I do not relish the notion of you enduring your father's pique for serving your sisters so well."

"Perhaps you should send me away if I am so much trouble."

"That is an interesting idea." Mama sank down on her favorite chair. "You are full of good ideas today."

Elizabeth screwed her eyes shut and leaned against the back of a worn wingback chair. Mama had never appreciated sarcasm. Why should that change now?

"Your father will object, no doubt, but he may be brought to see reason, yet." Mama tapped her fingers together in front of her face. "My sister, Phillips, in Meryton, has no children. She might welcome your company. Many gentlemen come from London for Mr. Phillips to write contracts. He is well able to put you in the way of some very eligible young men."

There was only one eligible young man in whose way she wished to be placed. Best Mama not know that, though.

"I shall not be sorry for you to be away from Rosings for a while. You have been there so long this time. I worried that you were being groomed as a companion for Anne."

Elizabeth bit her tongue. If Mama only knew!

"Your father might accept that, but I am not yet ready to surrender my hope to see you properly married—somehow."

Mama would not surrender her, but Papa would? Elizabeth's chest pinched. She wandered to the window.

"I shall write my sister directly." Mama's skirts swished, and the door shut behind her.

Elizabeth pressed her forehead on the cool glass pane.

Perhaps a visit to Meryton would not be so disagreeable.

But Mr. Darcy would not be there.

She closed her eyes, and hugged her shoulders. Would he actually come to call? Dare she hope? How good it would be to hope, even dream, but how very, very dangerous for her heart.

Safer to believe he regarded her as a friend to his sister, that there would be nothing more.

Cold tendrils suffused her chest and she shivered in the sunbeam.

That night, the comforts of her own room with its familiar, if cheaper, appointments and dear little treasures from her life, far outweighed the loss of Rosings's luxury. She slept more restfully than she had in weeks, unencumbered by the worry Miss de Bourgh would demand her attendance at any moment.

The first rays of morning danced through her window pane and teased her awake. She yawned and stretched. The counterpane embraced her, whispering she should sleep longer. Still, a morning ramble called to her more loudly. So, she hurried to dress and be on her way before anyone else arose.

The morning dew on Mama's flowers hailed her as she stepped outside. The garden, filled with color and fragrance, waved on the soft morning breeze, greeting her and beckoning her closer. She closed her eyes and drank in a deep breath. No matter where they lived, Mama always had a garden. Sometimes it was little more than a box of dirt filled with flowers, but somehow, she would make it grow and flourish. More than anything, the garden's perfume was the smell of home.

Would she still be welcomed here when Papa returned? He would be angry, no doubt. The only question was, to what degree? Nothing about the circumstance suggested his fury might be inconsiderable.

Would that his stay at Rosings continued longer.

She wished no ill on anyone, but perhaps if Miss de Bourgh turned her ankle? Or perhaps, Lady Catherine might lose her voice. A happy thought, indeed.

And one she should not be dwelling upon—no, not at all. How ungracious and unkind—

"Miss Elizabeth."

She started. "Oh, Mr. Darcy." If only he knew her uncharitable reflections.

"I am pleased to see you this morning. May I stroll with you?" He bowed.

"Yes … I … that would be lovely."

He gestured for her to proceed. "Are your family in good health?"

"Those at home, enjoy excellent health. Nearly half of them are at Rosings Park, though. You would be more cognizant of their health than I. So, sir, are my family in good health?"

A dear little dimple appeared in his right cheek. "Your sisters are in excellent health—and spirits."

Surely, he could not intend that as a compliment.

So all was not well with the new company at Rosings. Jane and Mary might make fitting companions for Miss Darcy. Their tender hearts could easily soothe Miss Darcy's anxieties, but Lydia and Kitty? She shuddered.

"Are they too high spirited for Miss Darcy?"

"Miss Lydia is a very lively girl."

"Lydia is generally regarded the prettiest among us—after Jane of course, and her disposition the most agreeable."

"Some company might say so. I am not among them, though." He paused and met her gaze with a penetrating look. "She is not your equal."

What if … dear Heavens … what if he examined too closely and found her wanting? Pray let him not look that close.

"I hope I have not disappointed you this morning."

"I do not take your meaning, sir."

"When we last spoke, I asked you if I might call upon you at your father's house."

Of course, having experienced Lydia, he no longer desired any connection with her. She hesitated midstep. Best she turn back now and leave those words unsaid. That would lessen their pain.

"You need not explain." Her eyes burned and she ducked her face away.

"Yes I do, for already I see you misunderstand." He lifted her chin toward him and trailed his fingertips along the side of her jaw.

How could so fleeting a touch possess the power to shake her to the very core? Why did he discompose her so? The approval, the warmth of his eyes strained her control to threadbare wisps. She must not weep and appear a fool.

"Your father was in high dudgeon yesterday."

"I am not surprised."

What might he have said in her absence? Surely he believed her exiled from Rosings for some transgression too great to name.

"I dare not risk calling at your house. I might be denied your company. So I purposed to meet you here, to walk as we did at Rosings. I apologize for my impropriety. My desire to keep company with you is stronger than my sense of protocol." He stroked her cheekbone with his gloved thumb.

She closed her eyes. Her skin tingled beneath his hand. How could hands so large and powerful be yet so gentle?

"Do you disapprove?"

How could she respond? To answer honestly was to invite fate to snatch away her happiness, but to fail to respond would wound him.

"You are hesitant to speak your true sentiments?" He lifted her hand to his lips.

She must not swoon.

"My sister wears the same mask when she fears someone will censure her opinions. I will not press you for an answer in words this time, as your eyes speak loudly enough. But, I pray you know you need not fear my disdain. How many times have we debated our ideas in these woods? I should hope by now, I have proven I would never scorn you for holding an opinion different from my own." His fingers tightened over hers.

Papa would have allowed her to dip in a meaningless curtsey and dash away without argument or comment, but not Mr. Darcy. He would not accept escape in place of honesty.

"You have indeed proven yourself. I fear, long held habits are not changed in an instant, though," she whispered.

"I am a patient man. I can wait. Allow me a different question." He offered her his arm, and they continued walking. "Tell me of your next birthday. When is it, and how old will you be?"

How could that matter ... oh! "In a fortnight, sir, I shall be one and twenty."

He squeezed her hand against his arm. "A fortnight is not so long. On that day, you will have a certain … independence? Be able to make certain … decisions?"

She stumbled over a leaf and gasped, clutching his arm for support. Could she make such a decision apart from Papa's approval?

He stepped in front of her and caught her other hand, standing too close. Far too close. Close enough that the warmth of his frame spread over her. The fragrance of sandalwood and something uniquely his own enveloped her, inviting—no demanding.

She balanced on a precipice, between everything she longed to escape and everything she ached to embrace. Invisible cords of duty bound her, clawing at her, demanding she obey.

"Elizabeth?"

She wavered, leaning heavily into him, her chest tight and breath labored. "Yes. Yes, I will … be able to decide."

He closed his eyes and released a tortured gasp. Tension sloughed away and—was that a silent prayer of thanks?

His eyes opened and poured out his soul. He had meant everything he had not said.

Half a step more and he nearly pressed against her, touching but not. He tugged her bonnet string and the knot came away.

She trembled, craving the stroke of his fingertips along her face.

He pushed her bonnet, and it tumbled back. A breeze swept her hair. She shivered as if naked in his presence. His shadow hovered over her, sheltering, covering her. His lips grazed her temple, the barest whisper of passion so intense, her knees quivered in his wake. He rubbed his cheek, dusted with traces of stubble, against hers.

"Do not doubt me, Miss Bennet. I am quite resolved. My only regret is this shall be the longest fortnight of my existence." His breathy whisper caressed her neck.

She pressed into him, relishing his scent, his strength. "Of mine as well."

The next several days passed quickly. Papa remained at Rosings. Lady Catherine, it seemed, still did not trust his promises not to advise Mrs. Collins. He might never forgive Elizabeth for this turn of events.

Mr. Darcy met her for a long walk each morning. She relished the company of the most agreeable man of her acquaintance. Even at the price of Papa's ire, it was worth every moment. Neither Mama nor Jane could guess the source of her good humor, and she was not disposed to share it.

Such fortune could not last. The day Papa returned home, he brought with him an abundance of rain. They were confined inside for three days complete during which Papa said little and remained ensconced in his book room.

Late in the morning of the fourth day, the clouds finally broke. He removed himself from his study long enough to call Elizabeth downstairs.

"Lizzy, I need you to go into the village. I have packages waiting at the apothecary and chandler."

A useful errand at last! Elizabeth raced down the stairs.

"Here." He shoved a neatly penned list in her hand. "He should have this already prepared for you.

Check everything against my list before you leave. Make certain it is all exactly as I have asked for."

"Yes, sir."

He refused to even look at her. Since her dismissal from Rosings Park, he barely spoke to her, wearing the same disappointed scowl every time she encountered him.

"Whilst I am out, would you like me—"

"Just do as I have asked, Lizzy, and only what I have asked." He pinched the bridge of his nose and looked away.

What would he do when he learned of Mr. Darcy's intentions? In a week, he could not forbid her, but what chance that he would approve? None, absolutely none.

"Papa, if only you will let me explain."

"No explanations, child. Consider yourself fortunate your mother has not been made privy to the conversations I have. It is a wonder you have not ruined Jane's hopes by your unseemly conduct."

"Unseemly? Who accuses me? I have done nothing."

"I will not debate this with you. There is simply no defense for what you have done."

"But—"

"Stop!" His hand twitched

She flinched.

"Just go to the village, and pick up these things for me. If you see anyone from Rosings Park, do not interfere with them." He flexed his hands and stalked away.

She clutched the banister, her knees quivering like a French chef's jelly. Who had turned him against her?

Miss de Bourgh? No, she would not have so quickly given up the possibility of making Elizabeth her companion. Tarnishing Elizabeth's reputation would not improve the chances of getting her way.

Miss Darcy was too shy to even speak to Papa and too sweet to be unkind. After the affair with Ames, none of the servants would have spoken against her, either.

Miss Bingley and Mrs. Hurst? She sank down on the bottom stair, head in her hands. How could she have overlooked it? The furtive glances at Mr. Darcy, the coy looks, the machinations to be near him. Miss Bingley sought his attentions! Of course, it was so simple, so clear. How could she have missed it? The vile harpy meant to insure Elizabeth stayed away from Rosings.

"Go now, Lizzy! I will not have you sulking about all day and getting caught in the rain. The gig is ready."

"Yes, Papa." Her throat cramped so tight the words barely squeaked through. She picked up her bonnet and spencer from the hall table and left.

Though the rain had stopped, deep grey clouds hung low overhead. What a fitting complement to the muddy roads and the state of her temper. Did Jane know her beau's sister was a vicious shrew, lurking in the shadows? Dreadful, despicable woman!

Elizabeth rushed through her visit to the chandler, hoping to escape the downpour hiding within the dark skies. Thunder clapped over the hills as she pulled the gig close to Mr. Lang's shop.

She hurried inside, list in hand. If fortune shone just a little brighter than the dreary sunshine, he would have her order ready. She could be off before Papa's ire grew in proportion to the brewing storm.

Blast and botheration! Another customer waited ahead of her.

"Miss Elizabeth?"

"Miss Darcy?"

"Oh, I am so pleased to see you. I have missed you so much this last week!" She extended her hands to Elizabeth and drew her close to kiss her cheek.

"And I you!" Elizabeth's heart pinched. The lack of Miss Darcy's society pained her almost as much as the loss of Jane's to Mr. Bingley. "Is someone unwell at Rosings?"

"Oh no, why do you—oh, of course. No, I am not here to purchase medicine. I am here for comfits." She giggled.

"Which ones?"

"The ginger," Miss Darcy mouthed behind her hand.

Elizabeth gasped. "I am shocked! Do you not know, Lady Catherine has been insisting he stop making them?" She pulled herself upright and peered down her nose. "Most unhealthful those. Such strong flavors are sure to imbalance a delicate system such as yours. Tea is the most proper manner for one to take ginger."

"The only thing they unbalance is Aunt Catherine."

Elizabeth chuckled into the back of her hand.

Mr. Lang shambled out. "Here you are, Miss Darcy. Ahh, Miss Bennet—what can I do for you today?"

"My father said you had an order prepared for him."

He slapped his forehead. "I knew I had forgotten something. I will finish it directly."

"Here, take my list if it will help."

"Thank you. He nodded and shuffled to the back room.

Miss Darcy opened the package of comfits and extended it to Elizabeth. They each popped one in their mouths, giggling.

"Oh, these are so good." Miss Darcy squealed. "I must bring a generous supply home to Derbyshire with me."

"Are you planning to return soon?"

Miss Darcy frowned. "We do not have a fixed date, but my brother talks about it often. He has been so unhappy at Rosings since you left. He and Aunt Catherine quarrel every day. He spends a great deal of time with Richard—one day I overheard them talking of settlement papers, but I cannot understand why. Fitzwilliam assures me he will not marry Anne."

But he did not tell her who he wished to marry.

Then again, what brother confided such matters in a younger sister?

"And Miss de Bourgh? How does she fare?"

Miss Darcy pressed in close, shoulder to shoulder with Elizabeth. "I am so glad I can tell you, for I dare not say such things to anyone else."

Elizabeth took Miss Darcy's hand.

Miss Darcy squeezed it. "Anne is much better, but while her strength improves, her temper does not. Truly, I am glad she will not be mistress of Pemberley. She is so—so much like her mother." She shook her head hard. "Even I know more about managing a household than she. Anne thinks because you demand it done, it is enough. She gives no respect to the cost or the labor or resources involved. You would not believe how much she demands in honor of her wedding: a carriage and clothes, new furniture. I still do not even know whom she will marry."

Elizabeth smoothed the front her of her skirt. "You do seem rather—"

"Unhappy? I am sorry. I try hard to be sanguine in this place. But I just cannot." Tears welled in Miss Darcy's eyes. "My aunt demands I play and perform every night. Without you to help me, I feel their stares crawling across my skin. Oh, it is awful!" She scrubbed her hands over her arms.

"I can well imagine how difficult that is for you."

"Sometimes Fitzwilliam tries to help me as you did, but it is not the same. Aunt Catherine says I will accustom myself to it. She insists I owe her the duty of entertaining her, but I will not adjust to it, and I do not owe it to her—do I?"

Mr. Lang shuffled into the storefront, arms piled with packages. "Your order, Miss Bennet."

"Thank you." She scanned the pile and mentally checked them off her list. "Would you take them to the gig?"

"Quite happily, Miss."

Miss Darcy followed her out. A flash of lightning and its accompanying thunder roared across the sky.

Elizabeth scanned the front of the shop. "Where is your carriage? The weather will not hold long—"

Miss Darcy scuffed the dirt with her toes.

"You walked, and with no one to accompany you." Who had influenced her to do such a thing? Surely not Miss de Bourgh. A nagging little knot formed in the pit of her stomach.

"You are out without a chaperone," Miss Darcy whispered.

Could words land with the force of a blow? Elizabeth pressed a hand to her chest.

Miss Darcy clapped her hands to her mouth. "I am sorry. I should not have said that."

No, she should not, but she only spoke the truth. "May I take you back to Rosings Park? I do not wish to see you continue on alone, and may be able to get you home before it rains."

"Thank you, I had not considered the weather when I walked out."

Mr. Lang helped them both in, and they were off at a brisk clip. The wind kept pace, sending slapping leaves and road dust toward them in angry swirls and gusts.

Miss Darcy rubbed her shoulders briskly. "You know, Rosings is not the same since you left. Everyone has been cross and prickly, and well, quite displeased with one another. Even the butler looks more cross than usual."

"Surely my younger sisters provide you some agreeable company."

"Forgive me, but they are not you, nor are the other ladies. You understand so much that they do not. They are all forever going on about my coming out and how I must be the belle of the ball."

"There is some truth to what they say. When you come out, you will be the center of attention for at least a season. How else will you be able to meet worthy young gentlemen?"

"Oh, no—do not speak of that. It would be wholly dreadful! I would never fancy that." Miss Darcy cringed.

"Think about it, a ball for you—or going to London to be presented in court? That would be so lovely! My younger sisters—"

"You are teasing me, and I am being very serious." Miss Darcy chewed her knuckle. "May I tell you a secret?"

"Secrets are dangerous things. Are you sure it is wise to share it?" Elizabeth swallowed hard. Would that she be surprised by Miss Darcy's confession, but it was hardly likely.

"I simply must. I cannot keep it to myself any longer." She clasped her hands together under her chin. "I shall not have to come out at all."

"What do you mean?"

"I am enjoying a courtship!"

No! No! No! Not him!

Elizabeth forced her hands to unclench around the reins. The horse should not pay the price for this conversation. "Was he the one who advised you to walk out unaccompanied?"

"He said it was a good way for me to become less timid. You yourself just said I am far too timid."

"That is not what I said—"

"You should see the way he looks at me, hear what he says to me." Miss Darcy sighed just like Lydia in the throes of a flirtation.

"Words can be untrue and looks affected for a man's purpose."

"You would feel differently, if only you knew him as I do. Then you would think me the luckiest girl in the world." She hugged herself. "Mr. Wickham—"

Elizabeth guided the gig to the edge of the road and stopped the horse. She turned to Miss Darcy and grasped her hands. "You must not permit yourself to be under the power of Mr. Wickham, not for any reason."

A damp wind cut through her spencer and a chill settled in her chest.

Miss Darcy pulled her hands away. "Why would you say such a thing? He is courting—"

"No, you must refuse him, cut him off entirely."

"I will do no such thing."

"You must, I implore you. Have I ever given you reason to distrust me?"

"No, but you do not know him as I do."

"I know things about him you do not."

"That is what my brother says! You sound so much like him. You only want to ruin my happiness." Miss Darcy turned her shoulder and wrapped her arms over her chest.

"What have I to gain by making you unhappy?"

"Perhaps you want him for yourself. Aunt Catherine said he was intended for you!"

"I have no interest in him, despite your aunt's desire otherwise."

"But you must, why else would you—"

Elizabeth pressed her forehead and drew a deep breath. "You know Mr. Michaels, whom your brother has asked to train Mr. Wickham in estate management?"

"Yes, and Mr. Wickham has told me he has been doing a very poor job of it. Do you know, after just a week, Mr. Michaels abandoned him to go to London?"

"Pray, hear me out. Mr. Michaels calls upon my sister Mary, and he feels very protective over my younger sisters. He developed concerns about Mr. Wickham's character and went to London to speak to those who are familiar with him. What he discovered was not favorable. Mr. Wickham is no gentleman by any stretch of the definition. Mr. Michaels found evidences of intrigues and affairs, gaming debts, drunken brawls and unpaid merchants."

"Surely there has been a mistake." Miss Darcy grabbed the gig's side rail.

"When Mr. Wickham and Mr. Bingley were sent away from Rosings to my mother's care, Mr. Wickham lavished attention on my youngest sister, Lydia. Since he returned to Rosings, he called upon her thrice or four times a week."

"Mr. Wickham has been calling on your sister at the same time he has been attending to me?" Miss Darcy covered her face with her hand, shoulders heaving.

Elizabeth slid her arm across Miss Darcy's shoulders and pulled her close, rubbing her back and whispering soothing sounds.

"No, no. I cannot believe this. I will not." Miss Darcy sniffled and fumbled for a handkerchief. "My brother and cousin, they did not approve. That is why we kept it secret."

"You did not think they had good reason?"

"My brother harbors resentment towards Mr. Wickham's open, appealing nature. So many people like Mr. Wickham, but not Fitzwilliam. He is jealous."

She brushed a tear from Miss Darcy's cheek. "Be thankful he is so attentive and protective of you. It is far worse to have … to have no one to step out and protect you. Pray, talk to your brother."

"He is prejudiced against Mr. Wickham. I will not believe—"

A carriage with the calash drawn up bore down on them from the direction of Rosings Park. It pulled up close to the gig.

"Georgiana!" Mr. Darcy leaned around the hood.

"She is well, sir."

"Where have you been? What possessed you to go out alone?"

Miss Darcy turned her face away. "Miss Elizabeth insisted on bringing me home from the apothecary's."

"She is well, sir, but you must speak to her. It is a matter of some urgency." Elizabeth met his gaze and gasped. Never had she seen so much appreciation directed at her. "Pull a little closer and she can step across to you."

He carefully positioned his equipage and reached for Miss Darcy. Elizabeth steadied her waist. With one hand he guided his sister, the other grasped Elizabeth's wrist too firmly for her to pull away.

"She is in danger from Mr. Wickham," Elizabeth whispered. "She did not believe my warning. Perhaps if Mr. Michaels …"

Lightening flashed. The horses jumped and started.

"I will attend the matter immediately. You have my word. You must get home. I will call upon you soon. Thank you. I cannot say that enough." He squeezed her wrist hard.

She nodded and urged her horse into motion.

The winds conspired against her, and her haste proved insufficient. The clouds burst a half mile from the house, soaking her through well before she arrived home. The packages remained a little drier, covered with an oilcloth beneath her seat.

Papa met her, umbrella in hand, at the front steps. She ducked under its shelter, little good that it did. A little more time in the rain could hardly make her any wetter than she already was.

"Lizzy! Look at the state of my packages!" He snarled as he gathered parcels from the gig.

Was she supposed to be able to control the storms and keep them at bay until a time more convenient and agreeable for them all?

"Why did you take so long? Did you not see the storm was close to breaking?"

"He had other customers. I could not force my way ahead. He was not prepared when I arrived. It was only because I had a copy of your list—"

"No more excuses." He stalked to the house, leaving her standing in the midst of the torrent.

Frigid raindrops slapped the back of her neck and dripped down her bodice. She splashed toward the house. What point in running now? She wrenched her ankle and nearly fell as she trudged up the front steps.

"Can I trust you with nothing anymore?" He dropped the wet oil cloth on the floor and stomped away, leaving her leaning against the foyer wall, searching for words.

At least, she had done some lasting good for her friends, and they appreciated it. Her birthday could not come soon enough.

Mama burst in and scolded her for dripping rainwater on her freshly cleaned floor. She grew sympathetic when Elizabeth began shivering, teeth chattering. She took Elizabeth, limping on her sore ankle, to the kitchen where a hot fire chased off most of the chill. Cook offered her a footstool and a cool compress for her foot, and the throbbing eased to a vague, dull ache. After a repast of hot broth and bread, Mama tucked her into bed where she slept through until morning.

The rains continued for many days. Papa remained testy and locked within his bookroom.

But why? His dour moods had never lasted this long before.

Elizabeth leaned against the wall just outside his door. Clouds held back the morning light and heavy raindrops pounded the windows. Should she try to talk to him again? No, he was usually dour in the mornings, especially when the weather was foul. Perhaps later today, he would accept his tea and French cream from her hand. She squeezed her eyes shut. The effort had been a spectacular failure yesterday.

No doubt, he was distressed at being kept from daily calls at Rosings, but this was more than that. His resentment seemed so directed at her. Yet she was safely away from Lady Catherine and could do nothing more to agitate *her*. Unless ... was he concerned over how Kitty and Lydia would conduct themselves at Rosings?

Of course!

She let her head fall back against the wall, hairpins scraping softly against the dull blue paint. Divorced as he was from them, he could not curb their high spirits. He must be sick with worry. Bad enough that Lady Catherine was put out with one of his daughters. What could it mean to the family if she found the younger ones wanting as well? That could be disastrous ... and her sisters were there because she had been dismissed.

So this was all her fault. No wonder his spleen was directed at her. Had she not been so frightfully selfish…

Best not try to bring tea today. She dabbed her eyes with her apron and trudged to the morning room.

"I am so glad you are come." Jane looked up from her sewing. "Mama is poorly this morning, and Mary waits on her. I felt quite alone."

"It is oddly quiet without Kitty and Lydia in the house, is it not?" Elizabeth sat down and picked through the work basket for something to mend.

"I am sure Lady Catherine had no idea of how much energy she was inviting into her home."

"I fear the prospect weighs heavily upon Papa right now."

"He has been so discomposed and so terse with us all, especially you. I expect he has not even acknowledged your birthday today."

In truth, no one had.

Elizabeth stabbed her needle into the torn apron. "Have you missed Mr. Bingley much these past few days?"

Jane glanced toward the window. A sunbeam parted the clouds and bathed her in its glow.

What must it be like to be so angelic?

"I do miss him so very much. Oh, Lizzy, I wish you could have spent more time with him. I am certain you would esteem him as much I do."

"If he makes you this happy, of course I think well of him." Elizabeth forced a smile. How lovely it must be to be able to freely speak about her *tendre'*.

"I hope he might make me an offer soon. We have talked a little, and he seems disposed toward it, if his sisters and friend support him."

"Are you comfortable with that? Should he be able to be so easily persuaded—"

"You think he is not steadfast?"

"I did not say that. I wonder, though, that he should need so much support for his decision. Does he not have faith in his own judgment? Would you not prefer that he should be able to stand his ground in the case of opposition?"

"Do you believe they might object to me?" Jane's face crumpled.

Pray, let her not cry!

"Not at all! I cannot imagine anyone objecting to you. You are everything anyone might want in a sister or a wife."

"Then I do not understand your concern. What is wrong with enjoying the support and encouragement of others?"

"There is nothing wrong in it. Only, perhaps, too much of it may not be a virtue."

"Not everyone is like you, able to bear the censure and displeasure of those around them." Jane pulled at her needle a little more forcefully than necessary. "While you may stand toe to toe with Papa and Lady Catherine, we are not all so bold."

"It is not a matter of boldness, but commitment to one's purpose. How would you feel if his sisters were able to dissuade him from his attachment to you?"

"I … I … that would be very difficult indeed, but they have been very kind to me. Why would they do such a thing?"

"I am pleased they have shown you kindness." Elizabeth stuck her finger with her needle and sucked off a drop of blood. "I hesitate to tell you, but perhaps it is best you know. Mr. Bingley's sisters have been disparaging me to Papa."

"Surely you have misunderstood. What have they said?"

"Nothing in my hearing, but I am well aware that someone has been whispering things to him."

"So you do not know it is them."

"It is obvious—"

"Is it not possible you might be wrong in your deductions? You place great faith in your abilities—"

"But you cannot believe anyone would be disagreeable or spiteful?"

"Not without ample reason. People are generally quite good and kind."

"Perhaps in your company, they are. Not all of us evoke such pleasing qualities in people." Some incite quite the opposite.

"I realize Papa is being unfair to you, but you need not be so bitter."

"Then you must know my bitterness is my only comfort." Elizabeth shoved her mending aside and gripped the edge of the table. "Mama has quite given up hopes for me. She wants to send me off to Aunt Philips in hopes I might take in Meryton. I have, after all, ruined my chances in Kent."

"Lizzy!"

"I am sorry." She shaded her eyes with her hand. "I should not allow my own dark thoughts to intrude upon your happy musings. I should not be so selfish."

"I do not like to see you so discomposed. If only you would—"

Hill's distinct rap sounded on the door, and she peeked her head in. "Mr. Bingley and Mr. Darcy are come to call. I wager they wish to go walking." Hill waggled her eyebrows and winked.

"Tell them we will be out in just a moment." Jane folded her sewing.

Hill handed them bonnets, gloves and spencers, curtsied and disappeared.

"How thoughtful of Mr. Bingley to bring along a companion for you to walk with when you chaperone us. A walk in company may be just the thing to improve your spirits."

"That was very good of him." Elizabeth fastened her bonnet and spencer, but she misaligned the buttons twice before successfully finishing.

What would Mr. Darcy say to her now he had talked with his sister? Had she successfully dissuaded Miss Darcy from Mr. Wickham or had she only made things worse?

The gentlemen paced the foyer and spoke softly between themselves. Mr. Bingley cut a fine figure, but next to Mr. Darcy, he seemed a bit boyish and unfinished.

"Miss Bennet! Miss Elizabeth." Mr. Bingley's easy, open manner fit so well with Jane's serenity. The two must have been formed for one another. "Would you care for a stroll now that the sun finally obliges?"

"Indeed we would, sir." Jane curtsied.

He offered his arm and led her out.

Mr. Darcy lingered back, brows low over his eyes, the same expression he donned for discussing difficult subjects. What had happened with Miss Darcy?

He bowed. "Shall we join them?"

"It would be more proper than leaving them to themselves." She cocked her head and lifted an eyebrow, a gesture that usually earned a dimpled cheek.

He clasped his hands behind his back and followed her out the door.

Fresh, storm-cleaned air filled her lungs, but her chest ached with each breath. Large drops slid from the leaves overhead, dripping on their faces and shoulders.

Mr. Darcy stared at his feet. The gravel crunched underfoot, squishing up tiny pools of water left from the storms. The edges of her nankeen half boots turned dark with the moisture, dots of mud spattering the tops with each step.

What weighed on him so? She glanced over her shoulder.

"What are you looking for?" he asked.

"There must certainly be some great cat, from India perhaps, hiding in the trees, waiting to drop down upon us."

"Excuse me?"

"Your countenance is so very dour, your shoulders bowed. You must be deeply troubled by something." Or perhaps by someone.

He stared at her, looked skyward, and shook his head. "Are there no secrets from you?"

"Only very rarely, sir. It is one of my most unappealing traits, so says my mother and youngest sisters."

One, two, three silent, muddy steps.

"They are quite wrong."

She chuckled. It was far more proper than screaming. Would he not simply come out with what was troubling him? "You find another trait of mine less appealing?"

"You invite me to criticize you as openly as other women beg compliments."

"I must have some feature of distinction, do you not agree? All women long for something which sets them apart from the rest." She adjusted her spencer's collar.

How could she explain—could he even understand? Inviting criticism dulled the pain when the biting remarks came. Censure, like most things in life, was far easier to tolerate when properly managed and controlled.

"I would that you stop. It is not an attractive performance."

She gasped and nearly stumbled over—wait, there was nothing in her path—her own feet. "What then would you have me do?"

Three, four, five steps.

Silence.

Oh, this was not to be borne!

"Do not trifle with me any longer Mr. Darcy. If I have offended you or your sister, just come out with it, and let the words be spoken. This stupid dance we are doing is entirely ridiculous. I will not participate any longer." She stopped just short of a large puddle and crossed her arms over her chest.

He gaped and eyes wide. The corner of his lips twitched.

A tremor coursed down her spine. If he laughed at her, she would surely return home and leave Jane to her interview with Mr. Bingley.

"You believe me offended?"

"What else explains your very peculiar behavior? You cannot tell me there is anything normal about your actions this morning."

He clutched his temples with one hand and huffed out a labored breath. "I suppose not."

"I am glad we have that established."

"You have known me long enough to recognize I am neither glib nor easy speaking important things."

"Did I injure Miss Darcy with the revelations about Mr. Wickham's attentions to my sister or Mr. Michaels' discoveries?"

"She would not speak to me at all yesterday—she disappeared as soon as we arrived at the house." He dragged his hand across his mouth. "I finally found her this morning, in a little used room at the back of the house. She spent the night there, weeping. It seems, after speaking with you, she sought out Mr. Michaels and then confronted Wickham. He failed to produce sufficient evidence to discount the claims against him."

"All on her own?"

"Indeed. I am taken all-a-mort, but most astonished by what you inspired in her. She is very unhappy to be sure, but none of that was of your doing. It was a necessary pain, and I expect it will be of brief duration."

In the distance, Jane and Mr. Bingley sat on a bench along the side of the path. Mr. Darcy gestured to a bit of stone fence shaded by a generous clump of trees. They sat.

"And you, sir? Are you distressed?" She looked away. Better to wait for his words than to see it in his eyes.

He snarled something primal and clenched his fists. "Distressed is not the word I would choose in this case. I would have laid cane upon Abel had I found Wickham this morning. I will remove him from Rosings this very day and bar him from all of my properties. If he ever should so much as look at my sister again, I shall let Fitzwilliam turn loose his unsavory connections and resolve the matter once and for all." He pressed his fist into his palm until his knuckles popped.

"She is very fortunate to have diligent protectors in you and the colonel."

"And in you."

"I did nothing."

His gritted his teeth and screwed his eyes shut. "Do not disparage what you have done for her! She and I are both deeply grateful. Do not devalue it."

She wrapped her arms around her shoulders. "Yes, sir."

"I suppose that whole affair makes what I want to say much more difficult, now."

Her stomach roiled as if she had swallowed blue vitriol. Why had she dared hope?

"I fear you will dismiss what I say as motivated by gratitude, not something much more substantial."

"Excuse me?" She turned to look at him.

"You must allow me to tell you how ardently I admire and love you."

Her jaw dropped in what must have been a most unladylike gape. She willed it shut, but it would not cooperate.

"Miss Elizabeth?"

"I ... yes ... I ... forgive me, sir. What did you say?"

He laughed and tugged at his collar, a scarlet flush crept toward his jaw. "I confess, that is not the reaction I anticipated. Perhaps I should—"

"No, please." She touched his elbow. "I … you … I expected something so very different."

"So you did hear me." The creases beside his eyes eased, and he took her hand. "What did you suppose I would say?"

"It does not signify."

"Yes, it does, particularly if you would count me among those who so freely criticize and blame you."

"I … I feared I upset Miss Darcy—and perhaps you as well."

"So you do expect—"

She closed her eyes and fingered the buttons of her spencer. "It seems I do not know what to expect at all."

"I wish you did. It is your birthday, is it not?"

She gasped. "Yes, it is."

"I have not forgotten, and neither have you."

Tears, stupid, foolish tears, leaked down her cheeks—just a few, thankfully.

He tipped her chin up and stroked them away with his thumb. "No doubt my Aunt will object, and your father is not likely to approve, but dash them all! I cannot imagine the prospect of returning to Pemberley alone, never to see you again. Pray, my loveliest Elizabeth, end my suffering, and say you will be my wife."

He had not forgotten! Thank heavens she was not standing, for her knees would never have held. "Mr. Darcy—"

Bodies crashed through the trees beside them.

They sprang to their feet. High squeals and low rumbles—was that laughter?—filtered forth.

Two figures appeared: Lydia, kicking and squealing, aloft in Wickham's arms. Her lips were swollen full red and her hair sported fallen curls.

"Hold fast there. I will have you home in a thrice!" Wickham's collar was rumpled and his eyes brimmed with carnal longing that would not long be held in abeyance.

"Unhand her!" Darcy jumped toward Wickham.

Wickham dropped Lydia to her feet. "Good morning to you, old friend. How pleasant to encounter you here." He bowed.

Lydia giggled and tucked her fichu into her dress.

"Lydia! What are you doing? Why are you not at Rosings? Does Lady Catherine know you are out?"

"La! You are such a stuffy old thing. Must you object to a bit of harmless fun?" She glanced over her shoulder at Wickham and batted her eyes.

"Whatever fun you think you may be having certainly is not harmless. Can you not see the very great harm to be done to all our reputations?"

"How? There is no one to see us."

"Are Jane and Mr. Bingley and Mr. Darcy and I no one?"

"What were you two doing sitting so close?" Lydia cocked her head. "For one so concerned about propriety, it seems you are a bit of a hypocrite."

Wickham straightened his cravat. "Indeed, Miss Elizabeth. One out of favor with Lady Catherine should not be seen so close to her favorite nephew. Would you not agree, Darcy?"

Darcy's gritted his teeth. How dare he stand there, so smug and so guilty, denouncing Miss Elizabeth's behavior? His balled fists trembled at his side.

"You are so quick to condemn others, Lizzy. That is a most disagreeable habit." Miss Lydia balanced her hands on her hips. Her shoulders bobbed in time with her words.

"Indeed." Wickham's self-satisfied grin begged to be forcibly removed. "Perhaps she is jealous of your good fortune." His eyes raked Miss Lydia's figure, stopping entirely too long on her generous bosom.

"You should stop wasting your energies. You will not provoke me today," Miss Elizabeth said softly, very, very softly.

The hair on the back of Darcy's neck rose. Oh, may that voice never be turned on him. What fools they were not to recognize the very great peril her whisper represented.

"Excuse me, sir." Elizabeth turned to him. "I shall return to the house now. My mother should be made aware of this—turn of events." She glanced at Miss Lydia, whose countenance lost some of its previous color.

"Lizzy, no! You cannot! After that dreadful Mrs. Collins told Mama about us riding in the gig together, she demanded to chaperone us herself."

Miss Elizabeth shrugged and walked away.

Gah! She had not answered his question!

Miss Lydia ran after her. If only he might do the same.

"That was a spot of bad luck." Wickham rubbed the back of his neck.

"Bad luck? That is all you see here—bad luck?" Darcy threw his hands in the air.

"My, my, you are upset." Wickham circled Darcy, clucking his tongue. "I dare say we interrupted something quite personal."

"My affairs are none of your concern."

Wickham's eyes narrowed, and the corner of his mouth turned up. "What sort of conversation did we interrupt?"

"Leave it!"

"So, were you going to set her up—"

Darcy slammed Wickham against a tree trunk. "Do not make such insinuations."

Wickham laughed, the coarse, raucous roar of a common pub.

"How dare you!" Darcy snarled and drove his fist into Wickham's gut "That is for my sister. Georgiana told me everything! You actually aspired to call me brother—"

Wickham doubled over and coughed. "My affection for her—"

"What affection? Did you not just have Miss Lydia—"

"That bit of muslin? She is not the sort one marries. She is worth a paltry sum at best."

"For one in your position, that sum is not paltry."

"My intentions toward your sister are wholly honorable—"

Darcy pinned him against the tree trunk. "Be away from here and away from Pemberley. You will be gone from Rosings today. Take your horse and be gone."

"What of my trunks?"

"Tell the butler where you wish them transported."

"You could provide me the use of your coach."

"If you so much as look at my coach, Fitzwilliam will advertise your whereabouts to any who will listen. There are a number of gamers, to whom you owe money, seeking your whereabouts."

Wickham's cocksure smile faded into a hard, defensive line.

"If you are seen on the premises again, you will be thrown into the arms of the magistrate and charged with trespassing." Darcy released his hold.

Wickham straightened his cravat. "I say, that is an awfully harsh way to treat your old friend."

"You are no friend of mine, and I suspect you never have been. Get yourself from Rosings before I have Fitzwilliam assist you."

Wickham snorted and stomped off.

Darcy glanced at Bingley and Miss Bennet, lost in their own happy idyll. Would that his fortune had been so good.

Miss Elizabeth and her sister had just stormed into the house. He could not call in the midst of that, but tomorrow, he would have his answer. If Providence favored upon him, he would share Bingley's happiness.

## Chapter 7

Elizabeth flung open the front door. It banged against the wall, the handle leaving a dull mark on the paint. Of all times to be interrupted! What was Lydia thinking? Thoughtless, stupid, selfish girl! Gah!

"Lizzy?" Mama's not–yet–but–nearly–irate voice called down the stairs. "Where is Jane?"

"Walking with Mr. Bingley."

Mama descended the stairs, clasping her hands together, just a hint of triumph in her air. "Walking with Mr. Bingley? Most promising, especially with a little privacy now. You have done very well indeed!"

Lydia slammed the door behind her. She pushed Elizabeth aside and scooted between her and Mama. "Ask Lizzy who she walked with."

"I will happily discuss it with Mama, after you tell her with whom you were keeping company." Elizabeth crossed her arms over her chest.

"Lydia? Why are you not at Rosings?" Mama stopped on the last step, looming slightly above them.

The air between them chilled.

"But Lizzy …"

Mama's look would sour wine to vinegar. Lydia withered beneath her glare.

"Lydia Elaine Bennet! We discussed this quite clearly before you went to Rosings—"

"I was not—"

"Do not lie to me."

"I did not mean to go out alone with him. I had my basket packed with—"

Ah, Lydia's favorite trick, diversion. She was so fleet of tongue, she could make a barrister forget what case he argued.

But Mama was no mere barrister. She grabbed Lydia's upper arm and shook her. "Lizzy, tell me what happened."

Lydia's cheeks lost all color. She turned to Elizabeth and mouthed 'no'.

"Whilst I sat on the fence to allow Jane and Mr. Bingley a more private conversation—"

"Whilst you sat with Mr. Darcy." Lydia hissed in Elizabeth's face.

Mama gasped.

"Who came to thank me for the service I rendered his sister. I took her home from the apothecary's so she would not be caught in the storm. It would not do for her to risk bringing illness to Miss de Bourgh." Elizabeth stomped, almost on Lydia's toes.

Lydia jumped back and squealed.

Surely Mama would be displeased about Mr. Darcy, but not nearly so much as about Mr. Wickham. "Whilst he conveyed their thanks—"

"That did not look like thanks he conveyed. He sat far too close and—"

"Mr. Wickham crashed through the trees and almost into us—"

"He was holding your hand and—"

"With Lydia in his arms, hair mussed and her gown ... it was entirely obscene the way her skirts were falling, exposing her legs and—"

"I hurt my ankle and could not walk."

"Funny how you seem to have no difficulty with it now."

Lydia shifted her weight and picked one foot off the floor. "You are just angry because we caught you with Mr. Darcy!"

Mama yanked Lydia closer. She yelped and grabbed at Mama's gripping hand.

"I expressly forbade you to be alone in Mr. Wickham's company. You had only to wait until—"

"I did not mean to be with him ... besides Lizzy..."

"Was not alone with a man! Nor was she disobeying—"

"But she kept company with Mr. Darcy." Lydia pumped her fist and stamped.

So much for her injured ankle.

"Clearly, she risked her own health and well-being to improve our situation with Lady Catherine. She considered the effect of her actions on her family, whereas you," she shook Lydia hard, "could not be so bothered."

"She is not supposed to be near Mr. Darcy or anyone from Rosings."

"That is not your concern." Mama threw a quick scowl at Elizabeth.

Ah, yes, the promise of a long discussion yet to come. What joy would be hers. Perhaps she ought to spend her afternoon packing her trunks for Meryton.

"Do you not realize the jeopardy to your reputation and Jane's and Mary's futures? Not to mention how Lady Catherine will react." Mama rattled Lydia again.

"How will she know? Who will tell her? Besides, who cares about her?"

"Do not say that. Do not ever say that. Your father's position is not fixed for life," Mama's face colored, redder than the garden roses, "like Mr. Collins's."

Elizabeth cringed. Mama's raised eyebrow promised more sharp words would come later.

"If he were to be dismissed, we would have to return to London and reestablish ourselves there. Have you any idea how the stain of your father's dismissal would color any attempts at finding new patients? Whatever you may want to believe, what that woman thinks of us is vital to the welfare of our family. I am not going to allow you or anyone else to put us at risk."

"You told me to encourage his attentions if I liked him."

"I also told you to behave like a lady. Come!" She dragged Lydia upstairs and to her room, Lydia squealing and protesting all the way.

Elizabeth sank down on the bottom step. Was it possible Mama resented Lady Catherine's overbearing rule as much as she appreciated the generous patronage?

Perhaps so. What a very remarkable thought.

Strident voices echoed through the house. If Mama was this angry with Lydia—whom she never scolded—how would Papa react? She shuddered. Tonight might be an excellent night to have a sick headache and keep to her room.

Tension from her shoulders crept along the back of her neck. A headache was not far off. She rubbed her temples.

Of all the places to find Lydia, in the arms of the man who had used Miss Darcy so ill. How could such a lovely moment turn so very, very wrong?

The front door swung open, and Jane danced in on a sunbeam and fresh breeze.

"Oh, Lizzy, I am the happiest of creatures."

Elizabeth rose and dusted her skirt. "Is it as you hoped? He made you an offer?"

Jane clasped her hands under her chin and twirled in the middle of the front hall like a princess in a fairy story. "He did! Oh, he did! I shall never forget his words … they were so perfect. He pledged himself to me, heart and soul, promising to love and protect me all the days of my life. I have never heard anything so beautiful."

"I am very pleased for you."

"I am so perfectly happy." Jane pranced toward the stairs. "I must tell Mama."

Elizabeth caught her elbow. "Now may not be the time."

"What do you mean?"

"You are unaware of what transpired with Mr. Wickham?"

"Mr. Wickham? What happened?"

"Jane dear!" Mama appeared at the top of the stairs, her color high and tense creases around her eyes and mouth.

Jane swept up to her. "I have the most wonderful news!"

Elizabeth hugged her waist and wandered away. Best let them enjoy Jane's glad tidings without her. The weight in her chest would surely prevent her from showing the requisite enthusiasm. Her own joy had been ruined by a thoughtless sister. How could she inflict the same upon Jane?

The family gathered for dinner. From outward appearances, everything looked very normal, but the air felt charged with an impending thunderstorm. Mama prattled on about Jane's good fortune, encouraging Jane to speak, but then cutting her off mid-way. Jane shrugged it off and glowed in the reminders of her good fortune.

Mary also had good fortune to share, which she had earlier confided to Elizabeth. She anticipated Mr. Michaels's offer of marriage soon, but she said little to that end. Who could blame her though, when any happiness she might share would be dim in the shadow of Jane.

What would Mama think if she knew not one, but three of her daughters were on the brink of marriage? How pitiably ironic that two of her daughters dared not share the news that could triple her joy for fear the reactions their news would bring.

"I do not see why I may not return to Rosings." Lydia poked at a potato and pushed it around the plate.

"That is not an appropriate topic for the dinner table." Mama's spine stiffened. She looked over at Papa, a little color fading from her cheeks.

"She invited me and Kitty. Will she not be angry if I am not there?" Lydia huffed.

"You coughed this afternoon. You will remain here until your father is certain that you will not compromise Miss de Bourgh's health."

"I did no such thing. I want—"

Papa slammed his fist on the table. Glasses rattled. Elizabeth jumped and clutched the seat of her chair.

"It seems what you want is to emulate your older sister and ruin us in the eyes of our patroness." He leaned on the table and glowered, first at Lydia, then at Elizabeth.

Mama stared, slack-jawed and wide-eyed. "Ruin us? What have you done Lizzy?"

"Why do you not tell your mother how you conducted yourself at Rosings?"

Elizabeth's mouth went dry, and she shook her head. "I have no idea what you are talking about."

"I trusted you. I lavished attention and favor on you. All the while, I believed I could trust you to behave like a lady and remember your station." He braced his hands on the table and half rose in his seat.

"I have done everything you have asked. Why else would I sit countless miserable hours at Miss de Bourgh's bedside, doing all those disagreeable tasks she required? It was because you wanted me to. How have I failed you?"

He slowly took to his feet, face florid and hands quivering. "When did I ever instruct you to have assignations with the butler?"

"The butler? How could you think such a thing?"

Mama came off her chair. "Elizabeth! How many times have I told you not to interact with *her* staff?"

Papa growled and shoved his chair under the table. "How could you possibly forget your station and permit Lady Catherine's nephew to take liberties—"

"I told you, Mama! You should have seen her and Mr. Darcy!" Lydia pointed at Elizabeth.

"Mr. Darcy, too? It is not enough that you threw yourself at Colonel Fitzwilliam!" Papa tore his napkin from his collar and threw it on his plate.

"What—"

"He was seen whispering to you in the drawing room."

"That is not what happened!" Elizabeth stood, hands locked in a death grip on the edge of the table. "And if I spoke to him at all, it is because you ordered me to! Or do you not recall asking me to gather intelligence for you?"

"So you admit you permitted—"

"No, I did not! I do not know what untruths Miss Bingley and Mrs. Hurst told you. They are nothing but jealous harpies—"

"How can you speak that way about Jane's future sisters?" Mama cried.

Jane leaned in. "I am certain this is an unfortunate misunderstanding. They are kind and thoughtful—"

"Whatever they are, it is neither kind nor thoughtful. Do not trust their regard for a moment."

"How can you say that, Lizzy?" Jane's eyes filled with tears.

"Now look what you have done." Mama draped her arm around Jane. "How can you make your sister cry on a day that should be so happy?"

"I am not the one who was caught cavorting in the arms of my lover in the woods. Why is everyone turning this on me? Is not Lydia—"

Lydia sneered. "There you go again, diverting attention to me, so you can hide your own—"

"Enough!" Papa's voice rattled the windows and cut though Elizabeth's chest like a surgeon's lancet. "I will not tolerate such disorder in my home!" His blazing eyes bore into hers.

"If you think me so much trouble, why do you not just send me to Aunt Philips and be done with me? I will pack my trunks." She threw her napkin on the table and stormed out.

"Elizabeth!" Papa shout rattled the chandelier.

She dashed up the stairs.

"Mrs. Bennet, you will attend me in my book room, now!" Papa's fist connected with the table again and sent shivers up Elizabeth's spine.

She slammed the door to her room and locked it. Clutching the key, she leaned against the door and slowly slid to the floor.

What had just happened? What possessed her to shout at Papa, to defy him so openly? Until this very moment, the thought would never have occurred to her. Why now?

She screwed her eyes tight to hold back the tears. What had she done? She ruined Jane's happy day and proved everything that had ever been said about her. She was a selfish, headstrong, foolish girl.

Did Mr. Darcy have any idea what a wretched excuse of a woman to whom he had made an offer of marriage? If he did not, dare she tell him? Would he even listen if she did? He hated it when she repeated her family's opinions in his presence.

Perhaps he saw something else in her.

Perhaps there was something else in her, something her father would never admit to seeing.

Perhaps.

She heaved a heavy breath and pushed to her feet. How convenient her trunks remained in her room. Some of her things were even still packed from her stay at Rosings. She pulled the trunks away from the wall and flung them open.

Had Mama even written to Aunt Philips? She never mentioned receiving a letter from Meryton, but Mama was so bad with correspondence. Papa would probably send her to Meryton directly, regardless. Might as well as not put her things in order for the trip.

What of Mr. Darcy? Surely Papa would not allow him near the house to speak to her again. Perhaps, Mary might help her get word to him through Mr. Michaels.

She wandered around her room, gathering items to pack: her mother's hairbrush and looking glass; the seashell Uncle Gardiner had given her from one of his travels; a sketch Mother had made of her and Jane when they were little girls, and a ragdoll Mother had helped her make when she first learned to sew. She wrapped them in petticoats and tucked them in amongst her gowns. Jane would tell her she was overreacting, but Papa was angry enough, he might just not allow her to come back, ever. There were some things she could not bear to lose.

Someone scratched at the door. "Lizzy?"

Oh, Jane. She closed her eyes and sighed. Jane was peace itself, but even her presence did not offer a balm to her wounded spirit.

She tiptoed to the door. "Yes?"

"I … I am worried about you. Pray, let me in."

She leaned back against the door. "I am not fit for company right now."

"Since when have I been company? I am your sister."

"You deserve better than me right now. I fear I will only squelch your happiness, and that is unfair to you. I am sure Mary will be better companion to you right now. Perhaps you might make wedding plans together."

"I heard Papa say he was making arrangements to send you—"

"I expected as much. I am sure it will be better that way."

"I just wanted you to know, once I am married … you will always be welcome."

A huge lump formed in her throat. Sometimes Jane knew exactly what she needed to hear.

"Lizzy? Lizzy, are you well?"

Elizabeth sniffled. "Yes … thank you. You are very good to me."

"Will you not let me in?"

She fingered the key.

"Perhaps I might be able to be able to help you talk to Papa. I think if you were to apologize—"

Apologize? She choked on the very idea. Her head fell back softly against the door. "I have a headache now. Thank you, though." She let the key drop into her apron pocket and trudged away from the door. Today she would not apologize. Perhaps she should, but no, not today.

Muffled, angry voices continued to filter upstairs, stopping long after the full moon painted long shadows with the trees. Instead of dressing for bed, Elizabeth paced the length of the room, keeping her steps soft lest she call attention to her movement.

Why could she not celebrate her own offer of marriage as Jane did? Mr. Darcy had proposed to her! He loved her—by his own admission, he declared it so. The things she most desired, the honest love of a good man, he offered. Better still, she loved him, so dearly, in return. He was indeed the best of men, more than she could have ever dreamed. In every aspect—every aspect but his connections with Lady Catherine, he was an entirely desirable match.

For herself alone, she would accept him without another moment's consideration. But what of her family—her father? The duty she owed them was so unclear.

Mama could hardly wish her to refuse his offer. Love match aside, he was of too great a consequence to turn down lightly. How many men worth ten thousand a year would she meet in her lifetime?

But, Lady Catherine would be incensed. Papa, and perhaps even Mr. Michaels, could lose their positions. Mr. Darcy esteemed Mr. Michaels enough to help him find another position, but Papa? What would become of him?

Was it right for her to ruin Mama and Papa's security to selfishly pursue her desires? Or did Mr. Darcy's significance and ability to help her family justify the fact she loved him?

She pressed her cheek against the glass, its cool smoothness a soothing compress to her turmoil.

Something moved outside.

A familiar carriage trundled up the lane, cutting through the moonlight like a black swan on the water. Though darkness obscured the crest, the distinct outline proclaimed it Lady Catherine's. Another, the older one she sent for company, followed behind. Whatever for? At this hour of night? No one traveled so late unless the need were truly dire.

The coaches slowed near the house.

Someone must be dreadfully ill.

She hurried to the door, but stopped before turning the key. Surely they sought Papa, and he would require assistance ... but no. After tonight, he would not want her presence, certainly not near Lady Catherine.

What was she to do? She paced back to the window. The driver handed Lady Catherine down from the carriage. What could be of such grave import as to bring out the great Lady herself?

Elizabeth perched on her bed, her heart thudding like racing hoof beats. She clenched her hands, but without horses at the end of her invisible reins, it made little difference. She must remain out of the way and not interfere. No doubt this was very bad news. It would not do to further importune Papa in the face of what would be a difficult circumstance.

Thunderous pounding rained upon the front door!

She jumped to her feet. Could Lady Catherine have knocked in such an unladylike manner? A fist assaulted the door again, but with the whole house abed, none was near enough to answer it.

Blast and botheration! She was not made for idleness.

In one leap, she flung her door open and flew down the stairs. She wrenched the stubborn front door open only to stare into Lady Catherine's flaming eyes.

"Good evening, your ladyship. What brings you here at such a remarkable hour?" The words tumbled out on their own accord, flat and involuntary. She could hardly expect a proper formal greeting under these circumstances.

"You can be at no loss, Miss Elizabeth, to understand the reason for my journey hither. Your own heart, your own conscience must tell you why I come." Lady Catherine pushed her way inside and loomed over her. Moonlight streamed in through the open door, backlighting her with an eerie glow.

Elizabeth stepped back, bracing against the wall behind her. "Indeed you are mistaken, Madam. I cannot at all account for the … honor of seeing you here."

In truth, it was no honor. Terror described the encounter much more fittingly.

Creaking doors and shuffling footsteps from upstairs filled the air between them.

Lady Catherine poked Elizabeth's chest. "You ought to know I am not to be trifled with."

Papa, in his dressing gown, thundered down the stairs. Usually his steps were so light. Elizabeth gulped.

"What the devil is going on, Lizzy? How dare you … oh, your ladyship, excuse me." He bowed. His nightcap flopped down and slapped his face. He flipped it back as he rose.

"What is going on?" She slammed the front door shut with her elbow. Darkness enveloped the front hall. "I shall tell you. A report of a most alarming nature reached me this very evening. I was told that not only your eldest was at the point of being most advantageously married to Mr. Bingley, whom I handpicked for her—"

"Indeed it is true, your ladyship. He made her an offer this morning." Elizabeth stammered, eyes slowly adjusting to the dim moonlight filtering in through the windows. "Although it is very happy news indeed, I hardly comprehend how it warrants such an extraordinary visit."

"Pray, your ladyship, come in, and sit down. Allow us to bring you some calming tea. It was late in the day when I heard the news. I intended to tell you first thing in the morning. I had no idea it would cause you such distress." Papa gestured toward the drawing room.

"Why should that distress me? I have known all along how it would go. My point of alarm is you, Miss Elizabeth Bennet." She towered over Elizabeth.

"Lizzy!"

"I am told you entertained an offer from my own nephew, Mr. Darcy. I know it must be a scandalous falsehood." She flipped her hand in Elizabeth's face. "I would not injure him so much as to suppose the truth of it possible. Thus, instantly, I resolved on setting off for this house."

If this was evidence of her instant resolve, when had she learned of it, and from whom? Not even Jane knew of Mr. Darcy's offer. The only ones who had any reason to even suspect it were Lydia ... and Mr. Wickham.

"Your ladyship, if you believed it impossible to be true, I wonder you took the trouble of coming. What could your ladyship propose by it?"

"What do you think would drag me out in the middle of the night, foolish girl? I insist upon having this report universally contradicted. Declare to me there is no foundation for any of this."

Hill brought a candle into the front hall. The candle light flickered off faces lining the upper stairs: Mama, Jane and Mary.

"Go on, Lizzy, put her ladyship's mind to rest." Papa's voice remained mild, as it always did in her ladyship's presence. But seething anger burned in his eyes.

"If you wish your report contradicted, then why did you not disbelieve it from the start?" Elizabeth folded her arms over her waist and clenched her hands into tight fists. "I do not pretend to possess equal frankness with your ladyship. You may ask me questions which I shall not choose to answer."

"Elizabeth!" Papa stomped toward her.

Lady Catherine cut him off. "This is not to be borne. I insist on being satisfied. Has my nephew made you an offer of marriage?"

This was neither the time nor the place for that truth to be told.

"You ladyship has declared it to be impossible."

"It ought to be so. It must be so, while he retains the use of his reason." Lady Catherine leaned so close their noses nearly touched. Her breath stank of stale coffee and brandy. Probably too much brandy. "But your arts and allurements may, in a moment of infatuation, have made him forget what he owes to himself and to all his family. You may have drawn him in."

She sidestepped toward the candlelight. "If I had, I shall be the last person to confess it."

Mama trundled down the stairs and stood near Hill. "I can assure your ladyship, my daughter is not—"

"Do you forget who I am?" Lady Catherine whirled on Mama. "I am not accustomed to such treatment as this."

"I most profusely apologize. You have caught us unaware and unprepared to entertain company. If you will but come to the drawing room, we will—"

*She* turned to Elizabeth. "I am almost his nearest relation in the world and am entitled to know his dearest concerns. There are no secrets to be kept from me."

"You may claim such relation to him, but who are you to me?"

Papa grabbed her upper arm in a grip so tight tears stung her eyes. "Lizzy! You will apologize immediately!"

"I plucked your father up out of the London gutters to such a position of ease and favor. I am entitled my say in your affairs."

"My father was not in the 'London gutters' as you so colorfully call them. Your patronage to him does not entitle you to know my dearest concerns. Nor will such behavior as yours ever induce me to be explicit."

Papa shook her, though he looked more ready to slap her. "You will give Lady Catherine the answer she requires immediately. No more of your lip."

She pulled against him, but could not free herself.

"Let me be rightly understood. This match to which you have the presumption to aspire can never take place."

"I do not know that you are in a position to stop it."

Papa's grip tightened again. She squeaked as her fingers grew cold and tingly.

"Darcy is engaged to my daughter. That is all the position I need to put an end to your aspirations. Now what have you to say?"

"Only this, if he is engaged to Miss de Bourgh, you can have no reason to suppose he will make an offer to me."

Lady Catherine exhaled and turned aside. Papa released Elizabeth's arm and jumped out of *her* way. Lady Catherine strode two steps into the darkness and returned to Elizabeth.

*Her* back to the candlelight, shadows obscured nearly every facial feature. Her words boomed from a faceless, black form. "Are you lost to every feeling of propriety and delicacy? Have you not heard me say that, from his earliest hours, he was destined for his cousin?"

"What is that to me?"

"It should be everything to you!" Papa's eyes flashed.

"But it is not." Elizabeth glanced at him briefly. "If Mr. Darcy is neither by honor nor inclination confined to his cousin, why is he not to make another choice? If I am that choice, why may I not accept him?"

"Because honor, decorum, prudence, nay interest forbid it. Yes, Miss Elizabeth, your own self-interest, for do not expect to be noticed by his family and friends. You will be censured, slighted and despised by everyone connected with him. Your alliance will be a disgrace; your name will never even be mentioned by any of us."

Elizabeth stared and Lady Catherine blinked.

The dragon flinched.

*She* must realize she had little control over Mr. Darcy. This was her last, desperate move to have her way. Elizabeth squared her shoulders.

The dragon would not win today.

"These are heavy misfortunes, but the wife of Mr. Darcy must have such extraordinary sources of happiness necessarily attached to her situation that she could, upon the whole, have no cause to repine."

"Obstinate, headstrong girl! I am ashamed of you. Is this your gratitude for my attentions to you and to your family? Is nothing due to me on that score?" She swooped upon Papa. "I came here with the determined resolution of carrying out my purpose. I will not be dissuaded from it. I have not been used to submit to any person's whims. I have not been in the habit of brooking disappointment."

"Indeed you shall not, your ladyship," Papa said in his softest, most dangerous voice.

Mama sidled back.

Elizabeth steeled her spine. The dragon was only posturing! *She* had smoke, but no flame.

"That will make your ladyship's situation at present more pitiable. But it will have no effect on me."

"Tell me, once and for all. Are you engaged to him?"

"I am not." Not yet, but the morning would change that.

Lady Catherine pressed her hand to her chest and heaved a labored breath. "And will you promise me never to enter into such an engagement?"

"I will make no promise of the kind."

The air around her froze, icy and brittle and sharp.

"I am shocked and astonished. I expected to find a more reasonable young woman. I shall not go away till you have given me the assurance I require."

"Promise her, Elizabeth. Promise her now!" Papa stomped toward her, but she dodged his grasp.

"I certainly shall never give it. You have widely mistaken my character, if you think I can be worked on by such persuasions as these. How far your nephew might approve of your interference in his affairs, I cannot tell. You have certainly no right to concern yourself in mine. Importune me no further on the subject."

"Not so hasty, I am by no means done. Are the shades of Pemberley to be polluted by the likes of you, with no wealth, no connections, no refinement to your credit? Do you not consider a connection with you must disgrace him in the sight of everybody?"

Elizabeth's eyes narrowed. "You can now have nothing further to say. You have insulted me in every possible method. I have no further response. You know my sentiments."

"You are then resolved to have him?"

"I am only resolved to act in that manner which will, in my own opinion, constitute my own happiness, without reference to you …" she turned to Papa, "… or to any person so wholly unconnected with me."

"And this is your real opinion? This is your final resolve! Do not imagine your ambition will ever be gratified. I hoped to find you reasonable; but depend upon it, I will carry my point."

"Since you have been entirely unsuccessful up to now, what fantastical plan have you for the working of this miracle?"

"That is enough, Elizabeth." Papa grabbed her arm again and shook her with each word. "You will not speak so to Lady Catherine. Get upstairs to your room right now. Pray, forgive her, your ladyship." He threw her toward the stairs.

"Enough." *She* flung open the front door, revealing a young maid and Ames. "Go pack her trunks."

Elizabeth clutched the banister. "Pack my trunks?"

"I will suffer your presence here no longer, Miss Elizabeth. You disrupt my family, disturb my daughter and refuse to gratefully accept your proper role in this society. I have no place for you here."

"I am going nowhere. This is my home—"

"You have no place here either." Papa's voice sliced their air with surgical precision.

She gaped at him.

"She will be sent to her aunt in Meryton at first light—"

"That is not acceptable. I will not have her here another moment. If neither of you can manage her, how will any of your relations accomplish the task any better? My coach is here to carry her away as soon as her trunks are packed."

"No! I am not going." Elizabeth pressed her back against the wall.

"Where do you intend to send her?" Mama whispered.

"Papa? Mama?" She looked from one to the other.

Mama's face, even in the wane candlelight, lost all color.

"That is none of your concern. I have resources to accommodate a foolish, impudent girl where she will have ample opportunity to learn a proper appreciation for the condescension of her betters."

"I will not—"

"Yes, you will." His words stopped the blood in her veins and the room wavered, dreamlike before her.

She clung to the stair rail lest she topple over.

"You are out of control. I warned you, but you chose not to listen. This is how it must be."

"But—"

"Not another word." He turned away. "Hill, take them to Elizabeth's room."

She sank to the bottom stair as bodies moved past her, ignoring her as they ignored furniture. Had she wished to speak, her tongue would have failed. What words could be uttered at such a moment as this? Activity and shouts swirled around her, but lead filled her limbs, leaving her to observe, as though in the audience of a play.

How ironic that she had already accomplished most of her own packing. Lady Catherine would appreciate the speed at which she would be found ready.

Ames carted her trunks though the front door. Jane, weeping and shuddering, and Mary, only slightly less vocal in her distress, hugged her and whispered promises of help. Both pressed small purses into her hands before they turned aside. Mama trembled and clung to Hill's arm, speechless—something Elizabeth had never seen before. They all clustered at the front door, watching as Ames silently handed her into the coach and shut the door.

The maid was not waiting there for her. Through the foggy side glass, she saw the girl climb up with the footmen on Lady Catherine's carriage. So, she would not have a chaperone, and her reputation might be ruined. A fitting parting gift. At least a warm lap rug lay rumpled on the seat beside her, probably forgotten by her ladyship. She pulled it over her, but it had little effect on the cold overtaking her heart.

An hour later, the sun crept up the horizon, and the landscape around her took on clear forms. She pressed her forehead to the cool side glass, searching for anything that might be helpful. The road felt familiar, and a fingerpost confirmed. She was being carried to London!

Thank the hand of Providence—wait no, London might not be their final destination. From London, she might be dispatched … anywhere. Lady Catherine had many properties and connections. She could find herself in a desolate cottage, a fine country house, a remote girls school, or even … no stop, this line of conjecture would not help!

Botheration! Nothing in the coach gave any clue.

The horses would require rest soon. A coaching inn must be near. She might be able to convince Ames to allow her to attend the necessary. Perhaps then she might—

What might she do? Escape?

Even if she slipped away, where would she go? She fell back into the squabs. Lady Catherine's stale rose scent rose in a cloud and clung to her. Would that she never smell roses again!

Thankfully, she had a little money. If she managed to break away, she might purchase passage on the stagecoach, or even the mail coach.

But where? What would she do in the meantime, alone?

Had she ever been so alone? Though she traveled around the village at Rosings without a chaperone, she knew everyone there, and they knew her. She was never truly alone there. She was now, though. So very, very alone.

How could Papa abandon her?

Then again, how could she have expected him to stand against Lady Catherine?

Her insides squeezed so tight breath hardly passed. Though dire, her situation might be worse. Jane would marry soon. She had only to manage until then, and she would have a place to live. They surely would not deny her now—would they?

She dragged the back of her hand across her eyes. There would be time enough for that later. Where would she go until the wedding, and how might she contact Jane? Charlotte would help, surely she would. Mr. Collins did not read Charlotte's post. A message to Jane might be sent through her—

The coach slowed and stopped. She peered through the glass. Where was the inn? Only a small, forlorn farmhouse broke the landscape. Why would they stop here? Was this their destination? Why? Her heart raced. How could she escape?

The coach swayed with the weight of men climbing off the box. The driver shambled away toward the farm house.

Ames unlatched the door, climbed inside and pulled the door shut behind him.

"Are you well, Miss Bennet?" He shuffled his feet and rubbed his hands along his thighs.

She scooted as far away as possible. "As much as might be expected under the circumstances."

He had recovered so well from his accident. Perhaps he might ... no, he owed too much to *her*.

"About that—" he slumped forward, "Please, Miss, you gotta understand—there weren't a soul at Rosings who wanted to go with the Lady to fetch you. Not a one. I would have said no myself, but my uncle, he made me."

"Indeed? Made you?" Tom was a friend, but like everyone else, he too—

"Yes, matter of fact, he planned everything."

"Planned what?"

"You got friends, Miss. You got friends."

Friends. She pressed her fist to her lips and blinked back the burning in her eyes.

"There be a bag of coins in your smallest trunk—tucked in your wool muff, Millie said—we could not see you off without means."

She gasped. "I had no idea."

"I think the Lady saw nothing neither." He winked.

"Where are you taking me?" She peeked out the glass.

"Not where she sent you. That is the best part." He grinned and folded his arms.

Great heavens, he was proud of himself, and Tom too, for acting outside of *her* notice.

"I do not follow."

"That farm belongs to the driver's brother, and a horse has gone lame."

"But the horse—"

He held up his hand. "The horse is gone lame. You are going to sit at the farmhouse while it's walked back to Rosings and replaced."

"How does—"

"You are very clever, Miss, and will run off while we are managing the horses. We will search ever so hard, but you are nowhere to be found."

"You are going to allow me to just walk away?"

"Heavens no! Uncle Tom would ring me a fine peal and rub me down with an oaken towel if I were to so much as turn me back on you. No, Miss, he said you has some kin folk in London? Millie said you asked her to post a letter to Cheapside?"

"Yes, My Uncle and Aunt Gardiner."

"Be they Bennets—"

"No, they are my mother's family."

"So they will take you in?"

"I think so … they have not answered my letter, but they are my best hope."

"Then that is where you are going … unless you rather somewhere else."

She chewed her lip. If she ran away now, she would be disobeying Papa and Lady Catherine. It would sever all ties with both of them, probably forever.

"You ain't thinking about going back, is you?

Perhaps she should. She shivered, Papa's cold eyes flashing in her mind. No, she dared not face him again.

But if she did not, would she ever see Mr. Darcy again?

What if she never had opportunity to give him an answer?

What if this was her only chance to escape the Queen of Rosings Park?

She hugged her sides and rocked softly. "I cannot go back. London is the best choice. But how? This carriage would be recognized, and someone will tell *her* where I am. She seems to have spies everywhere."

"We are far cleverer than she believes. Uncle sent one of the farm wagons ahead. The driver is bringing it 'round, and we'll load up your trunks. I'll drive you to London while the driver takes the 'lame' horse back to Rosings. I'll be back before he returns, and we should be to Rosings by nightfall with the tale of your clever escape."

"I am all astonishment."

How many had Tom rallied to her cause? How many endangered themselves on her behalf?

"It is agreeable, yes?"

"Yes, yes. I am just stunned you would all go to such trouble for me."

"We mightn't be the upper crust, but we do not forget our friends or thems that done us a good turn. You been both." He tipped his head.

"Lady Catherine will certainly be furious. You will lose your position. I cannot permit—"

"Don't be worrying, Miss. The farmer's wife and daughters will take the blame. They promised to watch over you." He waggled his eyebrows.

"Let me guess. He has no wife."

"Ain't never been shut up in the parson's pound." Ames grinned so broadly he might pop with the pleasure of it.

Would that she might share his enthusiasm.

"What about you?"

"If she sacks me, so be it. I am alive because of you, Miss. Besides, Adele and me, we been saving up. We'll just take it as a sign from Providence that it be time to buy that pub we been talking about. Either way, it be good for us. Never planned to stay at Rosings forever."

She drew breath to speak, but he lifted an open hand.

"Not another word of that. I'm just sorry the best we worked out for you was a farm cart. Here it comes now. We'll load it up and set right off. I expect you'll be in town by breakfast."

Ames disappeared into the farmhouse and returned in plain clothes. He looked so different without his livery. How odd, seeing him in an old work shirt and slops dispelled most of the dark cloud that had followed her from Rosings.

He helped the driver transfer her things to the cart and cover them with feed sacks. A few minutes later, the driver helped her from the coach.

He spread the rug from the coach on the cart seat. "It wouldn't do to sully your gown, Miss."

"Thank you so very much. I do not know what to say."

"Nothing more needs saying. You always been so intent on taking care of the likes of us. It is time to do you a good turn." He tipped his hat.

"That and Uncle Tom would nigh give any of us a moment's rest if he didn't know you to be safe." Ames flicked the reins, and the farm horse plodded on.

The wagon lacked the coach's springs and padding. Every rut and rock in the road jarred her bones.

But sunshine and friendship—true friendship—atoned for those small discomforts.

London rose on the horizon, shrouded in fog. Her heart fluttered—how would she explain her sudden appearance, and in such a vehicle?

Why had Aunt Gardiner not written back?

Perhaps they would not want her.

Would they be very angry at the impropriety of her appearing with her pile of trunks on their doorstep and no invitation?

"You said they lived on Gracechurch Street, in Cheapside, Miss?"

"Yes, yes—do you know the way?"

"In fact I do." He guided the cart through a narrow turn. "Don't worry none. I know it don't look it, but I can get this cart through any street. It won't be much longer, Miss."

Street sweepers and shopkeepers, street vendors and urchins populated the thoroughfare, each on their own errands. Did they secretly wonder about hers, though they seemed to ignore the farm wagon with a lady perched atop? Or was she as invisible as she felt?

The Gardiners' house appeared in the distance. Her breathing turned shallow and her hands cold. Would they even be able to take her? What if they already had guests or—

Stop! Simply stop! There had been sufficient disaster for one day. Inventing more—no matter how real it felt—was only foolishness.

Ames stopped the wagon in front of the second-rate town home at the center of the block of townhomes. Angular columns lined the freshly painted front door. Though not a great, first rate home, it was certainly the grandest on the street and far nicer than any her father had ever leased in London.

Oh, but it was too early for a morning call. Would the family even be awake? Perhaps she should wait—no, Ames had to return, and she had nowhere else to go.

She sucked in a deep breath of funny smelling city air and rapped the brass door knocker upon the imposing black door.

Behind her, two shopkeepers called to each other across the street, though she could not make out their conversation.

How long could it take to answer the door? She chewed her lip and drove her nails into her palms. Should she knock again, or would that be rude?

The door barely creaked as it swung open. The Gardiner's housekeeper, a grizzled old woman nearly as wide as she was tall, opened the door. Her frilly mobcap, with the distinct coral ribbon she always wore, framed her face. She scowled a moment then smiled her familiar gap-toothed smile.

"Miss Lizzy? As I live and breathe, no one 'ere told me you was expected."

She grabbed the doorframe lest her knees give way. "I ... I ... it was a rather unexpected trip, I fear."

"Well, do come in. I'll send the—wagon?" She peeked out the door and cocked her head, raised brows furrowing her forehead. "—around to the mews. You will be staying for some time?"

"I cannot be sure, but I do hope so."

The housekeeper ushered her inside.

"Who calls so early?" Aunt Gardiner bustled into the front hall, a bundle of letters in her hand. "Elizabeth?"

"Aunt Gardiner." Elizabeth tried to curtsey, but her knees gave way. The housekeeper and Aunt Gardiner caught her by the elbows and helped her to the parlor.

The comfortably familiar room, with its friendly pillows and warm colors, invited her in and promised her welcome. No formality, no pretense, just the safety and ease of family.

"I am delighted to see you, to be sure. When I did not hear back from you, I wondered if you had refused our invitation. What could have brought you all this way at this hour of the day—and alone?" Aunt handed the post to the housekeeper and waved her out. "Did not your father travel with you?"

"No, no one." She barely forced the words out.

"No maid accompanied you?"

"Only the driver."

Aunt's grey eyes turned stormy. It was too much!

Elizabeth crumpled into a heap on the carpet and wept into her hands. Quiet cries grew into wracking shuddering sobs that threatened to tear her heart open and spill along the hearth.

At some point, she knew not when, Aunt knelt alongside her and held her tightly. Sometime later, heavy steps entered. Uncle Gardiner dragged a piece of furniture close by and sat near her. The show of support only pulled more wrenching laments from the darkest places of her soul.

How long could one weep? Surely a sensible girl would have ceased her carrying on by now and been able to manage a conversation. But she was not sensible—there was nothing sensible about anything that had happened to her. Nothing made sense anymore, and perhaps it never would again.

Aunt pressed a handkerchief into her fist.

She fixed her eyes on it until her hands stopped shaking and applied it liberally to her face.

"Will you not tell us what has happened?" Aunt brushed damp hairs back from Elizabeth's forehead.

Elizabeth untied her bonnet and pulled it off. Aunt took it and laid it on a small inlaid table behind them.

Sunbeams streamed through the window, embracing Elizabeth and reminding her she was no longer in Kent, no longer in the grasp of the Queen of Rosings Park.

"I am so sorry …" She scrubbed her face with her palms.

"You need not apologize. No doubt there is an excellent explanation."

Uncle Gardiner growled. "Of course there is, and her name is Mrs. Bennet." He sprang to his feet and slammed his fist into his palm. "I told you things would come to this, that she was not a fit mother for my dear sister's girls."

"It was not Mama," Elizabeth whispered.

Aunt Gardiner helped her to the couch and sat beside her. "Why did you not write back to us? I have been anticipating a letter from you for days. We were pleased to invite you—"

"You invited me?" She clasped her hands and pressed them against her lips, rocking ever so slightly.

"Yes, of course we did. You know you are always welcome with us." Aunt chewed her thumbnail. "You did not receive the letter, did you?"

"No, I did not. Mama has the habit of reading our correspondence and sometimes it does not reach us in a timely fashion."

Uncle threw his hand in the air. "She reads your correspondence? The ill-bred, ill-mannered—"

Aunt cleared her throat and he stopped.

"She wanted to send me to Aunt Philips in Meryton. I imagine she did not regard it necessary to show me an invitation from you."

"Why would she send you to Meryton, to a woman not even related to you?"

"Why would she send you anywhere at all?" Uncle added with a muttered epithet under his breath.

Aunt took her cold hands and held them in the penetrating warmth of her own. "Tell us what happened. We need to know."

"Mama wanted to send me away because I am so vexing, because I did not accept Mr. Collins, or Mr. Wickham. Is it so wrong to refuse a man who is utterly disagreeable in every respect?"

"Of course not. But how is it you have come to us and not to Meryton?"

"Lady Catherine, it was she who … who banished me." She pressed the back of her hand to her mouth. More tears would help nothing.

"Banished you? That is not possible." Uncle Gardiner returned to his seat. "You cannot mean to say she whisked you away in the middle of the night, your father permitting it under his nose?" He rolled his eyes.

Elizabeth sniffled. "I know you unlikely to believe me, but that is just how it happened."

Uncle Gardiner blanched and leaned in close. "Tell me precisely what happened."

Her voice unsteady, Elizabeth stammered out the tale. In the middle of her story, Uncle jumped to his feet and paced the length of the room. Even in her own ears, the story sounded outlandish, even fanciful, more like a gothic novel than anything that might actually happen.

"And your father stood by the entire time, never once attempting to protect you from the harridan." He snarled, fists knotted and shaking at his sides.

She pulled her wrap more tightly around her shoulders.

"And it was her ladyship's servants who undertook to thwart her plans?"

"I have, from time to time, undertaken to assist on their behalf." She twisted the handkerchief into tight knots and plucked it loose only to tie it again.

"Knowing you, my dear, time to time means quite regularly." Aunt stroked her back. "I expect they see you a better mistress to them than the Lady they serve."

"Pray, might I stay with you, at least until—"

"Not until anything!" Uncle slapped his thighs. "Your home is with us now."

"Truly? I am not inconveniencing you—"

"You did right to come to us, my dear." Aunt squeezed her shoulder. "We are very glad to have you for as long as you wish."

The tight strings that had been holding her together snapped and unleashed another fit of tears. How could she weep years' worth in a single day?

"I will write to your father straight away—"
"Pray, Uncle, do not!"
"Why?"

"What matter is it to him? If he knows where I am, he may tell *her*—" She shoved her fist to her mouth. She would not cry again!

Aunt patted her back and looked up at Uncle. "Calm yourself, my dear, we will keep our counsel for now. It cannot hurt for him to feel the weight of his foolishness for a while, can it?"

"No indeed. He deserves any suffering that may come of this." Uncle knelt beside her and tipped her chin. "And you need never fear *her* again, child, for this is one house into which she will never have admittance. I care not who she is, nor what her connections may be. She has injured my family, and I will not stand for any further interference. You are done with *her* forever."

She stared deep into his eyes. He meant every word.

---

Darcy rose before dawn and cursed the darkness. He could not leave the house before first light, though he would have liked nothing better. Why did the sun take so long to rise today of all days?

He paced along the windows. At last, enough light to dress by. Without his valet's help, it would take longer, but perhaps the occupation would make the time pass more quickly.

He tied his cravat and slipped on his coat as the sun rose high enough to set the wispy clouds aglow. At last!

Finally, he could seek out Miss Elizabeth, who must be taking a walk this glorious morning. Dear God, if she did not, he would surely run mad.

He would have his answer from her—her promise to marry him before the sun rose much higher. Then all would be right with the world.

He burst forth from his room and trotted down the stairs. No one but the staff would be about at this hour to interfere with his errand. Still, he tip-toed past Aunt Catherine's throne room—when had he begun thinking of it in Miss Elizabeth's terms? The corner of his lips crept up—

"Darcy." Aunt Catherine's shrill, ear splitting voice shattered the air.

He jumped and turned.

She appeared in the doorway of the parlor.

Something about her was not right, unkempt, disheveled. The Lady with never a hair out of place seemed rumpled. Had she not slept the night?

"You will attend me, now."

"No, I am going out for a ride." Every nerve tensed, as on a hunt, waiting for the hart to break through the bushes, but today he was prey, not predator.

Her taffeta wings ruffled and she peered down her hawkish nose. "You will attend me now. Whatever you wish to do can wait."

He knotted his hands to absorb the tension from his shoulders. "I will give you five minutes, no longer." Had she been a man, he would have held his ground, but Mother's rules of deference were far too ingrained. He stalked into her lair.

She perched upon her throne, partially obscured by early morning shadows. "You will not be in such a hurry once you have heard me out."

He squelched the desire to look over his shoulder for whatever lay in wait to ambush him in this ominous, dismal chamber. He dare not appear vulnerable in her presence. "What could you possibly have to tell me so early in the morning?"

"I know what you have been about, nephew, and I am most displeased."

"What are you talking about?"

"I told you how to settle the matter with Miss Elizabeth Bennet, but you chose to ignore me."

"You insisted I dishonor her, ruin the reputation of her sisters—"

"What matter? The Bennets are below us and of no consequence. It is Anne for whom you have been destined from birth. Your mother and I agreed, deemed it so, planned it so, from the very moment of—"

"Without ever consulting either of the two parties who must consent."

"Anne will do as she is told."

"But I will not. I have never been yours to command, nor will I ever be. I have tolerated it with good humor, for my mother's sake, but no more."

"You would abandon her? Your flesh and blood, your family?"

"Fitzwilliam will marry her."

"Richard? What is he—"

"We have already decided it between us. He has been exerting himself on her behalf. She appears well pleased with his attentions."

"You would give up Rosings to your cousin?"

"It is not the prize you think it is."

She clutched the arms of her throne and rose, ready to pounce. "How dare you!"

"Rosings is in disrepair and debt, far deeper than you understand. That is why I hired Michaels—"

"That sapscull—"

"—is trying to save you from your creditors, though you fight him at every turn."

"Why should I listen to a common—"

"Because he knows his business."

"It should be your task, you who are family—"

"I have Pemberley to manage. I will not endanger it to spend my days fighting you to rescue your ill-managed property!"

Her voice dropped into tones soft and almost sweet. "If you marry Anne, it will be yours."

"Fitzwilliam can have it. If he can make it solvent, he deserves it all."

"And you made this decision without consulting me?"

"Much as you decided Anne and I should marry." His lip curled. "Perhaps you do not like matters taken out of your hands any more than I do. It is a done thing, and there is nothing you can do about it."

She stood to full height, slowly growing into a towering presence, backlit by a single wavering sunbeam. "Not so fast, young man. I have already solved the problem."

Her manner—a mix of smug and dangerous—sent a cold shiver slithering down his spine. He edged back in spite of himself. "What problem?"

"Miss Elizabeth Bennet."

He bounded across the distance between them and stopped short of grabbing her shoulders and shaking her. "What have you done? If you have harmed her in any way—"

"Not harmed, simply removed."

"Removed? What are you talking about?"

"I removed her from Rosings, removing all your distraction from marrying Anne."

He clenched his jaw, fists quivering. He must not lay hands upon her. "How was she removed?"

"I sent my coach to carry her away last night."

"In the middle of the night? How dare you endanger her—"

Aunt Catherine sneered and snorted. "Oh, she will be safe enough, and safely away from you. Now you are free to do your duty."

"Where have you taken her?"

"You cannot believe for an instant I would tell you where I have placed the woman you attempted to propose to—against my explicit wishes—only yesterday."

"How would you know anything of my personal and private business?"

"How can you think anything escapes my notice? There are those among us more loyal to me than you—and I reward loyalty handsomely."

Wickham! Who else? He would pay dearly for his treachery.

"Tell me where she is!" Had she only been a man, he would—

"You will never see her again."

"You think your servants cannot be bribed?"

"Only I am aware of her final destination. My driver will hand her off to another—probably already has, who will finish her journey. There is no one here to pay for the information."

"And this is your final resolve?"

"Absolutely."

"You cannot imagine this will in any way compel me to change my mind regarding Anne. Nothing whatsoever will induce me to matrimony with your daughter. What say you to that?"

"You shall change your mind. A Darcy is a duty bound creature."

"Not to you."

She laughed.

Laughed! As though she had triumphed.

He pulled himself up, taller still, and glared down at her. Oh, the harridan was not accustomed to being reminded she was not all powerful. Closer still, he exhaled on her face.

She flinched.

"Then hear my resolve. You will never see Georgiana or me again. We will never darken the doors of Rosings again, nor will you be welcome on any of my properties, ever. We will never attend another event where you are present. I will not hesitate to let it be known that you have grievously harmed my family. I will hire away your steward, who would likely have quit on the news of what you have done to his future sister, something you should fear much more than the withdrawal of my company."

"I shall hire another. Such men are easily acquired."

"Remember that when you find yourself turned out of your home and consigned to debtor's prison, but do not write to me for assistance. And know this; I shall not rest until I have found Miss Elizabeth. If any harm has come to her, be certain, Aunt, you will feel the pain of it." He stalked out, shouting for his valet, the butler and any other servant in earshot.

Half an hour later, he stormed out of Rosings. His valet would pack his things while Bingley oversaw their party's removal to the inn in town. From there,

Hurst would take his wife and Miss Bingley to London. Fitzwilliam, now Darcy's trusted lieutenant, agreed to remain behind to see if any further information might be had from the staff.

Darcy mounted his horse and took off at as fast a pace as he dared. An undergardener reported the carriage had been seen on the road to London. Perhaps he could follow—

Not far out, he encountered one of Lady Catherine's drivers, leading a horse.

"What is the meaning of this? Where is the carriage? More importantly, where is Miss Bennet?" He slid off his horse and dropped down in front of the sweaty, bedraggled driver.

The man dodged eye contact. "The horse threw a shoe, sir, a'fore we got to the first coaching inn, and is gone lame. The footman stayed, but I come back—"

"Yes, yes," Darcy's heart raced. Perhaps she might not be so far off and this horrible nightmare—

He jumped back into the saddle and sped away.

If only the horse could move faster. It would not do to kill it. Bloody fragile creatures when one needed them most!

But, every step was a step closer to his dearest Elizabeth. What dangers might she be facing even now, broken down along the side of the road?

Any kind of scoundrel might be imposing upon her. Providence protect her! Could not this bloody horse go just a little faster?

There, in the distance, near a tumble-down tenant farm, Lady Catherine's carriage!

This ordeal would end in just moments. She would be safe with him and promise to be his wife. All would be right once more.

What?

Where was the footman? He should have been guarding the coach. He would sack the man himself for endangering—

The curtains were pulled back from the side glass and dear God—there was no one inside!

He pulled his horse up short. The farmhouse! He urged the horse to a gallop. Once there, he barely paused to dismount and nearly stumbled in his haste to get to the door. He knocked, but no one answered.

Certainly someone must be about. This was not one of Rosings' many vacant properties. He searched the outbuildings and found the farmer in the barn.

Yes, he saw the horse unhitched and led off. No, he had seen no one else from the coach. Yes, he would send word if he had news of a young woman.

Darcy staggered to his horse. No one disappeared without a trace. Where could she have gone alone and on foot?

Wait, she might not be alone. What of the footman?

He raked his hair and screwed his eyes shut. How many footmen were in Lady Catherine's employ? Surely not that many. Who had he not seen this morning?

He pinched his temples. Long Tom's nephew … Ames? He had been absent.

Ames! That could not be a coincidence. The young man owed Miss Elizabeth a particular debt, and his uncle was her self-appointed protector at Rosings! His chest released and he dragged in a desperate breath.

They must have found some way—perhaps the driver knew as well. The whole of Rosings staff esteemed her. They could all be part of this! Perhaps she was not lost at all, but safely in their care

Thank Providence, there was good reason for hope. He must return to the manor and begin asking questions there.

On the way back to Rosings, the road took him past the Bennets' house. The very sight of the place, bathed in the warm morning sun as though there were nothing wrong in the world, made his stomach churn. He turned his face aside and focused on the tree-lined lane before him. No point in wasting his energies on what would not aid his cause.

A short distance beyond, Miss Bennet walked along the middle of the road. She seemed in a daze, dragging her feet in the dust, and weaving from one side of the road to the other. His horse slowed as it approached her, but she gave no sign of awareness or recognition.

"Miss Bennet?"

She jumped and looked at him. Her eyes were red and face drawn as Georgiana's had been after crying all night over Wickham.

He dismounted and maneuvered his horse to obscure any view of them from the Bennet's house. "Are you well, Miss Bennet?"

"They sent her away—with no warning, nothing. I have not even a direction to which I may write her."

"Your parents made no objection?"

She pressed a wrinkled wet handkerchief to her cheeks. "No, they just … just … let Lady Catherine…"

Her sobs wrenched his self-control. He bit his tongue hard. There was language a lady ought not be subjected to, no matter how satisfying it might be. "I most heartily apologize …"

She cried harder. "What good are apologies when my sister is gone, and no one knows nor cares where she is?"

"I care."

She looked up at him.

"I just came from looking for her."

"You found her?"

"Not yet. The coachman brought back a lamed horse. I expected to find her on the road with the carriage, but it was empty when I came upon it."

She pressed her fist to her mouth and screwed her eyes shut.

"But I saw no signs of foul play: no damage to the coach; her trunks were gone, but the ropes not cut. There is reason for hope."

"Hope? How is that a reason to hope?"

"A footman went with her, Tom's nephew."

She gasped.

"He owes her a substantial debt. Neither he nor Long Tom would permit anything untoward to happen her."

She swallowed hard and blinked rapidly. "Do you think …"

"Be assured, I will not rest until I have found her. I have asked her to be my wife."

"When she came last night she said something about it, but I could hardly believe."

"It was not merely Aunt Catherine's paranoid speculation."

"Oh my heavens! I am astonished she would not have told me."

"I have removed my family from Rosings and her influence. I will recover your sister. In the meantime, I must ask something of you."

"What? Anything." Hope returned to Miss Bennet's eyes, so like Elizabeth's, his throat pinched.

"First, tell no one of my suspicions, lest they be reported back to my aunt."

"Certainly."

"Have you any friends or relations in London or on the way there to whom Elizabeth might turn for refuge?"

Miss Bennet chewed her knuckle. "Our Aunt and Uncle in Cheapside, our mother's brother. He and Papa are barely on speaking terms."

"Excellent, give me their direction and—"

"I will write to them."

"No, you must not. If she is there, we must not allow anyone else to suspect. I know it is difficult. I promise, I will send word to you of whatever I discover."

"Jane!" Dr. Bennet called from some way down the road.

She wiped her eyes once more and emerged from behind Darcy's horse.

"Yes, Papa."

Darcy stepped out behind her.

"Get your things. Stop sulking about. I need you to attend me to Rosings. Miss de Bough has had another spell."

"That is Lizzy's role."

"And she is not here, so you shall—"

"No, I shall not."

The birds stopped calling, the breeze fell away and the air was silent.

"What did you say?" Bennet's face shifted through three different shades of red, none appealing.

"I will not attend you, Papa. I have neither the stomach, nor the skill, nor the patience for it." Miss Bennet squared her shoulders and stared directly at Bennet.

Had he ever seen her like this? Had Bingley?

"What skill or patience? And as to the stomach, you have little choice but to develop it at some point or another. I insist you return to the house and—"

"I am not going with you. Perhaps you have forgotten. Lizzy was your assistant, not me. She understands your recommendations for each ailment and has what you need at your fingertips before you ask. I cannot do that."

"I am not expecting—"

"Yes, you are. You will demand I be her and, when I cannot, you will shout and swear at me just like you did to her."

He shook his head furiously. "I never raised my voice or upbraided her—"

Miss Bennet laughed a coarse, bitter, choking sound. "That is not the common opinion in our home, or at Rosings. Everyone hates the way you speak to her."

"Rot and nonsense! I esteemed—"

"If you esteemed her so highly, why did you allow Lady Catherine to take her?" She covered her face and sobbed.

"Enough! Not another word. Gather your things and attend me."

Darcy might not have Elizabeth under his protection, not yet, but this one thing, he could do now. "Miss Bennet, my sister and I have taken rooms at the inn. I fear she will be lonely without female companionship. Would you accept an invitation to stay with her?"

She peeked up and whispered, "Oh yes, that would be delightful. Thank you."

"I forbid it." Bennet stomped toward them.

"Do you ride—can you—" He glanced at his horse.

"If you help me mount."

He boosted her onto his horse, eyes averted, as she awkwardly arranged herself and her skirts. He adjusted the stirrup. It was not a lady's saddle, but if she had half Elizabeth's horsemanship, the short ride to the inn would be safe enough.

He handed her the reins. "I will send someone for your things later."

"Thank you." She set off, shoulders squared and back straight. She definitely shared her sister's skill.

Dr. Bennet stood, sputtering, in the middle of the lane. "How dare you interfere with my family!"

"How dare you abandon your daughter!"

"I did not abandon her. She is in the care of—"

"No one."

"Nonsense, Lady Catherine—"

In one long stride, Darcy met him nose to nose. "Has no idea of where she is, nor does the driver."

"That is not possible. How would you know?"

"Because," Darcy poked his chest hard enough to force Bennet back a step. "I went looking for her. I, not you, her father—"

"She was in Lady Catherine's care."

"Aunt Catherine has never cared for someone below her and never will."

"She is my patroness. I owe her—"

"Your daughter as a sacrifice? I have nothing more to say to you, sir, and I hope never to see you again."

"You have Jane."

"She is the guest of my sister and welcome to stay with us until she marries my friend. She is, as I understand, of age—as much as Miss Elizabeth—"

Bennet's face blanched. That should not satisfy him so, but it did.

"You cannot force her back to your house, and I certainly will not. Good day, sir." He turned and stalked down the road, Bennet still stammering behind him.

The mile's walk to the village inflamed Darcy's temper, nearly raising lather. Pedestrians gave him a wide berth on the street, which was probably best, all told. Ideally, he would retrieve his horse quickly and be on his way to question Long Tom at Rosings.

He hurried by the pub. The inn was next door, and just beyond, his horse and freedom of movement.

Something caught his eye. There, in the window—Wickham!

His hands clenched and arms corded with the not-at-all-unconscious desire to unleash his rage. Words, polite or otherwise, left him. His vision narrowed to a single, despicable focal point, and everything else disappeared.

He stormed into the largely empty tavern. Stale food and body smells assaulted his nostrils. A serving girl dodged away from him, nearly spilling the drinks on her tray.

Wickham scrambled up from the table, ale sloshing from his tankard. Three dandies at the table with him turned tail and disappeared into the abundant shadows.

"Darcy." A wide smile, Wickham's favorite distraction, stretched his mouth, but his eyes narrowed. His gaze flicked from Darcy to the nearest door and back.

Darcy snarled and planted his hands on the table so hard it nearly tipped. "I will ruin you."

"Come now, you can hardly be so animated over a common bit of muslin." Wickham edged back.

Darcy side stepped around the table. "This is your fault."

"What is?"

"She is lost."

"She is on a jaunt to London. You can find her easily enough."

Darcy stomped closer. "She vanished on the road and is gone."

Wickham gulped.

So he had no part in Aunt Catherine's scheme. How fortunate for him.

"She will turn up. I do not see what is your worry." Wickham tossed back a last gulp of ale and dropped the tankard, clattering on the floor

"First, you try to interfere with my sister, now her?"

"What is the little chit to you?"

Darcy roared and backed him against the wall. "You knew well enough to bring a report to my aunt."

Wickham's lip pulled back in an all too familiar expression. "You know she was meant for me. It might be construed—"

Darcy grabbed his collar, lifted him until his toes barely touched the ground, and shoved him into the wall. "I will ruin you. Every barrister, solicitor and landowner from here to Pemberley will know your name, your face, and every mark and scar on your scrawny frame. I will see to it you will never find employment in Derbyshire, Kent or any other county to which I am connected."

Wickham wrenched himself out of Darcy's grasp. "You really intended to marry the chit."

"I still do. I will find her; have no doubt."

"Then what is the to-do? You will get what you want. Why bother with me?" He tugged his waistcoat straight.

"No one interferes with those connected with me and walks away unharmed. I told you to remove yourself from Kent once before. You chose to ignore it. I give you one hour to remove yourself from this village."

"Else what?"

Darcy twisted Wickham's cravat in his fist.

Wickham gasped and slapped at his hand.

"Else further, unnecessary unpleasantness will ensue."

"You have not got it in you."

"Fitzwilliam does. He was most displeased over Georgiana. Twice now, I dissuaded him from pursuing you, saber drawn. I convinced him his pistol would be ungentlemanly."

Wickham's smile faded.

Darcy released him. "One hour, be gone or I will have you shot as a trespasser."

Wickham straightened his collar and sauntered past Darcy.

Only Father's finest lessons in self-control kept Darcy from throwing a punch as he passed. But brawling like a common rogue would only delay finding Elizabeth.

Darcy rode to Rosings, pressing the horse as hard as he dared. Though he approached the back of the house, an observant groom hurried up to take his horse.

He took the kitchen steps at breakneck speed, scaring a scullery maid into nearly dropping her burden. He snarled at the cook to bring Long Tom.

It was not like him to frighten the servants. After all, it was not their fault, and in all likelihood, he owed them a great debt. But if his angry energy did not discharge somewhere, he might combust in a great shower of spark and flame.

Long Tom arrived in mere heartbeats. He stood—just stood—and looked down at Darcy until he must know every thought, every agony that wracked Darcy's being. Darcy bit his tongue lest he lose his most likely ally. Finally, Long Tom beckoned for him to follow.

They wove through the warren of tiny, windowless service rooms until they found the butler's pantry. Tom gestured him inside and shut the door.

Darcy paced along the short wall, not an arm's span from Tom and his flickering candle. Tom shoved a chair toward him, but if he sat now, the inactivity would surely kill him.

"Lady Catherine is quite displeased at the driver's news." Tom said, his voice low, even, and unaffected.

No signs of agitation. Darcy's heart unclenched a fraction. The man could get frantic; that he was not was a good sign.

"The household staff is in an uproar over it as well. A few of the younger maids have walked away from their posts." Tom dipped a rag in a jar of silver polish.

"I am in an uproar." Darcy snapped. "Yet, you are not."

Tom blinked. "It is incumbent upon my position—"

Darcy slapped the wall behind him. "Enough!"

Tom flinched, just a tiny bit, but it was sufficient to be satisfying.

"I have neither the time nor the patience for word games. No prevarication; I came here because—"

Tom's scowl tightened. So that was how he maintained order below the stairs. Quite effective, that expression.

Darcy squeezed his eyes shut and pinched the bridge of his nose. "Nothing at Rosings escapes your notice."

"That is true, sir."

"Then, no doubt you observed Miss Elizabeth and myself."

"While it is not my place, I have wondered—"

"…at my intentions toward her?"

Tom's eyebrow lifted just enough to be noticeable.

Darcy snorted. "You have greater respect for her than her father does."

"And you, sir?" Tom's shoulders flexed, but he might as well have crossed his arms over his chest and tapped his foot.

Darcy scratched his head. Why was he having this conversation with the butler and not—hang it all! "Yes, I respect her and yes, my intentions are wholly honorable. I had just made her an offer of marriage when that bounder Wickham burst in and proceeded to make a mess of everything."

"Marriage?"

Something in Long Tom's tone suggested he did not quite believe. Perhaps he had heard too many of Fitzwilliam's brandy infused ramblings. But he was not Fitzwilliam. Long Tom ought to realize that.

"Yes, nothing less."

"Did she make you an answer?"

"We were interrupted before she could."

"So she did not accept your offer?"

He was a servant; how dare he! Darcy raked his hair and stalked away. The spleen of the man … but Darcy would have answered Bennet had he asked these questions. They were not inappropriate, or disrespectful for a father to ask. He sucked in a deep breath and released it over ten counts.

"A fortnight ago, I asked her permission to make her an offer after her twenty-first birthday, which she granted me. I consider that strong grounds to have expected a favorable response."

Tom pursed his lips into what, for most people, would have been merely a frown, but on him looked quite menacing. "That is acceptable."

"You will help me recover her?"

Tom blinked.

"Your nephew—by your intervention I am sure—rode with her and secreted her off to safety."

"I do not know where she is."

Darcy stared into Tom's eyes. The man spoke the truth.

"I am correct as to your plans, though."

Tom only blinked.

"Then I know how to act." Darcy strode to the door but paused before he turned the handle. "You and Ames have my deepest gratitude. I will send you word when I recover her. I shall not forget your faithfulness." He opened the door.

"She deserves a man who properly esteems her, sir. I wish you joy."

Darcy looked over his shoulder, but Tom had turned his back and begun to polish a silver coffee pot.

Clouds moved in and caught him in a torrential downpour as he made his way back to the inn. How could the elements so conspire against him? Without Tom's oblique assurances Elizabeth was safe, he would have set out in the darkness and weather. Bingley, Georgiana and Miss Bennet together begged him to wait for the safety of first light, so he capitulated.

He awoke the next morning to more blinding rains and a raging head cold. Though he tried to leave in spite of it all, the ringing in his ears turned to dizziness, and he could not stand. His valet urged him back to bed, where he spent the next two days. He did not bear his confinement well.

On the dawn of the third day, both the weather and his cold subsided. He adjusted his coat, ready to call for his horse.

A frantic rap at his door presaged Miss Bennet, clutching a wrinkled note in her hands, cheeks tearstained, eyes red.

"What is wrong? Elizabeth?" He took her elbow and led her to a chair, calling for his sister and her maid. They dashed in.

"Pray, Miss Bennet, tell me of your news." His voice had a sharp edge that usually forced Georgiana into hiding, but it was the most pleasant he could muster. Hopefully, Miss Bennet would be made of sterner stuff.

"This just came from my … my sister Mary. The house is in an uproar. Papa forbade them sending word, but Mary… Mary—"

"What happened?"

Georgiana grabbed Miss Bennet's hands and glared at him.

"The night I left…Lydia…oh, it is too shocking. Lydia is gone."

"Gone? Aunt Catherine?" Georgiana gasped.

"No, no. She has gone off—eloped—"

"Wickham?" Darcy and Georgiana said simultaneously.

Miss Bennet nodded.

"Servants saw them take the road for London."

"I will see to this. Take care of her, Georgiana." Darcy stormed out.

He took to the road as soon as his horse could be made ready and made haste toward London.

Wickham was a low and loathsome being, but this stooped farther than he ever imagined possible. Despicable creature meant to use Lydia to extort him.

Elizabeth would be his wife, but he would not have Wickham for a brother. With the foul weather, Wickham and Lydia were not likely to have reached London much before he would arrive. He would find them, and if necessary, would employ tactics befitting Fitzwilliam, but Miss Lydia would never, never bear the name Wickham.

He stopped at the first coaching inn. The innkeeper confirmed Wickham and his 'lady' had indeed been there and claimed to be on their way to London. Darcy penned a brief note for Fitzwilliam to be posted with the next mail coach and continued his journey.

## Chapter 8

ELIZABETH SAT CURLED in the parlor's window seat contemplating the weather. Thick grey clouds that painted the London skies with the deepest feelings of her heart had rolled in and remained stubbornly in place for several days. They drenched everything and everyone in torrents of rain. She had cried so many tears in the past few days. How pleasant to let the raindrops flowing down the window pane take their place this morning.

Ever-patient, Aunt Gardiner extracted the entire story from her, never criticizing, never judging. No one, even Jane, had ever listened to her so gently, so completely. On one issue, though, Elizabeth had not been entirely forthcoming. At some point, she would have to confess the full story of Mr. Darcy's offer, but not until she could think of it without storms of tears flowing unchecked.

She dragged her palms over her cheeks. Her hands shook again. The trembling haunted her every night since she arrived. Whenever Elizabeth closed her eyes, *she* intruded to carry her off once again. She drove the heels of her hands into her eyes as if that would stop the frightful images haunting her dreams.

No! She must not allow the wraiths of Kent to follow her here. Safe and surrounded by those who truly loved and cared for her, she must be grateful and content. What more could she want for?

Her throat clamped down almost cutting off her breath. She leaned against the cool, damp window. Only one other thing did she lack, and that she might have to relinquish forever.

The knocker clattered against the front door. That must be the post, late and soggy once again. If only she might have hope for a letter, but none knew where she was, and possibly no one even cared.

Elizabeth needed some occupation. She should get the workbasket from the other side of the room and join Aunt in the morning room where the light was better for sewing. Perhaps in a few minutes, once Aunt finished reading her letters. She clutched her temples.

"Elizabeth."

Heavens! That was Aunt's something-is-wrong -with-the-children- voice. She ran to the morning room.

Aunt slouched at the table, pallid in the dreary cloud-filtered light. Her bearing was always perfect—something was dreadful wrong. A stack of letters lay between her tea cup and plate. An open letter balanced barely in her fingers.

"What happened? You are so pale."

"Pray, sit down. A most astonishing letter just came … from Mary."

Elizabeth's limbs went cold and numb. Mary had little reason to write to Aunt Gardiner. She crushed her apron in her trembling fingers and paced in the narrow space between the table and window. "Oh no, it is Lydia, is it not? She has done something dreadful."

"How do you know?"

"The letter has no black trim, no one has died. I expect Jane's betrothal is secure. If it were not, you would be sad, but that would be no reason for you to lose all color in your complexion. Likewise, had Papa suffered some disfavor with Lady Catherine, your posture would not be so collapsed. The only other likely misfortune …" She screwed her eyes shut and chewed her upper lip. "Lydia has put herself in the power of Mr. Wickham. Mama probably restricted her freedom to see him, and Lydia responded as only Lydia might."

"I should not be so surprised, I suppose, but it still astonishes me how much you are able to discern. Is it of any consolation that Mary's opening remarks related your cruel and unexpected removal from home? I think it was her first purpose to ensure that we knew what had happened to you. She is quite distraught."

"My situation is nothing to Lydia's. What has been done to recover her?"

"Mary does not say, but notes Lady Catherine is most displeased with the entire state of affairs. She threatens to dismiss your father if Lydia is disgraced."

Elizabeth braced her hand along the window frame and hid her face in the crook of her arm. "I warned him of the very great danger Mr. Wickham presented. I warned him. You must believe me. I tried to avert this …"

"No one is blaming you."

"Mama insisted they must be properly chaperoned. Oh, she was so angry to find how Lydia had been behaving. She tried to rein Lydia in. I tried … but Papa dismissed me as though—" the words tangled over her tongue and were carried away in a sob.

"I do not know what to say. I am as shocked as you."

"What am I to do?" Elizabeth wrapped her arms around her waist and huddled against the window. Mr. Darcy must know of Lydia's folly by now. He could hardly desire to be associated with her now.

"There is very little for you to do."

"But I should … I must …"

"This is not something you can fix my dear." Aunt moved to her side laid an arm over her shoulder. "Whilst I am very troubled to hear of your family's difficulties, Lydia is your father's concern. She is a stupid, foolish girl who certainly knows how to behave better than she has. For all her faults, I am convinced Mrs. Bennet did not teach her to behave thusly."

The housekeeper peeked into the morning room. "Missus?"

"What is it now? Pray excuse me." She hurried from the room.

Elizabeth sank down to perch on the windowsill. Cold little pools soaked through her dress. How was all this possible? What was worse, her removal from Rosings or Lydia's disappearance? Respectable, and believable, excuses might be made for herself, but Lydia? The family might never recover. Mr. Bingley and Mr. Michaels might even be persuaded to cast off her sisters.

Elizabeth shivered harder. She pulled up the corner of her apron and dragged it across her face. Little good tears accomplished. Perhaps she should scream and carry on, flail about and stomp her feet until things suddenly worked to her favor. It always seemed to work for Mama—at least it did when Papa was there.

"Miss Elizabeth?" The housekeeper appeared again. "Missus says there is a caller for you in the parlor.

A caller? Who …

She flew past the housekeeper, nearly tripping on the carpet edge. Aunt lingered in the doorway, an imposing, dark figure behind her.

"He says he is acquainted with you from Kent and has been concerned for your wellbeing." Aunt stepped aside.

"Mr. … Mr. Darcy?" She dodged around Aunt Gardiner and flew to his side. A proper lady would have stayed in her place and allowed him to come to her, but she could not have restrained her feet had she bothered to try. "You are here? How did you … even *she* does not know where—"

"Thank Providence you are safe!"

Strong arms, encased in a damp coat that smelled of sandalwood, enveloped her. A heavy cheek pressed the top of her head. She fell into his chest, too shaken to stand.

"You cannot imagine the agonies I have suffered," he whispered into her hair.

She clung to him, unable to speak. Surely he felt her quaking—

"As soon as I discovered what my aunt had done, I took off in search of you. I found the empty carriage and thought the very heart had been torn from my chest. Pray, do not hold me hostage any longer. I must have your answer."

She clutched the lapels of his coat. If only she could breathe!

"Will you be my wife?"

She tore away from him. "I cannot!"

He caught her wrist. "Because of your sister and Wickham?"

She stopped, frozen mid-step and gasped.

He drew her close. "I know everything, and I am undeterred." His arms encircled her again. "Now, Miss Elizabeth, give me my answer and your hand."

His voice was strong, but a tiny tremor in his hand betrayed him.

He had come after her. He alone took the trouble to discover her sanctuary. How had he done that?

"Yes, Mr. Darcy," she whispered against his chest. "I will be your wife."

He sagged against her. "How I have dreamt of you saying those words."

She turned her face him. His eyes shimmered—did he feel this as deeply as she?

He leaned in to her and touched his lips to hers. Her knees melted beneath her and she fell against him. His strength was sufficient for them both, his kiss breathing strength and security into her soul.

A man cleared his throat from the far side of the room. She stole a quick look over Darcy's shoulder.

Uncle stood in the doorway beside Aunt, his expression more bewildered than annoyed. "You were right, Maddie. There is clearly a part of the story to which we have not been made privy."

Elizabeth edged back from Darcy. How cold and empty it felt to be even that far away from him. "Uncle, may I introduce Mr. Darcy."

Darcy stepped toward him. "I am deeply indebted to you for your service to—"

"My niece, my family, my flesh and blood?" Uncle crossed his arms, a possessive, protective set to his shoulder.

"My betrothed." Darcy glanced back at Elizabeth.

Aunt's eyebrows rose. Elizabeth nodded, blushing.

"It would seem, sir, we have a great deal to discuss." Uncle looked very serious and not a little surprised. He gestured Darcy toward the door.

Darcy took her hand and laced his fingers with hers. "We do have much to discuss; however, I insist Elizabeth is part of the discussions from the start. She does not deserve to be compelled to puzzle our conversation together from looks and postures and odd words and deeds."

Aunt snickered and bit her knuckle while Uncle chuckled.

"What do all of you find so very humorous?" Elizabeth whispered.

"Do not be offended, my dear." Aunt rushed forward and took Elizabeth's face in her hands. "We are all so accustomed to you being cognizant of what is going on with everyone. It is difficult to remember how much you were never told. We just assume you will know, regardless."

Darcy leaned into her. "Let us begin things correctly. You should be included in discussions that impact you and your family. There is, after all, no hope that it can be kept from you."

His soft smile was too dear and the respect—oh, that was the look in his eyes! She gasped.

"You are no silly woman to be kept from serious matters. I value, and will continue to value, your good sense and judgment. We may not always agree, but I will always honor you in our household."

She swallowed hard and held his hand very tight. Perhaps if she held on tight enough, she might finally stop trembling.

Uncle cleared his throat.

"I shall arrange for tea—" Aunt stepped out.

"In my study, if you please." Uncle beckoned them to follow.

Uncle's study was a cheery, tidy room with street-facing windows on one wall and bookcases along the rest. Everything was just enough in order to imbue the room with tranquility, and not so much as to suggest a rigidity that left one feeling vaguely unwelcome.

Uncle pulled four lyre-back chairs and a small inlaid table into a cluster near the windows and gestured for them to sit. "Now, Mr. Darcy, why do you not begin for me at the beginning?"

Darcy colored and shifted in his seat. Clearly few men questioned him, and even fewer tradesmen dared to do so.

"I met Miss Elizabeth in my aunt, Lady Catherine's, drawing room." He took her hand and brought it to his lips.

To hear him tell it, she was every bit as lovely and angelic as Jane and far more interesting for her impertinent wit. Was that truly how he saw her?

Aunt herself brought in the tea tray with plates of biscuits and sandwiches.

"When I discovered what my aunt had done, I set out immediately to find her. But her friends were determined to protect her, even against me. It took me far longer to work out where she might be than I hoped. During that time, Miss Bennet accepted an invitation from my sister to join us until such time as she is married to my friend Bingley."

A gasp caught in Elizabeth's throat.

"Does that meet with your approval?"

Surely he knew that it did, but her watery-eyed nod seemed to delight him nonetheless.

"Then the storms kept me back—though I am grateful, for it permitted me to receive the news of Mr. Wickham and Miss Lydia."

"How much of Rosings' staff is aware—"

"Long Tom appears to have orchestrated everything, though he did not actually say as much …"

"He does communicate a great deal in what he does not say."

"I cannot be sure how many were directly involved, but everyone I saw below stairs was in an uproar. I made an offer to Michaels and he has accepted—"

"So Mary will—"

"Yes. I have a cottage set aside for my steward, and I think she will find it quite—"

"Eh-hem. Excuse me, but I do believe there are several more timely matters to deal with." Uncle drummed his fingers on the table. "What efforts have been made to recover either of Mr. Bennet's daughters?"

Elizabeth held her breath.

"I told Mr. Bennet that Miss Elizabeth had been lost on the road. He seemed shaken by the news, but expressed faith that my aunt—"

"So he has done nothing."

"I do not know that for a fact, sir, and I would not so disparage—"

"Stop. I do not need you defending that—"

"Mr. Gardiner." Aunt cleared her throat and flashed him a look that would stop a highwayman—or a pack of small children—in his tracks.

Uncle sighed. "And with regards to Lydia?"

So Papa had made no effort—demonstrated no concern she was missing? Elizabeth rose and wandered to the far corner near the bookcases, vaguely registering he had done hardly more on Lydia's behalf.

He did not care. Papa truly did not care. How long had she deceived herself?

"Are you well, Lizzy?" Aunt whispered, standing over her shoulder.

"I do not think so." What did one say when an empty spot opened up in one's belly and twisted in on itself until the knot grew so tight it might never come undone?

"Your father has always been a passive man. In truth, I never expected very much, but he has reached new lows. He will never be welcome in this house again."

Elizabeth sniffled. "I know you mean well, but—"

"But it changes nothing. Neither does it suddenly make him a good father."

A good father. Aunt was right, he had not been. Her knees buckled and she caught herself against the shelves, nearly knocking a heavy tome from the shelf.

He never had been all the things she had convinced herself he was.

"Did he ever care for any of us?"

Aunt held her shoulders. "I prefer to believe he did, though he surely did not know how to do it well."

"I insist, sir, whatever is to be done, whatever inconvenience is to be borne for her recovery, let it be mine." Darcy's voice rose just enough to be noteworthy.

Aunt and Elizabeth turned toward them.

"Where have you looked?" Uncle leaned his elbows on his knees.

"I believe your Mr. Darcy is much more like your uncle than your father. He is one whose actions will speak his care for you much more loudly than his words," Aunt whispered.

Darcy wore the same expression now that he did the night they had met, whilst he hovered over Georgiana. If anyone could find Lydia, he would be the one.

Over the next several days, Darcy did exactly as Aunt Gardiner predicted. Each morning, he visited to discuss his plans for locating Mr. Wickham. Each day was spent following through with those plans, sometimes with Uncle Gardiner's company, sometimes on his own. His own business probably suffered neglect, but he would not be deterred. Each evening, he returned to take dinner with them.

While Papa and Mama dismissed Uncle Gardiner as a tradesman, therefore below them in all things, Darcy did not. Clearly, the Gardiners had neither his wealth nor consequence, but he offered respect and courtesy at every turn. He was a gentleman in the truest sense of the word.

On the evening of the fifth day, they sat together in the parlor after dinner—the drawing room having been abandoned days earlier as too formal. The snug room with its comfortable furnishings and signs of life and family littered throughout fitted their time together so much better.

The children were brought in for their evening time together. Elizabeth joined her cousins on the couch, helping them with their samplers while Aunt played an old harpsicord. Darcy and Uncle Gardiner sat on the floor with the boys, marching tin soldiers across the carpet. One of the boys dragged a box of wooden blocks near. They began building a fort, with the two men debating the relative merits of moats and turrets in such serious tones, she bit her tongue not to laugh.

How Lady Catherine would rail! A gentleman did not do such undignified things. But the children took to Darcy in an inexplicable way, vying for his attention and edging each other out to be close to him. Odder still, once the initial panicked look faded from his countenance, he became easy in their presence and even invited their attentions.

How at home he seemed here, his smile easy and his posture relaxed. This was a side of him she had not encountered before. What a very different sort of father he would be.

He looked up at her, his gaze wandering to the little girls cuddled close to her. His eyes misted and his head bobbed in a tiny nod that he could hardly have been aware of. He approved—of her, of what she was doing, of her dearest relations—

A sharp rap echoed from the front door.

The housekeeper rushed in, tense lines etched beside her mouth, and whispered something to Aunt, who jumped to her feet. She hurried to Uncle and crouched to whisper in his ear.

His mien grew dark and stern. "Lizzy, take the children upstairs and help them to bed. Mr. Darcy, forgive me, but I must ask you to leave now, through the kitchen."

The kitchen? Why would he dismiss Darcy like a servant?

A chill that nearly froze her joints flooded through her. No! No! It could not be! Elizabeth fought to stand.

The boys began a protest, but Darcy took their hands. "You must help your sisters and do what your father says."

He followed Elizabeth to the stairs. "Do not fear. I trust him to protect you." He kissed her hand and dashed downstairs.

Elizabeth guided the children up two flights of stairs to the nursery. Their discomfiture forced her focus away from her own anxiety as she helped them undress and tucked them in to bed. She read them several stories, more than she ordinarily would, needing the comfort as much as they.

Only when the youngest two were fully asleep did she creep down a flight of stairs, to the bedroom level. Familiar, angry, voices rumbled up from the study.

His voice! Why had she bothered to hope it would not be him?

Her heart throbbed so loudly, she could not hear as she raced to her room and shut the door. She reached for the key.

*I trust him to protect you.*

Darcy had made a special point to tell her that. The key clicked in the lock and she clutched it tightly. Its hard, cold weight reminded her of Uncle's promises. She was not alone and friendless. It would not help matters to allow fear to overtake her. No, she must trust in those who truly loved her.

But fear was so much more familiar, so much easier. It had been a constant companion for so long, it seemed she had forgotten something when it was not by her side.

She curled up in the small chair near the window and listened. The waning moon cast a sliver of silvery light into her room, just enough to cast eerie shadows on her wall. With the study almost immediately below her, it was impossible not to hear the turmoil.

"What do you mean you do not know where she is?" Uncle Gardiner demanded in a tenor she had never heard from him before. Pray let him never find cause to use it upon her. "You entrusted her to that woman—"

"I did not—"

Oh, the look of offense Papa must be wearing; the one that generally accompanied his bristliest moods.

She tucked her knees under her chin and wrapped her arms around her legs lest she make a dash for the door. She did not need to soothe him. It was not her place.

Aunt Gardiner said it was time to allow him to feel the consequence of his choices. Had she any idea how difficult it was?

"What sort of father are you? You permitted her to take Lizzy."

"Enough, Gardiner! What was I to do?"

Uncle's heavy fist slammed into something very solid. "Damn it! Protect her! Is that not your duty?"

"I had no idea the foolish girl would run away."

Foolish? She screwed her eyes shut and held her sides until the knifing pain in her ribs faded. He called her foolish—is that truly all he thought of her?

"You blame Lizzy for this?"

"If she were not so headstrong—"

Headstrong too? All her efforts to understand him, anticipate him and make things easy for him, and she was headstrong? She hunched against the back of the chair and covered her face with her apron.

"I have heard enough, Bennet! Get out!"

"I need your help to find her … to find both of them." Papa sounded a bit defeated.

"Precisely why should I do that?"

"Who better to help but their flesh and blood?"

Uncle snorted. "You threw away Lizzy, and what connection is Lydia to me? Mrs. Bennet made it clear she does not deem Cheapside a suitable place for her daughters."

"Do not hold her biases against me."

"You did not choose to correct them."

"Then do not hold them against my daughters."

Heavy footfalls, that she felt as much as heard, echoed. Uncle Gardiner must be pacing. Papa's steps were always lighter.

"What has been done toward their recovery? It has been days, even with the foul weather—speak man, what have you done?"

"I … I … I spoke with Hurst and with those at the pub in town Wickham frequented." Papa only stammered when he was very, very agitated.

"In all this time, that is all?" Uncle probably threw his arms in the air—he always did that when flabbergasted.

"They were not very helpful, and I had patients to attend."

"And what of Lizzy?"

Elizabeth held her breath so as not to miss his answer. Surely he must have done something.

But none came.

"You have done nothing?"

"I trusted Lady Catherine—"

"Damn foolish move."

"I do not need your criticism. Besides, Lizzy needed to learn—"

"Learn what?"

"She disobeyed Lady Catherine. I could not risk the family on her willful—"

"Willful? Lizzy? She is the last person I would ever call willful. She is thoughtful, kind and caring beyond what you or your bloody patroness deserve."

Silence.

Papa could not agree with Uncle's assessment of her. No, to him she was merely foolish and headstrong. She balanced her forehead on her knees, throat tight and aching. Crying would probably make her feel better, but at long last, she had no tears left.

"I need my daughter back."

No, not his daughter. His servant, perhaps; his secretary; his maid; his not-apprentice who took on tasks that would sully a gentleman's hands; but not his daughter.

A soft scratch at the door drew her attention.

"Lizzy? Pray, let me in," Aunt Gardiner whispered.

Elizabeth unfurled from the chair and unlocked the door.

"I was afraid you would be able to hear them." Aunt sat on the bed and patted the spot beside her. The moonlight painted her face, highlighting the tight lines beside her eyes.

Elizabeth dropped down on the bed and hugged a pillow to her chest. "He came looking for me?"

"He came because he learned Mary wrote us and thought we might be of assistance in finding Lydia."

"Why did he believe you would know anything of Lydia's whereabouts?"

"Desperation, I suppose. He is clutching at straws to recover her and not lose Lady Catherine's favor. Apparently, the great lady was distressed at misplacing you. News of Lydia nearly threw her into apoplexy. She is most unhappy with the Bennet family at the moment."

"I am certain the only thing that bothered Lady Catherine was that her plans were thwarted. My loss would mean little to her."

"You may be right. In either case, it has put your father at our doorstep."

Elizabeth rubbed her eyes with the back of her hand. "Will Uncle help Papa find Lydia?"

"I expect he will wish to speak with Mr. Darcy first. He has, after all, already invested much in the search."

"He is a good man."

"Yes, the very best sort. Mr. Gardiner and I are pleased to welcome him into our family."

"Should I go down to Papa?"

"That is not for me to say."

"What would Uncle wish for?"

"To throw your father out on his arse like he has wanted to for years." Aunt's lips twisted in wry smile. "Forgive me dear, you did ask."

Elizabeth giggled. "I suppose I did. Do you think he will call again?"

"I have no way of knowing for certain, but I expect he will. He is more likely to persist in demanding help than in any search effort."

"Then perhaps I shall not tonight. I do not think I have the strength to encounter him."

"My dear, as far as your uncle and I are concerned, you need never confront him again. You are one and twenty. He cannot compel you back to his home."

"He said he wants me back."

"I heard him say that too, but I do not consider you so shatter-brained as to take such a statement at face value. Look at me."

Hers was a tone of voice that brooked no disobedience. No wonder her children were so well-behaved.

"I have no doubt you have considered what your father truly wants and are only waiting for permission to accept it. You have permission. Do not allow what you want to believe of your father to color what you see is actually there."

"But am I not to honor my father?"

"Does it honor him to believe lies about him?

"Is it wrong to hope there is good?"

"Misplaced hope is a dangerous thing and only puts you in the way of being further disappointed in him."

"But I want him to be ..." She crushed the pillow to her stomach. How ironic that she could not even say it.

"I know my dear, but often, we do not get what we want."

Uncle roused them all early the following morning to call upon Darcy. No one could predict when Papa might return, and Darcy deserved to be informed of the events of the previous evening. They climbed into Uncle Gardiner's modest carriage far earlier than polite calling hours, but this visit would not be strictly polite.

Elizabeth would rather have sat in the box with Uncle Gardiner, but the impropriety would be too much. After driving herself so often in Kent, her hands itched for the reins, or at least an open air view of the road. Aunt Gardiner tried to distract her with conversation, but their talk always returned to the same, uneasy topics until they neared Darcy's house.

Though Gracechurch Street was a pleasant situation, it was nothing compared to the street that held Darcy House. The place was quite grand—a large first-rate home in the center of the block of townhouses flanked with elegant ironwork and sporting fresh paint. The Gardiners' home looked almost shabby by comparison.

What would Darcy think if he saw the run-down second rate home she and her family had occupied during their tenure in London?

The housekeeper let them in immediately, not even asking for a card. Darcy must have told her they were welcome at any time. Dear, dear man.

Darcy met them in the grand front hall, his boots echoing on the marble tiles. "What is wrong?"

Uncle Gardiner snorted. "Must there be something wrong for us to call?"

"Certainly not." He reached for Elizabeth's hand and drew her closer. "But I know your look too well. There is something wrong."

Uncle grumbled as he unbuttoned his coat. "I imagine you already suspect what happened last night."

The housekeeper took Uncle's coat and Aunt's wrap.

Darcy helped Elizabeth off with her spencer.

"Yes, and I have not had an hour of sleep for it. Come."

He led them down the corridor into his study. Fresh, ivory paint and several mirrors made the space bright and open and bespoke a simple, elegant taste. How well it suited him.

Darcy's study smelt of books and leather and of him. A huge mahogany desk resided near the window, looking like it had been birthed in that very spot. Not far from it, a small writing desk nestled between the large desk and the bookcase. The marks on the carpet told the path it had been dragged and confirmed it as a new addition. Delicate lines and graceful carving on the legs lent a feminine air in the very masculine room.

"A man after my own heart." Uncle sat near the desk. "One can never have enough books."

Darcy pulled a chair from behind the writing desk and gestured for Elizabeth to sit. He nodded toward the desk and lifted his eyebrows. "Is it to your liking?" he whispered.

She ran her hand along the finely carved edge. "Yes … very much."

His eyes twinkled, but turned dark and serious as he pulled a chair close to her and sat. "What happened last night?"

"Bennet came. He wants help finding his daughter."

"Daughters." Aunt cleared her throat.

"Hardly. He needs to find Lydia to secure his position in Kent. He might like to find Lizzy, if it is convenient, but he is hardly engaging in the effort."

Darcy dropped to one knee beside Elizabeth and enclosed her hands in his.

"I did not see him myself." She turned away from his searching gaze.

"But you heard his bluster."

Apparently, he already had seen enough.

"I heard much of what Papa had to say."

He pressed his forehead to her hands. "I am so sorry. I can only imagine what vitriol spewed from his mouth."

"It is nothing I have not heard before." The words cut her throat almost as deeply as Papa's words cut her heart.

"You think that makes this better? You should never have been subjected to such abuse in the first place."

"It does not signify."

He cocked his head and his eyes narrowed. "You are a very bad liar."

He was the only one who had ever forced his way through her façade. How naked—and safe—he made her feel.

Aunt coughed. "The question now, I believe, is how shall we proceed?"

"Given that casting him out of London entirely is not within the realm of possibility—"

"Uncle, please!"

"Pray forgive us, Mr. Darcy. As you may imagine, there has been a tension in the family since the death of our dear sister." Aunt shot Uncle a glare usually reserved for the children.

Darcy squeezed Elizabeth's hands and returned to his seat. "How much stock do you place in his efforts to recover Miss Lydia?"

"Little to none."

"Just as well." Darcy reached into his pocket. "I might have news of her." He handed Uncle a folded paper. "While not my first choice, I have availed myself of some of Fitzwilliam's old army connections. They are often in the way of useful bits of information."

"In exchange for a bit of blunt, no doubt." Uncle harrumphed.

Elizabeth gasped. "How much?"

"It is of no matter, and I have no wish to speak of it again." Darcy raised an open hand.

"But it is not right for you to bear—"

"Shall I remind you of the service you did my sister on many occasions, not the least of which was opening her eyes to Wickham's character?"

"But that was not—"

"It was a favor I shall repay in kind; doubly glad because I may serve you by it."

They stared at one another until Aunt Gardiner coughed. "You said there was news?"

"Ah…yes. I had planned to investigate today. While I do not know for certain, there is a man who claims to have seen Wickham at cards recently. He says Wickham won, which usually means he will stay for some time. Generally, he flees when his gaming debts mount. There is an inn …"

"If you give us the direction, my wife and I will go there directly," Uncle said.

"I had thought to go myself."

"Lydia can be very headstrong. I believe I may have a better chance of persuading her to leave with us than either of you gentlemen." Aunt Gardiner turned to Elizabeth. "I prefer you do not join us. I fear she would only be distracted by your presence, Lizzy."

"What am I to do then?"

"Stay here with Mr. Darcy. Wait for us where we know you will be safe from your father." Uncle nodded at Darcy.

"I would be pleased for you to stay here. I might show you about your future home and make note of what you may wish to change. Your rooms, in particular."

"My rooms?" She blinked and glanced about the room. He had already welcomed her into his sanctum. This would be her home.

He laughed softly. "The thought had not occurred to you?"

"I…ah, no. I have not actually given it a great deal of thought." A hot blush crept along her cheeks.

Aunt chuckled. "I think it a very reasonable plan. I am sure you have much to discuss with the…eh…housekeeper."

Uncle rose and bowed from his shoulders. "We will return as soon as possible."

The Gardiners left without so much as a backward glance. Great heavens, he was alone with her!

The housekeeper peeked in. "Tea, sir?"

"Yes, in the drawing room—no, the parlor, and instruct the staff to wait until they are called. We are not to be disturbed."

"Yes, sir."

He placed his hand on the small of Elizabeth's back and guided her to the rear of the house. "My mother loved this room. I think you will find it to your liking as well."

Only family—and not all the family—received invitations to the parlor. His mother had decorated it in her own eclectic manner, definitely not according to fashionable tastes. She insisted that was what the drawing room was for. There, professionals had been consulted and opinion of society considered. But the parlor was for comfortable furnishings and the décor was chosen to please none but herself. Aunt Catherine pronounced it shabby. Lady Matlock called it quaint. In his eyes, it was perfect.

The room held her presence and treasured memories: the portrait of Lady Anne and her children over the fire place; the curtains in which he had hidden from his governess; the shelf with his favorite childhood books; and the ink stain on the carpet from when he jostled his mother's writing desk whilst she wrote a letter, now carefully hidden by an oddly placed foot stool. If anyone could appreciate this room properly, it would be Elizabeth.

He took her on a slow tour about the parlor, pointing out the odd trinkets and bits that turned up in the most unexpected of places. She asked for, and he obliged to tell, the stories attached to each item, some of them even Georgiana did not know.

She caressed a tattered, stuffed horse and replaced it on the shelf. "I think my chances of being happy in a family that treasures old tin soldiers and baby house chairs alongside a truly magical kaleidoscope and schoolgirl's sampler are very great indeed."

"Others have looked at these bits and baubles and muttered strained politenesses about them. But, I know you look at them and see the heart of the Darcy family as no one ever has." He returned a tin soldier to its post. "I wonder what we shall add to this collection."

She went to the open window and leaned into a sunbeam. "Your garden is lovely."

"It is nothing compared to you." He moved to her side. "You like the peonies?"

"I like everything I see. Everything is so well cared for and in order." She turned to him. "I think it is very much like you."

"I suppose it is." How did she do it, know him so well without ever once prying? "I hope you do not find it dull and predictable."

"You have been criticized for that."

There was no question in her voice, just a statement of fact.

"I expect by your cousin, Fitzwilliam, who I doubt has spent a great deal of time in this room. Dare I posit, he finds you tiresome and informed you that the most desirable ladies prefer a gentleman who can recite poetry as though he had written it for their pleasure whilst inspired by their beauty?" She dangled her fingers in the fringe along the edge of the curtain.

He chuckled. "How do you do it?"

"So I am correct?"

"Of course. But I no longer care what Fitzwilliam or his desirable ladies fancy. I only care what you prefer." He edged behind her, nestling his chest against the warmth of her back.

She leaned into him.

Thank heavens, he had said something right!

He slid his arm around her waist and pressed his cheek to the side of her face. Was he taking advantage of their privacy? Perhaps, but she would surely tell him if it was too much.

"You asked what I prefer." She rotated in his embrace and peered directly into his eyes. "I do not need poetry or flowery words. I do not need, nor do I want, surprises or excitement. They are entirely overrated. You are dependable and trustworthy, thoughtful and sensitive, and that is everything I have ever desired."

What was a man to do upon hearing such words? Only one thing came to mind.

She answered his kiss tentatively, but she answered. His dear, precious treasure!

The warmth of her lips on his, that he expected, but the heat coursing down his spine and suffusing into his being caught him unawares.

"You were not certain I would be pleased?" She pulled back and looked at him with her fine, probing eyes.

"I suppose no man ever is."

"Then I must be absolutely clear." She rose on tiptoes and wrapped her arms around his neck.

Every baser feeling and every finer one welled up and collided in his chest, exploding in an effusion of light and fire. He wanted her in every way possible, to possess and to protect, to ravish and to honor. He crushed her to him and devoured her kiss.

She met him with a fervor that matched his own, dainty fingers knotting in his hair. Her soft bosom pressed against the planes of his chest.

Dear Lord, what she did to him!

A soft knock at the door and they jumped apart. He stalked to the door. Should he sack or reward whoever stood behind it?

The housekeeper handed him a tea tray and walked away, making no attempt to peep inside. A reward was in order, indeed.

He kicked the door shut and turned back to her. She had moved away from the window, into the shadows of the corner by the bookcases, face hidden in the shadows.

The tea tray could not land fast enough.

"Elizabeth ... Elizabeth." He panted beside her, hand hovering over her shoulder. "Have I frightened you? Shall I open the door, ask a maid in to chaperone? I would not for all the world have —"

"No, not at all." She turned to him, uncertainty in all its forms written in every crease on her face. "Does it not trouble you that I am willing to be so improper?"

"Why do you keep asking me to criticize you, showing me fault to find in you? You ask for my disapproval as fervently as that Bingley woman demands praise. I cannot fathom it."

She distanced herself, arms wrapped around her waist and walked along the bookcase toward the fireplace.

---

Dare she try and answer his question? Could she expose such a very deep and intimate truth, something not even Jane comprehended? Surely it would be better not to, to leave the subject alone. Why ask for the heartbreak that would surely follow when he did not understand—or worse, he pretended to, but only grasped it in shallow, banal concepts?

Fingertips brushed her shoulder. "Elizabeth?"

He was there, so close beside her, almost whispering in her ear. His warmth, his scent, all called to her, demanding her honesty.

She turned her back to him. These were not things to be said whilst he could see her face. No, that intimacy was far too much. "I doubt you will understand. It is foolish, I suppose."

"More criticism? Why do you not let me be the judge of what I will call foolish?"

Why did he have to be so persistent? Could he not allow her this? "When one knows fault will be found with them, it is … more manageable if one—"

"Offers up what is to be criticized, like a sacrifice? It is less painful than having it torn from you?"

She spun and sought his eyes. "How?"

"My father was an exacting, demanding man, better at offering correction than care. He had many fine qualities, but …"

"Understanding was not among them?" She laid her palm against his cheek. "I had no idea."

"You need not be so concerned. Though he could be difficult to please, he was a good man." He pulled her into his chest.

His heart beat so loud, so strong. The rhythm reassured and comforted her as his strength encompassed her.

"I do not want such a sacrifice from you, Elizabeth. Pray, stop and let me not listen to anyone criticizing my beloved, even you."

She nodded against his chest.

In a single motion, his lips met hers, so warm and demanding, hungry. She surrendered into him and allowed her passion to flow, unchecked. Oh, that spot on her neck—how could he know what she herself did not? He kindled a craving for something she could not even name? If only he might never stop, holding, touching, kissing her.

He pulled back, panting, and rested his forehead on hers. "No woman has ever brought me to the edge of self-control as you have. You are the completion of everything I am, and I want it all so badly I can taste it. But you have had far too much taken from you. Though you might even give me what I most dearly desire now, we cannot begin our lives together that way. You are worthy of every respect, of everything right and proper. Though it may kill me, we shall wait."

The strain in his eyes was too real for his words to be hollow.

So, this was what it meant to be truly loved. Tears trickled down her cheeks.

"I love you and will spend the rest of my days making sure you know that. Trust me."

"I do."

Late in the day, the Gardiners trudged into Darcy's study. Though well-lit with candles and mirrors, their flames did nothing to brighten their weary visages.

"We found Lydia in an unsavory inn." Uncle Gardiner fell into a leather wingback that groaned under his weight.

Aunt leaned on the back of his chair as though she could bear the weight on her shoulders no longer.

Elizabeth covered her eyes. "Completely unaware and unconcerned with the nature of her surroundings."

"Sadly so." Uncle exhaled heavily.

Darcy pulled a chair out for her and Aunt Gardiner sat beside Uncle. "You can surmise it all easily enough. She refused to return with us."

"Great heavens." Elizabeth's knees faltered and she clutched the edge of Darcy's desk. "She refused?"

Uncle bounced his fists off the chair arm. "She said I was—oh, how did she put it—wholly unconnected to her or some such rot. No, it was that I was no relation to her. That was it—and as such, had no place to tell her what to do."

"Stupid, foolish girl!" How entirely like Lydia to stare salvation in the face and declare it a trespasser.

"What of Wickham?" Darcy's voice turned feral.

Uncle sniffed and rolled his eyes. "He sat there, reminding us she joined him of her own accord, and we could not accuse him of kidnapping. As neither of us were relations to her, we could not force her to come with us."

Darcy turned his back to her and he stalked across the room.

Did he think he could hide so easily from her? The weight of his steps, the carriage of his shoulders, even the pace of his breath all spoke far more loudly than she might ignore.

Elizabeth hurried to his side. "You think this somehow your fault?"

He knotted his hands in the back of his hair. "In Kent, I…we…"

"You confronted him and told him to leave not only Kent, but Pemberley as well, and preferably Derbyshire? Perhaps you went so far as to threaten to expose his character—"

His jaw jutted forward, and he nodded once. "This is his revenge upon me. This is—"

She pressed her face close to his. "Do not dare say it—this is nothing of your fault—nothing. You gave him a convenient opportunity, nothing more."

"I hardly think—"

"Consider the way he carried on with Lydia. I have no doubt they would have run off within a few weeks."

"Dare I ask how do you come to that conclusion?"

"A man like him would surely recognize the connection between your family, you and Lady Catherine, and mine. Families like yours prefer to stay out of the scandal sheets, making an ideal target for extortion. Meddling with Lydia and threatening exposure could induce you or your aunt to pay to cover the indiscretion, lest your family be tainted by association."

He slapped his forehead and muttered thinly veiled invectives. "Fitzwilliam would call me a fool for not anticipating that."

"I believe Mr. Wickham saw another, even easier opportunity at hand."

Darcy clutched his temples and grumbled. "And what might that have been?"

"He brought Lady Catherine intelligence of your offer of marriage to me and received a handsome reward for his services."

"Lizzy, how can you suggest—" Aunt Gardiner seemed genuinely shocked.

"Quite easily." She threw up her hands and paced across the room. "Consider, where is he getting funds for all his gaming? To pay for a coach to London? As I understood, his circumstances were modest at best."

A strangled groan died in Darcy's throat.

Elizabeth touched his shoulder. "All this rests on … on Papa and Lady Catherine, not you."

"She is right, Darcy." Uncle rose to his feet. "He could, and more importantly should, have stopped it. He needs to feel the burden of this and by God he will." He slammed a fist into his palm. "I will tell him where his bloody daughter is and leave him to deal with it. I wash my hands of the entire sordid affair."

"Pray forgive me, but I cannot allow this matter to rest. There are ways we may yet work on him, and I cannot simply walk away from this affair." Darcy returned to his desk, Elizabeth matching him stride for stride.

"One can hardly say you have not done enough." Aunt Gardiner said softly. "Indeed, one might even say you have done too much. Mr. Bennet will probably never say so, but we are grateful for everything you have done."

"Still, the thing seems undone to me. Pray allow me just one attempt to recover her. I must make that much effort on her behalf." Darcy took Elizabeth's hands in his and brought them to his lips

She pressed her forehead to his. "How can I deny you anything? Just promise me, you will allow me to help."

He caressed her cheek. "Is that not what my helpmeet is for?"

Papa called the early next morning, demanding to see Uncle Gardiner. Elizabeth kept to the nursery, to her young cousins' delight. She read them stories, voicing characters as she did for Miss de Bourgh. Their squeals and laughs obscured the sound of Papa's voice. Once or twice she almost forgot he was downstairs.

Almost.

Even after he departed, the specter of his appearance left her flinching and looking over her shoulder the remainder of the day. Worse still, Darcy sent a servant bearing word that he would not call upon them that day at all.

What a cruel punishment to bear on the heels of Papa's visit. Aunt Gardiner maintained his absence only spoke of his efforts in recovering Lydia and nothing more. No doubt she was correct, but one and twenty years of disappointments and forgotten promises made even the smallest unexpected turn a significant blow.

Yet the dainty writing desk in Darcy's study was unexpected as well. Should it not speak as eloquently? Not a clerk's desk that spoke of toil, or a spare piece of casegoods purloined from another room in the house, but a graceful, feminine escritoire that she might have selected for herself. He selected it for her, placed it near him, in his sanctuary, a silent testament to his desire to have her near. Yes, that act spoke loudly, and she must listen carefully to its message.

The following sunrise, bright and warm, felt a little better. Sunshine had a way of making things appear less awful. Tea and fresh buns in the morning room and sewing side by side with Aunt reminded her of such times with Jane. For a few moments, life felt almost normal.

The sharp, masculine rap of the knocker snuffed the feeling like a candle flame. Elizabeth poised to bolt. She held her breath, waiting for the caller to announce himself.

"Is Miss Elizabeth available?"

Darcy!

She dashed into the front hall.

The housekeeper waggled her eyebrows and grinned. "Shall I bring coffee to the parlor, Miss?"

Darcy shook his head.

"I think not. Let Aunt Gardiner know Mr. Darcy is here."

The housekeeper curtseyed and shuffled off.

Darcy offered his arm and they strolled to the parlor.

"I missed you yesterday," he whispered, though there was no one near to hear. His voice had that furry-rumbly note that made her knees weak.

"And I you."

"I carry pleasing news though."

"I am pleased enough that you are here." She leaned her head against his shoulder. "You need bring nothing else."

"You are indeed easy to please. Perhaps too easy. You will spoil me to be sure." He pressed his cheek against the top of her head.

She sat with him on the couch. A gentle breeze wafted through the window, fluttering the curtains at them.

"I still would like to hear your news."

"Actually there are two things of which I need to speak to you."

"Then tell me both."

"I expect the arrival of a party from Kent today. Mr. Bingley is bringing Georgiana and Miss Bennet."

She gasped. "Jane will be here, today?"

"Indeed. Perhaps, after the day's business is accomplished, you might join me at Darcy House."

"That would be wonderful! I long to see her and Miss Darcy."

"Do you think it possible that the Gardiners might permit you to stay with us?"

Aunt Gardiner cleared her throat from the doorway. "Elizabeth stay at Darcy House?"

"With my sister and Miss Bennet, madam." Darcy rose and bowed. "I thought that with Mr. Bennet about, you would not wish for Miss Bennet to come here. Especially in light of the other intelligence I bear."

"And what would that be, sir?" Aunt pulled a small lyre-backed chair close to the couch.

"I have made arrangements for Miss Lydia's recovery."

Darcy's coach was plush, well sprung and did not reek of Lady Catherine. The buttery leather smelled of him and of safety. Elizabeth pressed close to him, his shoulder strong and comforting.

No, she should not be riding in it alone with him, much less sitting beside him. But the curtains were closed, and Aunt Gardiner had agreed to Darcy's plan: when they reached the Tower Green, he would leave the coach at one corner, she at another. After they met again, Lydia should be with them, and they could openly ride together to the Gardiners.

If everything went well … but so many things might not. What if … no, such thoughts were not helpful now. Her heart raced painfully.

The coach rolled to a stop, and the groom opened the door.

Darcy took her hands. "Promise me, you will allow my man to stay with you,"

"I am not accustomed to being accompanied."

"You are used to being neglected, and I cannot abide by that any longer."

She swallowed hard. "I shall find a way to inure myself to it."

He kissed her hands. "Thank you."

The door shut behind him and the coach trundled off again. The wheels crunched along the road, counterpointed by the clop of horse shoes.

The carriage turned a corner and stopped.

"Miss?" The groom poked his head in and handed her out.

A path lined with tall bushes, reminiscent of her beloved hedgerows beckoned. Surrounded by green, she could almost quiet her soul enough to think. But, she was not here for contemplation—perhaps another time. For now, she must focus.

She followed the path through several meandering bends. The groom shadowed her, several steps behind. That would take some getting used to.

A flash of red caught her eye—a couple walking. His jaunty step felt far too familiar, as was the girl's fawning clutch on his arm.

Wickham and Lydia.

She ducked into the bushes and hid in a particularly dense clump of something or other. It did not matter what, though she really ought to be able to remember the name!

She peeked around a thick trunk. They continued their approach.

"Why are we here at such an unfashionable hour, my love?" Lydia whined.

"Because, my dear, I have some business to conduct."

"But why bring me? You know I care not a jot for such things."

"Be patient. It is not my preference to bring you into such matters, but I had little choice."

"I do not understand."

"Hush," he hissed. "Ahh, Darcy."

Elizabeth clutched a low hanging branch. She must not run out to meet him, not yet.

"I have brought her, as you asked." Wickham's voice sent chills down her spine, or was that merely the sharp breeze that rustled the branch she clung to?

"Why did you want me here? What have you to do with any of us?"

"I needed to see that you were well, Miss Lydia. The Gardiners—"

"I told them already that I have no wish to leave my dearest Wickham. I will not change my mind."

Lydia tossed her head and stomped her foot, her red cloak swishing around her.

"I do not expect to change your mind, Miss Lydia. However, Mr. Wickham might."

Lydia snorted. "We are to be married."

"I understand you believe so." Darcy spoke to her in the same tolerant tones he used with his own sister.

He considered her family as his own, even now! Dear, sweet man.

"Did you bring it?" Wickham asked.

Lydia pulled at his arm. "Bring what?"

"I do not carry any blunt."

"Why would Mr. Darcy bring money?"

Darcy tugged his shirt cuffs straight and planted his feet hard in the gravel path. "As a bribe. He demands to be paid off in order to marry you."

"What?" Lydia plucked at Wickham's lapel. "But my love, you will have my dowry."

"Which is only one thousand pounds." Wickham scraped her hand from his arm.

"Is that not sufficient?"

"Silly girl, do you know how little a thousand pounds supplies?"

Darcy stepped a little closer. "Certainly not life in the style to which either of you are accustomed."

"I need ten thousand pounds for that." Wickham crossed his arms. A self-sure, arrogant smile lit his features.

"Ten thousand." Lydia giggled. "Mr. Darcy is going to give us ten thousand pounds? What a wonderful gift. We shall be so—"

"No, he is not." Elizabeth crashed through the dense bushes, sharp limbs pulling at her skirts. She stumbled, and Darcy caught her elbow. She was not supposed to expose herself so soon, but one more stupid word from Lydia, and she might well do herself an injury.

Lydia gasped. "Lizzy! You have been here in London all this time?"

"He is not giving you any money. He is not giving you anything!" Elizabeth braced her fists on her hips and glared.

Darcy's eyebrows twitched and the tiniest of dimples appeared in his cheek only to disappear a moment later. "I see you paid close attention to Aunt Catherine's technique," he whispered, lips not moving.

So, Colonel Fitzwilliam had taught him that trick. They would have to talk more about that later.

"What business is it of yours, Lizzy? If he wants to give us money, who are you—"

"My betrothed." Darcy placed her hand in the crook of his elbow and pulled her so close she felt his warmth though her spencer.

"All the more reason for a gift then, for we shall be brother and sister." Lydia grinned, an expression that all but demanded to be slapped off her face.

Perhaps this time Elizabeth would do it.

"You say, for ten thousand you will marry her?" Darcy held Elizabeth's hand to his arm, as though to reassure her he would not deviate from his stated intentions.

Even knowing what he had in mind, she bit her tongue so hard tears stung her eyes.

"A bank draught in that amount will settle the matter and even see that we stand up in a proper church." Wickham winked, though tiny beads of sweat formed along his brow.

"Ohh, I shall have my sisters for bridesmaids. They all will be so jealous!"

"And if I do not produce such a bank draught?"

Wickham blinked. "You would not dare. You value your family's reputation far too much."

"So you will not marry her without a bribe?"

The temperature dropped. Elizabeth looked for clouds, but the sky remained clear.

"Bribe?" Lydia's eyes grew wide, as though she had not heard it the first time he used the word.

"That is what you call paying someone to do which they would otherwise refuse." Only the tension in Darcy's arm beneath Elizabeth's fingers revealed the depth of his anger.

Lydia clutched at Wickham, pulling him to her. "Refuse! What nonsense! We are in love."

"Even a couple in love must have something to live on, my dear." The endearment sounded more like a curse on Wickham's tongue.

"What did Mr. Darcy mean that you will not—"

Wickham dragged Lydia, squealing, a step closer to Darcy. "Seven thousand, Darcy. That, with the dowry, will be sufficient."

"I think not."

Darcy demonstrated every strength, every determination Papa lacked. She pressed her lips hard to hold back her smile.

"What do you mean, 'You think not?' She has been entirely and wholly compromised. You cannot take her back."

"You said we would marry!" Lydia blanched and wavered. She might just swoon—for real, not just as a ploy to receive attention.

"You want her, take her." Wickham shoved her toward Darcy.

Elizabeth barely caught her as her feet caught in the loose gravel. Lydia sputtered and collapsed in Elizabeth's arms.

"Enjoy your damaged goods. Whilst I tell everyone of the fine romp I had with your sister."

"I think not." Darcy jerked his head.

Four ruffians and Colonel Fitzwilliam appeared out of the thick bushes and shadows. Wickham made to run. Fitzwilliam caught his arms before he took three steps.

The colonel's movements were so economical, she barely recognized what had happened, his countenance so dark and savage, she shrank back.

"No, you have travel plans, Wickham." Colonel Fitzwilliam twisted Wickham's arm hard behind his back.

Wickham winced as he was forced up on his toes.

"You shall come with me and discuss the exact details. I can present you with two alternatives, depending on just how much talking you insist upon." He passed Wickham into the hands of two of his associates and turned to Elizabeth and bowed. "Pray, accept my deepest apologies for my aunt's actions. I hope this small service is a token of my sincerity."

"Thank you," she stammered.

Fitzwilliam trundled Wickham away. They stared after them until the men disappeared around a corner.

Darcy came to her side and held her shoulders, sheltering her with his body. "Your father should be at Gracechurch Street by now. I will return Lydia to him. You need not confront him yourself."

His warmth penetrated her soul; his strength suffused her being. She was not the woman who left Kent … and that was a very good thing indeed.

"No, I think it is time I face him."

"You do not have to do it alone. Neither Gardiner nor I—"

She brushed his lips with her finger. "I know, and I am grateful. I am ready for this."

"I will support you then. I have no doubts as to your capability."

"Let us go and be done with it." She squared her shoulders.

They conducted Lydia to Darcy's nearby carriage.

He handed Lydia in. "I will sit on the box. Perhaps she will talk to you."

Perhaps.

At the very least, she might observe Lydia and learn as much or even more than a conversation would tell. Lydia huddled in her seat, pulling her cloak tight around her. The coach rocked as Darcy climbed onto the box.

Elizabeth settled into the facing seat and arranged her skirts. "Did he buy that for you? I remember you asking Papa for one."

"Yes. Papa said it was an extravagance we could not afford." Lydia dabbed her eyes with the edge of her hood.

"That was not the only thing you liked about Wickham?"

"He…I…we…we were to be married!" She dissolved into a fit of hysteria fit for a gothic heroine. "He said he loved me."

The tears were real, even if the histrionics were overdone. Lydia fancied herself in love. Poor dear, for all her foolishness, she had been well and truly deceived. Wickham's cruel dismissal must have broken her heart.

Elizabeth slid the side glass open. A bit of fresh air would do them both good. Lydia disconsolate was a difficult creature to manage. If past experience were any guide, her petulance and stubbornness would be high and her complacency and repentance low. But, this problem of Papa's would not be dropped so neatly in her lap for remedy.

Not this time.

Never again.

She pinched the bridge of her nose. Willow bark, she needed willow bark tea before her headache made it impossible for her to concentrate. Could she just hide at Darcy House for the duration? The longer she watched Lydia mutter and snivel, the greater the appeal the idea held.

The coach slowed and stopped before the Gardiners' house.

Lydia, more irate than recalcitrant, refused Darcy's help from the carriage and marched up the steps herself.

Darcy helped Elizabeth down.

"Thank you for everything," she whispered. "I fear my sister—and likely my father—will never say it, but thank you."

"I did it for you, not them, so their thanks are of little matter." He laced his fingers in hers and brought them to his lips. "I cannot tell you how pleased I am to do something to hasten your father's departure from London and our lives."

"I am relieved she is found, but cannot bring myself to hope Papa's withdrawal will be so simple." She chewed the inside of her cheek.

No, Papa always managed to complicate things when it was most inconvenient he do so.

"Trust me. We shall be finished with this soon." He squeezed her hand and escorted her to the door.

The housekeeper ushered them inside. Darcy strode in, calling for Uncle Gardiner.

In a flurry faster than the eye could follow, the front hall was filled with agitated speeches and irate people, stomping and elbowing for access.

"Lydia." Uncle Gardiner caught her arms.

"Elizabeth!" Papa stomped toward her, florid and sweat beading on his forehead.

She jumped back out of his reach. Papa was beyond angry—there was no name for the frightful passion on his face. Dreadful did not begin to capture the magnitude of his displeasure.

Darcy stepped between them. She clutched his arm, drawing on his strength to stand in the face of Papa's fury. She would do this.

"Move aside." Papa's voice was soft and measured and dangerous. He expected capitulation and would brook no disobedience.

"I think not." Darcy matched Papa's force with the same tempered power he exerted with Wickham.

Papa tried to dart around Darcy but found himself cut off three times. Finally, he managed to crane his head past Darcy's broad shoulders. "What the devil are you doing here, Lizzy?"

Who was Papa to the Gardiners and Darcy? She would not falter now, not in the presence of such support.

"What matter is it to you? You did not care when I left. Why should it matter whether I am here in London or prisoner in some isolated farmhouse put upon by—"

"I will not tolerate your insolence!"

"If you wish respect, then you shall first offer it." She trembled as a dam within ruptured and far too many unsaid words surged to the surface.

"Pray, everyone to the drawing room." Aunt clapped sharply and stillness fell over the crowded front hall. "Move along, all of you."

She ushered everyone along and closed the door behind them. Elizabeth lingered back with Darcy, putting as much distance between herself and Papa as possible.

"Now, sit. Lydia, with your father, there." Aunt gestured to a pair of lacquered armchairs.

"You—" she pointed to Elizabeth and Darcy, "there."

They sat on the two chair-back settee. Elizabeth clasped her hands in her lap and studied the gold and ivory striped upholstery. If she held them tightly enough, perhaps Papa would not see her quiver. Surely he would think it a sign of her soon coming repentance when nothing could be more untrue.

Uncle stood near the fireplace. Aunt joined him.

"Now, let us discuss this matter as befits civilized beings." Uncle glowered at Lydia and Papa.

"It is their fault." Lydia pointed at Elizabeth and Darcy.

"You will speak when you are spoken to and not before," Uncle snapped.

Lydia huddled into the chair.

That should not be so satisfying a sight.

Uncle lowered himself into his mahogany and dark leather council chair, just reminiscent enough of Lady Catherine's throne to give him precedence in the room. "Now, Bennet, your wayward daughter is returned, what have you to say?"

Papa braced his elbows on the chair's arms. "What is Lizzy doing here? You knew I sought her, and yet you deliberately hid her presence?"

"Do not blame them. I did not desire to be found." Elizabeth straightened her spine and dug her heels into the carpet. "After the utter disregard—"

"That is not how you speak to your father." He sprang up and stomped toward her.

Darcy jumped up and intercepted him. "She is my betrothed. You best consider your words carefully."

"You?" Papa whirled on him. "How dare you interfere in my family? I have not condoned your match, nor will I. Lady Catherine has forbidden it and apart from her approval—"

"I am one and twenty. I do not need your approval." Elizabeth rose slowly and took Darcy's outstretched hand. "You abandoned me, refused to protect me—"

"From what did you need protection? Lady Catherine would have cared for you. How did you get here?"

"It does not signify." Elizabeth forced her lips into a smile which meant anything but pleasure, something Papa would never recognize.

"I asked you a question."

"One I do not choose to answer. Sir."

Papa's eyes bulged and he sputtered.

Oh, he did not like that answer, not at all. How unfortunate for him.

Elizabeth rose on her toes to look him directly in the eye. "Suffice to say, though I have no illustrious patroness, I am not entirely friendless."

"No, she is not," Uncle said.

Papa's face turned a remarkable color, one probably not considered healthy. "You do not understand my position."

"Yes, I do. I just do not respect it." Uncle joined Darcy in the middle of the room. "You chose the easy road, not the admirable one, as you always have. I am ashamed to ever have called you brother."

Papa glared back, or at least he tried to. His resolve failed, and he shrank back to Lydia's side. "What am I to do with her? Lady Catherine demands I am not to return unless she is properly married."

Lydia jumped up. "He would have married me, but Lizzy—"

"He demanded ten thousand pounds to marry her. Perhaps you are in a position to pay his demands? You are most welcome to, but I shall not." Darcy's even tone did not waver.

"Lizzy told him not to do it. It is her fault I am—"

"Hush, girl. You were the one who treated that scoundrel to both ends of the busk." Uncle crossed his arms and scowled, an expression every bit as effective as Aunt's.

Elizabeth gasped and snickered. The language she had heard before, but not from so proper a man as Uncle Gardiner.

The veins in Papa's forehead throbbed. "They must be made to marry. How else can I resume my service to Lady Catherine?"

"That is none of my concern." Darcy brushed invisible dust from his hands. "Wickham will soon be on a ship for the West Indies where I have interests to keep him gainfully employed and a satisfactory distance from my family."

"The West Indies?" Lydia sobbed. "How could you do this to me?"

"I would not subject anyone to a union with a man like Wickham."

"Then what am I to do with her? I cannot bring her back in her … her condition, or Lady Catherine will dismiss me."

"My condition? What is wrong with my condition?" Lydia shrieked.

"Be quiet, girl! We do not need your lip. Perhaps …" Papa looked at Uncle.

"No, we will not take her. Have you forgotten? Mrs. Bennet is no relation to us and declared Cheapside too mean a setting for her daughters."

"More importantly, she is not a fitting model for our daughters, and our first responsibility is to them." Aunt cast a sharp look at Lydia.

"You took Lizzy."

Something inside her shattered into tiny shards and rained down upon the carpeting.

"I am not a fitting model? I—the one who has served and obeyed you at every turn? Who endured with good nature and equanimity Lady Harridan invading my trunks and closets? Not even Mama tolerated the intrusions with the grace and good humor I have. And do you know why?"

His face went blank as though she spoke some savage, foreign language, unfit for a gentleman's ears. No, he had absolutely no idea.

"The same reason I treated that cruel harpy you married with all the respect due a mother. She was no mother to me. But for your sake, I bore her insults and neglect in silence. I did not come to you to mend the thousand daily piercings of my heart, never troubled you with the bitterness of my soul that she inflicted."

"She has been a paragon of virtue concerning you. It is you who have always been a difficult and ungrateful daughter to her."

"I—not the daughter who ran off to elope and gave away her virtue to a fop—I am the one you choose to fault?"

"Have you forgotten all this came about because you disobeyed Lady Catherine's orders to stay away from him?" He pointed at Darcy.

"Have you forgotten it was you who ordered me to try and ferret out the mysterious case he wished you to consult on?"

Darcy's jaw dropped.

"You will not speak to me this way!" The way his hands quivered, had she not been surrounded by Darcy and Uncle, he probably would have slapped her.

"You are quite correct. I will not, for I have nothing further to say to you, ever." She turned on her heel and marched from the room.

There, it was done and said and could not be recanted now.

She made it to the base of the stairs before her knees collapsed and she fell into a heap on against the banister.

Darcy's gaze followed her out. A poor influence? Elizabeth? She was beautiful in her fury. Had she ever unleashed it before? Bennet's expression suggested not. Pray she never turn it on him! His Elizabeth was a force to be reckoned with.

He subdued the prideful smirk that would ruin the somber demeanor he needed now.

"How dare she!" Bennet stormed toward the door.

Gardiner caught him by the arm a half step before Darcy reached him. "You will leave her alone, or I will pitch you into the street myself."

Bennet stammered unintelligible angry sounds, as ineffective as the man who uttered them.

"And I will help him." Darcy blocked the doorway.

"But she—"

"Concern yourself with the daughter you still have." Gardiner pointed at Miss Lydia.

"What am I to do with her?"

The poor girl lost all color.

"What do you mean? Shall I not go home—" she inched toward her father.

He turned his shoulder to her. "You have no home in Kent."

"Papa!"

"You are ruined. I cannot permit you back. I refuse to lose my position because of your folly."

"You would cast me out? But I am—"

"You have left me no choice."

Miss Lydia wailed. "We were to marry. It is not my fault. Mr. Darcy might still make him an offer so that we may. Make him! He must, he must!"

Gardiner grabbed Miss Lydia's arm and deposited her in a chair.

"It all comes back to you, Darcy! You see what you have done to my family," Bennet snarled. "Shall you now decry me to your aunt and make your triumph complete. Why are you so determined to ruin me?"

"I have done nothing. It is all your own doing." He closed his eyes and huffed. Hopefully, Elizabeth would not despise him for this. "However—"

No one moved or breathed. Even the breeze from the windows ceased to blow.

"Because of my esteem for Miss Elizabeth, I do not wish to see her distressed in any way."

"You will return Wickham?" Lydia sniffled.

"I am not going to aid nor abet any scheme that results in him becoming related to me."

"You will take her to live with you then?" Bennet's eyes lit with relief he did not deserve to feel.

The spleen of the man! Poor Georgiana could not tolerate any more of Miss Lydia than she had already been forced to endure at Rosings.

"Certainly not."

"What have you in mind, sir?" Mrs. Gardiner asked.

"I know of a school whose headmistress is known for her skill in improving the characters of ... high spirited young ladies. I will accept the cost of her transport and two years attendance. You will pay for her clothing, pocket allowance, and anything else additional. At the end of that time, if the headmistress deems her reformed, I will assist in finding your daughter a suitable situation. If not, I will wash my hands of her, and she will be entirely your responsibility." He turned to Gardiner. "If you and your wife would be willing to keep her whilst I make arrangements—less than a fortnight, I expect—I would be deeply in your debt."

Gardiner glanced at his wife. "I believe we can accommodate that. What say you, Bennet?"

"What can I say?"

"What about me? I do not want—"

"Hush!" Mrs. Gardiner snapped. "You are in no position to be making demands."

"And you," Gardiner poked Bennet, "you can acknowledge the generosity of the offer which so neatly solves your problems with no actual effort and little expense on your part."

"I do not offer for your sake but for Elizabeth's. I need no thanks from you."

Bennet snorted. "I suppose she has already thanked you—"

The glimmer in Bennet's eye!

Darcy grabbed him by the lapels, lifted him on his toes and shook him with each word. "Your daughter has never been anything but a perfect lady. If you ever insinuate otherwise, you will most heartily regret it." He dropped Bennet and stalked out.

Elizabeth met him in the front hall, cheeks stained with tears she should not have been forced to shed.

"I heard what you were willing to do for Lydia. It is far better than she deserves."

"It is the least you deserve. I cannot imagine you ever resting easily knowing a sister, even that one, had been cast out."

"You are right. I suppose it is entirely too softhearted of me—"

"Do not criticize the woman I love."

She looked at him, eyes shimmering. He took her face in his hands and kissed her forehead.

She sniffled.

Dash it all. He pulled her into his arms and pressed her into his shoulder. "My dearest, Elizabeth, I am proud of what you said to him, that you stood up to him, and that you will be my wife."

Her shoulders heaved and she sobbed into his coat. Hopefully, this was a good thing. Georgiana had told him sometimes ladies cried for happiness. It was difficult, though, to see anything that resembled happiness out of this day's events.

"I would carry you off to Gretna Green right now except that you ought to have a proper settlement and wedding."

"You are too good." She peeked up.

"No, trying hard to be good enough."

Soft footsteps approached. Mrs. Gardiner appeared just behind them.

Darcy braced himself for censure, but no such look came. He held Elizabeth tighter.

"I fear Mr. Bennet is on the verge of becoming very unreasonable. Perhaps it is best that you go, lest further uncomfortable scenes ensue. We will do our best to calm him and make him accept your very gracious offer. I also think it wise for Lizzy to accept your sister's invitation to Darcy House." She cocked her head at Elizabeth. "Assuming, of course, that you find that idea agreeable."

"I would like that very much."

"I will send your things along, soon." She kissed Elizabeth's cheek.

Mrs. Gardiner handed him Elizabeth's bonnet and pelisse, and he helped her into them.

They left through the kitchen door. This was not the first time Bennet had driven him out like a servant, but it would be the last.

How had it become so late? Sunset already faded into the greys of evening. They waited silently in the carriage house whilst the coach was readied.

The coachman opened the door for them, and he followed her in, drawing the curtains over the side glass. She huddled into the squabs, hands clasped tightly in her lap. Perhaps he should not, but he sat beside her and draped his arm over her shoulders.

"Is this agreeable? I will move if you but say the word."

"Very agreeable." She laid her head in the hollow of his shoulder, precisely where it fit so well and felt most natural.

"Pray, tell me what you are thinking."

"It is difficult to give it voice. I have never permitted myself to even consider it."

"If you need it, you have my permission to speak it now."

She sighed. "I was taught to respect him and his station. I am disappointed in my father, and I am angry—angry at so many people and things right now."

"With me?"

"No, not with you. To you, I am very grateful."

"Is that all."

"And very much in love."

He held her a little tighter. All was now right in the world.

## Chapter 9

DESPITE THE REASONS for it, little could satisfy him more than bringing Elizabeth to stay at Darcy House, where she might be protected and cared for properly. No doubt she was well aware of his contentment, but still, it was probably best not to speak of it just now.

The housekeeper met them in the front hall as they walked in. "Miss Bennet's rooms are ready for her, sir."

He shrugged. "I took the liberty of suggesting you might be joining the house party."

"Your staff is nothing if not efficient." She smiled up at him.

The amusement and approval in her eyes warmed him down to his toes.

"Miss Georgiana and Miss Bennet have already supped, sir, and have taken to their chambers for the evening. They were much tired from their travels."

"Very good." Indeed it was. Even Georgiana's company was hard to look forward to right now. "We will ring when we desire a supper tray."

The housekeeper curtsied and disappeared.

He took her arm and guided her to his study, shutting the door behind them.

She stopped short and turned to him. "I do not know how to thank you—"

"Shh, no talk of him. He and his business have no place here, in our home. I will not invite him, nor welcome him here."

"But…"

He pressed her lips with his finger and led her to his favorite chair, pulling her into his lap as he sat.

She leaned into his chest, molding herself to him. He took her face in his hands and she cuddled close. Their lips touched, gentle at first, but passion flowed just beneath the surface.

Her arms twined around his back, fingers working their way into his hair.

Did she comprehend the fire they left in their wake? A yearning ache opened within him—one only she could fulfil. She shifted across his lap.

That made the longing worse—definitely, definitely worse. He could not endure …

They broke apart, gasping for breath.

"We must talk about our wedding, dearest. I cannot suffer much delay."

"Of course." She slipped off his lap and retreated to the window. The evening's first moonbeams revealed the delicate flush of her cheeks, the rapid rise and fall of her chest. She was as affected as he.

The distance was too much, far too much. He stood behind her and wrapped his arms around her waist. Somehow, he would find enough control.

He whispered in her ear, "We may do anything you desire for our wedding and our wedding tour."

"You have no preferences?"

"Only that it makes you happy and it be soon, very soon."

She laced her fingers in his. "You are very good to me."

"Would that you always say that of me, my dearest. Now, shall I send for a tray?"

"Not yet, if you please. I should very much like to just stand here, close to you, and consider our future together until I cannot think of anything else."

"As you wish, my lady, as you wish."

He slept little that night, enduring the torture of having her so close by, but not in his arms where he might comfort her. Early the next morning, he stood at the door to her chambers. He poised to knock, but he hesitated. She was an early riser by habit, or at least she had been so in Kent. Yes, last night had been so late and so very difficult. If she still slept, it would be inconsiderate to wake her. But would she feel neglected if he did not seek her company first thing?

No, he could not lie, even to himself. As pleasing as it sounded, the truth was, he selfishly desired her company. Perhaps he should master that impulse, but not on the very first morning with her under his roof.

He knocked softly as a compromise.

"Come in." Her sweet voice contained only a shadow of its usual brightness.

He swung the door open.

Oh, heavens, she was lovely, silhouetted in the sunbeams! The morning sun did too many exquisite things to her. His self-control should not be so taxed so early in the day. But it was entirely his own doing, and he would prove himself worthy of her. He locked his hands on the doorframe lest he give way.

"Did you sleep well? Was the room to your liking?"

None of those things were what he wanted to know, but they seemed the right and proper things to say. How was he to greet her when what he truly desired was so improper?

She turned to face him. "The room is delightful, the most comfortable I have ever known. Sleep was an entirely different matter through no fault of yours, your staff, or your home. I do not imagine you slept either."

That look in her eye! How did she do it? Without a word, she discerned even his deepest hidden musings. His cheeks heated. "Only a little, and only because I knew you were safe here with me."

She tilted her head and lifted her brow. Could someone laugh without making a sound? If this was a taste of his future life, then it could not begin soon enough.

He offered his arm. "Join me for breakfast?"

She went to him. "It is early for that, is it not?"

"Yes, but—"

"Is it possible that you hope to share a meal together, without additional company? Our sisters are dear to us both, but still you are not a great lover of company, especially in the morning?" She slipped her hand in the crook of his elbow.

Someday he might grow tired of having no secrets, but for now, it was sheer pleasure to be understood so completely. He hummed a little sound of contentment that made her chuckle.

They finished the walk to the morning room in content silence. He whipped the waiting pot of chocolate and poured her a cup. Her eyes sparkled little like a little girl's.

Chocolate would grace their morning table every day.

"Are you in a mind for making plans?" He poured himself a cup of coffee.

"What kind of plans?" She quirked her brow.

Oh, the dear minx! Had she any conception of what her teasing did to him? Would she stop if she did?

"What do you think would be on my mind so early in the morning? The final details of when and how we may be married. I shall begin to work on the settlement with my solicitor today. I would like to present it to your uncle for his approval. I want Gardiner to know exactly how you will be cared for. He deserves the courtesy."

"I know of no other who would be so willing to submit himself to a man below him."

"His is a connection I do not repine. Anyone who loves you as they do is a welcome connection to me."

Oh, that she might always smile that way at him!

"It may be difficult to get Papa to release my dowry."

"That is the least of my concerns at the moment. We can resolve the issue over time if need be. Have you decided if you wish to stand up with your sister?"

"As much as I would like to stand with Jane, I do not wish to marry from Kent. I would be content to marry from Gracechurch Street, quietly, with my Aunt and Uncle, and any of your family you wish to attend. I know Georgiana and Colonel Fitzwilliam would sorely miss it if they were not among our witnesses. I need nothing more. If that appeals to Jane and Mr. Bingley I would be pleased to share the day with them."

"Do you truly want something so simple?"

"In that my parents are unlikely to ruin it, yes, it is exactly what I want." She stared into her chocolate cup as if she might hide her feelings from him so easily.

He caressed her cheek. "Then I shall make it so."

"Excuse me, sir." The housekeeper curtsied from the doorway. "Mr. and Mrs. Gardiner are come to call. It is very early. Are you home to them?"

"Yes, show them here."

"Very good, sir." She disappeared.

He leaned close and kissed her forehead. "It does not matter what news they bring. Nothing will interfere with us."

She cupped his cheek with her palm. "You are the very best of men."

With support like hers behind him, he could be whatever she declared him to be.

"The Gardiners," the housekeeper announced.

Elizabeth slowly rose and went to her aunt and uncle. "I am glad you have come."

"As are we." Mrs. Gardiner passed her tightly packed basket to her husband. She gripped Elizabeth's hands and kissed her cheeks.

"Please come, sit. Take breakfast with us." Darcy waved the housekeeper to set more places.

Elizabeth poured cups for them, an act as simple and natural as if she had always been mistress of the house.

"You have had a very long and difficult evening?" Darcy said.

Gardiner laughed, but with a touch of bitterness, not humor. "While that is true enough, I fear it is far too obvious to earn you credit for your powers of observation."

"Your smile suggests you obtained at least some level of agreement from him." Elizabeth lifted a brow in a delicate arch.

Uncle took a deep draw from his cup. "Yes, I will spare you the details. He did, sometime well into the small hours of the morning, accept your most generous offer."

"It is not unknown for the wee hours to be the best time to make him see reason." Elizabeth's eyes were far too sad—how many times had she been forced to do just that?

"I shall begin the arrangements immediately. I wrote to the schoolmistress last night, anticipating such a turn of events."

More precisely, he wrote because he could not sleep. It seemed one of the few useful things that might be accomplished in the middle of the night, but they did not need to know that.

"How has Lydia taken the news?"

Aunt Gardiner rolled her eyes. "She is angry and resentful—utterly unable to discern her great good fortune. She is as stubborn as her father—and more concerned with not getting her way than the blessing offered her."

---

"I hardly expected anything else." Elizabeth pinched her temples. She anticipated as much and should not be disappointed. Little help that was.

"Perhaps, you would join me in my study, Mr. Gardiner, and we might go over the plans for Miss Lydia's removal to Summerseat." Darcy rose.

Uncle Gardiner followed him out.

"Perceptive man." Aunt Gardiner smiled and glanced toward the door. "I imagine there are a few things we need to talk about?"

"Would you care for some chocolate?" Elizabeth whipped the chocolate pot back to a froth.

"I can hardly refuse a cup of chocolate, you well know that. But that hardly answers my question." Aunt took a cup from Elizabeth and sipped it daintily.

Elizabeth leaned back in her chair let her head fall back. "It is hard for me to believe last night actually happened. I was so callous toward Papa."

Cold tendrils from her words spread to her belly. She rose and sought a sunbeam in the window, but its warmth was not sufficient to drive away the emptiness. She clutched the frilly curtains in a knotted fist, knuckles white with the effort.

Aunt stood close behind her. "Elizabeth?"

"I was so angry … so very, very angry … what have I done? How could I have said such things to … to … my own father! What daughter says …" No, she must not cry!

Aunt's gentle fingers pried hers off the curtain. "Stop now. You are a sensible girl, and it is time for you to look at things that way. You were right to feel angry—it is long, long overdue—and you did the right thing. I am proud of you. You are so accustomed to allowing him his way that doing something different feels …"

"Wrong, dreadful, terrible, disobedient, disrespectful—"

"And yet, it is entirely the proper thing. You have our full support."

"How can something that feels so appalling be correct?" She chewed her knuckle.

"Because sometimes our feelings do not tell us the truth. You have been trained not to feel the sting of your father's outrageous behavior and so miss what is obvious to the rest of us. Everything you feel about your father is upside down."

"What am I to do?"

"Recognize that he no longer has a hold on you."

"Mr. Darcy would be pleased to hear you say that."

"No doubt. But that is not the whole of it. You must also release your hold on him."

"My hold? I … I never thought of that." But the idea would bear some serious reflection.

Aunt patted her arm. "It will take some time, but you will become accustomed to it all. I think though, you have dwelt on these things long enough for now. Would you care for a more pleasant diversion?"

Anything would be more pleasant than continuing to consider Papa. "What have you in mind?"

Aunt patted the top of her basket. "I brought with me some lace and trims I have been saving for a special occasion. I thought we might refresh your newest frock, the white muslin, for your wedding." She moved aside the sturdy canvas top cloth and pulled out a sheer white swatch, embroidered in white with a delicate floral pattern. "I think this should make a lovely overskirt and perhaps some pouffed oversleeves."

Elizabeth ran her fingers along the edge of the fabric. "It is exquisite."

"And this," Aunt Gardiner drew out a bundle of Honiton lace, "to line the neckline and decorate the bodice? I also have some lengths of bucks point lace to edge the overskirt."

"Are you certain? It is all so lovely."

"Absolutely. My girls are many years from needing a wedding gown and I prefer to see it used before it yellows with age. Between you and me, Jane, Miss Darcy and a clever maid if you can find one, I am certain it can be ready in just a few days."

Aunt and Uncle Gardiner excused themselves to attend to arrangements for Lydia long before Jane and Miss Darcy rose. Elizabeth fluttered in the morning room. Neither sewing nor reading kept her attention. Oh, when would Jane finally make an appearance? Still, she had to do something, so she pretended to review menus for the housekeeper.

So many unfamiliar dishes. Thankfully, the housekeeper brought Mrs. Darcy's book of receipts as well. What was in that ragoo of eggs?

"The house is very lovely, Lizzy." Jane stood in the doorway, wringing her hands.

Elizabeth rushed to take her hand and drew her inside.

Jane perched on the chair closest to the door and looked everywhere, anywhere but at her. Why?

"I am pleased you will be staying here with me. Aunt and Uncle Gardiner visited earlier this morning. I am sure they will call again tomorrow. Perhaps I may invite her to bring the children as well. It has been so long since you have seen them." All this was true, but had very little to do with what she truly wanted to say.

"I look forward to seeing them."

Elizabeth clutched her forehead. Enough of this! "Jane, what is wrong? Are you … are you upset with me?"

Jane jumped up. "No, heavens, no, Lizzy. Why would you think such a thing?"

Usually Jane would have come to her, but she remained rooted near the doorway.

"I thought perhaps, perhaps you might—oh Jane, so much has happened to our family! It seems like we are broken apart all in just a short time."

"I do not blame you, not at all. Nor do I repine the changes … at least most of them, for they are all for the better."

"Truly? Then I do not understand." Why did she remain so far away?

"Oh, I do not know how to say it. There has not been a day that I have not been tormented." Jane pressed her fingers to her mouth and closed her eyes, swaying slightly.

"By what?" What had Papa—or perhaps Mama—done in her absence?

"Mr. Darcy has not told you?" Jane turned aside and walked to the window with the curtain Elizabeth had abused earlier that morning.

"No, he has told me nothing."

"I am surprised, for he witnessed the entire awful scene. The day after you left us, Papa stood in the lane shouting at me to take your place. In that moment, I realized all you have endured whilst the rest of us stood by and allowed you to suffer."

Elizabeth blinked several times, burning prickles spreading along her cheeks and working their way down her neck. "What are you saying?"

"I am heartily ashamed of myself, most heartily. I had thought myself good and considerate, and so solicitous for your well-being."

"You have been."

"No, I have not. That is the whole point. I treated you little better than Papa." She hung her head and covered her face with her hand.

Elizabeth grabbed the edge of the table. "How can you say that? I have always turned to you for support."

"No, none of that required any effort on my part. It was easy to listen—listen and do absolutely nothing to change the circumstance."

"Do not underestimate—"

"It is hard to underestimate the value of nothing. I stood by whilst you were stolen away in the middle of the night."

"Do not be so hard on yourself." The plea sounded weak in her own ears.

How often had she defended Jane's quiet acceptance of all she endured? Almost as often as she had wished for someone to take up for her, someone to make her feel less ungrateful, less … wrong … for everything. But it never happened. Still, it was not fair to expect her sisters—

"When Papa began insisting I accompany him, I suddenly realized how dreadful it would be to be in your place. You never complained though. How you bore it all so patiently, I do not know. Yet, you still concerned yourself with the comfort of the rest of us. How could you do that, when he disregarded you at every turn?"

"Jane, please—"

Jane whirled to face her. "No, do you not see? When faced with the possibility of living your life, I refused. For the first time in my life, I stood up to him. I could not even endure the thought of it, much less a day of it."

"I am glad you did…"

"Do you not see? I should have stood up for you whilst you were still with us, cared for you, as you did for the rest of us."

"I never asked you to."

"You never asked, but you should not have had to. Perhaps if I had stood with you—"

"No." At least on this point she was certain.

"How can you be sure?"

"I have watched Uncle Gardiner and Mr. Darcy both oppose him with reason and good sense, and he is utterly intractable. Not only does he refuse to capitulate, but he further insists upon having his way as though by divine right."

"But if we—"

"No, if Uncle and Mr. Darcy could not change him, there is no hope we could have."

"Still, I hope in the future—"

"Sometimes hope, I am convinced, is foolishness. Some things will not happen. Papa will not change.

He will never admit that he might be wrong. To hold out for such a day is to court sorrow."

"How did it come to this?" Jane took a halting step closer, but only one.

"I do not know. I suppose, after making too many easy choices, one becomes incapable of making right ones."

"But you should not have had to suffer so."

"Who are we to take the place of Providence and determine what should or should not have been? It is over now. I am determined to look only to the future. I shall be very happy with Mr. Darcy, and I pray the same for you and Mr. Bingley."

"I shall never have your happiness apart from your goodness."

"You made it bearable for me. Do not be so hard on yourself."

Jane offered a weak half shrug and shook her head. "Do you think we should assist Kitty?"

"We will not. Darcy is already going to support Lydia at school. I shall not ask him to shoulder more of Papa's responsibility. And ... I know it sounds awful—I do not want anything connecting us to them."

"No, I understand. Truly I do." Her eyes did not agree with her words.

Surely she desired to comprehend it all, but did not. But was it that she could not, or that she dared not? What would happen to her sunny little world if she admitted a storm cloud like Papa might exist in all his storming, thundering fury?

"Kitty is not as silly and thoughtless as Lydia. Perhaps Mr. Bingley will be willing to have her with us."

"You and Kitty have never gotten along well."

"But to leave her alone ..."

"I caution you against tying yourself to Papa in any way."

"That seems so cruel."

"There are no half measures with him. Invite Kitty, and he will install himself and Mama in your house as well."

"Surely not. Mama would not so easily give up her own home. She takes such pride in being mistress of her own house."

"Perhaps it will be different for you. Know this though, Darcy shall never permit me anywhere he thinks Papa might appear, even if that is with you and Mr. Bingley."

"Why must you always be so concerned with what might go wrong?"

Jane could never believe ill about anyone. Elizabeth had always considered that one of Jane's greatest strengths. But perhaps, it was not.

"Darcy has offered that we might stand up together to marry," Elizabeth said softly.

"That is a lovely idea."

"I will not invite Papa and Mama, though."

"Mama will declare it quite heartless. She has always desired to see us both well married."

"I know she will be unhappy. Yet I am unmoved. If it is too cruel for you, then we need not wed together. Invite them to witness you and Mr. Bingley marry. While I wish to stand up with you, my dearest wish is … I … I want a moment whose memories will not be marred by them."

Jane laid her hand on Elizabeth's shoulder. "I understand. I … we …"

No, she had no idea at all. Her eyes, her posture, everything begged Elizabeth to change her mind.

Though she might desire to, Jane would never fathom the reasons Elizabeth would not be moved.

"Do not give me an answer now. Talk with Mr. Bingley tomorrow. Talk with Aunt Gardiner—she is a wellspring of good sense. I want you to be certain and have no regrets, whatever you decide. I shall bear you no ill will, whatever you choose."

"I do not wish to disappoint you."

"I have been disappointed the whole of my life. I come to expect it as much as breathing. I can survive it far better than the thought of forcing my decisions upon you. I could not bear anything that might cause you to resent me. That I cannot endure."

"But…please…" Her eyes pleaded.

Elizabeth closed her eyes and shook her head.

"Very well … I will do as you suggest and speak with both of them tomorrow. I … I am sorry this is all so complicated."

Elizabeth nodded and slipped from the room.

It was not complicated at all. But, Jane was so gentle, so sweet, perhaps she was not prepared yet to distance herself. Perhaps she did not need to.

Elizabeth hugged her arms around her shoulders and wandered through the French doors to the garden. Though different from Mama's, the garden here embraced her with a welcome of color and fragrance. Had Jane seen the garden yet? She would approve.

"Elizabeth?"

When had Darcy come out? Such troubled lines in his forehead. Oh, dear.

"You heard?"

"Enough." He wrapped strong, warm arms around her and pulled her to him near a bountiful peony bush. "How long do you wish to give them to decide?"

"A day or two, no more."

"Should I apologize for suggesting the notion?" He leaned his chin on the top of her head, pulling her just a little closer.

Did he realize how much she liked that?

"Not at all. It was generous and considerate. Their choices, whatever they may be, do not change any of that."

He sighed. "You said you expected disappointment."

She caressed a pink blossom. Of course, he had to have heard that. But then again, he already knew.

"It has saved me much heartache," she whispered.

"Do you expect it of me?"

"I do not know what to expect of you, Mr. Darcy. You are a surprise at every turn." She tapped his nose with her forefinger.

He rumbled with a swallowed laugh and bent to kiss her. The warmth of his lips spread to suffuse her entire being in tingles and light. How could he leave her so satisfied and so wanting all in the same moment?

He nibbled the side of her neck. "I hope I can continue to surprise you, in the most pleasant of ways, all the days of your life, my dearest, loveliest Elizabeth."

She shivered and surrendered to his attentions. Every nerve came alive and cried in anticipation of his touch. His hands were so large and strong, but gentle, as they whispered across her neck, her collar bone.

She fumbled with the knot in his cravat—why did he wear it still?

It fell away on the gentle breeze and fluttered to the ground. On tiptoes, she reached the salty, stubbled skin of his throat, suckling the pulse point there.

He groaned, every fiber of his being poured into a sound of longing so profound it was painful to hear. His hands claimed her shoulders, her back, her hips, pressing her to him with an urgency that sated the deepest yearnings of her soul.

He loved her, not for what service she might render or what convenience she might add to his life, but for herself alone.

"I am a dreadful selfish being to say this, my love," he rumbled in her ear, "but I would not regret Bingley standing up without us, for it would allow us to marry that much sooner."

"So it would, Mr. Darcy. Happy thought indeed." And in truth, it was.

Three days later, the sun rose, bright and clear, over a morning on which everything would change. In just a few hours, she would leave the name of Bennet behind forever, and she would cleave to her husband, bearing the name of Darcy ever after. Her sons would not even bear her father's name. Her eldest would be Gardiner, not Bennet. Nothing would keep her tied to that old life from this day onward. Now, she balanced on the precipice between past and future, all she wanted to leave behind and all she anticipated going forward. Though the past was—well, ghastly in so many ways—it led her to this place and for that, she would be grateful.

She lingered a few extra minutes in bed. A morning walk would have been nice, but the moment she left her room, someone would demand her attention.

Just a little more time for quiet and reflection was a luxury worth pursuing.

The clock chimed eight. She slipped out of bed and into her dressing gown for her last toilette as Miss Elizabeth Bennet. The girl who was serving as her lady's maid came in to do her hair.

Letty was a sweet, gentle young woman, eager to please, and niece to the housekeeper. Though she dressed hair well and was very clever with a needle and thread, her greatest strength was her ability to talk or not, as suited her mistress. Today, she simply hummed a sweet tune under her breath as she pinned and tucked and curled.

"Are you pleased?" Letty stepped back and tilted her head to and fro.

"Yes, I hardly recognize myself with all you have done." Elizabeth patted her curls. "I do not know how you manage to make this look so easily accomplished."

"Thank you, madam." Letty smiled, though she clearly tried to maintain a more proper decorum. "Would you care for some chocolate and a bite to eat before you dress?"

"Yes, that is an excellent idea." More because it offered her a few more moments alone than because she desired anything to eat.

Letty curtsied and disappeared.

At least, Elizabeth's reflection in the large silver mirror looked composed and confident. That was something for which to be grateful. The Earl of Matlock did not need to see how anxious she was.

She washed her face and hands and anointed herself with the fragrance and lotion that Letty had prepared for her. A touch of color to cheeks and lips, and she felt prettier than she ever had before.

The door peeked open and Letty slipped in, Georgiana on her heels.

"I hope you do not mind. I just had to see you for a moment." Georgiana bit her lip and shrugged.

"You are always welcome. Have some chocolate with me."

Letty pulled a small chair close to Elizabeth's dressing table and Georgiana sat down. Letty spun the chocolate mill between her hands, raising a healthy froth on the chocolate. She poured two cups.

"You look very beautiful this morning." Georgiana sipped her chocolate.

"Thank you. Would you like Letty to do your hair? She is quite finished with mine."

"Oh no, I could not—"

"Letty, attend Miss Darcy when we have finished our chocolate."

She curtsied. "Shall I return to help you dress?"

"No, my aunt will be here to help me. Assist Miss Darcy with that as well."

"Yes, madam." With a final curtsey, Letty ducked out.

"Are you nervous having so many people in the house today?" Elizabeth swirled her chocolate. The froth ebbed and flowed against the side of the cup.

Georgiana looked at her feet. "A little. Uncle and Aunt Matlock always make me a little uneasy. But I know most everyone so well, that makes it easier."

Elizabeth squeezed her hand. "Good. I would not have you uncomfortable on my account."

"I am very glad you will be my sister, you know." Georgiana set her cup on the dressing table. She steepled her hands and held them to her mouth, swaying slightly. "I never thanked you for warning me about Mr. Wickham."

"And I never told you how proud I was of you for confronting him as you did."

"How—"

"Your brother told me. He is proud of you, too."

"But I was such a fool!"

"No, a fool does not learn from her mistakes."

Georgiana blinked, a hopeful glimmer in her eyes. "Will your youngest sister be here today?"

"No, Aunt Gardiner is convinced she is determined not to learn from her mistakes."

"Oh … I like your aunt very well. She is a very clever seamstress. Your dress is so beautiful."

"It is not the kind of finery that your family would expect."

"Does that bother you?"

Elizabeth rose and walked to the armoire where her dress hung. She held it to her chest and ran her hand down the skirt. "It is exactly what I would have chosen for myself. But I do not wish to be an embarrassment—"

Georgiana rushed to her side. "You could never be an embarrassment to us. That is the purview of Uncle Matlock's family. Richard's sisters and brothers …" she shuddered.

Darcy kept assuring her that he had his share of uncomfortable relations to contribute to their family circle. It probably should not please her, but it was a bit of a relief.

"Nonetheless, I am glad to be wed here, in the house, away from prying eyes and those who would seek to find fault. I know our union will be reported in the society pages. I just hope it remains there and not in the scandal sheets."

Georgiana giggled. "You will not be the one to put our family there, I am sure of it."

She kissed Georgiana's cheek. "I am sure I will need you to remind me of that often. Go enjoy Letty's attentions, and tell her of how wonderful Pemberley is while you do. I hope to persuade her to come with us when we go."

"Oh! What a splendid idea! She does not like town at all." Georgiana hugged her briefly and left.

As much as Georgiana might appreciate the decision, it truly was a blessing not to have to travel to the church to be wed. No one unwelcome would disturb them today. That was the greatest gift Fitzwilliam might have given her.

Someone scratched at the door.

"Come in, Jane."

She was already dressed, in her favorite light blue gown, hair arranged with flowers. Jane was so beautiful. Anyone would pale in comparison.

No, Fitzwilliam would scold her for comparing herself to Jane. It was his opinion that mattered to her. He deemed Jane pretty, but not handsome enough to tempt him. Granted, it was difficult to believe, but the look in his eyes when he held her was impossible to deny.

"Your hair is already done." Jane's chin quivered, and she looked away. "I had hoped to help you with it."

"I am sorry … I did not expect you would still want to."

"You are upset with me for not—"

"No, I am not." She touched Jane's arm. "Not so long ago I would have been unwilling to risk Mama's and Papa's ire."

Jane sank down on the bed. "You must think me very weak."

"No. Not at all. I fear I am too hard." Elizabeth gripped the slender oak bed post. "And I am worried you do as well."

"I do not know what I think right now. I do not know what I should think."

The door swung open, and Aunt Gardiner swept in. "You should think of how you might serve your sister's happiness this day."

Jane gasped.

"I heard far more than I wanted to just now, and I am ashamed of you. Truly, Jane, it is Elizabeth's wedding day, and you should not judge what means by which she chooses to be happy. She is completely right to exclude those who have caused her so much pain. Today is for Elizabeth. For this one morning, can you not leave your feelings aside?"

Elizabeth gulped. Aunt Gardiner was never so harsh, especially not with Jane. "It is well—"

Aunt turned to her, hands firmly on her hips. "No, my dear girl, it is not. You are too accustomed to sacrificing your happiness to the convenience of others. Today of all days, I will not have it."

Jane rose and sniffled. "She is right, Lizzy. I am being selfish. Pray forgive me."

"Of course." She patted Jane's shoulder. "Think no more of it."

Of course they both would. Hard as it was, there was something gratifying about having her feelings matter. Another gift from Aunt Gardiner for her wedding, one that she must not overlook, even for Jane.

"Let us get you dressed, Lizzy. It is nearly time." Aunt took her dress from the armoire.

It took only a few minutes to finish her transformation from plain Elizabeth to fashion plate bride. A glance in the looking glass took her breath away. She really looked as though she was about to marry Darcy.

"You are truly lovely, Lizzy. The most beautiful woman here." Aunt Gardiner straightened the embroidered overskirt as they stared into the mirror.

"You do look very well indeed." Jane sniffed and turned aside.

No, it could not be … Jane was jealous? Of her?

Jane kissed her cheek and hurried downstairs, claiming the need to make sure everything was ready, but her ruse was too transparent.

"It is difficult to give the day to someone else when you are accustomed to being the center of attention." Aunt Gardiner closed the door gently. "Was I too harsh with Jane?"

"I am not accustomed to any finding fault with her."

"Neither is she. It will be difficult for her as she begins to move in society. There are always those who will criticize, especially one who is so self-absorbed. Unfortunately, it sours an otherwise sweet disposition. I will help her as I can as they will mix much more in my own circles than in yours."

"I am sure she will be glad of it."

"I am not certain she will, particularly not at first. Enough of that, though. Tell me about you. Are you anxious? Is there anything I can do for you?"

As if she had not done enough already. "Only promise me you will come to us at Pemberley this summer."

"You could hardly keep us away. The children will love a sojourn to the country, not to mention a visit with their favorite cousins. They truly are delighted with him."

The mantle clock chimed daintily.

Aunt Gardiner straightened a ribbon on her sleeve and blinked back tears. "Come, it is time. Your uncle is waiting."

He met them at the top of the grand, sweeping stairs.

"I will see if they are ready for you." Aunt hurried away.

He placed her hand in his arm. "You are certain about this Lizzy?"

"After all we have walked through, now you ask?" She chuckled and patted his hand.

"I had to ask. You know I think very well of Darcy. I would not have signed the settlement if I did not feel sure of him. But, my dear, should anything go amiss, remember you will always have a home with us."

"I would not have accepted his offer had I not been certain of him. But I will remember. I promise." She rose on tip toes and kissed his cheek.

Aunt reappeared. "All is ready."

He escorted her down to the drawing room, which her sisters had bedecked with flowers in preparation for Darcy House's first wedding.

Familiar faces dotted the formal, dignified room: the Gardiner children, Georgiana, Colonel Fitzwilliam, Jane and Mr. Bingley. A finely dressed couple who favored the colonel sat front and center—that must be the earl and his wife. Behind them, a gaunt skeleton upon whom an expensive suit hung. The viscount. Two couples beside him must be his siblings and their spouses.

The vicar stood in a sunbeam, at the front of the room, Darcy beside him.

His jaw dropped, and he caressed her with his gaze. Had even the Bard spoken so eloquently with all his words? Could he have even expressed half of what had been conveyed across the room for all to see? Heat rose in her cheeks.

Jane saw it too. She blushed and turned aside ever so slightly. Poor dear, intensity of any sort made her uncomfortable. She would never know the soul nurturing power of it.

Uncle tucked her hand in Darcy's arm. His fingers covered hers, radiating a heat equaled by the longing in his eyes. This man was her completion, her strength and her refuge.

"I will," she whispered and he slipped the ring on her finger.

The vicar presented them, Mr. and Mrs. Darcy.

---

Darcy claimed her arm again and escorted her out. Mrs. Gardiner would assist Georgiana in her role as hostess for the next few minutes. Strict propriety demanded they should stay, but another moment more in company and he might just run mad.

He could not speak on the infinite walk to his study, the one place no one would dare intrude. Surely she understood, if he had less to say, he might be able to speak, but he did not dare now.

The door shut behind them, and she was in his arms, warm and soft. It was not a dream, she was there with him, not for only a moment, but a life time.

There was something he wanted to say, needed to say.

Her fragrance overwhelmed him, driving every word from his mind and leaving him only able to press his lips to hers in a desperate attempt to express what he could not utter.

She understood, as she always did, and melted into him assuring him all was right in the world.

"So, Mr. Darcy, what say you of married life?" She snuggled a little closer.

"Entirely too full of other people." He kissed her again, until they had to part to breathe.

"Which is why Georgiana is going to stay with the Matlocks and Jane the Hursts for the next several days."

"They are? I knew nothing—"

"Of course not! What surprise would there be if you knew?"

"How …"

"I made the arrangements."

"You know me so well, Mrs. Darcy."

"Not nearly well enough, Mr. Darcy."

"Good. As soon as our company has had their fill of breakfast and cake, we shall bid them good day, and I shall employ myself in getting to know you much, much better.

# Epilogue

A MONTH LATER, ELIZABETH woke with the first rays of sun pouring into the windows of the master's bedroom. He lay next to her, snoring softly, one arm thrown over his eyes. A contented little smile graced his lips, even in sleep. He had not been without it since their wedding day.

She cuddled into his side and he wrapped his other arm around her. Their early morning walks had been replaced by leisurely conversations and time for *knowing* one another better, lingering long into the afternoon and evening. The idyll could not last forever. The concerns of business and family would make their demands soon enough. Perhaps then they would begin to walk in the mornings again, or just share coffee—for he never drank anything else in the morning—here in the confines of their sanctuary. Either way, mornings would remain their special, private time of day.

He murmured something content sounding and ran his hand along her side. "Good morning, Mrs. Darcy."

His voice had that delightful purry-rumble that made her insides shiver. They would not be leaving their chambers soon.

Hours later, sated and glowing, he rang for a breakfast tray.

They sat in the large dressing room at a small oak table borrowed from the mistress's dressing room. They had rearranged the furniture between the rooms so often in the days since the wedding, the housekeeper had taken to asking them each morning what would be their pleasure to move that day and how many footmen it might require. Darcy's valet entered, bearing a tray with coffee, toast, butter, and jam. A crisp letter with the seal of Rosings lay next to the silver coffee pot.

Darcy poured two cups of coffee and slathered butter on his toast.

"Are you not going to read your letter?" She stirred cream into her coffee. How did he drink the bitter stuff straight? She had yet to convince him to indulge in morning chocolate himself, so for now she shared his coffee.

"Not if I can avoid it."

"If it is good news, should you deny yourself of it?

"Good news, from Kent? I can hardly imagine." He turned the letter over in his hands.

"The handwriting is not Lady Catherine's."

He turned it right side up and stared at the direction. "You are correct."

"I would prefer you did not say that with such a tone of surprise." She cocked her head at him in the way that always made him smile.

"One day your overconfidence will have the better of you."

"I doubt it"

He cracked the seal and opened the letter. "Fitzwilliam writes. He says Anne's condition is very grave. If she is still alive as we read this, she has not long."

"We always knew Miss de Bourgh would never be cured."

"It will be very difficult for Aunt Catherine, accustomed as she is to ordering the world according to her preferences. She has never contended with a foe as resolute as death."

"We should go to Rosings and … Lady Catherine."

"After all she has done to you?"

"Perhaps because of it. She is family to me now. I do not want to live in continual dread of her."

"You know you need never see her again."

"I do, but I would prefer she not believe she can intimidate me into capitulation."

"Spoken like a true Darcy." He leaned across the table and kissed her.

"Colonel Fitzwilliam will need your help managing Lady Catherine. She is overbearing and tyrannical, and she does not respect him as she does you. But she loves her daughter and has watched her die slowly for years. That kind of torture takes a toll. I fear she will succumb to the strain. At the very least, she will need a capable steward to look after her concerns."

He shook his head with a look of disbelief that was almost—but not quite—comical. "You sound ready to take the job on yourself."

"I am not such a glutton for punishment, but you might consider encouraging Lady Catherine to have Mr. Michaels resume his role. I have every faith you could find another good steward for Pemberley."

He kissed her forehead. "I had hoped to see Fitzwilliam married to Anne by now. Losing Rosings will be a difficult blow to him."

"All the more reason he will need you."

"You always speak such good sense." He cradled her close and stroked her forehead with his cheek. "Very well, we shall go. But I insist that you do not go to your father's house. If you find it essential to see your sisters or your mother, they must come to Rosings. And I insist—"

"That I not see Papa at all?"

"That is too obvious a conclusion for me to give you any credit for your powers of deduction." He clasped her hands in his. "You do not wish to see him, do you?"

"No. I know there will be a chance of it whilst we are at Rosings, but I will not invite it."

"And I will not hesitate to throw him out on his arse should he give me any reason … like looking at you crossly or sneezing in your direction."

She chuckled and caressed his forehead with her fingertips. He brushed his thumb over her lips and leaned in.

His kiss was so warm, so soft, yet so demanding. She answered in kind, blood thrumming in her ears. What an intoxicating liquor, to be loved so completely. Dear heavens, she did not want to leave this room, much less Darcy House!

"We must go." Her voice hitched.

"So you tell me." He nibbled the soft skin just behind her ear, that particular spot that sent shivers to her toes. "But I think we can safely wait one more hour."

---

The warm colors of sunset crept onto the horizon as their coach passed the first of Rosings' gates. How had Elizabeth managed to get him out of the door so quickly? It would have been easy not to leave until morning, to spend just one more night alone with her. She was right though, the sooner they reached Kent, the sooner the business might be managed and they could leave.

The coach stopped at the parsonage. No doubt Elizabeth agreed to call upon Mrs. Collins more to humor him, than for any urgency to see her friend before anyone else. Mrs. Collins greeted her at the door and waved to Darcy. Elizabeth would enjoy her visit and he could confront Aunt Catherine without fear for her safety. When he was assured of her reception, he would send for her.

A groom met him at the front steps and Long Tom opened the door before he even knocked. The estate was efficient, if not welcoming.

Tom said nothing, but looked at him with an expression that demanded information, one that a father should have worn, but Bennet probably never would.

Impertinent and out of place, yes. But not entirely objectionable either, not after the service he had offered them both.

"She sends her greetings and her thanks. Mrs. Darcy stopped to call upon Mrs. Collins, but I expect to send the coach for her shortly. See my usual rooms are made up for the both of us. She will share my chambers."

The barest shadow of a smile lifted one corner of Tom's lips. Surely his face would shatter if he actually ventured a proper one. "Very good, sir. The mistress is currently occupied. If you desire audience with Colonel Fitzwilliam, he is in the steward's office."

"No need to show me there."

Tom bowed and walked away.

Was that lightness in his step? No, it could not be.

Darcy turned and strode for the office. An odd place to find Fitzwilliam to be sure. The door sat partially open, so he rapped on the door frame and peeked in.

Barely enough candles lit the small room. Papers lay strewn across the desk, before a haggard Fitzwilliam.

"Come, it is not as if I needed to concentrate." Fitzwilliam scrubbed his face with his hands.

"I can take my leave if you wish."

"Darcy! When did you arrive?" Fitzwilliam rose and dodged around a stack of ledgers on the floor.

"Only moments ago. The look on your face suggests I might not be unwelcome."

"Certainly not. Port?" Fitzwilliam was already at the decanter.

That certainly did not belong to the steward's office. From which room had he purloined it? Probably not a good sign.

"Thank you."

"I must say, you are the last person I expected to see here." He handed Darcy a glass.

"So am I, to tell you the truth. It was my intention never to darken these doors again."

"You got my letter?" Fitzwilliam moved a stack of papers off a nearby chair and waved him toward it.

"We did. Elizabeth insisted we set off immediately."

"Then you got my father's letter as well?"

"No. Has something happened with your brother?"

"Sit, sit," Fitzwilliam dropped into a large leather wingback. "You will find this all very interesting."

If the creases on Fitzwilliam's brow were any indication, the tale was very interesting indeed. Darcy settled into the newly cleared bergère.

"Andrew went on another binge, right after your wedding—disappeared for a fortnight. I know that hardly comes as a surprise. What is interesting is when he was finally recovered, Father put his foot down and demanded something be done. He threatened to cut Andrew off entirely if he did not mend his ways."

"Your father said that?"

"Indeed he did. Moreover, he wrote to ask my impressions of Bennet, if he might be of use. His letter arrived shortly after Miss Elizabeth—"

"Mrs. Darcy."

"After her sudden departure to London. I wrote to him and told him everything, good and bad, especially that. In spite of everything, he offered Bennet patronage in the hopes that he might be as efficacious in his care of Andrew as he was Anne."

"Bennet will be installed at Matlock?" Darcy raked his hair.

"Father swore to me he would write and tell you. He has been reluctant though, knowing your feelings about Bennet. He does not wish to alienate you or your charming new wife, but he is desperate."

"Had I not seen Bennet's success with Ames, I would find it difficult to forgive." Darcy took another draw from his glass.

"Bennet is already at Matlock and his family too, save the daughter betrothed to Michaels. She stays with the parson's wife."

"Who could blame her? Even Collins's society is better than Bennet's. I cannot see Aunt Matlock entertaining him at her table, not more than once at least. She does not suffer fools gladly."

"He will not find my father so generous a patron as Aunt Catherine. I know you are not pleased with his proximity to Pemberley, but remember he will not be close enough for daily visits —"

"But far closer than—" Darcy growled under his breath.

"Do not work yourself up into a bad skin. It will change nothing. Besides, Father has made it clear none of the Bennets are to set foot on Pemberley grounds without a direct invitation from you. It is not the kind of order Bennet is likely to ignore. I dare say, suffering Aunt Catherine's dismissal has reminded him of the necessity of pleasing his patron. "

"That is some small blessing."

"If he can effect any improvement in my brother, it will be worth the inconvenience."

"Unfortunately, you are correct." Darcy swallowed the last of his port. "What of Anne?"

"Anne has been failing since the turmoil began, and Aunt Catherine sent Bennet off to retrieve his wayward daughter.

"Who, by the way, will be shipped off to Mrs. Drummond's School for Girls shortly."

"An excellent place for such an article. Bennet should consider himself lucky you would place her there."

"That is another conversation."

"True enough. In any case, Aunt Catherine has barely left Anne's side since that sapscull surgeon took over her care. Blackguard though he is, Bennet is a damn sight better than Peters. Anne would have died long ago had he been charged with her care." Fitzwilliam rolled his eyes and tossed back the remainder of his port. "She has not awakened for two days now. Last time I was upstairs, I heard a death rattle. It will not be long."

"I am sorry. It would have been better for everyone had you been able to marry."

"Yes, as to that." Fitzwilliam crossed his legs and sank into the depths of the chair. "With Aunt Catherine occupied and without a steward—remind me to thank you for that later—it fell to me to begin the search for the papers that will be necessary at Anne's passing."

"Which explains the state of the desk and the floor."

"And my mind, thank you. I will detail the horrors of the state of her affairs later, but there is one particular detail you will find … interesting."

"Interesting?" That was not a word that boded well.

"Have you any idea of who is named heir of Rosings Park?"

Darcy winced. "No, I have no idea."

"It seems I am soon to be master of all you survey." Fitzwilliam raised his empty glass.

"You? Did Aunt Catherine know?"

"I can only assume she did."

Darcy rose and stalked the length of the room, dodging piles of paper and ledgers. "All the while she knew you were heir, and she was trying to push me to marry Anne? She dangled Rosings in front of me, as a prize for submitting to her will, knowing full well what the estate could mean to you?"

"So it appears."

Had she no shame? "I do not know what to say. I am all a-mort."

"As was I, when I discovered it. Apparently my father influenced Sir Lewis' decision—I found a letter to that effect. Aunt Catherine resented his interference and vowed to find a way to usurp his desire to give me precedence to which I had not been born. " Fitzwilliam rose and refilled his glass. He lifted the decanter toward Darcy.

"No. Thank you." She would cut off Fitzwilliam simply to revenge herself on his father? Stubborn, selfish, arrogant …

Fitzwilliam sipped his glass. "Do sit back down. It is not so bad at as that."

"How can you say that? What she did was unconscionable."

"You have far higher expectations of people than I. You are first born and in possession of a handsome estate. I am a second son and not a very distinguished one at that. And let us not forget, she doted upon your mother, but has never, ever liked my father."

"You are very philosophical."

"I suppose I could go glimflashy about it all, but to what point? What is done is done. She cannot be changed and you are not responsible for her choices."

"You do not resent me—"

"Heavens, no! It is not as though her favor brought you any joy." Fitzwilliam perched on the corner of the desk. "Besides, the suffering Aunt Catherine is about to experience will be apt retribution for whatever wrong she intended to do me."

"What do you plan for her?"

"You mean, will I throw her out? I will certainly not have her in the manor. She can move to the dower house or the town house in London, which I prefer all the more. I do not need the distraction whilst I try to repair the damage her rule has wrought. I will insure that she is cared for—within her means."

"A task fit for Sisyphus. Is there any way I can assist?"

"Michaels. Allow me to hire him back. I need his expertise."

"You will not be surprised to hear, Elizabeth already asked that of me."

"You are right, I am not surprised. You are a fortunate man, Darce. I can already tell marriage agrees well with you."

"It does indeed."

Fitzwilliam drained his glass again. "Much as I hate to say it, you should see Aunt Catherine."

"Lead me into the fray, cousin." Darcy rose and followed Fitzwilliam out.

They trudged up the stairs, the house around them eerily quiet. Not that the manor had ever been filled with the sounds of family and life, but now, the emptiness threatened to overtake them, claim them as its next victims.

The carpet in the hall absorbed the ring of their footsteps, reducing them to shuffling whispers insufficient to announce their presence. Still, Aunt Catherine appeared in Anne's doorways when they arrived.

How very old and worn she looked, pale and haggard, hair escaping its pins. Gone was the great Lady. In her place, a weathered shell of a woman, bearing only a distant resemblance to Catherine De Bourgh, stood watching, waiting for them to arrive. She clutched the doorframe and swayed slightly.

"She does not obey me." Her voice rasped, as though she had been shouting. She probably had been. "My daughter does not obey."

Fitzwilliam peeked in. Darcy peered over his shoulder. A slight, still form lay supported by many pillows and draped in blankets. Anne's suffering was over.

"She will not wake up. She does not get up." Aunt Catherine stared into the corridor, swinging in and out of the doorframe like a pendulum.

Darcy stepped back, but Aunt Catherine grabbed his arm. "Make her get up! This is your fault. You taught her to disobey me. You would not obey, you and that … that Bennet wench. You have taught her this. Now you must make it right."

"I cannot …"

She tried to shake him, but had not the strength. "You must. You owe me this. Do your duty to the family. A Darcy is a duty bound creature. Do your duty!" Her tone climbed, shrill and thin.

He took her by the shoulders and held her securely against her shaking.

Dawson and Mrs. Jenkinson appeared in the hall. Fitzwilliam beckoned them over.

"Take your mistress to her room." Darcy handed Aunt Catherine into their arms.

"Wait here just a moment." Fitzwilliam ducked into Anne's room and returned with a brown bottle. "Prepare her some tea and mix in a spoonful of this. Just one spoon and no more."

Mrs. Jenkinson took the bottle and curtsied. "Yes, sir."

They led Aunt Catherine away. She muttered and mumbled with every stumbling step.

"Is it wise to dose her with laudanum?" Darcy asked.

"I fear she may do herself, or someone else, an injury if we do not." Fitzwilliam followed their progress down the hall with his gaze.

"Do you think she will recover?"

"I do not know, but I can see what you are thinking. I will retain Dawson and Mrs. Jenkinson to care for her as long as it seems advisable."

"That is both wise and very generous of you, particularly in light of what she sought to do to you."

"You have not lived enough in the world. Her behavior is neither so surprising nor unusual." Fitzwilliam shrugged.

"I am not sure I like the world you have lived in."

"You are fortunate if you can keep yourself to higher things and stay untainted by the sins of mortal men."

"Sounds as though you do not like your world either."

"It is what it is, whether I like it or not." Fitzwilliam laced his hands behind his neck and stretched.

"I prefer to believe there is better than what you describe. How else might I explain Elizabeth?"

"She does defy explanation in many ways. I am happy for you, cousin. You are indeed fortunate, albeit in an unfortunate sort of way."

"What are you talking about?"

"You have found such a woman, yet she has no real dowry, not one worthy of much notice in any case, and she has such a family."

"It is a small price to pay." A very small one for a treasure so great. How much longer before he might hold her again?

"How long will you stay?"

"How long will you wait to bury Anne?"

"I have no need to draw things out. It would do Aunt Catherine no good either. Two days, three at most."

"We will stay until then."

Three days later, Aunt Catherine remained ensconced in her chambers, muttering and whispering to herself and the walls, while Darcy and Fitzwilliam accompanied Anne's body to the cemetery beside Hunsford's stone church. Mr. Collins spoke the appropriate words, and far more besides, as she was laid to her rest.

Something within insisted he should feel more grief, more remorse at Anne's passing. There was some form of sadness to be sure, but little else. Somehow that was unsettling. No doubt tonight, when they talked before they slept, Elizabeth would help him make sense of it all. She always understood such things. How he needed her beside him.

The next day, early in the afternoon, a groom readied a horse for him while Elizabeth supervised their packing. Only one more task remained to be done before they left for home, and for once, it was not a disagreeable one.

He rode into town, to a street he rarely visited. The pub was not entirely unappealing, but certainly not the sort of place he patronized. Quaint, that was the best word for it. Not the place to cultivate a den of ruffians, but neither a place for gently-bred ladies.

He walked in and paused until his eyes adjusted to the dimmer interior. Not too large, nor too small, and it did not smell—there was a great deal to be said of a pub that did not reek of debauchery. He strode to a table near a large window.

"Good day, Tom, Ames." He nodded and sat.

A serving girl approached, but he waved her away.

Tom sat straight as a poker, no expression betrayed on his face, exactly as he always appeared. Ames may have tried to emulate his uncle, but proved entirely unsuccessful. One had to be as singular as Tom to manage it.

"Pray accept our condolences for Miss de Bourgh, sir," Ames said, uncertainty muddled his voice. Junior footmen rarely conversed with gentlemen.

"What may we do for you, sir?" Tom asked exactly the same way he would had he been in the halls of Rosings.

"Nothing."

That did it. Tom's eyelid fluttered—a veritable guise of shock on the man. Fitzwilliam would never have believed it possible.

"Excuse me?"

"It is not what you may do, but what you have already done."

Ames looked aside, his feet shuffling beneath the table.

"You both exerted yourself to protect Elizabeth, my wife, and did so at great risk to yourselves, to your futures and livelihoods."

"Sir—" Tom frowned.

Darcy raised an open hand. "Please, stop. Elizabeth has been concerned for both of you since she left Kent. She does not know what I have planned. I have no doubt that she would approve. Had she been unencumbered from other burdens, she would have insisted upon it herself." He pulled a piece of paper from his pocket and slid it across the table to Tom.

Tom unfolded it and held it at arm's length to read. His face lost all color and his jaw dropped. "Dear God, sir!"

"What is it?" Ames snatched the paper from him. "Zounds, sir! Is this …"

Darcy bit his cheek. It would be in very poor taste to laugh, but the victory of seeing Long Tom finally react was almost too sweet not to savor. "The deed to this very establishment. It is the one you were considering, is it not?"

"Sir, we cannot—" Tom pushed the deed at him.

"Yes, you can, and you will. We cannot know what might have happened had you not intervened on her behalf. But you kept her safe, and delivered her into the hands of those that cared for her as deeply as I.

For that I must thank you in kind. Pray, honor me and her by accepting this." He slid the paper back at Tom.

"What does one say to such a gift?"

"Thank you comes to mind. It is what Elizabeth would recommend."

"Then thank you, sir. And tell her, we shall name it in her honor. We shall call the place … 'The Good Deed.'"

Darcy chuckled. Who would have thought Tom had a sense of humor? Elizabeth had told him so, but he had been reluctant to believe. "She will approve."

What a gift this story would be when he presented it to her on his arrival. Her eyes would light up that special way they did when she knew he understood her, and she would smile the smile that was for him alone. Yes, Tom and Ames might be pleased, but this gift was for her pleasure above all.

## Author's Note

**Laudanum: Panacea of Withered Poppies**

Although we commonly consider drug addiction and abuse a modern world problem, it began in far earlier times. Physicians of prior centuries were concerned with issues of both overdose and addiction to laudanum. Ames' accidental overdose in chapter 5 was based on a case described in an 1809 medical journal article, *An Account of the Effects produced by a large quantity of Laudanum taken internally, and of the means used to counteract those effects* by Alexander Marcet.

### History of Laudanum

The 16th century discovery of laudanum by alchemist Paracelsus, and its subsequent rediscovery in 1660 by English physician Thomas Sydenham set the stage for the opium trade of the following centuries.

The name laudanum comes from the Latin verb *laudare*—to praise. The tincture was widely praised for its ability to relieve pain, cough and diarrhea. By the 18th century, George Young published *Treatise on Opium*, a text that exalted the virtues of laudanum and recommended the drug for a broad range of ailments. In an era when cholera and dysentery regularly ripped through communities, killing victims with diarrhea, and dropsy, consumption, ague and rheumatism were all too common, laudanum's popularity is easy to understand.

By the 19th century experts also recommended laudanum to promote sleep, reduce anxiety, check secretions as well as treat colds, meningitis, cardiac disease, yellow fever, and relieve the discomfort of menstrual cramps. Nursery maids even gave it to colicky infants.

### Homemade Laudanum

Ease of acquisition further fueled laudanum's popularity. The opium poppy could be raised in home gardens and its pods used to prepare the tincture in one's own kitchen or stillroom.

The Receipt Book (1846) of The Honourable Ellen Jane Prideaux-Brune lists a receipt for laudanum and several home remedies based upon it:

#### *For rheumatism*

One spoonful of gum-guacum mixed with two teaspoonfuls of milk, add six drops of laudanum, and take it three times a Day.

This is the quantity for one taking.

#### *For a cough*

Two tablespoonfuls of vinegar,
Two tablespoonfuls of Treacle
60 drops of Laudanum.
Take a teaspoonful of this mixture night and morning.

Popular medical books for the era also offered laudanum receipts, including these for dysentery:
1) Thin boiled starch, 2 ounces; Laudanum, 20 drops; "Use as an injection every six to twelve hours";
(2) Tincture rhubarb, 1 ounce; Laudanum 4 drachms; "Dose: One teaspoonful every three hours."

And this for diarrhea:
Tincture opium, deodorized, 15 drops; Subnitrate of bismuth, 2 drachms; Simple syrup, 1/2 ounce; Chalk mixture, 1 1/2 ounces, "A teaspoonful every two or three hours."

### Laudanum in Patent Medicine

Laudanum found its way into many patent medicines where it would be combined with everything from spices to tincture of cannabis to chloroform. Such formulations were marketed as cures for migraines, diarrhea, insomnia, neuralgia, consumption, dysentery, "women's troubles," and nervous afflictions.

Perhaps more troubling were patent formulations made specifically for children. Steedman's Powder quieted teething babies. Infants' Quietness, Soothing Syrup, and Godfrey's Cordial, calmed colic and fretfulness even in newborns. Some of these potions enjoyed such wide spread popularity that nearly all the families of a county might use them, despite the inherent danger of death by overdose. In very small children even a few extra drops could kill.

Laudanum use, both in patent medicines and home remedies, was highest in the marshy, low lying fens. Frequent outbreaks of marsh fever led fen-dwellers to seek relief where ever they could find it. Laudanum was far less expensive than the antimalarial quinine, so the opiate became the medicine of choice. Laudanum's euphoric effects kept marsh fever suffers coming back for the drug even after they recovered from the fever. Many became addicted.

### Addiction

As early as 1700, the medical community knew of opium's addictive nature. Dr. John Jones's medical treatise, *Mysteries of Opium Reveal'd*, was probably the first work on the subject, describing in accurate terms the "dull, mopish and heavy disposition," as well as memory loss and agonizing withdrawal symptoms common to opium users.

Dr. Jones explained that once the honeymoon period in which opium users tended to be over-achievers known for their "expediteness in dispatching and managing business, self-assurance, courage, contempt of danger, and satisfaction" ended "intolerable distresses" would set in.

These intolerable distresses include:

*Physical dependence/addiction where the body adjusts to the presence of the drug and requires it for 'normal' functions.

*Respiratory Depression or distress which includes shortness of breath or slow and irregular breathing.

*Constipation

*Dysphoria, a saddened or depressed state of mind, especially in users with a physical dependence.

*Constriction of the pupils even in the absence of high levels of light.

*Intense itching

Over time, the addict would require more and more laudanum to achieve the same desirable euphoric effects. Moreover, withdrawal from laudanum caused symptoms even worse than the side effects from use. At the mildest it produced:

*Cold-like symptoms, such as a runny nose, watery eyes, and increased perspiration

*Insomnia and frequent yawning

*Muscular aches and abdominal cramps

*Nervousness and agitation

*Goosebumps

*Nausea, vomiting, and diarrhea

In more severe cases it could result in life threatening:

*Cardiac arrhythmia

*Seizure

*Stroke

*Dangerous dehydration

*Suicide attempts

Since it was available at chemists, groceries and pubs, at under a penny for a quarter ounce, there was little pressure for addicts to stop using.

### Legislating Laudanum

In the Victorian era as laudanum use spread to Britain's upper and urban working classes, wide public debate raged. Advocates emphasized the drug's beneficial uses as well as England's active opium trade to China.

Many doctors, however, expressed concern. Some feared that indiscriminate laudanum use masked the symptoms needed to diagnose other illness, caused accidental poisonings, and induced suicides. Worse still, laudanum withdrawal and overdose symptoms were treated with laudanum itself.

These concerns resulted in the 1868 Pharmacy Act. The act required that only registered chemists and pharmacists could sell opium derivatives. Although the amount and frequency of sales were unrestricted, each bottle had to be clearly labeled as poison. Later legislation required pharmacists to know customers personally, and to meticulously record each narcotic sale. However, it was not until well into the 20th century that opiate use in Britain and abroad drastically declined.

### References

Victorian Medicine: Use of Laudanum and Treatment of the Sick

http://freepages.family.rootsweb.ancestry.com/~treevecwll/vicmed.htm

Alexander Marcet. An Account of the Effects produced by a large quantity of Laudanum taken internally, and of the means used to counteract those effects. *Medico-Chirurgical Transactions*. 1809; 1: 77–82. PMCID: PMC2128802

http://www.ncbi.nlm.nih.gov/pmc/articles/PMC2128802/

Laudanum Detox and Withdrawal

http://www.projectknow.com/research/laudanum-detox-and-withdrawal/>

Withdrawal from Laduanum
http://www.withdrawal.net/learn/laudanum/
Side effects of laudanum
http://www.livestrong.com/article/95368-side-effects-laudanum/

# Acknowledgments

So many people have helped me along the journey taking this from an idea to a reality.

Abigail, Jan, Dave, Ruth, Anji, Joy, Debbie and Debra Anne thank you so much for cold reading, proof reading and being honest!

And my dear friend Cathy, my biggest cheerleader, you have kept me from chickening out more than once! Thank you!

*Other Books by*

*Maria Grace*

**Given Good Principles Series:**
*Darcy's Decision*
*The Future Mrs. Darcy*
*All the Appearance of Goodness*
*Twelfth Night at Longbourn*

***Remember the Past***
***The Darcy Brothers***
***A Jane Austen Christmas: Regency Christmas Traditions***
***Mistaking Her Character***

Available in paperback, e-book, and audiobook format at all online bookstores.

# On Line Exclusives at:

www.http//RandomBitsofFascination.com

Bonus and deleted scenes
Regency Life Series

<u>Free e-books</u>:
*Bits of Bobbin Lace*
*The Scenes Jane Austen Never Wrote: First Anniversaries*
*Half Agony, Half Hope: New Reflections on Persuasion*

## About the Author

Though Maria Grace has been writing fiction since she was ten years old, those early efforts happily reside in a file drawer and are unlikely to see the light of day again, for which many are grateful. After penning five file-drawer novels in high school, she took a break from writing to pursue college and earn her doctorate in Educational Psychology. After 16 years of university teaching, she returned to her first love, fiction writing.

She has one husband, two graduate degrees and two black belts, three sons, four undergraduate majors, five nieces, six novels in draft form, waiting for editing, seven published novels, sewn eight Regency era costumes, shared her life with nine cats through the years, and tries to run at least ten miles a week.

## She can be contacted at:

author.MariaGrace@gmail.com

**Facebook:**
http://facebook.com/AuthorMariaGrace

**On Amazon.com:**
http://amazon.com/author/mariagrace

**Random Bits of Fascination**
http://RandomBitsofFascination.com

**Austen Variations** http://AustenVariations.com

**English Historical Fiction Authors**
http://EnglshHistoryAuthors.blogspot.com

**White Soup Press** http://whitesouppress.com/

**On Twitter** @WriteMariaGrace

**On Pinterest:** http://pinterest.com/mariagrace423/

Printed in Great Britain
by Amazon